Protector

Protector

Book One in the Demon Hunter Series

A novel by
TL GARDNER

Q-Boro Books
WWW.QBOROBOOKS.COM

An Urban Entertainment Company

Published by Q-Boro Books

Copyright © 2007 by TL Gardner

ISBN13: 978-1-933967-13-4
ISBN 10: 1-933967-13-7
LCCN: 2006936055

First Printing July 2007
Printed in the United States of America

10 9 8 7 6 5 4 3 2 1

Cover Copyright © 2006 by Q-BORO BOOKS all rights reserved
Cover layout/design by Candace K. Cottrell
Cover Photo by Ted Mebane
Editors: Candace K. Cottrell, Leah Whitney

Q-BORO BOOKS
Jamaica, Queens NY 11434
WWW.QBOROBOOKS.COM

The Nephilim were on the earth in those days—and also afterward—when the sons of God went to the daughters of men and had children by them. They were the heroes of old, men of renown.

Genesis 6:4

Protector

Prologue

Do It, Elijah, pull the trigger.

Huge tears clouded Elijah Garland's vision and his sobs filled the moonlit bathroom. He inhaled deeply, closing his light brown eyes, searching for the courage to obey the voices.

The voices. How long had he been hearing them now— nine years? Ten? Elijah stared up through the large skylight to the bright silver moon, its light reflecting off the barrel of the chrome nine-millimeter handgun he held in his hands. He laid his neatly braided head back onto the hard edge of the bathtub, lifting the gun up to his temple.

His slender, ebony finger trembled as it hovered over the trigger.

Do it, Elijah!

His heart raced and his chest heaved in the soft light of the bathroom. Feeling the trigger against his finger, he shut his eyes tight, concentrating, searching for the courage.

"Fuck! Fuck! Fuck!" he cried out, dropping the gun to the cold linoleum floor in anger and despair.

Outside, only half a block away from the two-bedroom

apartment Elijah shared with his roommate, Darryl, just off of the waterfront in the Old City section of Philadelphia, police were taping off a crime scene.

A young, beautiful, black woman, her brown eyes locked in a lifeless stare at the cold moon—an expression upon her face that could have easily been interpreted as bliss—lay dead on the cold concrete. Only a few feet away from her lay the body of a middle-aged black man, his right hand clutched tightly over his left ring finger. Their bodies were still warm as the police searched the area for the murder weapon. But they wouldn't find it there—it was in Elijah's hands.

"God, help me, please!" Elijah cried out, dropping his head into his hands as he sobbed. Then he snorted derisively, thinking about his foolish plea.

Why would God help you, Elijah? You're a sinner!

He felt his throat constricting as he tried to swallow the truth the voices shouted into his mind. It was true; he had led the life of a sinner, ignoring God and his commandments. Why would anyone help him? Who would care if he died today or tomorrow?

No one cares about you, Elijah!

Elijah closed his mouth and forced air into his lungs through flaring nostrils, a determined expression finding his tear-streaked ebony face. His eyes went down to the nine millimeter on the floor and he thought of how totally alone he actually was. All of his life he had felt alone. Especially after his grandmother had died.

Elijah felt another wave of sorrow wash through him when he thought of her. She had raised him from birth, taking over his young mother's matronly duties, for she had only been sixteen at the time—still a child herself and she didn't want him. His grandmother, Ruth Garland, taught him everything he knew—everything, except how to be a man and take care of the responsibilities that came along with being a man. But then, how could she? But what she *did* teach him—more than anything else—was how to love. It was all he knew. He grew up wanting only to bring a smile to his grandmother's face, wanting only to please her. After her death, Elijah began his search. Latching onto one woman after another, he unconsciously tried to replace the woman he had lost, only to find that all women were not as loving and devoted to him as his grandmother had been.

Elijah's heart would never fully recover from losing her, and the pain began to pile up inside of him with each failed relationship. Elijah's only escape from reality was the few hours at night when he would close his eyes and dream. There, in his dreams, he created his own world where he could give back the pain and heartbreak he endured in the real world. He created demons to battle, imagining they were the tormentors of his soul. Armed with twin blades and a shirt of chain mail armor, he would release the pain, tearing into the demons and their master he had named Reality.

The dreams began to get as out of control as his real life spiraled downward. Time after time, Elijah would fall in love, only to have his heart torn apart. The demons in his dreams were growing stronger with every letdown he experienced in the world, and the voice of Reality was getting louder and louder. Soon he would create an alter ego, a mirror image of himself, not with the love and compassion his grandmother had instilled deep in his weary heart. No, this other self was rage incarnate. This alter ego had no conscience, no remorse, and no sympathy. It would gather and accumulate all the tears, letdowns, and heartbreaks Elijah experienced in the real world and release the pain and hate back upon Reality and his children. The alter ego's only purpose was to destroy and kill.

He was content with his life then, satisfied with the give and take that he exchanged with Reality, accepting the voices that would constantly whisper that happiness was not meant for him. It was something he knew would only be found in death.

Then came Taysia.

Elijah felt his tears beginning anew. He sobbed heavily upon the bathroom floor, images of the beautiful black woman lying dead on the waterfront flashing into his mind. He remembered when they had first met and how Reality had toyed with him, dangling her love in front of him like a baited hook to a finless fish.

Elijah was blessed with good looks—light brown eyes and a handsome smile. His full lips, framed by a neatly trimmed goatee and thin mustache, won him plenty of affection from the ladies. He stood a bit over six feet tall and every muscle in his 175-pound frame looked to be chiseled from stone, so it wasn't hard for him to find a willing woman. But he was also cursed—he believed—never to find true love.

He met Erica in a disco when he was twenty-eight. She was pretty, and the sweetest woman he had ever met. But she was ten years younger than he was, and he knew from the beginning their relationship would not last. He went with it anyway, enjoying the sex and companionship she offered. The trouble began when Erica introduced him to her best friend, Taysia.

They had both felt the connection the moment they laid eyes on each other. Taysia was the most beautiful woman with whom he had ever imagined himself. Her body was perfect: slim at the waist, round in the behind, and bosomy. Her light brown eyes seemed to glow above her full, beautiful lips, and her angelic face, framed by the micro braids that hung down past her shoulders, was breathtaking, to say the least. Elijah's heart belonged to her that first day, and she knew it.

They both fought their desire for one another, neither of them wanting to break Erica's kind, childlike heart. Taysia was like a big sister to her, and Elijah—well, he felt more like Erica's guardian than her man. But as weeks passed, Elijah and Taysia found it hard to resist that which they both felt was meant to be.

The girls both worked at a club as waitresses, and Elijah would drop Erica off every night, walking her inside just to see Taysia. It was on one of these nights that Erica had called out from work, and had stayed with Elijah in his apartment on the waterfront. She had gotten a call from Taysia, who had been stranded by her ride at the club. Erica wasted no time asking Elijah to go and get her, and to take her home. Elijah tried to play it off, complaining he was tired and didn't feel like it, but in reality, he was overjoyed.

A smile slowly worked its way to Elijah's tear-streaked face as he leaned his head back against the tub, reminiscing. He remembered how they had sat in uncomfortable silence as he drove her home, and how they had sat in front of her house and talked briefly about nothing. But when Elijah had walked her to the door, always being the perfect gentleman, something happened that would change both of their lives forever. As Elijah stood there, waiting for her to find her key in the darkness, his eyes roamed down to her shapely waist and her flat belly, exposed by the cut-off T-shirt she wore along with her hip-hugger jeans. Elijah felt his heart melting as he watched her.

"Thank you, Elijah. It was really sweet of you to come and bring me home," she had said, smiling awkwardly as she stared up into his eyes. "Erica is very lucky to have a man like you."

Elijah had sighed at the mention of Erica's name, his shoulders slumping. He shook the feeling away and decided to let things end there, but when he looked up and saw those beautiful, full, perky lips . . . "Taysia—"

"Elijah . . . please don't," Taysia had whispered, cutting

him off before he could go any further. Her eyes turned away, and he could see there the same thing he was feeling in his own heart.

Elijah swallowed his emotions and his hormones and stepped away from the door. "Okay . . . goodnight, beauty," he said softly.

He watched Taysia open the front door and wave. He thought for an instant he had seen a spot of moisture on her cheek, just before she closed the door. He knew then Taysia was the only one for him. She was the one to make the demons in his dreams go away and he would have her. But first he would have to deal with Erica.

For two weeks, Elijah tried to break up with Erica, and for two weeks, the dreams and the voices increased.

Night after night the dream returned, and it was always the same: Reality forging up images of his dead grandmother, faces of loves long lost to Elijah, and any other hurtful images that would weaken him in his battle. But Elijah slowly came to accept his loss, learning to channel the sorrow and pain he felt upon seeing the images of his grandmother dead, into pure rage. This is how he battled Reality, and when Reality realized he was losing the upper hand in these dream battles, there was always . . . reality.

Elijah had no way of defending himself against Reality here in the real world; there were no blades to fight back with, no platinum armor to absorb the blows, no alter ego that could step in and take up the fight for him—and there were rules. And so back and forth they went. Whenever Elijah would begin to get an upper hand, Reality would give him love or happiness in the real world, only to snatch it away—fuel for torture in Elijah's dreams.

When he met Taysia, things had changed. In his heart, Elijah was beginning to tire of the repetitive chaos of his dreams. Whenever Reality would throw a new log onto the fire of pain and sorrow that ate away at his soul, Elijah would give in to his alter ego, allowing himself to float away from the carnage and brutality. He soon began to focus on one thing, one last chance for happiness, ignoring the voice of his other self that warned him of impending doom—the doom of true love.

Then one Sunday, as Elijah and Darryl relaxed at home playing baseball on their big screen TV, he received the phone call. How his heart had raced when he recognized Taysia's voice on the other line. She told him she was in the area, just doing some shopping, and had decided to give him a call. Elijah met her five minutes later on the busy avenue lined with small shops known as South Street. They walked and talked as Taysia window-shopped. Elijah found himself unable to stop smiling as he walked along with the woman of his dreams.

They stopped on the waterfront, enjoying the view of the water beneath the warm sun. They talked then about everything, explaining how they had feelings for each other, but how neither of them wanted to hurt Erica. Taysia told him about all the nights she would go to sleep dreaming of him. She also told him how she had cried the night he had given her a ride home. Elijah also explained to Taysia how he felt like more of a guardian than a man to Erica, and how he would end it that very night. They left it at that and spent the remainder of the day just enjoying each other's company.

Later that night, Elijah kept his word. In his mind, he told himself, as he gazed into Erica's tear filled eyes, that it was not just because of Taysia that he had to do this. It was, as he had explained to Erica, that he felt almost guilty about their relationship because Erica was so young and had so much of life to experience. He didn't want her to miss out on anything because of him. She was too young to be tied down. Elijah felt his own tears on his cheeks as Erica had run out of the apartment sobbing heavily. She truly loved Elijah, and would have given up any experiences he thought she was missing out on to be with him. No one had ever treated her the way he did. Elijah cried all the way to the telephone.

An hour later, Taysia and Elijah walked along the beautiful waterfront, holding hands under the bright full moon. Another figure walked along the waterfront also, but this one in the shadows, following the two figures as they slowly walked along in bliss. Elijah stopped and turned to Taysia with joy in his heart. For the first time in his life, he had found happiness, and he had decided to reach out to it and hold it in his hands forever. He remembered staring at her soft smile as a breeze blew in off the water, gently lifting the strands of her hair across her face. He had waited for this moment all of his life. His eyes fell upon her wet lips, and he knew that to taste of them would be the beginning of his trip into paradise.

"Taysia," he began softly, his smooth voice causing Taysia's heart to melt, "I have waited for you all of my life . . ."

Taysia's warm smile stole the thoughts from his mind, and he sighed heavily, not knowing what else to say.

"And I've waited for you," she replied in a whisper, stepping into his strong embrace as she stared up into his eyes.

He longed to say the words to her, and to hear her say them back to him. He fought to control his emotions, feeling her soft hand reach up to catch the tear that fell from his eye, ignoring her own.

"Taysia . . . I love you," he whispered, his lips inches away from happiness.

"And, Elijah . . . I—"

Elijah looked up to see the stranger suddenly step out of the shadows of the trees, his hand going into his coat, and then the moonlight glinting off a shiny metallic object aimed at him. Elijah's heart raced as he realized the man had a gun. Before he knew it, his reflexes propelled him the ten feet that separated him from the man, and his hand reached out for the man's arm just as the gun went off.

Elijah and the man then struggled for the weapon, fear giving Elijah the upper hand. Adrenaline coursed through his veins. He tried to wrestle the gun from the stranger. Their arms locked in between their bodies and another shot went off, followed by two more. They both fell to the ground, Elijah staring down as the stranger's eyes went wide and he took his last breath. Elijah pushed himself up off the man, checking his own body, searching for a bullet wound, but he found none. Shouts rose up from the street in the distance. He turned then to look for Taysia and his heart stopped.

Her body lay where he had left her standing. A wave of dizziness passed over him. He fought to breathe, staggering over to where she lay motionless in a small pool of blood. He dropped down to his knees, half to try and help her and half because he could not stand any longer. He blinked slowly, unsure if what was happening was truly real. His breathing came in short gulps of air. He slowly reached down to pull her head up into his lap. Taysia stared wide-eyed at him, confused and afraid. Elijah's tears then fell unabated. His head slowly began to shake from left to right, his mind refusing to believe what his eyes were seeing.

"No." His mouth moved but no sound came out. Tears blurred his vision.

Her voice was barely above a whisper. "E-Elijah . . ."

Elijah was forced to focus when he heard her call to him. Her eyes were no longer confused—no longer afraid. They were calm and placid, the bright moon causing them to glisten from her tears. Elijah felt his body tremble as he sobbed heavily. He knew then, just as she did, that this was the end.

"I love you, Elijah."

For a brief moment his body calmed, his tears ceased to flow, and he sniffled, staring down into her eyes.

"Kiss me . . . please."

Elijah felt himself falling apart as he leaned over, his body tremulous and heaving once again. Then his lips met hers for the first—and last—time.

And it was heaven.

When Elijah brought his head back up and stared into her eyes once more, he saw no life there. At once, his sorrow turned to anger, an anger he had never known before. Even in his dreams his alter ego would have blanched at the madness in Elijah's eyes. He stared down at his bliss.

A gut-wrenching cry of anguish filled the waterfront as Elijah cried out to the night. He cursed his very existence, cursed God and everyone else who had anything to do with him being here. Then his eyes went to the gun, glittering in the light of the moon next to the dead man's body.

Elijah's tears were now a memory. He slowly picked the gun up from the bathroom floor. His heartbeat was calm and tranquil. He heard her soft voice repeating over and over again in his mind. *I love you, Elijah . . . kiss me, please.*

He placed the gun in his mouth.

He had found the courage he was seeking.

Yes! Do It, Elijah!

Elijah did it.

Chapter One
A Visitor

Gabriel calmly walked over to the porcelain bathtub and nimbly hopped up onto its edge. Kneeling over at an almost impossible angle, he inspected the bloodstains there. He touched the dried blood, bringing his fingers to his nose and sniffing quickly. He cocked his head to the side curiously, contemplating his next move.

"You know," he said absently, still deep in thought, "they have a word for what you're doing. I think it's . . . voyeurism?" A wry smile formed on his lips. "Yeah, that's it. Voyeurism. Do you know what that means?" He paused, sniffing the air. "I said, do you know what that means, Aaron?"

There was a moment of stillness, with only Gabriel's words reverberating off the tiled walls of the bathroom.

Then suddenly, the skylight above him exploded into a shower of broken glass, followed by the body of his formerly unseen attacker. Gabriel stood and turned before the man could get his footing, kicking him square in the chest and sending him flying backward out of the room to crash heavily threw the hallway closet door.

"Voyeurism, Aaron," Gabriel began in his usual sarcastic

tone. He slowly walked toward Aaron's bruised, slumping form. "It *is* illegal. . . . You do know that, right?" He watched in amusement as Aaron struggled to his feet, dust and debris falling from his long, brown hair.

"Whatever it is you're about, Gabriel, we will know," Aaron whispered, emphasizing his words by launching into a series of attacks, punching and kicking at speeds faster than the human eye could track.

Gabriel blocked them all too easily. He then ended the exchange with another kick, this time sending Aaron through the wooden banister and down the carpeted stairs to crash heavily upon a glass end table.

"It's illegal, Aaron!" Gabriel smiled, slowly walking down the steps, his eyes adjusting to the bright sunlight illuminating the room.

The beige vertical blinds that hung in front of the large bay window swayed as Aaron reached out his hand, looking for support to pull himself up.

"Although the monkey's laws are not quite as severe for this as I would like," Gabriel continued smugly, coming up to stand over the bruised angel amidst the broken glass.

Aaron forced himself to get up. He came at Gabriel once more, swinging impossibly fast and connecting with nothing.

Gabriel was gone.

Aaron closed his eyes as he realized his mistake. He knew Gabriel was on an entirely different level than he. Aaron was only a foot soldier, completely outmatched.

He accepted his fate as soon as Gabriel gave it to him.

Gabriel appeared behind him in the blink of an eye, his fist halfway into Aaron's back and his lips at his ear. "You know," he whispered as his fingers searched for Aaron's heart, "this is the part I really hate. It didn't have to be like this!" he said angrily, feeling his fingers close around Aaron's heart. "Tell our Father I said hello. And tell Him I'll have this war thing cleaned up in no time," he added as he crushed the soft muscle in the palm of his hand and ripped it from Aaron's body.

Aaron fell to the carpeted floor with a soft thump. The bright afternoon sun shining in through the blinds was the last image he saw.

Gabriel leaned over the fallen angel's still body, staring down at him sympathetically, watching as Aaron's eyes slowly melted away in death.

"You were given a choice, my friend," he sighed softly. "You chose wrong."

Then he gently reached out with two fingers, closing the eyelids over Aaron's now empty eye sockets.

He turned away, again his mind on the business at hand. He waved a hand backward casually and flames erupted in the large apartment, burning only what Gabriel wanted to be burned—Aaron's remains. He walked outside onto the bustling street, ignoring the shouts as shoppers and sightseeing tourists pointed to the smoke coming from the second floor window of the apartment. He had Elijah's scent now. All that was left to do was to find him.

Chapter Two
Keeping Vigil

Michael watched Gabriel step out onto the sunlit side-walk, his jet black hair flowing behind him from the cool October breeze that wafted across the rooftop on which he was perched. As Gabriel quickly made his way through the crowd of pedestrians gathering in front of the apparently burning apartment building, Michael wondered exactly what it could be that he was up to.

Gabriel paid Michael no mind; he sensed his presence, but he had no time to dawdle with his older brother right now. His plan was moving along as scheduled.

Gabriel stopped when he reached the next corner, his eyes searching the busy street for a suitable means of transportation. It was rather warm for early October, and he felt the occasional stare as he stood on the corner wearing his long, brown, trench coat. But that was trivial. He watched the long line of cars coming down the small, busy, one-way street await their turn at the stop sign in the busy shopping district known as South Street. The blare of angry horns, blowing in contempt and impatience, filled the area. A bright yellow taxi cab turned the corner and stopped in the middle of the street, bringing more loud, angry horn blasts as it held up traffic.

A scantily dressed woman, her long, blond hair hanging loosely about her bare shoulders, stepped out of the cab and went about her way, silencing the angry motorist behind the taxi who lustfully stared at her as she passed. Gabriel stepped out into the street, ignoring the loud horn blast and screeching tires as he walked directly into the path of a passing car. He opened the door to the taxi, knowing where to begin his search.

"Take me to the nearest hospital," he told the cab driver, his mind still at work. The driver slowly pulled off, eyeing his new fare curiously in the rearview mirror.

"The nearest hospital? There's three of them in the area. Which one do you want to go to?"

Gabriel glanced at him peculiarly; he had no idea which hospital to go to. He looked out of the window for some sort of clue.

"Come on, pal, I ain't got all day!" The cab driver huffed impatiently, driving slowly as he waited for the destination, the angry horn blasts behind him beginning to irritate him.

Gabriel waved his hand casually at the driver.

"I mean . . . take your time," the driver said weakly, looking around, confused.

"Excuse me! Officer!" Gabriel shouted from the window as the cab came to a stop at the next intersection.

The officer tipped his black cap up and back as he stepped up to the cab. "Yeah? What's the problem?"

"Umm, yes sir. Maybe you could help me," Gabriel began smoothly. "You see, my friend was in an accident yesterday and I don't know which hospital they took him to. If an ambulance picked someone up from this street, where would they take him?"

"Well, most likely that would be Central. Down on Sixth,"

the officer replied, extending a hand with his index finger up to the impatient driver behind the taxi as he talked with Gabriel.

"Most likely? What do you mean most likely?"

"Look, buddy, you asked me and I told you—"

Gabriel rolled up the window, cutting him off. "Take me to Central."

If he had to search every hospital in the city, then so be it. The driver nodded and pulled into the heavy traffic on the always-busy street.

A young, heavyset, light brown-skinned woman sat back in a large pink leather chair, clicking the channels on the television mounted on the wall of the hospital room. Her eyelids sagged as she tried to focus on the small color set. She glanced down at her silver wristwatch—it was 9 PM. Her white, button-down shirt and gray flannel pants were a bit dusty, and her hair unkempt.

She was tired.

She had sat in this very spot for almost seventy-two hours in her work uniform, keeping vigil. Her eyes drifted over to the heating unit beneath the large window and heavy gray curtains. She frowned softly, rolling her eyes away from the flowers arranged there, knowing the people who had sent them probably didn't give a rat's ass what happened to her brother anyway. The loud clicking of high-heeled shoes out in the bright hallway didn't rouse her from her musings. She was immune to it. Eva, her mother, had spent the last seventy-two hours running in and out of the room, searching for doctors to ask the same old questions over and over again. It was a wonder her shoes were not worn to the sole. Her oldest brother lay in the bed next to her in a coma. He had put a bullet through his own head.

She lounged back lazily in the oversized chair, glancing

over at her brother's still form in the soft light. He had died. Of that they were certain. Somehow the doctors had brought him back. But he had sustained a substantial amount of brain damage, and the doctors held little hope that he would ever recover from his coma. But Kenyatta wasn't worried in the least. She knew her brother. She knew his crazy ass would survive; somehow she just knew it.

She had not even shed a tear when they had told her and her mother the news, but her mother had fallen apart. Kenyatta didn't—*couldn't*—know the pain her mother felt. She knew they had an argument the last time they had talked, but there was a deeper sadness in her mother's tears, a sadness she couldn't understand. Maybe it was guilt, she figured.

Her brother had been raised by their grandmother, who had died when Kenyatta was only eleven. He had lived with them off and on after her death, but her mother and Elijah would always end up getting into an argument and her brother would end up leaving. Kenyatta didn't know why she loved Elijah so much, and she didn't know why she always looked forward to his visits. All he would do was play with that stupid Dungeons and Dragons stuff and pretend he was in his own weird world.

Her mother entered the room, interrupting Kenyatta's thoughts. "I brought you some breakfast, Kenyatta."

"Thank you," she answered, watching her mother come to sit gently on the side of the bed. She looked at the sandwich she handed her disdainfully. "Where you git this from?"

"From the machine," Eva answered absently, staring down at her son lovingly.

Eva was just as tired as her daughter, and the bags underneath her lively brown eyes showed it. Her burgundy-tinted micro-braids hung about her shoulders lazily. Eva was almost 50, but didn't look it in the least. Her tight-fitting black dress had brought many derogatory comments from her free-lipped daughter, and even more stares from the men in the hospital.

She ran her fingers through his hair gently. She couldn't help but feel responsible for it all. The last time she had spoken to her son they had argued. Eva had been angry with her ex-husband, and she had taken it out on all of her children. She had overheard Elijah call her ex-husband's wife 'Mom' while talking to her on the phone.

She had gone off, hollering and screaming for Elijah not to call that bitch 'Mom' in her house. She knew her ex-husband was not the father of her oldest child, but what she didn't know was that Elijah knew it, too. She had lived with the lie for so long that she had actually forgotten about it. She could only stare in disbelief when her son had turned on her in anger and shouted, "If that's the case, then why in the hell should I call him Dad?" He then stormed from the house, slamming the door behind him.

"I don't understand why his hair turned white." Eva gently brushed his thick, white locks back.

"If yo' ass died and came back, yo' hair would probably turn white, too," Kenyatta replied lightly, laughing easily. "Shit, he probably saw Jesus."

"Shut up, Kenyatta." Eva laughed, a tear forming in her eye.

"Ma, I don't know why you're crying," Kenyatta said, standing up to stretch. "Elijah ain't going nowhere. He's too fuckin' crazy to die."

"Yeah, I hope you're right."

"Good evening, ladies."

They both turned around as a man dressed in a doctor's uniform walked into the dimly lit hospital room, his dusty, brown boots clicking loudly on the shiny tiled floor as he entered.

"How's my boy?" he asked, walking by Kenyatta to stand next to the bed.

Kenyatta looked to her mother curiously. They had not seen this doctor before. Her mother shrugged helplessly as the doctor bent over Elijah's body, inspecting him.

"Who the hell are you?" Kenyatta finally asked, causing the doctor to pause and sniff the air.

"I'm sorry," the strange doctor replied, turning to regard Kenyatta with a smile, "that was very uncouth of me. My name is Dr. Gabriel Smith. And you are?"

Before she could answer, he spoke again. "No wait, don't tell me." He inhaled deeply. "You must be the sister."

"So what? Did you come here to tell us the same thing that all the other doctors have told us?" Eva asked sarcastically.

Gabriel turned to regard her, looking deeply into her eyes, causing her to look away nervously. "You must be Mom." He placed a hand on her shoulder.

She shuddered at his touch. His hands were like ice.

"Well, Mom, don't worry. That's not why I'm here." His smile stole her anger away.

"Then why are you here?" Kenyatta asked, drawing his attention away from her mother. She didn't back away from his icy gaze. "If you can't make him come out of his coma, then you might as well leave. Unless you some kind of miracle worker or something, we don't need you," she added, defiantly crossing her arms over her heavy breasts.

"Kenyatta, be quiet. He's just doing his job," Eva said, coming to his defense, although she didn't know exactly why she was doing it. There was just something about this strange man, something almost familiar, like she knew him from somewhere—somewhere in her past.

"No, no, it's okay," Gabriel said, calmly walking over to stand in front of Kenyatta. "You know, I like you," he began quietly. "You're so . . . so . . . so defiant. So belligerent. Not a

care in the world. I bet if the . . . the . . . What's the leader of
your country called again?"

Kenyatta and her mother both looked at each other curiously.

"The President?" they replied in unison.

"Yeah! The President! I bet if the President were standing
right here in front of you, asking you how it was going, you'd
probably tell him to kiss your ass, wouldn't you?" Gabriel
asked, smiling wide.

"If he pissed me off you gotdamned right I would. He
ain't special. He bleeds just like I do." Kenyatta frowned.

Gabriel's smile spread as he looked back and forth from
Kenyatta to her mother. "God, I love this girl!"

"Does any of this have to do with my son?" Eva asked seriously.

"Your son?" Gabriel glanced at her oddly. "Oh! Yes, Elijah,"
he said, as though he had just remembered why he was there.
He turned and gazed down at Elijah. "Don't worry, Mom,
Elijah is going to be just fine."

"You sound very sure of yourself. What do you know that
the other doctors don't?" Eva asked.

Gabriel smirked. "Everything." He leaned over Elijah,
placing his lips to Elijah's ear. "Come back!" he whispered
fiercely.

A look of concern found Eva's face. "What are you doing?"

Gabriel turned a serious gaze her way. "Do you pray, Mom?"

"Y-y-yes. Yes, I do," she stuttered as his eyes locked with her
own.

"Why is that?" His icy stare dug into her very soul. "Why
do you pray?"

"I-I-I don't know."

Kenyatta stood silently, for she could not answer the question herself.

"Who do you pray to?" Gabriel pushed, his tone growing

deeper, almost threatening as he closed the distance between them.

"God, of course!" Eva replied frantically.

She felt Gabriel's breath on her neck as he leaned close. Chill bumps ran up her arms and legs when he spoke.

"Does he answer your prayers, Eva?" he whispered, calling her by name.

Fear gripped her heart. "How do—"

"I knew your name before it was even a whisper in your mother's feeble mind. I watched as she gave birth to you on the bathroom floor in that dingy little apartment. I was there when you were six years old and your father broke both of your arms for pissing in the bed. Remember that nasty accident he had? It wasn't an accident. And I was there, in that dark alley, when you were sixteen and still as pure as the Virgin Mother Mary. When you conceived—" Gabriel paused, glancing back to her son's resting body.

Eva was paralyzed by the fear that now coursed through her veins. Images of that dark night jumped into her mind. That night so long ago. She had been raped by a man. . . .

"Yes. You remember. But worry not," Gabriel whispered. "You have no reason to fear me. I'm actually one of the good guys. Or should I say, I have chosen my sides wisely."

Looking around the room one last time, his eyes fell upon Elijah once more. Then he leaned in close to Eva again. "Pray without ceasing, Eva," he whispered, "for the time will soon come that you will be judged by your faith."

A voice came from the door. "Hey, who are you?"

It was Elijah's doctor, coming to make his rounds.

Gabriel ignored him as he walked to the door. "Shhh." He put a finger to his lips as he uttered the sound, silencing the doctor as he walked out of the open door and into the bright hallway.

Chapter Three
Rebirth

"Welcome, Elijah."

Elijah slowly opened his eyes and the darkness melted away. He was in the cavern again. The same cavern he would battle Reality in whenever he would dream. He focused his senses on the voice. The same voice, always it was the same voice.

"Welcome . . . home."

Elijah's eyes slowly perused the dimly lit area. Something was different this time. There was no threat. No leering evil. Reality and his children were not here to attack him.

"We can leave this place now."

Elijah brought his hand up and tilted his head to the side, shielding his eyes from the bright light that suddenly appeared in front of him. Slowly, his eyes dilated, adjusting to the developing light. He could make out an opening in the cavern wall, an opening that had never been there before. The light, he realized, was the bright golden glow of the sun.

He felt the comforting vibrations of the twin blades upon his hips as the sun shone brightly in the afternoon sky, filling him with warmth as he stood in the entrance of the cavern.

A vast green forest lay before him, the tops of the evergreen trees rolling out into the horizon, their scent filling his nostrils with crisp freshness. Elijah stared out at the marvelous scene and down to the ancient stone steps. Weeds and plants grew amongst the many cracks and crevices in the old stairs that disappeared down into the forest.

He understood then.

With a smile and a great leap, he began his descent, and for the first time in his life, he had no worries, no fear, for finally he had found an escape from the pain; he had finally found the courage to come home.

His thoughts were interrupted by the sound of footsteps and voices when he reached the bottom of the stone stairway. His heart raced at the thought of his first encounter. Would it be human? Or an elf? Maybe even a dwarf! Would he even be able to understand their language? His anxiety carried him swiftly to the edge of a clearing in the heavily wooded forest. He stopped and peered around a tree.

Elves! he exclaimed to himself, recognizing their sharp facial features.

His heart must have been beating a thousand beats per second as he prepared himself for his first encounter. He took a deep breath, steadying himself, trying to bring his pulse back to normal.

"Well . . . here goes nothing!" he said, walking from around the tree and out into the open.

Then he felt himself being pulled away. He tried to scream in protest, but no sound came forth from his lips. He felt the darkness then, enveloping him. Closing his eyes, he tried to concentrate, tried to force the darkness away. It was no use; soon, there was only silence, as the darkness swallowed him.

Gabriel perched silently on the ledge of the roof, waiting. His eyes focused on the brightly lit entrance of the hospital below. He had coerced Azrael, the collector of souls, into doing him a small favor. In return he had offered him—in a very polite way—his life.

As he sat under the moon's soft light, a gentle breeze blew his stark white hair across his smooth face, carrying with it a familiar scent. Gabriel sniffed the air, recognizing the smell. "Hello, Michael." Gabriel didn't bother to turn from his perch.

"Gabriel," Michael greeted him and walked to stand next to him, his long black hair blowing in the breeze. "Always the bringer of change," Michael stated absently, his eyes peering in the direction of the hospital where Gabriel had visited.

"Shouldn't you be commanding your army of angels up there?" Gabriel replied, sounding somewhat annoyed.

"Better that I keep an eye on your dealings, than fight a losing battle."

"God! Do you have to do that? You know, Michael, you should really get out more. No one talks like that anymore. And besides, it's really annoying!" Gabriel chided, his gaze never leaving the front of the hospital.

"What are you about, Gabriel? And why is Azrael so flustered after your meeting with him?"

"I have already killed one of our own this day, Michael. It would be wise for you to keep Zadkiel off my heels."

"Agreed," Michael began, dismissing Gabriel's threat. "We are hard pressed without you, Gabriel. And it is rumored that more of our ranks are becoming sympathetic to Camael's cause."

"Who?"

"Raguel and Haniel, I suspect," Michael replied, naming the angels.

"Fear not, Michael. For soon, you and I both will be able to devote our undivided attention to the war."

"If that were possible, the war would have been over when

it started. We cannot allow Satan and his demons to run unchecked on earth. Without our presence, man will lose faith," Michael said.

"They will lose faith with or without our presence, dear brother. But I agree with you; we cannot allow Satan and his minions too much freedom," Gabriel began. "And unlike you, I have decided to do something about it. Go back and lead your armies, Michael. I will join you shortly. And together we will be victorious. Worry yourself not about man. I will take care of that," Gabriel added, his lips slowly curling into a smile.

"How will you do this?"

Gabriel sighed lightly. "Have I ever let you down before?"

Michael's silence spoke a thousand words. It was not so long ago that Gabriel had spent time outside of God's grace. He had not obeyed a command exactly as it was given, and he had been punished.

"That was a long time ago," Gabriel voiced. "I know what I am doing. Go, Michael, return to your armies," Gabriel said with finality.

"Very well. I will await your return."

"Nooo!"

The tormented scream echoed through the entire floor of the hospital. Kenyatta dropped the soda she had been holding, staring wide-eyed at her now awake brother.

"Elijah!" Eva shouted, startled from her nap.

She jumped up out of the chair and ran to the bed. She grabbed her son's hand eagerly, tears glistening on her cheek.

"Elijah?" she whispered again, as her son lay unmoving, eyes closed.

Elijah knew immediately that his nightmare had returned. He cursed to himself. No matter how hard he tried, happiness just wouldn't be still enough for him to hold on to it.

He had always felt death would be his release, his only hope of holding on to happiness. It had taken him twenty-nine years of pain and suffering to finally find the courage to end it. And in the end, he had failed at that, too. He could still taste the scent of the evergreens upon his tongue, could still hear the whispered voices in the forest.

"Hey, Mom," he whispered, opening his eyes. It took him a moment to bring the room into focus.

"Elijah, I'm so sorry!" Eva began, her tears falling unchecked now. "This is all my fault—"

"Mom, its okay."

But it wasn't okay. Elijah had always wondered just what his life would have been like if he would have known his father, if he'd been raised in a normal family, if his mother hadn't forced him to come back home after his grandmother died. To tell the truth, it *was* her fault. But it didn't matter to Elijah now. Nothing mattered.

"It's about time," Kenyatta said dryly, walking over to the bed. She leaned over and put her arms around her big brother.

Elijah started to say something smart in return, but found himself suddenly choked up. He returned his sister's hug warmly, trying to fight the tears away. "Get off me, cow," he finally managed to say.

"Kiss my cow ass!"

Eva sat back and watched the exchange. A smile found its way to her tear-streaked face. She had her family back.

"Kenyatta . . . are you crying?" Eva asked her daughter.

Kenyatta turned away, picking up a tissue to wipe the tears. "No. I ain't crying. It's something in my eye," she lied.

Eva laughed. "Yes you are! Man, I ain't seen you cry in a long time."

"She's crying 'cause she's hungry!" Elijah said. The gloom slipped away for the moment as they shared a warm bit of laughter.

It didn't last long for him; his mood quickly changed from light to somber. "How long have I been in here?"

Eva tried to force her smile to remain, but it slowly faded away. "Three days. The doctors didn't think you would ever wake up."

"But they don't know your retarded ass like I do. I told Mommy you would be fine," Kenyatta interjected.

"Where are my clothes?" Elijah wanted to be alone and out of the cold hospital room.

Eva frowned. "Why? You can't just get up and leave!"

"Why can't I?" he replied, snatching the IV and other monitors off his arm and wrist.

"Elijah, stop! You have to let them make sure everything is okay."

"I'm fine. Does it look like anything is wrong with me?"

"Besides being crazy?" Kenyatta put in, walking over to the closet to retrieve his clothes. She wanted to be out of there, too.

"Just wait a minute, boy," Eva said forcefully. "Let me see your head."

Elijah obeyed, pausing to let her unwrap the bandage on his head.

"You haven't looked in the mirror lately, have you?" she asked as she pulled the remaining bandaging off.

"Why? Am I ugly now?"

"Oh, my God." Eva's hand went up to her mouth, her eyes wide.

"What?" Kenyatta and Elijah asked together.

"Oh, my God," she repeated.

"What?" Kenyatta asked again, walking over to see what was so shocking. "Damn!" She stared at Elijah's wound—or lack of it.

The wound was totally healed. It was as if it had not been there. There were no scars, no stitches, and even the hair had grown back.

"That's impossible." Eva was still in shock.

"What?" Elijah demanded.

His mother took his chin in her hand and turned his head to inspect the back of it. She pushed his white hair to the side to find nothing.

"I don't understand," she said, looking at Kenyatta helplessly. "He's completely healed."

"Good. Then we can go the hell home now," Kenyatta replied flatly, turning away.

"Kenyatta, you don't find that strange?" Eva turned Elijah's head back and forth again as if she expected to find the wounds she must have somehow overlooked.

"Ain't no stranger than his hair turning white." Kenyatta put her hands on her hips.

"My hair turning white?" Elijah exclaimed, twisting his head back trying to shake off his mother's grip. "Ma! Let go!" he shouted, finally breaking free.

He threw back the sheet and stood up. He paused, feeling the blood in his veins begin to circulate. He clenched his fist at his side a few times. A strange feeling flowed through him. Then he remembered. It was the same feeling that filled him in his dreams: when the rage would take over as he fought off the demons.

"What's wrong?" Eva saw Elijah pause. She rushed around the bed to support him, but he waved her away.

"No, no. I'm fine," he whispered.

Fine was not the word for it. Elijah felt more alive than he had ever felt in his life. His jaw dropped open when he stared into the mirror above the small sink in the corner of the room. "What the fuck?"

Every hair on his head was white, even his facial hair. He ran his hand over his neatly trimmed goatee, a smile slowly working its way to his lips. He liked it. He ran his fingers through his thick mane, now as white as snow.

"Kenyatta, you have to braid my hair."

Kenyatta shot him a frown. "I ain't braidin' shit. I don't do hair."

"You know your grandfather's hair turned white before he was fifty," Eva commented, walking over to stand next to her son.

"Yeah, you sort of look like Longboy," Kenyatta added, laughing.

"Kiss my ass, Kenyatta," Elijah replied absently, ignoring the reference to their deceased alcoholic grandfather. "Hand me my pants."

"Elijah, you can't leave yet. At least let the doctors check you out first."

Kenyatta rolled her eyes and picked up her jacket. "Ma, you got some nerve. As many times you've walked out of hospitals? Please. We out."

"Yeah, but I didn't have a bullet wound in my head!" Eva protested.

"And neither does he. You saw that for yourself," Kenyatta answered back, gathering her things.

"B-b-but—"

"But nothing, Mom. I'm out of here," Elijah stated, slipping on his faded blue jeans.

"But what about the police? They have officers outside waiting. What the hell happened that night anyway, Elijah?" Eva asked.

"Oh. That." Elijah sighed heavily as memories of that night entered his mind. "I don't know. Some guy tried to kill me, I think." He pulled his blue T-shirt over his white hair.

"His name was Marcus Hooks," Eva said as Kenyatta rolled her eyes and placed her hands on her hips impatiently. "That name mean anything to you?"

Elijah repeated the name over in his head, trying to remember. Then he stopped, his eyes closing as he remembered where he had heard that name before. "Andrea." He whispered the name, remembering the married woman he'd had a brief affair with almost a year ago.

"Who is Andrea?" Eva asked.

"A name from the past. Someone I had forgotten about, but evidently her husband remembered." *So that's it. My only chance at happiness, taken away by my own sinful past.*

Elijah sighed heavily once more as he thought of the events that had transpired three nights earlier. *My heart's desire died from a bullet that was meant for me . . . How fitting.* Elijah's demeanor quickly changed when he looked up into his mother's concerned eyes.

"Well, you can't leave. You have to tell the police that," Eva said.

"Ma, come on. We're leaving," Kenyatta said, ignoring Eva's words, walking toward the door.

At the same moment a short, bald doctor entered the room, accompanied by a slim, black nurse.

"What's going on?" Dr. Hollace asked, looking around the room at each of them curiously. Then he realized his comatose patient was no longer comatose. "How? W-when?" He walked over to stand in front of Elijah.

Elijah sat down on the edge of the hospital bed, looking around for his Timbs.

"Mr. Garland," the doctor began, regaining his composure, "how are you feeling?"

"Fine," Elijah replied. "Kenyatta, where are my shoes?"

"Right here." Kenyatta bent over to pull his shoes out from underneath the other side of the bed.

"Mr. Garland, you can't leave," the doctor commented flatly. "You have to be cleared, and the police want to talk to you. And you still have wounds—" His words dropped from his lips when he saw that the wounds he was referring to no longer existed. "That's impossible. How?"

Elijah ignored him as he tied up his black Timberlands.

"Mr. Garland, please. You can't just walk out."

Elijah smiled, tying up his other boot. "Oh no? Watch me."

"Mr. Garland, don't make me have to call security. Please, just give me until the morning, and we'll discuss your release then. Please."

"You can call whomever you wish. No one is going to keep me from walking out of this hospital tonight." Elijah stood to look the doctor in the eye.

"Mr. Garland, please! You have to stay. We cannot allow you to leave in your condition!"

"Just what do you mean, in my condition?" Elijah asked, staring down at the doctor.

Dr. Hollace backed up a step, feeling Elijah's gaze burning into him. He motioned to the nurse. "Get the officers outside," he said nervously.

"And what is my condition, Doctor?" Elijah asked again, taking a step toward him.

"Elijah, please. Just wait until the morning," Eva said, walking over to stand in front of Elijah.

"Mr. Garland, you have to understand. It was only three days ago that you put a gun to your own head and tried to kill your—"

"No, if I'm correct, I *did* kill myself," Elijah interrupted sarcastically.

"Well, technically, yes, you did. But you still have to be evaluated by a mental health professional, and the police also want to question you. . . . And then there's the fact that your wounds have healed completely in such a short time. There are still tests we have to run. You just can't leave yet. I'm sorry, but it's out of the question," the doctor finished, his resolve strengthened by the return of the nurse, accompanied by two police officers.

Kenyatta sighed when the officers entered. "Ohhh boy. Y'all done fucked up now."

"Is there a problem, Doctor?" one of the officers asked loudly, walking over to stand next to him.

"It will be in a minute," Kenyatta muttered, chuckling as she walked toward the door. "Ma, come on. You better get out of the way, 'cause it's about to be some shit."

"Shut up, Kenyatta, no it's not. Elijah, listen to me. Just stay until the morning and we'll see what happens then. I'll stay with you," Eva said. "Now just sit down."

Elijah let her guide him back to the bed.

"Kenyatta, come here," Elijah called to his sister.

"Yes, Mr. Garland. Please listen to your mother," Dr. Hollace pleaded.

Elijah ignored him and pulled his sister in for a hug. "Meet me outside in five minutes," he whispered into her ear. "Okay. I'll stay," he said aloud, letting his sister go and sitting back onto the bed.

Eva looked at the two of them suspiciously.

"Thank you, Mr. Garland." the doctor said.

"Ma, can you please go and get me a cheesesteak?" he asked, looking at his mother innocently.

"Yeah, Ma, come on. I'm hungry, too," Kenyatta added, pulling at her mother's arm.

Outside in the hall, one of the officers immediately called their supervisor to report the change in Elijah's status.

"Right now?" Eva asked. "Where we going to get a cheesesteak from this late? It's after ten o' clock; nothing's open." Eva knew they were up to something, but she didn't want to let the doctor know it, too.

"Ma, I know where we can get one at. Come on," Kenyatta said.

"No. Wait a minute," Eva replied, trying to buy some time.

"Ma, please. I'm starving. If you don't go, I'll get up and go get it myself. And I won't come back."

"Can't you wait a minute?"

"Never mind," Elijah said, sliding forward to get out of the bed.

"Okay, okay, but you better not leave." She lowered her voice so the doctor couldn't hear.

"I won't." Elijah sat back on the bed and threw his feet up. The doctor moved in.

"Can I check a few things real quick?" he asked, pulling out his stethoscope.

"We'll be right back, okay?" Eva said, moving to get out of the doctor's way.

"Okay, Mom," Elijah replied impatiently.

Eva and her daughter walked out of the room.

"What were you two whispering about in there?" Eva asked while they stood waiting for the elevator.

"You'll find out," Kenyatta muttered, stepping onto the elevator.

"What's that supposed to mean?" Eva paused just outside of the elevator door.

"Nothing, Mom, just come on!" Kenyatta pulled her reluctant mother onto the elevator.

"This is just incredible," the doctor was saying as he examined Elijah's head. "I've never seen anything like this before," he added, sounding mystified. "Even the scars from your IV are completely healed!"

"That's all wonderful, doc," Elijah said, interrupting the doctor's rambling. "I suppose you would like me to stay, so you and your little friends can find out why," he stated, smiling.

"Yes . . . yes, of course," the doctor replied absently, caught up in his findings. "I mean, that is, we just want to make sure you're okay," he added quickly, trying to clean up his words.

The doctor stepped back, deep in thought. He would have to call the head surgeon immediately. What he was seeing before him was medically impossible. A wound that would normally take months to completely heal had disappeared in less than three days! This was something big. The possibilities were limitless.

"If you will excuse me, Mr. Garland, I must get your chart from the nurse's station. I'll be right back." The doctor slipped his clipboard underneath of his arm and walked toward the door. He had to act quickly. He didn't know how long they would be able to keep the patient there to run the required tests.

"Excuse me, officers. May I have a word with you?" he said as he walked out of the room and approached the officers.

"Everything okay, doc?" one of them asked.

"Actually, no. You see, this patient attempted suicide and we believe he may try to get out and try it again. But that's not the only problem." He looked around nervously. "You see, we think the patient may be carrying some type of virus. A virus that could possibly be very deadly," he lied, lowering his voice to a whisper.

The officers looked at one another.

"A virus?" the second officer asked worriedly.

"Oh, don't worry; it's nothing for you to be concerned about. It cannot be spread by touch," the doctor added quickly, sensing their trepidation. "I'm going to call the chief surgeon now to find out how he wants me to handle this. But it is imperative that the patient does not leave."

"Don't worry, doc. He's not going anywhere any time soon. Until you guys clear him, that is. Then he'll be escorted downtown to the courthouse."

"Are you sure it's not contagious?" the other officer asked.

"I'm positive. Now, I'm going to make a phone call. Whatever you do, don't let him leave!" he exclaimed in a whisper. Turning, he headed for the nurse's station, leaving the two officers in the hall.

"What do you think, Jones?" the tall, black, heavyset officer asked his partner.

"Well, he's a little guy; shouldn't be too much of a prob-lem if he tries to leave," he replied, pausing to retrieve a pair of latex gloves from his pocket. "All we have to do is keep him here until they decide if he's gonna be released." He pulled the gloves on with a loud snap. "Then we'll take him downtown."

The other officer followed suit, pulling out his own gloves and snapping them on just in time to look up and see the pa-tient stroll casually into the hallway.

Elijah stopped when he exited the room, looking one way and then the other. He spotted the elevator just beyond the two officers, who were now walking his way.

"Sir, I'm going to have to ask you to return to your room," Jones said firmly, stepping to intercept Elijah, his partner close behind.

Elijah felt the adrenaline rush through his veins as the of-ficer closed the distance. But he felt something else also. He felt a sense of power flowing through him, a power that he had never experienced before—at least not here.

Suddenly the two officers approaching him, one standing at least six feet four inches and weighing about 245, and the other standing about three inches shorter but looking to weigh about the same, seemed to be a very minuscule obsta-cle for Elijah.

Elijah thought nothing more of it as he caught the first of-ficer's outstretched hand in his own. Stepping into him, he pushed the officer's arm back and down, causing him to bend backwards awkwardly and howl in pain. Elijah heard the loud pop as the officer's elbow snapped out of joint, but he paid it no mind. He saw the other officer reaching for him. With his free hand, he almost casually pushed the scream-ing officer away. The officer's body flew into the closed door of a patient's room, shattering it into splinters as he contin-ued to slide across the smooth, shining floor, bouncing heavily off the cooling system on the wall on the far side of the room, and leaving a deep indentation.

"Hey! Get the hell out of here!" an old man shouted angrily from his bed at the officer's groaning, prone form.

The other officer paused to watch his partner fly through the heavy wooden door. "What the hell?"

Soon, he, too, was sliding across the floor of the very same room, leaving an indentation of his own in the cooling system.

The half-senile old man looked down at the semiconscious officers curiously. "Is this about the missing Viagra?"

Dr. Hollace watched it all in awe, along with the other members of the staff. They all stood watching, their jaws hanging open in disbelief.

Elijah walked on. He paid no attention to the ease at which he had dispatched the officers.

"Stop him!" Dr. Hollace shouted, snapping out of his shock. "Quick! Call the front desk downstairs. Tell them there's a patient coming down on the west elevator. They are not to allow him to leave!" he shouted at a nurse sitting behind the desk of the nurse's station. "Someone call the police now!" he exclaimed, running for the stairs. The patient was already on the elevator.

Elijah looked up at the numbers over the elevator door. He was on the fifth floor. The elevator seemed to crawl downward, coming to a stop on the fourth floor. The doors opened and a rotund nurse walked onto the elevator, pushing the button for the third floor. Elijah eyed her in contempt. The doors slowly closed and the elevator once again continued its crawl.

"You lazy bitch," Elijah said slowly, as the elevator came to a halt once again.

"Excuse me?" the nurse exclaimed, turning to look at Elijah incredulously.

"You heard me. I called you a lazy bitch," Elijah said calmly, looking her square in the eye.

The nurse stumbled off the elevator, staring back at Elijah in disbelief. Elijah closed his eyes, regretting his harsh words and wondering why he had voiced them. He couldn't understand the strange, invulnerable feeling flowing through him. He knew he would never have said anything like that to anyone; he had been raised too well for that—so why now? He thought no more of it as the door closed, and this time it didn't stop until it reached the ground floor. Three security guards stood ready in the lobby, hurrying staff and visitors alike out of the brightly lit area. The men watched the elevator door slowly open.

Elijah could see the exit from where he stood. He paid the three guards no attention as he strolled off the elevator in the direction of the glass doors.

"Take him down!" one of them yelled as bystanders suddenly found themselves scrambling to get out of the way.

The first guard came at Elijah directly. Lowering his head, he charged forward, attempting to tackle Elijah to the ground. Elijah stepped to the side. Turning slightly, he grabbed the guard by the back of the neck, spinning him in a complete circle to aid the guard's momentum, and then he let go, sending the poor man slamming into the closing elevator door, bending the hard steel before he fell unconscious to the lobby floor. The other two guards stopped in their tracks. Elijah walked on.

"What are you doing? Stop him!" Dr. Hollace shouted.

The guards looked at each other, back to the doctor, and then to their fallen friend.

"Fuck that. You stop him!" one of them replied.

Elijah walked through the automatic doors and paused, deeply inhaling the familiar scent of the city. What a contrast it was to the crisp evergreen scent he had experienced in his dream. *Was it a dream?* His eyes went up to the night sky, and the same moon that had stared down on him and his now dead Taysia was there, staring back at him. Slowly he lowered his gaze, letting the memories fade as he spotted his ride. There was Kenyatta and his mother, sitting in his mother's black Chrysler Sebring convertible, waiting.

"Stop!" Dr. Hollace screamed as he ran out behind Elijah. But no one was there to help.

He watched helplessly as Elijah jumped into the car and Eva slammed on the gas, leaving a set of thick, black rubber marks in her wake. He ran behind the car, trying desperately to see the license plate number through the thick, white smoke.

Elijah leaned forward in between the passenger and driver seats with a smile on his face. "Can we go and get my cheesesteak now?"

Chapter Four
Sacrificial Lamb

If Gabriel could have seen what went down inside of the hospital, there wouldn't have been enough room on his face to contain his smile. As it was, Elijah was awake and free. That was all he needed to know. Now all that remained was contact.

Elijah would have to learn his place, and Gabriel would show him exactly where it was. But he had to be careful. Gabriel had watchfully guided every stage of Elijah's life, every moment of heartache, every tear, carefully nurturing the rage so that when the time came, he would be able to handle the power. Gabriel just had to make sure Elijah didn't blow up in his face. It was a possibility. It all depended on Elijah. If he saw Gabriel as the cause of all his suffering and chose death—again—rather than servitude, then Gabriel would be forced to start from the beginning. He didn't have time for that.

Gabriel's smile disappeared when he noticed the lone human form down on the sidewalk in front of the hospital, staring up at him. He knew immediately that this was no normal man, but a man possessed by a demon, for no man could look upon an angel unless allowed.

Gabriel's attention was drawn to his feet. Tiny spiders appeared, crawling from all over. There were hundreds of them, all moving in the same direction. They crawled past him and onto the roof behind him. Gabriel sighed and leaned his head back slowly, closing his eyes. He felt the dark presence behind him, but he didn't turn.

"Tell me, Gabriel," the cold voice whispered, "how is your faith?"

Gabriel ignored the question.

"How does it feel to be loved the most?" the voice continued. "Oh, forgive me. I should be asking man that question. After all, that *is* who He loves most," the voice added, moving up to the edge of the rooftop to stand next to Gabriel. "Isn't that right?"

"Why are you wasting your time here? Shouldn't you be somewhere possessing little girls and making them puke on priests?" Gabriel replied sarcastically, his eyes still on the hospital below.

"Amusing words, dear brother," Lucifer answered, turning on Gabriel quickly.

Before Gabriel could react, he felt his arm twist up into the small of his back, and his hair snatched back violently. Then he felt Lucifer's breath on his neck.

"I know why you're here," he whispered into Gabriel's ear.

"That makes two of us." Gabriel grimaced as Lucifer pulled his head back farther. He was bluffing, trying to get Gabriel to let him in on some information.

"Where is he?" Lucifer growled. "Where is your little pet?"

Gabriel scowled in pain. Lucifer twisted his arm up higher, almost lifting his feet off the ground. Gabriel went with the momentum. Kicking out, his foot finding the edge of the roof, he flipped himself up and over Lucifer's head.

Kicking out with both feet, he used Lucifer's back as a springboard; he flipped once more, the force sending Lucifer over the edge of the roof. Gabriel landed on his feet, dropping down to one knee, ready to move. He felt the ripples in the air behind him as Lucifer reappeared. Gabriel dove forward into a roll immediately, lessening the blow that glanced off the back of his head. He twisted and stood, facing The Fallen One.

"Come on, brother," Gabriel whined sarcastically. "There are little girls down there waiting for you. Must we waste this time fighting? And you know time is not something you have a lot of."

"I could kill you now," Lucifer said coldly, brushing his long black hair out of his remarkably beautiful face. "But that would accomplish nothing."

"Nothing you do accomplishes anything. Don't you know that?" Gabriel smirked. "I mean, seriously! You possess a few priests, blow up a few buildings, and kill hundreds and thousands of people. I mean, who cares? We all know how it's going to end anyway. Am I right? Or am I right?"

"If that is so," Lucifer began, his gaze stealing the mirth from Gabriel's tongue, "then why are you here, archangel?"

Gabriel could find no response. He watched Lucifer turn away, his black trench coat flowing behind him.

"And Gabriel," Lucifer paused, glancing back over his shoulder, "I will find him. And I will kill him, just like the rest," Lucifer said with finality.

Gabriel watched his form explode into a thousand tiny spiders, all scattering into the darkness. He stamped his boot down angrily as one of them ventured close to his foot.

Somewhere in Eastern Pennsylvania, in a large underground bunker, Charles Kreicker stood in the center of a huge pentagram, his arms outstretched as the chants rose around him in the dark room. The only light came from the squat red candles placed at each point of the star, drawn out in what looked to be blood.

Charles reveled in the power he felt. He was the youngest ever to lead the cult of which he had been a devout follower since the age of seventeen. He was now twenty-two, and the congregation had grown greatly since its beginning. He thought it very ironic, as he looked around the room at all of the loyal followers, their white robes and hoods pulled over their heads as they chanted in unison, that he had become their spiritual leader.

His parents were devout Catholics. Charles had spent more time in church coming up than he had spent sleeping. He had only joined the cult to make a statement, just to piss his parents off. He never really took these ceremonies all that seriously. It was basically just for show, at least as far as he was concerned. But it had become harder and harder to fake the ceremonies as the cult grew. Now it was almost impossible.

It had even branched out. Others, who lived too far away, had started their own sects, all claiming to be a part of the original. Some sects were merely white supremacists, and did not take part in the ceremonies like this one, but they all held on to the ties of the original cult. He had thought about leaving the cult for a while, but had then thought better of it as he came to realize the power the cult held in society. They had members everywhere, from the police force to the FBI. The group definitely had its perks. He knew his place though; he was simply a figurehead. With his long blonde hair and bright blue eyes, he stood out as the poster boy for white supremacy.

He had meetings once a week with the older and stronger members, the real leaders of the cult. They would guide him and give him his instructions. Some of them wished to remain anonymous, sending a representative with a letter, which he was then instructed to burn. Others stayed in contact through the Internet, using the Web site that he had created for himself.

He let his eyes roam across the room, wondering briefly why it was so humid in early October. Thin lines of sweat were beginning to run down his pale face, and the air smelled of sulfur. From his vantage atop the raised altar, he could see to the far end of the dark chamber, where all the white robes gathered. He took a deep breath as he realized he was near the end of the ceremony.

He looked down at the squirming form of the young girl, her hands tied and feet bound in chains. Charles felt his heart skip a beat as he stared at the sweat glistening on her naked body. They had been through this act a hundred times before. He looked into her fear filled eyes, and she began to squirm more forcefully, heightening the act.

Tonya was an excellent actress. His eyes moved to the ceremonial dagger lying next to her. The chants escalated, the congregation sensing the culmination of the ceremony. Charles reached slowly for the dagger, his eyes falling on the tattoo of a rose on the back of his hand between his thumb and finger, the symbol of their order.

The Order of the Rose.

His hand closed over the hilt of the dagger and he began the words.

"Satan, our great and all powerful Lord." He recited the words from memory, bringing the dagger up and holding it in both hands, just above Tonya's heart. "We worship you with this sacrifice, a pure and untouched symbol, a symbol of our faith."

The chants ceased, and all eyes looked to Charles and the upraised dagger. Not a soul seemed to even breathe a breath, all waiting for the dagger to fall. Charles could almost feel the power in the poignant room. He could sense their desire to see the dagger fall. Charles fought back the sudden urge to vomit, as the evil in their hearts over-whelmed him. He could never get used to that. He raised his arms into the air slowly, drawing anxious gasps from the gathering.

"A symbol of our faith!" he shouted, making his voice fluc-tuate to get the maximum effect. "In you!" he exclaimed, his eyes finding Tonya's as the moment was upon them.

Charles froze where he stood. Chill bumps ran across his skin as he looked down at Tonya. Her eyes, once a vibrant shade of brown, were now black as coals. She stared up at Charles, a devilish grin spreading across her face. Charles couldn't move. He was frozen with fear. This had never hap-pened before.

"Kill her, Charles," a low rasping voice demanded from out of Tonya's lips. "Kill her now!"

Charles felt his skin beginning to burn. He felt something in his head, some sort of evil presence. Sweat rolled down his face as he found himself suddenly struggling to retain his soul. But the demon was strong, and soon Charles was watch-ing it all from somewhere inside of his own head. He looked up at the dagger he held above his head and watched in hor-ror as it disappeared, only to be replaced by another wickedly barbed blade. This blade would not collapse as the other one would, and Tonya would surely die.

He tried to scream, but he could find no sound. The blade fell swiftly, plunging into Tonya's heart. Howls and screams of ecstasy erupted throughout the room. Charles watched it all in horror; he saw the surprised and confused look now in Tonya's eyes, as the blade, guided by his own hands, dug wickedly at her heart. He looked on in disbelief as he reached in and violently snatched her still beating heart from her chest.

Dalfien chuckled at the revulsion in his host and raised the girl's heart into the air for all to see. Cries and praises to Satan rose up all around the room as he lowered the black muscle to his mouth. Charles tasted the blood as his teeth tore into the heart. Then he felt the darkness take him.

Dalfien looked over the gathering, judging them all one by one. He grinned wickedly; every soul in the room held nothing but a desire to serve his father. A silence fell across the congregation as they awaited his guidance. He would enjoy his time here, but first, there was his father's business to tend to.

Chapter Five
Ravenous

Kenyatta and her mother watched in open-mouthed amazement as Elijah finished his third cheesesteak. They had stopped at Lorenzo's, a popular cheesesteak shop that stayed open twenty-four hours, not far from Elijah's apartment on South Street. The two women continued to gawk at Elijah as they sat near the front of the brightly lit store, ignorant to the stares of the young couple who had just entered through the double glass doors.

Elijah closed his eyes in bliss, devouring the last bite of his third steak. He let the soft, seasoned meat roll over his pallet, mixing with the mayonnaise, ketchup, and Cheez Whiz. *Damn, that's some good shit.* He smiled as he brought a large napkin up to wipe the excess mustard and ketchup mix from the corner of his mouth.

Elijah felt like he could eat three more of the famous sandwiches.

He was famished.

"Are you ok?" Eva asked, looking at her son with concern.

"What do you mean?" Elijah asked.

"Nigga, you just ate three giant cheesesteaks!" Kenyatta

exclaimed, sitting forward in the hard plastic chair to stare at her brother.

"So? I've been in a coma for the last three days. That's one cheesesteak for each day." Elijah smiled.

"What happened in the hospital, Elijah?" Eva asked.

"What do you mean what happened? I left."

"They didn't try to stop you?"

"Yes, they tried," Elijah replied, looking around the shop, feeling the curious eyes on him.

The small shop brought back a few memories to Elijah. Lorenzo's had been one of his usual hangouts on late nights; often he would bring Ericka here to get a bite to eat after she had gotten off work. His eyes went to the rear of the shop and the long counter. A young couple holding hands stood in front, staring up at the large menu over the window of the counter. Elijah eyed the foreign men behind the partition, trying to place the faces. They wore white cook shirts stained with flour and other substances he couldn't make out. He let his attention go back to the room itself; the cook he'd had a fight with must have been fired or was off for the night.

"They tried?" Eva asked, bringing Elijah back to the table.

He didn't understand what was happening to him, and really wasn't in the mood to talk about it.

"What's that mean, they tried?" she asked, staring Elijah in the eye.

"I'm thirsty," Elijah said suddenly, standing up and walking toward the counter. "I'm going to get another soda."

"Ma, you worry too much," Kenyatta said. "Why can't you just be happy that he's okay?"

"I am, I am. I just don't understand what's going on."

Kenyatta frowned. "Why you always got to be so damned curious?"

"I ain't curious," Eva began. "I mean, don't you want to know why he healed so fast? That doesn't seem strange to you?"

"Curious, like the fuck I said." Kenyatta chuckled.

"Oh, just shut up, Kenyatta," Eva said, frustrated. "I don't even know why I waste my breath talking to you."

"Because you know I make sense," Kenyatta said, smiling. "You need to stop playing Inspector fuckin' Gadget and just relax. You know what they say: curiosity killed the rat."

"The cat, you damned fool!" Eva corrected her, laughing lightly.

"Cat, rat, bat, kitten. I don't give a shit. Whatever it was, it killed the little muthafucka," Kenyatta returned absently.

Elijah returned to the table as they shared a laugh, carrying a jumbo drink that was already half empty.

"What's so funny?" he asked as he sat down.

"Kenyatta says I'm being too curious. Do you think I am?"

"You always have been. But I can understand why. I mean, it's only natural for a mother to be concerned," Elijah answered.

"Then why do you think you healed so fast?"

"Ohhh boy. Ma, will you please leave that shit alone! What difference do it make? Would you rather his brains be hangin' out of his head for the next three months? Damn, the shit is gone. Leave it alone!" Kenyatta rolled her eyes in disgust. She was never one to dwell on anything, good or bad.

"Yeah, but three days, Kenyatta?" Eva was determined to get some answers from somewhere.

"What makes you think I know why?" Elijah asked.

"I bet you that strange doctor had something to do with it," Eva said excitedly.

Elijah looked up. "What doctor?"

"The doctor! I don't remember his name. He came in the room and leaned over you and it looked like he whispered something into your ear. You remember, Kenyatta?"

"That muthafucka was touched, too," Kenyatta replied.

Elijah glanced at Kenyatta. "What do you mean?"

"He was crazy. Asking me some off the wall shit about the president and shit. I don't know what he was saying to Mommy, but she was fucked up for a minute."

Elijah looked at his mother. "What did he say to you?"

"Nothing, I don't remember," Eva said uncomfortably. But she did remember. She remembered very clearly every word he had whispered to her.

"Bullshit. She remembers. I don't know what he said, and I don't really care, but I know it fucked her head up. If she wants to sit here and lie about it, then fuck it," Kenyatta said.

"Kenyatta, you don't know what I remember. And I ain't got to lie about nothing," Eva said defensively, her tone letting Kenyatta know she was approaching that line.

"Anybody own a black convertible sitting outside? 'Cause the cops are about to give you a ticket," one of the cooks yelled out as he strolled into the shop. When he spotted Elijah, he did a double- take.

Elijah recognized him as the same cook he had fought with—and embarrassed.

"Oh, shit!" Eva shouted, jumping up to grab her things. "That's us! Come on!"

Elijah stood to follow them as they ran out of the steak shop. But something told him to slow down. He watched from the front of the store as his mother and sister approached the officers.

Something was wrong.

There were three police cars parked around her car. It didn't take six cops to write a parking ticket. Elijah walked to the corner and casually stepped around it, turning to peek back around to see what was happening.

"Is this your car, ma'am?" one officer asked Eva as she approached.

"Yeah, why? What's wrong?" Eva asked, realizing this wasn't about a ticket.

"Are you Mrs. Garland?" another officer asked.

"Yes. Why?"

"Where is your son?"

"My son? I have three of them. Which one are you talking about?"

"Hey, Joe! Check the steak place!" he called back to another officer. "Take them both downtown," he then ordered, walking toward the steak shop.

Kenyatta's, eyebrows arched abruptly. "Take who downtown?"

"Take us downtown for what? What did we do?" Eva asked the two remaining officers.

"We need to ask you two some questions. Now you can come peacefully, or we can place you under arrest."

"Under arrest for what?" Kenyatta exclaimed.

"For aiding and abetting."

"Aiding and abetting who?" Eva demanded.

Elijah watched the four officers walk into the steak shop. He knew they were looking for him, but he wanted to be sure his mother and sister were okay. He watched as they were led to one of the police cars and placed in the back seat.

"Hey! Come over here!"

Elijah broke into a run as the officer coming out of the steak shop spotted him.

"We got him! He just ran around the corner!" he yelled back into the shop. He ran to the corner and stopped in his tracks as the other officers caught up.

"Better get the cruiser; we got a track star," he said as they watched Elijah turn the corner, already at the next block.

Elijah turned the corner and sprinted as fast as he could, the small row of houses lining the block becoming a blur. He knew he was a speedster, but as he reached the next corner, he knew he was running *too* fast. He slowed a bit and made the turn. In moments, he was at the next corner.

He pulled up short of the last building, wiping the water

from his eyes and face. He peeked around the corner at the steak shop. The last cop car was just turning the corner in his pursuit. He smiled to himself, and casually walked up to his mother's car. Reaching under the front bumper he found her extra key.

"I love you, Mom," he whispered, jumping into the car. He paused for a second, a confused expression on his face.

"Where the hell am I going to go?"

He sped off into the night, unsure of his destination. He knew they would be at his old apartment, so that was out of the question. He also knew his mother was a law abiding citizen, so all of her papers on the car and on her license would no doubt be correct. So her house was not an option either.

Kenyatta, on the other hand . . .

Elijah pulled up to the entrance of the Tasker projects slowly, looking for cops. Seeing none, he pulled the car into the trash littered lot and parked it behind his sister's unit. He walked up to the door, looking around nervously. A smile came to his face when he turned the handle to her front door.

It was open.

He closed the door and walked over to the couch. Although it was in the middle of Ghetto Central, Kenyatta's home was beautiful once you made it through the front door. Kenyatta's boyfriend, The Drug Dealer, as Elijah simply referred to him, gave her anything she wanted. He snorted as he walked past the big screen TV and the huge entertainment system to his left. *All of this money and they leave the door wide the fuck open.* He quickly pulled the purple curtains closed and flopped down on the comfortable black leather couch. His stomach growled in complaint as he laid his head back. Alone for the first time since his rebirth, his thoughts wandered.

There were so many questions. And he had no idea where he would get the answers. He sighed deeply, his thoughts going back to the happiness he thought he had finally found. It had taken him so long to find the courage to do what he knew was his only hope at finding peace. And somehow, he had failed at that, too. No. He had succeeded. He had been there. The doctors had even said it themselves. Elijah sat up on the couch, trying to put it all together. Someone, or something, had brought Elijah back. It wasn't the doctors—couldn't be. They were in as much shock as everyone else. Elijah knew he didn't come back on his own. He wanted the exact opposite.

He looked down at his hand, flexing his fist open and closed repeatedly. And what of this strange feeling of power? Why, all of a sudden, did he feel so full of life? His hands went up to his head, and he ran his fingers through his thick, white hair. And what about the wounds? His mother was right; it was not possible for someone to heal that quickly.

Elijah stiffened as he felt a chill run through his body.

Something was about.

Elijah stared at the front door warily. Slowly rising to his feet, he stalked silently over to the window. He saw a shadow flit past the bottom of the front door. An envelope slid underneath the door. Elijah ran to the door and snatched it open. He looked all around, but there wasn't a soul to be seen anywhere. He closed the door and looked down at the envelope curiously. Bending over he picked it up and opened it. Inside he found a roundtrip plane ticket to—

"Jerusalem?" Elijah exclaimed in shock. "Hell naww! I ain't going to no fuckin' Jerusalem!"

Elijah inspected the ticket further. The departure time couldn't be right. It said three AM. That was in less than three hours.

"I am not going to Jerusalem," Elijah whispered to himself, dumping the remainder of the envelope onto the glass coffee table.

Along with the ticket, there was a credit card with his name on it. He almost overlooked the small piece of paper that fell out last. There was one word written on it.

WHY?

"Jerusalem it is then," he whispered to himself.

Whoever had sent these tickets had some answers. He had no other options anyway. The police were searching for him, and he desperately wanted to know why he was not allowed to stay in bliss. He wanted to know who was behind his new life.

He ran upstairs to the bathroom, searching through Kenyatta's makeup and toiletries. He found a wig and some black mascara. He would need to hide his hair. Slipping a stocking cap on, he then fitted the wig, cutting it short so it resembled an afro. He took the mascara and carefully colored his mustache and goatee. Then he found a piece of paper and left a note, telling his mother and sister where he had gone. Then he left out, heading for the airport.

Chapter Six
Interrogation

Kenyatta tapped her foot on the floor impatiently. She had been led to a small, unremarkable room that held a single square table and a lone metal chair. The officer told her someone would be with her in a minute and locked the door behind him when he had left.

That was almost two hours ago. Damn that brother of hers. He was always getting her involved in some shit. But she loved his crazy ass. After all, Elijah and her little brother, Kendell, were the only family she had. And although he didn't know it, Kenyatta looked up to Elijah with a respect that she herself was ashamed of. And she would be damned if she would admit it. Even though they had spent almost all of their lives at each other's throats, Kenyatta knew without a doubt her brother would die protecting her, and would give her anything she asked for if it was within his means.

When Kenyatta had first heard her brother was dead, she refused to believe it. Ever since they were small, Elijah would always disappear for months, even years, but he would always pop up out of nowhere, alive and in perfect health. How she would miss his crazy ass when he was gone. So she had no other choice but to believe her brother would return to her.

"Hello, Mrs. Garland."

Kenyatta looked up from her thoughts to see a young black woman enter the room. She wasn't a cop; at least she didn't have on a uniform. She was kind of small, only about five foot five, and looked to weigh no more than a buck thirty. Her hair was cut short and styled nicely. She wore very little makeup, except for a bit of red lipstick on her full lips.

"You wastin' your time, 'cause I ain't sayin' shit until I see a lawyer." Kenyatta crossed her arms and looked away.

"Nice to meet you, too," the woman replied, walking over to stand in front of the table opposite Kenyatta.

"Ain't no nice-to-meet shit," Kenyatta began angrily. "I been sittin' in this fuckin' room for almost three hours. I'm hungry, I have to go to the bathroom, and I want a fuckin' cigarette. And like I said, I ain't sayin' a fuckin' word until I see a lawyer."

"My name is Agent Ebonee Lane, and I'm sorry you had to wait so long, but your brother is in some serious trouble. I'm with the FBI. My partner and I have been assigned to his case—"

"FBI? Fuck did he do? Die wrong?"

"No, Mrs. Garland. Your brother is wanted for questioning in the deaths of two individuals and for assaulting two police officers." She paused to angle a serious stare at Kenyatta. "And if he doesn't turn himself in soon, it will look really bad for him if they pin him with a murder rap."

"That's what the fuck everybody is chasing him for?"

"Mrs. Garland—"

"Kenyatta," Kenyatta corrected her, loosening up a bit.

"Kenyatta, we received a call from a doctor claiming that a

man with a gunshot wound to the head got up and walked out of the hospital three days later without so much as a scratch. That alone gave us a reason to investigate. But the doctor also informed us that the patient was carrying an unknown virus, a virus that he claimed to have never seen before, but one that he knew was deadly," she explained.

"A virus? Ain't nobody say nothing to us about a virus."

"That's because there is no virus, at least as far as his initial blood screenings are concerned. The doctor told us he had taken his own tests, but had somehow lost the results. I also find it difficult to believe that a patient whose body could heal a gunshot wound in three days could not wipe out a virus of any kind," Agent Lane continued. "Kenyatta, you must believe me. We only want to help your brother. If we could just talk to him, bring him in and get this mess cleared up . . ."

"Look, Officer Lang, Lane, Lame—whatever your name is—even if I did know where my brother was, I wouldn't tell you. But the fact of the matter is, I don't have a clue where he is."

"Do you have any idea where he might go if he thought someone were after him? Family? Friends?"

"Look, Mrs. FBI lady. I told you I don't know where he is."

"Any luck?"

Kenyatta looked up at the newcomer that walked into the room and stood next to Agent Lane. Kenyatta chuckled to herself. He looked like a Nazi with his tight suit and buzz hair cut.

"No, she doesn't know where he is," Agent Lane replied with a sigh. "How about you?"

"No luck. She claims she doesn't know anything either," he stated, walking around the table, staring at Kenyatta.

Kenyatta frowned. "Fuck you lookin' at?"

Agent Lane watched him curiously. This was her first assignment, and she had already decided she didn't like her partner. Even though he hadn't really done anything to warrant the dislike, she just got this nasty vibe whenever he looked at her. It felt like he was looking down on her, the same way he was now looking at Kenyatta.

Agent Parks ignored Kenyatta, and chuckling lightly, walked out of the room.

"Fuck was that about?" Kenyatta asked, looking up at Agent Lane.

"I don't know," Ebonee replied absently, her eyes still on the door.

"That's your partner?"

Ebonee sighed heavily. "Yeah. That's my partner."

"Damn. I feel for you," Kenyatta said, chuckling.

Ebonee smiled weakly. "Thanks." After a moment of thought on her new partner, she looked back at Kenyatta. "Look, Kenyatta, I'm serious about wanting to help your brother. But I don't know what these other fools will do if they catch him. Especially dickhead." She leaned close so no one would hear her but Kenyatta. "So please, if you hear from your brother, call me, and only me." She handed Kenyatta her card and turned to walk out of the room.

Agent Parks met her in the hall.

"I just got a call from central. Our man purchased a plane ticket," he said, walking by her.

Agent Lane had to hurry to keep up. "A plane ticket?" she asked, trying to keep pace with his long legs.

"That's what I said. A plane ticket," he replied sarcastically, not bothering to slow in the least.

"To where?"

"Jerusalem."

She stared at his back incredulously. "Jerusalem?"

Parks continued, getting into the car and starting it. Agent

Lane had to run to catch up. She slammed the door of the car angrily.

"Look, Parks, if you have a problem with me, then why don't you just come out and say it?"

"Okay, I don't like you. And I don't like this bullshit case. The sooner we're done with this, the better."

"Excuse me? Have I done something to offend you?" Agent Lane asked.

"Your skin color offends me," Parks mumbled under his breath.

"What was that?" Ebonee asked, staring at the tattoo on his right hand.

"I said, let's just get this case over with so we can move on."

"Yeah, let's do that," Ebonee whispered, trying to make out what it was on his hand. It looked like a rose. "Let's do that," she repeated, turning away and leaning her head back into the seat. This was going to be a long case.

Dalfien paced angrily in front of the large window, his eyes staring out at the vast green fields that surrounded the huge complex. He hated waiting. He wanted nothing more than to have some fun with these foolish men, but those plans would have to be put on hold. He had been sent here with explicit orders. To disobey or stray from those orders would be foolish. But Lucifer had given him no further orders, so once he was finished with his business, the fun would begin. He continued staring blankly out of the window, watching as a large bird alighted on the seven-foot fence surrounding the facility. He smiled wickedly when the bird suddenly squawked in pain, its wings fluttering uselessly in the setting sun as it fell into the tall grass, electrocuted. His thoughts were interrupted by the phone.

"Yes?" he answered, drawing upon his host to use his voice.

"Hello, Charles, how have—"

"What news have you?" Dalfien interrupted, turning away from the large window. His voice echoed off the brown wooden walls of the hollow room; there was no furniture other than the old desk and the semi-comfortable chair.

"Not much. Nothing too much out of the ordinary. However, there is one case we're working on, but I don't think it's what you're looking for."

"Where?" Dalfien asked.

"Well, this guy in Philadelphia decided to blow his brains out—"

"The man I'm looking for is alive, you imbecile," Dalfien said coldly.

"Hold your horses, I'm not finished. Like I was saying, he was admitted to the hospital, only to walk out three days later without a scratch."

"So?"

"So? The guy blew half his brains out and walked away without a scratch in only three days! You said you were looking for anything strange or out of the ordinary. I'd say that's about as strange and out of the ordinary as it gets. And one more thing: the guy only weighs about a hundred and seventy pounds."

"So? What's so amazing about that?" Dalfien asked, suddenly very interested.

"I'll tell you what's so amazing about it. He took out two of Philadelphia's finest without so much as lifting a finger. Eye witnesses said he threw them about twenty feet."

"Have your men brought him in yet?"

"Not yet, but we will have him soon enough,"

"Where is he now?" Dalfien asked, his gaze going back to the window and the dead bird, his mind forming a plan.

"He purchased a roundtrip ticket to Jerusalem, so he'll probably be boarding in about fifteen minutes. The local authorities have men on it. Hopefully they'll apprehend him for assault there and then we can move in."

"That's not good enough. I want him arrested and brought here," Dalfien instructed. "Do you know what he looks like?"

"Check your e-mail, Charles. I've already sent you a digital image of him."

"Perhaps a greater crime will further facilitate his capture," Dalfien thought aloud. "I want him brought directly to me when he is captured. See to it that it happens."

Dalfien glanced down at the large oak desk and the blank computer screen and frowned. He had no idea what this contraption was for. He would have to free the human for a moment. He focused on images of his intent, ensuring that Charles would understand, and then he released his mind back into the world of consciousness.

Charles blinked rapidly, then looking down at the computer he went to work, quickly bringing the image of the man into view. Charles was gone in the next instant.

Dalfien concentrated on the picture, burning it into his memory. Then he sat down in the chair. Closing his eyes, he concentrated, opening up a telepathic link to his own plane of existence. He found what he was looking for in no time.

The imp shrieked angrily at the intrusion, but settled down quickly enough when it realized who was calling to it. Imps were minor demons, often used for such services as messengers to the greater demons such as Dalfien. Dalfien filled the imp's mind with images, giving it instructions.

The imp would obey, for fear of death.

Its mission clear, the imp headed off in search of the doorway that would lead it to the place that Dalfien had burned into its mind. Satisfied, Dalfien focused on the telepathic doorway that would lead him back to his host. He found it, but with a little difficulty. The link was weakening. Dalfien tore through the dark plane with blinding speed, passing through the door just as it was about to collapse in upon itself. Charles cried out in fear as Dalfien, once again, forced his mind back into the darkness. Dalfien chuckled. He would take great pleasure in torturing Charles this night.

Chapter Seven
Sleeping Dogs

Elijah walked briskly through the dark airport parking lot, stopping once to check his disguise in the reflection of a car window. Everything was fine. With one last look, he pulled the collar of the black trench coat up around his ears, not because it was nippy out, but because he just liked the added security. He proceeded down the busy sidewalk quickly, passing gates D and E and trying to avoid eye contact with any of the skycaps and baggage handlers busy at work helping passengers load and unload their luggage. His flight was scheduled to depart from gate F in about fifteen minutes. He had waited until the last minute because he didn't feel comfortable sitting down in one place for too long.

Hopefully this little trip would provide him with some answers. He stepped hastily through the automatic door at gate F, entering the semi-crowded baggage claim area. He noticed two police officers standing near the escalator talking. Confident in his disguise, he walked right past them, pulling up the hood of the long, black, leather trench coat, which he had borrowed from Kenyatta's closet. He looked one of them in the eye as he passed, and the officer turned away,

completely ignoring him. He just kept on talking to his partner.

"Did you hear what I just said, Frank? Frank?" the officer
said, trying to get his partner's attention. But Frank's eyes
were somewhere else, as was his mind.

The imp struggled to gain control of the officer's body;
possessions were not one of the imp's strong points. Luckily,
this particular human was weak. Still, it took every bit of the
imp's strength to hold him out.

"Frank!" the other officer yelled, grabbing at his arm.

Frank ignored him.

The imp had seen through Elijah's disguise the moment
he had arrived. Frank's eyes followed Elijah up the escalator,
and then he turned to follow.

"Frank! Where are you going?" Frank's partner called out
to him.

But Frank couldn't hear. Frank was too busy trying to fight
the imp out of his mind. He tripped as he walked up the escalator. For an instant Frank had pushed through. "Smitty!
Help!" he managed to mumble before the imp forced him
back out.

The officer once again pushed his way up through the
crowded escalator. Elijah heard the confusion and glanced
back over his shoulder. As he stepped off the escalator, his
eyes locked with the pursuing police officers and he nearly
panicked.

Elijah looked around, his mind racing. He saw the check-
in counter for his flight, and the single woman dressed in
light blue, standing behind it staring at a computer screen.
He was no more than fifteen feet away, and most of the passengers were more than likely already boarding. He decided
to circle back. If there was a confrontation, he didn't want
the airline clerk to see he was involved. If he got away, then
maybe he could still board the plane.

The officer stopped when he saw Elijah coming back

down the escalator on the other side. Elijah stood perfectly still, staring into the cop's eyes intently. He wasn't completely sure if it was indeed he who the cop was after, but the look in the estranged officer's eyes told him the truth.

But there was something else. Another feeling assaulted Elijah's mind as the officer crouched down, preparing to leap across the five feet that separated the escalators. Elijah sensed something about this officer, something horribly evil. But he had no time to dwell on his feelings, for at that moment, the officer leapt across the expanse, tackling Elijah down onto the hard steel steps of the escalator.

Elijah felt the pain in his arm as the jagged edges of steel ripped into his flesh. Rage began to flow through Elijah's body. He struggled to push the officer off of him, and passengers around them stared and pointed. But the officer was strong. Too strong, Elijah thought, as he remembered the ease in which he had dispatched the two officers at the hospital. He didn't want to hurt him, but he was trying to kill Elijah.

Finally Elijah succumbed to the rage. He pushed the officer's face back with his left hand as the officer straddled him, choking him. Then he let loose with a right hand, knocking the wind out of the officer's chest and sending him into the glass wall of the escalator. Before the officer's body could fall, Elijah kicked him again in his chest, sending him up and over the side of the railing.

Elijah leapt to his feet and grabbed at the falling man's hand. Screams erupted from somewhere below. They were still about twenty-five feet from the lower level and the hard gray cement floor. He caught the sleeve of the officer's navy blue jacket and held on fast, slamming him roughly into the side of the escalator. The officer looked up, an evil grin on his face. The imp's job was done. Now he could have a little fun. Bringing his feet up, the officer kicked at Elijah's hand, forcing Elijah to let go. The imp grinned wickedly as it watched the ground rush up at it. Then at the last moment, the imp released his hold on the officer's mind, just in time for the officer to realize his fate. Elijah sprinted back up the escalator and was at the check-in counter before the officer's second bounce off the ground.

"Can I help you, sir?" the check-in agent asked, not bothering to look up.

"Yeah, I have a ticket for the three o'clock to Jerusalem," Elijah said hastily, glancing back over his shoulder toward the escalator. He prayed there were no 'good Samaritans' on his heels.

"Do you have any bags to check, sir?" she asked, looking up at Elijah.

"No," Elijah replied, handing her the ticket.

"Okay then, sir. I have you confirmed for the three o'clock to Jerusalem, no baggage to check. Would you like a window or aisle?" she asked happily.

"Window."

"Smoking or—"

"Smoking! Definitely smoking!" Elijah exclaimed. He could use a few drinks and some nicotine to calm his nerves.

"Okay, here you are, but you better hurry. They're making the boarding call right this moment, sir. Thank you for flying—" She looked up from her computer screen to see no one there.

Elijah walked briskly down the ramp, still looking back over his shoulder at the escalator. They came up then. Four cops—all with their weapons drawn.

Elijah knew better than to run now. They weren't sure where he had gone, and running would definitely give him away. So he walked on through the glass tunnel, his heart racing.

When the gray carpeted ramp curved around a bend, Elijah sprinted to the security checkpoint. He stepped through, pausing as the lone airport worker waved a metal detector up and down his body. And then he continued on his way. He couldn't see the police anymore, so he relaxed a bit. Finally, he reached the boarding gate. He gingerly stepped up to the small podium and handed the flight attendant the ticket. Still staring back down the ramp, he stepped casually into the long tunnel that would take him to the plane. He proceeded to the rear of the aircraft, ignoring the curious stares from the passengers already settled in their seats. A flight attendant approached him and asked to see his boarding pass. Inspecting it, she looked back up at him curiously, her large brown eyes glowing.

"You're in first class, sir. That's the other way. Follow me," she said with a smile. She looked down at the boarding pass again, reading the name. Elijah sighed when he caught a glimpse of her nice round behind as she led him to his seat. For some reason, the sight did nothing for him. The woman stared at him again as he sat down. Elijah closed his eyes, trying to force himself to relax.

"You don't remember me, do you?" The flight attendant smiled down at Elijah.

Elijah was at a loss; there was too much going on in his head to try and remember who she was. She was cute, though, Elijah noticed. Slim and brown skinned, with big brown eyes. "Should I?"

"Yes you should! You stood me up!" she exclaimed, smiling. Elijah cocked his head to the side, still not remembering.

"Remember? The turbulence?" she offered, putting her hands on her hips.

"Oh, yeah. I do remember. How have you been? Terry, right?" Elijah asked, his memory providing him with some tidbits. He had met Terry on a flight back from Germany a few years ago.

"Don't even try it! You read my name tag," she said, laughing. "I'll come back and talk to you later, okay?"

"Yeah, okay," Elijah replied absently. He just wanted to rest. He felt the plane moving then, and his fears dissipated slowly, not disappearing until the plane was fully in the air and on its way. Elijah looked out of the small window at the night sky. Memories flooded his mind. Memories of loves long past. Katrina, Olivia, Crystal . . . Taysia.

Taysia.

She had died in his arms. Her last wish—to taste his kiss. He could still see her face. Still hear her lovely voice. He had known her embrace was happiness. He had finally caught it, had held it so close. And then it had been stolen away from him. Ripped unmercifully from his grasp. Her death was his own. But even in death, somehow he had failed. For now here he sat, staring out at the night sky, wondering once again. "Why?"

Elijah never paid any attention to the nasty wound he had received on the escalator. But then, why would he? There was nothing there for him to pay any attention to.

Agent Ebonee Lane and her partner walked into the terminal just as the police were taping off the scene.

"Whatcha got?" Parks asked one of the investigators.

"Homicide, pure and simple," he replied, looking up at Agent Parks.

"Pure and simple?" Agent Lane asked curiously.

"That's what the man said," Parks commented dryly. "What happened?"

"Looks like Frank recognized the perp. He approached him and tried to apprehend the suspect, the suspect then resisted, tossing the officer over the side of the escalator," the investigator explained, yawning lazily as he nodded toward the double set of glass and metal mechanical stairs.

"Sounds pretty simple to me," Parks replied, slipping his hands into his trouser pockets.

"Were there any witnesses?" Ebonee asked.

"Plenty, but only one will tell you anything—his partner. But from his vantage point, he couldn't see the struggle."

"Where was he?" Ebonee asked curiously, her brown eyes showing a hint of doubt.

"Why don't you ask him? He's right there." He pointed to an officer standing with a cup of coffee.

"Thanks, but I don't think that will be necessary," Parks said quickly.

"What do you mean it won't be necessary? It is necessary," Ebonee rebutted, her heels clicking on the cement. She turned and walked toward the officer.

"Well, you go ahead and waste your time," Parks replied, huffing as he watched her walk away.

"Hi. How are you? Agent Ebonee Lane, FBI," she said, introducing herself to the officer.

"Hey. Mike Smith," he greeted, nodding his head, but never looking up from his coffee.

"What happened here, Officer Smith?"

"I'll tell you the same thing I told them: Frank saw the guy and went after him. Unfortunately, the guy tossed him over the railing," he said calmly, lowering his cup momentarily and staring out of the large glass windows of the terminal.

"You don't sound too concerned. Did you know him well?" Ebonee asked, a curious expression crossing her face. She followed his gaze to the large window and the street beyond. The sky was just giving way to the soft light of the coming dawn. Skycaps and passengers went about their business, loading luggage into the trunks of awaiting cars, occasionally glancing into the terminal at the police who were finishing up.

"No. We were only together for about a week," he replied, taking another sip of coffee.

"Where were you when he was thrown over the railing?"

"I was standing right about there." He pointed to an area near the bottom of the escalator.

"Why were you so far away?"

"What do you mean?" he asked nervously.

"You said you and your partner were standing there when he saw the suspect," she said, pointing to the spot he had indicated. "Why didn't you give pursuit also?"

"W-w-well, because I-I-I didn't see him at first," he said, stuttering. His eyes shifted uneasily and he made a point to look at everything but the agent's suspicious stare.

Ebony waited a moment, digesting the officer's peculiar reactions. He sipped at the coffee again, his thick, black mustache hovering above the rim of the cup, almost as if he were trying to hide behind it.

"Officer Smith, I don't think you ever attempted to assist your partner. In fact, I think you turned your back on him," Agent Lane said calmly, going on a hunch. She watched as he sipped again, this time a line of the black liquid escaping past his lips to run down his chubby chin.

"What are you trying to say?" Officer Smith asked, wiping at the coffee with his free hand and glancing around nervously.

"What happened that made you turn your back on your partner, Officer Smith?"

"Look, I tried to get to him, but I was too late. When I turned around he was already in the air. I never even saw the guy who did it," he confessed, looking Agent Lane in the eye for the first time.

"But what made you turn your back on your partner in the first place?"

"Well, I don't know what it was exactly. He was acting all weird," he answered, this time looking straight ahead as if he were reliving the incident.

"Weird in what way?" Ebonee pressed.

"I don't know, just weird. His eyes rolled back in his head, and he wouldn't answer me. He just ignored me. He didn't say anything when he started up the escalator. I called to

him, but he ignored me. I don't even know how he could
have seen the guy. He was looking straight at me the whole
time we were standing there having a normal conversation."

"So you didn't follow him because you thought he didn't
want to be bothered? Has he ever acted strangely like that
before?"

"No, not since we've been together, at least. But you gotta
believe me. If I would have known he was going to make an
arrest, I would have been right there," he continued, looking at Agent Lane seriously.

"But you couldn't have. He didn't say anything about it,"
Ebonee replied, reassuring the man.

"Y-y-yeah, that's right. Hey, you're not going to tell anyone, are you?" he asked fearfully.

"Only if they ask," she replied with a smile.

She walked away from the man with more questions than
answers. Looking around the quickly filling terminal, she
spotted a young black woman standing alone with two young
children. She walked over to them.

"How long have you been standing here, ma'am?" she
asked the woman.

"Long enough," the woman replied, as if she knew what
was about to take place.

"Long enough to see what happened here tonight?"

"Well, my back was turned, so I didn't get to see what actually happened."

"I saw it! I saw everything!" the woman's daughter exclaimed, jumping up and down.

Ebonee looked at the mother.

"My baby don't lie. If she says she saw it, then she saw it,"
she said evenly.

Agent Lane glanced back down at the little girl. Her bright
smile was missing a few teeth and her long ponytails bounced
as she hopped up and down. Ebonee looked back at the
mother. "May I?"

"Go ahead. My ride is late, so I got plenty of time," she said, smiling as she reached down to pick up the smaller boy.

"Hi. What's your name, sweetheart?" Ebony asked, smiling at the child.

"Tiara," she replied happily.

"Tiara, huh? That's a pretty name. How old are you, Tiara?"

"I'm eight," she answered quickly.

"Tiara, did you see what happened to the policeman?"

"Yes."

"Can you tell me what you saw?"

"Yes."

"Okay. What did you see?"

"I saw the policeman jump all the way over there." She pointed up at the escalator.

"Wait a minute," Ebonee interrupted her, trying to understand what she meant. "You saw him jump? Where was he when he jumped?"

"He was going up on the other one."

"So he jumped from that escalator over to the other one?"

"Yes," the child answered, still smiling.

"Okay. Then what happened?"

"He started beating up this man, and they was fightin' and then he was chokin' him," the little girl explained excitedly.

"Wait, wait. The policeman was choking someone?"

The child nodded emphatically. "Yes. He was chokin' the man. Then the man pushed him and kicked him over the thing. Then the man was holding the policeman by the arm so he wouldn't fall, but the policeman tried to kick him in the hand, and he let go," she finished, taking a deep breath.

"You sure? The man was holding him?" Ebonee asked.

"Yes."

"Well, Tiara. Thank you very much. You be good, okay?" Ebonee rose to her feet to look at the mother. "You have a very observant daughter."

"Observant my ass. She just newsy as hell," the mother replied, laughing.

"Well, you've been a big help, thank you," Ebonee said, turning to walk away.

She made her way over to the body of the dead officer. Kneeling down, she inspected his arms. She found a purplish bruise on his left wrist. She looked up at the escalator. The little girl said he had jumped from one escalator over to the other. Agent Lane walked over to stand in between the two escalators just as paramedics rolled a gurney up to the officer's body. Looking up, she stretched her arms out in between the moving metal stairs. Her hands fell short of both escalators by about a foot. She looked back over to the plump form being hefted up onto the stretcher by two men.

"Impossible," she whispered to herself. But then, their man had walked out of a hospital with a gunshot wound to the head, fully healed. In three days!

Elijah yawned as he looked around the quiet airplane. He leaned back in the soft leather seat, his legs stretched out in front of him. This was his first time flying first class.

"I guess a black man does have to die to fly first class," he whispered, smiling.

He looked around the small cabin again, trying to spot Terry. He didn't feel like being bothered, so if he saw her coming he would pretend to be asleep. *Wow, death can really change a person.* He had no desire whatsoever. He remembered how sex was once the only thing that had brought him satisfaction. How he longed for it, needed it. How he had to have someone in his bed at all times, just to chase away the loneliness.

But all those emotions had died with Taysia. He could care less if he ever held another woman. His heart had turned to stone, it seemed. The chains that once bound his heart, preventing him from slipping and falling prey to heartbreak, had fallen away into dust at Taysia's touch. And then, without her love to keep it safe and warm, his heart had shriveled up and died—as had he.

He reached up to run his fingers through his hair, then realized he still had the wig on. Confident no one would be looking for him in Jerusalem, he pulled the wig off. He ran his fingers through his bushy white hair, closing his eyes.

"Excuse me."

Elijah looked up to see a tall white man smiling at him. His wavy white hair hung lightly down past his shoulders and he had an almost angelic look about him.

"Is anyone sitting here?" the man asked.

"Ummm . . . no, no," Elijah replied, looking at the man oddly.

For some reason he felt like he knew him. The man sat down and leaned back in the chair, a smile on his face as he wiggled around in the softness of the seat, crossing his legs comfortably.

"Those seats in coach are just so uncomfortable!" he said, winking at Elijah. Elijah couldn't help but smile at the stranger, with his dusty brown cowboy boots and trench coat.

He turned his head and looked out of the window. It was daytime now, and the sun was shining brightly in the clear blue sky. The man sat forward in his seat and stared at Elijah. Elijah could feel his eyes on him; he turned his head and did a double-take. The man was sitting there, eyeballing him with this stupid grin on his face.

"You okay?" Elijah asked.

"You don't remember me, do you?" the man asked, his eyes never leaving Elijah's.

Elijah raised his eyebrows, at a loss. "Uhhh . . . no?" He smiled awkwardly, unsure of himself.

The man stared at Elijah for a moment longer.

"You really don't," he said, sounding like he was talking more to himself.

"Sorry?" Elijah offered, shrugging his shoulders helplessly as he tried to keep himself from laughing.

"Oh well," the man began, shrugging his own shoulders, "my name is Gabriel. Nice to . . . uhhh . . . meet you." He extended his hand.

Elijah's laughter slipped through. "Nice to . . . uhhh . . . meet you, too. My name is—"

"Elijah. Yeah, yeah, I know all of that," the man said quickly, causing Elijah's smile to disappear. "I suppose now you're going to ask me how I know your name, right?"

"Actually, I really don't care at this point," Elijah answered, turning to look out of the window once more.

That caused Gabriel to pause. Sitting back, he adjusted himself in the comfortable leather seat. "You know, this is a lot easier than flying the other way."

Elijah furrowed his eyebrows and frowned, turning to regard the strange man again. "The other way?" he asked, almost afraid of the answer.

Gabriel sat forward suddenly and stared hard into Elijah's eyes. "Look, let's cut the crap. I don't have time to dick around leading you by the hand. Have you ever seen an angel, Elijah?" His expression was dead serious.

"What the hell are you talking about?"

"You don't question me! I asked *you* the question, now answer it!" Gabriel said forcefully, his eyes burning into him.

Elijah was taken aback by the stranger's sudden aggressiveness. "No . . . I haven't," he answered quietly.

"Well, now you have. You're looking at, and talking to an angel, Elijah—an archangel."

"You expect me to believe that you're an archangel?" Elijah asked, laughing lightly.

"That's not all I'm expecting you to believe, Elijah," Gabriel replied calmly, leaning back in the seat once more. "You were born for one reason and for one reason only: my reason. I gave you life, Elijah. I watched you grow up from a little crying brat to the man—and I use that term loosely—that you are today," Gabriel explained.

"Yo, man, you talkin' crazy. I think you need to go back to coach," Elijah said, shaking his head and looking away.

Elijah couldn't deny Gabriel's words. But he wouldn't allow himself to believe them, either.

"Still in denial, huh?" Gabriel asked, smiling as he sat forward once again, his eyes burning into Elijah's soul. "Let me ask you this. I want you to think back. Think back to the last time you had a common cold. That's not too difficult, is it? Shouldn't have been too far back. I mean every *man* catches a cold every now and then. Do you remember?" Gabriel pressed, his eyes never leaving Elijah's.

"Of course I remember," Elijah stated, defiantly. But honestly, he couldn't remember ever having a cold.

"Keep lying to yourself. I want you to think about something else. You're a good looking guy, of course. How many ladies have you slept with without using protection? No, no. I'll make it simpler. How many have you slept with and used protection? Come on, Elijah. How many?" Gabriel asked with a smile.

Elijah sat back in the seat, a seat that had suddenly become very uncomfortable. He had always thought himself very lucky when it came to that. He had not once caught anything.

"Elijah, you've ran naked through more microwaves than a coffee cup, and not once did you ever get burned. That's some luck, isn't it?" Gabriel asked, getting silence in return. "Still in denial? Okay. Think about this: how many times have you been in a hospital? When was the last time you broke a bone?"

Elijah shifted uncomfortably in his seat. He had never broken a bone in his life, and he had never been in a hospital unless he was just visiting.

"You remember that time when you were six years old,

and you were hit by a Cadillac? Boy, I swear, you must have flown at least ten feet into the air! Do you remember that, Elijah? Do you remember who picked your little skinny body up out of the street and carried you home?" Gabriel's words cut into Elijah's mind like a knife.

Elijah stiffened as he replayed the memory over in his head. He had never remembered who had carried him home that day. He went back to that time, trying to remember every detail. He was there then. He felt himself being carried by someone, but he couldn't see clearly through the tears. But then the image cleared and he saw Gabriel's face as clear as he could see the chair in front of him. He inhaled deeply, and his eyes opened wide. Chill bumps flowed over his skin.

"You were outside playing football in the street an hour later! What about that time in Germany when the car you were in skidded off the road at 120 miles per hour. How many times did it flip? Four, five times? And you walked away with a headache!" Gabriel exclaimed, laughing lightly.

Elijah dropped his head down into his hands. What did it all mean? Everything the man said was true. He had always thought he was just lucky or something. Then Elijah relaxed and sat back as the truth set in. He looked calmly over to Gabriel, his gaze now burning with a fire of its own.

"What about the pain, Gabriel?" he asked coldly. "What about the suffering, and the tears? Were you there then, too? Were you there when my grandmother died and left me all alone? Fatherless? Motherless? Did you comfort me when I cried at night?"

Gabriel sat back in the seat, but his eyes never left Elijah's. He accepted the anger in those eyes as he thought about his deed.

"The pain was necessary. You had to learn that man's world was not your own. You had to learn to deal with the rage in order to control it at the proper time. Now is that time, Elijah,"

Elijah's demeanor shifted. His eyes suddenly filled with hate as he thought of the implications. "And Taysia?" His voice was barely a whisper and dripped with venom.

Gabriel smiled at the sight. Elijah would do just fine. He saw the power in his eyes, the unyielding strength.

"Did you orchestrate her death as well?"

"Get your hormones in check, son. I created you, and I can destroy you. Remember that," Gabriel said calmly. "As far as the girl is concerned—" He paused, wondering how much he should reveal to him. "I had no part in that. I actually kind of liked her. She was hot, wasn't she?" he added with a smile.

Elijah found no humor in his words. "She was my last hope," he whispered after a moment, his gaze shifting to the horizon and the white fluffiness of the clouds.

Gabriel stared at Elijah, deep in thought. A rare, sympathetic expression crossed his face. He knew all too well the pain Elijah was feeling, for he had orchestrated it in his life for years to prepare him. He had actually known Taysia's death would push Elijah to the limit and signify his rebirth. He had actually planned it. But Gabriel was not prepared for the sheer power of the love that the two would share. So pure and so real. "Heavenly," Gabriel whispered to himself as he reflected. Their love was something Gabriel found he could not deny, no matter how much he had planned.

Elijah looked over at Gabriel curiously as he spoke, seemingly to himself.

"I couldn't do it," he whispered, his eyes staring blankly forward. Then he turned to regard Elijah. "But that was my plan . . . her death. You know, I just find it so amazing the more I experience man. You're so fragile, yet . . . yet . . . so . . . full of hope! I filled your entire life with pain and heartbreak!

Yet, each time you saw the chance for love you jumped right at it! I didn't think you would ever break. But when I brought her into the picture, I knew that she would be the deciding factor. I felt the connection between the two of you before you even met. Then I watched as the two of you embraced for the first time, ready and willing to devote yourselves to each other, completely and sincerely. God, it was wonderful!" he added, smiling. "Too wonderful. So wonderful, in fact, that I forgot the reason I had brought her to you. I decided to leave you alone. I couldn't bring myself to destroy something that was obviously God's will. For only he could create something as pure and beautiful as was your love. So I walked away."

"Then why?" Elijah began, confused. "Who?"

"You already know who, Elijah," Gabriel stated, his tone serious again.

Elijah turned his head back toward the window and the clouds again. Slowly, his facial expression changed from one of deep sadness to one of unyielding resolve.

"Where do I begin?" Elijah asked with calmness in his voice that signified his determination.

A smile spread across Gabriel's face as he looked into Elijah's eager eyes. "London," he replied with glee.

"But what's in Jerusalem?"

"Nothing. This airplane will make a layover in London. Here." Gabriel paused to hand Elijah a small piece of paper. "Go to this address. Someone will be waiting for you there. They will explain to you everything you need to know."

"Gabriel—" Elijah began, his expression once again softening. "Taysia . . . did she—"

"I believe you'll find that out for yourself," Gabriel answered, rising with a wink. "Now I must leave you for a while. Good hunting!"

Gabriel turned and walked back through the curtain that

separated coach from first class, leaving Elijah with a dumb-founded look on his face.

"I'll find out what?" Elijah asked, standing to pursue Gabriel. He threw back the curtain and stepped through, but Gabriel was gone. "And what the hell does 'good hunting' mean?"

A lump caught in Elijah's throat as he stood there. A sense of wholeness he had never known before filled him. He had always considered himself a fatherless child until then. Gabriel had been with him from the beginning. Perhaps his intentions were somewhat questionable, but he had been there nonetheless. More importantly, he was there now. "My father is an angel. . . . Wow," he whispered, smiling warmly.

"Archangel, son!"

Elijah chuckled lightly, hearing the words in his mind.

"Hey, Elijah! Looking for me?" Terry exclaimed, smiling brightly. "Hey! What happened to your hair?"

"I died," Elijah whispered sarcastically, ignoring the curious stares from the few passengers who were not asleep.

"Why did you choose that color? Oh, never mind, I like it. You should let me braid it!" she rambled, her sentences sounding like one long word. "Here, come on!" she said, leading Elijah back to his seat. "I can do it right now! I just love a man with long hair! I think it's sexy!" she added, turning him to face the window and kneeling in the seat next to his.

"Ain't you supposed to be working or something?" Elijah asked.

"Please, everyone is sleeping, and my buddies will cover for me," she answered, pulling her comb through Elijah's hair.

"But won't it take too long?" Elijah asked, looking for any reason to get her away from him.

"Don't worry. I braid fast, and we still have ten hours before we get to London," she said, pausing to lean her lips down to his ear. "And if I don't finish, you'll just have to come with me to the hotel and let me finish there."

Elijah didn't have to see her face to know that she was grinning from ear to ear. Helplessly, he let out a long sigh. It was going to be a long ten hours.

"Agent Lane!" Parks called out to his partner as she stepped out of the bathroom in the now busy airport baggage claim area. "Come on. The Deputy Assistant Director is here. He wants us to report right now," he said, turning to walk away.

"The D.A.D.? Why? Where is Special Agent in Charge Warminster?" she asked curiously, quickening her pace to keep up with him in the crowd.

"I guess we're going to find out soon enough."

"Where is he?"

"The airport security office," Parks answered, stopping at an elevator.

"Oh, here." Ebonee handed Parks a set of keys. "You left these in the car."

Parks grabbed the keys and threw them in the pocket of his blazer.

"You're welcome," Ebonee said sarcastically.

Parks ignored her, stepping onto the elevator. They exited on the underground level of the airport and then proceeded down a long, bright, unremarkable hallway until they came to a set of double doors. Parks knocked, and they entered. Ebonee stopped next to Parks as they stood before the director. He was an older man. Gray streaked his thinning black hair. His bloodshot blue eyes stared long and hard at Agent Parks. Agent Parks shifted nervously under his gaze.

Ebonee eyed the director, trying to find some sort of clue to his intense stare. But his face was completely emotionless, his eyes cold and judging.

"Agent Lane." His voice startled her, and she jumped unintentionally as the director finally turned his gaze to her. "I'm Deputy Assistant Director Scott. Welcome to the FBI."

"Ummm, thank you, sir. It's a pleasure to meet you," she replied.

"The pleasure is all mine, Agent Lane. I've reviewed your record. Graduated in the top 3 percent of your class—impressive," he began, watching Parks out of the corner of his eye. Parks huffed impatiently, rolling his eyes. "So far you've done an excellent job. But I'll be taking over from here," he explained, turning to stare at Parks again.

"But, sir, this case is just starting. And I thought we were supposed to be reporting to Special Agent in Charge Warminster."

"Agent Lane, I understand that this is your first case and you want to do well, but I will not be questioned by a rookie, or anyone else for that matter. As far as Special Agent Warminster goes, he is on vacation. Now, you have a room at the hotel. I suggest you use it until you're notified that your assistance is requested!" the director exclaimed, turning on her threateningly. But she didn't back down.

"But don't you even want to hear my report?"

"No need. Agent Parks here will fill me in on everything. Now go get some rest."

"But, sir, there are some things about this case that Parks doesn't—"

"Goodbye, Agent Lane!" the director said with finality.

Ebonee stared at him in disbelief for a moment. There were facts about this case that led her to believe that their fugitive, and he was that now, may not have done all he was being accused of. In fact, the way she put things together, he actually tried to save a man's life after the man had attacked him. Something was wrong here.

"Yes, sir," Ebonee replied, sighing heavily. She tucked the folder under her arm and walked out of the room. She glanced around, making sure no one was watching. Then she reached into her pocket and pulled out an earpiece, inserting it into her ear. She listened closely as the tiny receiver she had planted on the keys relayed the conversation in the room.

"Can you get rid of her?" Agent Parks asked wishfully.

"Silence, you dimwitted fool!" Director Scott yelled, walking over to stand in front of Agent Parks, whose shocked expression made him even more disgusting to look at. "I have worked too hard to get to where I am today, only to have it destroyed by a halfwit like you!"

"I-I-I don't understand," Parks stuttered, unsure of what to make of his brother's anger.

"That's the smartest thing you've said all day. Look at yourself. You look like a gotdamned Nazi! The only reason you made it this far is because of The Order. Your father was a close friend of mine, and I promised him I'd look out for you." Director Scott's expression softened at the thought of his old friend. "Son, this is not a game. This is not some silly little hate group you now belong to. It's taken us years to establish this network. And if you're going to be a part of it, then you can't be running around with your hate on your sleeve for all to see. There aren't going to be any lynchings. You are not going to go out and hang a nigger from a tree or burn a cross on someone's lawn. This is not the fifties or the sixties. We work in more subtle ways now. A controlled oppression, if you will. And the sooner you learn that, the better. Understand?" Scott asked, turning away.

"Yes, sir,"

"Good. Now, to the business at hand—Charles Kreicker is here."

"He's here?" Agent Parks had only heard about the man.

He had never been privileged to witness one of the famed ceremonies Charles was known for.

"Yes. It seems the hermit has come out of his shell," the director said. "This Elijah fellow must be extremely important for some reason or another. I've never heard of him ever leaving the compound," Scott mused, more to himself.

"Have you spoken to him?"

"Not directly. That wouldn't be ideal. Although my sources tell me he's not the same man we once knew. He's changed."

"Changed how?"

Scott looked at the young man peculiarly. He wondered if Park's ideals had been fully corrupted by the darker side of the sect. The side devoted to Satanism. He truly hoped that was not the case. He and the other, more prominent leaders sitting on the council had tried hard to ensure that the foolishness of worshipping Satan did not get out of control, but Charles was a very good motivator, an exceptional speaker of words. And the real leaders of The Order had seen this. So they had used him. Charles was simply a figurehead, and nothing more. But now it seemed that Charles, after surprising them all by actually killing the young girl at one of the monthly ceremonies, had developed a sense of power, a sense of authority that put the ruling members of The Order on alert.

It seemed that Charles did not want to play the puppet any longer, but so far, he had done nothing to warrant any actions to be taken against him, which was a larger problem in itself. Most of The Order's followers knew nothing of the council's existence. Charles was like a god to them. They worshipped him. The council knew if their hand was forced against Charles, it would cause havoc. They had spent too much time grooming Charles into the leader he was now, and finding a replacement for him would not be easy.

"It's not important," he said after a moment, deciding to

leave it at that. "What is important is that we apprehend the fugitive. When we do, we'll take him to Charles and find out what this is all about. Now are you sure this guy killed that officer?"

"Without a doubt. His partner witnessed it all."

"Strange," Scott whispered to himself, recalling the conversation he had with Charles only a few hours ago. He had told him they would have a reason.

"What's that, sir?"

"Nothing, you can go. We'll wait to see if he shows up on the return flight," Scott said, waving his hand at the door.

"What about Agent Lane?"

"I'll deal with her. You just focus on catching Mr. Garland."

Agent Lane pressed urgently on the door-close button as Parks walked out of the room. She leaned against the wall of the elevator, slamming her palm against the useless button as Agent Parks walked curiously toward the elevator. Finally, the door slowly began to close.

"Is that you, Agent Lane?" Parks asked curiously, looking at the closing door suspiciously.

"Come on, come on," Ebonee said excitedly, waiting for the door to open on the ground floor. She felt her pocket for the miniature tape recorder she had been given. Finally, the door slid open slowly.

"Agent Lane."

Ebonee nearly passed out as she looked up at Agent Parks, who stood in the opening of the elevator door.

"Didn't you hear me calling you downstairs?"

"God! You startled me!" Ebonee said, gasping as she caught her breath.

"You're very jumpy all of a sudden. What's going on?" Parks asked, forcing himself to smile.

"And you're very pleasant all of a sudden. What's wrong

with you?" she replied, frowning at the smile that was as fake as a three-dollar bill.

She pushed past him and headed for the exit.

"Wait a minute, I'll take you to your room."

"No, that's okay. I think I can manage all by my little bitsy self," Ebonee replied sarcastically. "Thanks anyway, though." She walked faster, trying to put some distance between them.

"No. That was not a question." Parks stepped in front of her and reached slowly into his pocket, his eyes never leaving hers.

Ebonee's heart raced as she watched him reach into his pocket and pull out . . . car keys.

"Besides, I have the keys," he said, smiling as he dangled the keys in front of her face. Then he turned and walked away.

Ebonee closed her eyes and exhaled deeply, trying to calm her nerves. She followed Parks out to the car, and he drove her to the hotel, which, thankfully, was only a few moments away. She jumped out of the car without a word as soon as it stopped in front of the hotel.

"Hey! Lane! Where's the fire?" Parks called out as she walked swiftly through the doors of the hotel.

"It would probably be on my lawn if you had anything to do with it," Ebonee whispered to herself as she walked up to the front desk.

"Can I help you, miss?" the clerk asked, smiling easily.

"Yes. Do you have a room for Ebonee Lane?" She felt the weariness beginning to set in. She had not been asleep in almost thirty-two hours; she needed the rest.

"Yes, Ms. Lane. If I could just see some ID. I'll give you your key and you'll be all set," the clerk replied, looking up from the computer screen.

Ebonee pulled out her wallet and handed her ID to the clerk, who checked it and then handed it back to her.

"Okay. Thank you, Ms. Lane. Here you are. You're in room 122. Enjoy your stay." The clerk smiled as she handed her a small plastic card key. Ebonee accepted the key and turned to walk away.

"Oh! Ms. Lane! Someone left this for you," the clerk said quickly, picking up an envelope with Agent Lane's name on it.

"What is it?" Ebonee asked, turning back to regard the clerk curiously.

"It's a letter, I guess," she replied, handing the envelope over the counter. Ebonee took the envelope, looking at it curiously. She opened it to find a simple message:

Let sleeping dogs lie.
You wouldn't want to get bit.
—A sleeping dog

Ebonee looked up at the clerk. "Who left this?"

"I don't know; someone just left it sitting on the desk."

Ebonee spun around, her eyes searching the lobby frantically. She saw the man almost immediately. Standing in a corner, wearing a long, beige trench coat over a plain, dark suit. He stared at her intently, dragging lazily on a cigarette.

"You look like you've seen a ghost."

Ebonee jumped at the voice that came from behind her. She turned to see Parks, still with that fake-ass smile, looking at her.

"Why don't you put some fucking bells on or something!" she said angrily, spinning to look for the strange man, but he was gone.

"Hey, look, I'm trying to be nice here," Parks said reluctantly.

"Well, don't do me any favors," Ebonee replied, turning to walk away. "I'll be in my room." She left Parks standing in the lobby alone, his cheeks red as a beet.

She took the stairs to the first floor. Spotting a payphone in the hallway, she went to it.

"FBI, Internal Affairs Division. How can I direct your call?" the operator asked.

"Assistant Director Moss, please," Ebonee replied, looking around nervously.

"Please hold," the operator instructed. A moment later the operator was back. "I'm sorry, but the director is on vacation. I'll connect you to Director Glenn."

"No, wait!" Agent Lane tried to get her attention, but it was too late.

"Assistant Director Glenn speaking. Hello?" Glenn answered, as Ebonee tried to make sense of it all.

Director Moss was on vacation? That alone gave her caution. She had known the director for the entire five years she had been in the bureau. She knew he would never go on a vacation with her in the middle of an investigation, especially one of this scale.

"Agent Lane?"

Ebonee held the phone away from her ear, looking at it incredulously.

"Are you there, Lane?"

Ebonee slammed the phone down on the hook and looked around frantically. The implications made her head spin. She leaned back against the wall, trying to think. She walked back toward her room, absently slipping her hand into her pocket. She felt the miniature tape recorder and paused. Then she went back downstairs to the front desk.

"Excuse me, but what room is Agent Parks in? You remember? The man who followed me in?" she asked, her eyes scanning all around the lobby for the stranger.

"Yes, ma'am, he's in room 115."

"Thank you."

She made her way back up to the first floor, walking along the carpeted hall in the direction of room 115. As she approached, she pulled out the tiny ear plug and inserted it into her ear.

". . . But why?" She picked up Agent Parks' voice.

"Listen, Agent, we don't ask questions. We just follow orders. The less we know, the clearer our conscience will be. Now can you get her into this room?" another voice asked, a strange voice.

"I don't think so," Parks replied.

"Then we'll have to go in," a second voice said, a voice she recognized.

Ebonee froze as the handle to the door of the room began to turn. She watched a tall black man, wearing the same type of trench coat and dark suit as the original stranger, walk out of the room. Their eyes locked, and they both froze. Time seemed to stand still until Ebonee snapped to her senses.

"Richards?" she said in a confused whisper.

They both went for their guns, but Ebonee was quicker. She emptied out a clip in the man's direction as she backed up, looking for an escape route. The hallway was too long for her to try to make it back to the stairs. She glanced over the waist-high glass railing and looked down. There was a small man-made pond directly below her. She thought about jumping. The other two men jumped over the wounded man and came out blasting.

Ebonee jumped.

Turning in the air, she returned fire. She hit the water with a splash. Luckily, the pond housed a rather expensive collection of Coy, and the water was deep enough to break her fall. She scrambled out of the water as the men approached the rail, taking their shots with abandon. She dove

behind a now empty bar and landed on top of the shaking
bartender, who was screaming at the top of her lungs. Suddenly the gunshots ceased, and all Ebonee could hear was
the torturous screaming of the bartender.

"Ohhh myyy Goddd! I don't want to diiiieee!" the bartender screamed and cried, over and over again.

Ebonee tried to listen for some clue to her assailants'
whereabouts, but she couldn't hear anything over the
screams of the woman.

"Shhh! Hush!" Ebonee shouted at her.

But the woman only screamed louder. Ebonee looked at
her angrily. "If you don't shut the fuck up, I'll shoot you my
gotdamned self!" Ebonee Lane yelled angrily, pointing her
gun at the terrified woman.

Suddenly there was silence, except for the sound of the
running water of the pond and a few pieces of glass falling—
and the loud click.

Ebonee's eyes opened wide, and she looked at the silent,
whimpering woman. She had heard that sound too many
times in her years in the service, but more importantly, she
knew what always followed that sound.

"Run!" she yelled to the woman. She sprinted out from
the cover of the bar.

The explosion helped her on her way, as the grenade blew
the bar to pieces. She landed in a heap up against a wall. She
shook her head, trying to dislodge the dizziness. She looked
to the left and saw an exit to the parking lot. She forced herself up and ran for her life.

Gunshots erupted again as the other man reappeared on
the first floor. He looked in the direction of the exit for
which Ebonee was running, and ran for it, hoping to cut her
off before she got there. The gunfire ceased as both he and
Ebonee ran out of bullets. Ebonee knew she wouldn't beat
the man to the exit, but she had no other choice. She heard

another click from somewhere behind her. They would reach the exit at about the same time; maybe she could dodge him.

Ebonee hit the ground hard as the man tackled her, knocking the air from her lungs. She rolled over in time to see the man reaching for her neck. She forced herself to her feet. Grabbing the man's hand and twisting his arm, she pulled it forward across her body with his own momentum aiding. Stepping to the side, she slammed her left hand into his twisted arm at the elbow, snapping it like a twig. The man started to howl in pain, but was interrupted when Ebonee's foot came up and connected with his chin.

She hit the door running.

Gunfire rang out again as she ran through the adjoining airport's long-term parking lot. The two men, for the wounded man was now back in the hunt, had reached the exit and were now pursuing her through the parking lot. She saw a black convertible pulling out of a parking spot, and ran for the door. Opening it, she dove into the passenger seat.

"What the fuck?" Kenyatta shouted, looking down at the curled-up form. "Oh shit! Ain't you that lady cop from downtown?" Kenyatta exclaimed, recognizing Ebonee.

"Drive!" Ebonee shouted.

"Oh shit! You bleedin'!" Kenyatta exclaimed again, seeing the blood on Ebonee's jacket.

"Drive, gotdammit!" Ebonee yelled, just as a bullet exploded one of the backseat's side windows.

"Oh shit!" Kenyatta yelled, slamming her foot down onto the gas pedal.

The car exploded through the lowered arm at the cashier's booth, careening out into traffic. Ebonee looked up to see all the traffic coming at them.

"You're going the wrong way!" she exclaimed.

"I'm going away from those muthafuckas shootin', ain't

I?" Kenyatta paused to veer out of the way of a large truck. "That sounds like the right fuckin' way to me!" she added, swerving back and forth across the expressway.

Soon they were out of sight and were able to get off the expressway without causing any serious accidents.

"What the fuck was all that about?" Kenyatta exclaimed, looking for a place to pull over. But she got no response. She glanced over at Ebonee's still body.

"Oh shit! Bitch, don't you die in my mother's car!" Kenyatta shouted, causing Ebonee to stir. She had taken a bullet in the shoulder and had lost quite a bit of blood.

"I'm going to take you to the hospital!" Kenyatta said.

"Nooo . . . no hospitals. No hospitals and no police . . . please," Ebonee moaned weakly.

"Fuck you want me to do then? Let you die?" Kenyatta asked incredulously. But Ebonee had once again passed out.

"Oh no you don't! Wake the fuck up! Come on! Wake up!" Kenyatta shouted, pushing at Ebonee with her free hand. She heard Ebonee groan, and felt a little better.

She remembered her next door neighbor was a certified nurse, so she headed home.

"Gotdamn Elijah's black ass. I'm going to fuck him up when I see him," Kenyatta said calmly to herself, shaking her head in total bewilderment.

Elijah stepped out of the taxi and looked up at the huge building. It was the largest church he had ever seen in his life. He unconsciously put his hand to his head and then stopped as he remembered that his hair was now in cornrows and he couldn't run his fingers through his hair anymore.

"Close the bloody door, will ya? I've got a call!" the cab driver yelled.

Elijah turned and slammed the door as hard as he could.

"Oops."

Glass went everywhere as the door slammed shut with a loud bang.

"Bleedin' maniac! Are you daft or what?" the driver exclaimed, getting out of the car to stare at Elijah.

Elijah stood there for a second, his hand covering his mouth, feeling totally the fool. He tried to fight back his laughter, but didn't do a very good job.

"I'm sorry. I'll pay for it.... Here." Elijah pulled out a stack of money and put it in the driver's hands.

The man looked down at the stack of money and raised his eyebrow questioningly. It was way more than needed, he knew that. But did the American?

"Is that all you have? 'Cause it's gonna take a lot more to get this bloody thing mended!" he shouted angrily.

"I think it will be enough to fix this window," Elijah began, his smile disappearing in light of the man's greed. "And . . ." he walked to the front door of the car and pulled it open, "this window," he finished, slamming the door hard, sending glass flying once again.

The man looked at him in disbelief with his mouth open, catching flies.

"And," Elijah began again, as he saw the man making no move to leave.

Elijah started for the other side of the car.

"No! No! It's okay, that's plenty!" the man shouted, jumping into the car and speeding off.

Elijah smiled and turned back to the church. He walked up to the gigantic wooden doors and looked for a doorbell. There was none. He raised his hand to knock, but then stopped as he thought about how ridiculous that would be. Then the door suddenly opened. A short, portly priest dressed in a long white robe beckoned Elijah inside with the wave of a stubby little hand. Elijah looked up at the huge door one last time, and then with a shrug, followed the priest inside.

A second taxi arrived no sooner than the doors of the church had closed. A large burly man stepped out, looking up at the church; he felt the Protector's presence. El'Rathiem had been warned of the Protector's arrival by Dalfien, and he knew exactly where to look. This was not the first time a Protector had treaded upon his domain. Each time, this was the place he would find them. El'Rathiem had killed the last two Protectors with little difficulty, and figured to do the same with this one.

"You ain't the Pope or nothin' like that, are you?" Elijah asked, breaking the eerie silence with a smile.

"A Protector with a sense of humor. That's rather odd," the priest replied as he led Elijah through the enormous sanctuary.

"What do you mean, Protector?" Elijah stared at the priest's back curiously. "You mean there are others?"

"Very few, I'm afraid. Some never made it past the steps of the church," the priest answered nonchalantly.

"Why? What happened to them?"

"Their hearts were ripped from their chests while they still pumped blood," the priest replied, waiting for the customary sucking in of air, followed by some wild exclamation demanding to know why. But it never came.

"Well, that's encouraging," Elijah said sarcastically.

It was the priest's turn to smile now as he stopped to regard this Protector in the dim light of the candles. "You are truly different from the others. You seem almost . . . willing. I sense no fear of death in you."

"Death," Elijah snorted and rolled his eyes. "Been there and done that, pops; it's overrated. Now what am I here for?" he asked, his shoulders sagging at the memory of the place he was so cruelly ripped away from.

The priest gazed at him a moment longer and then turned to continue their walk. "To learn, my son," he said, sounding a lot like the prophets in those old holy movies.

"Well, what do you have to teach? Will it take long?" Elijah asked, frowning. He was not known for his patience.

"Long? No. What I have to teach is actually quite simple."

"Good, 'cause I'm a very simple man." Elijah paused and cocked his head to the side. "Wait, that didn't come out quite right."

The portly priest paused again, glancing back at the Protector. This time he couldn't resist his laughter.

Elijah looked at the round laughing priest curiously. "What? What's so funny?" he asked seriously, causing the robust man to laugh even harder.

Finally, the old priest was able to catch his breath and speak. "Oh, my. Do forgive me. It has been quite some time since I have laughed so sincerely," the priest whined, taking a deep breath as he continued on.

He led Elijah to a staircase that descended behind the pulpit to a closed door. Elijah paused as a sudden wave of chill bumps ran the length of his arms. It was the same feeling that went through him when the officer had attacked him back at the airport. "This way," the priest directed, unlatching what seemed to be a hundred and one locks and deadbolts that sealed the portal shut.

Finally, the door slowly creaked open. The priest stepped inside and lit a match, holding it up to a torch that sat in a sconce upon the wall, igniting it. Elijah stepped through the doorway and his eyes went wide as the light from the torch spread across the small room.

"What in the hell—" Elijah slapped his hand over his mouth. "I meant heck." He looked back at the priest sheepishly, causing the priest to chuckle again.

Weapons of all sizes and types lined the walls of the room: spears, swords, axes, and many more.

"Ummm . . . why does your church have an arsenal?" Elijah asked, looking back at the priest curiously. "My church never had anything like this!"

"Take what you wish, Protector. They are all blessed by the archangel, Michael, himself. They will never fail you," the priest said when he had finished his latest bit of chuckling. "I will wait above."

Elijah walked the length of the room, picking up various items, swinging swords in the air, checking it all out. Then something caught his eye. Along the back wall, amidst all of the bright shining silver and gold weapons, there stood out a darkness.

Elijah's heart raced as he laid eyes on the dark blades. They were black, each one about four feet long with a slight curve from the hilt to the tip. He knew these blades well. They were the swords from his dreams. He reached out tentatively, lightly touching the hilt of one sword. Slight vibrations passed from the sword into his fingers and up through the rest of his body, comforting him. He picked them both up and held them up to the light. Strange symbols were engraved along each blade. He thought about putting his thumb to the cutting edge of one of the blades to check its sharpness, but thought better of it. He knew they were razor sharp. He looked down, and there, folded neatly on a small shelf, was an outfit made of black leather and silver chain mesh. He wasted no time changing. He slid the boots on and fastened the belt around his waist, sliding the blades into their sheaths on the belt. Then he put back on his black trench coat.

"Cool," Elijah whispered to himself as he looked into a shield at his reflection. His self admiration was cut short though, as the chill bumps again found his skin. But this time, they were accompanied by a loud scream.

Chapter Eight
First Blood

Elijah turned the corner at the top of the ancient stairs and froze. Standing in the front of the pulpit, was a large burly man. He stood with his arm outreached and up high. At the end of that arm, the portly priest twisted and squirmed while clutching wildly at the man's hand around his throat, his feet kicking madly at the air.

The man, inhabited by El'Rathiem, turned his head to regard Elijah. Then he unceremoniously tossed the priest to the side, where he landed heavily with a groan.

"Taking advantage of a defenseless priest?" Elijah began walking toward El'Rathiem.

Elijah ignored the chills that still ran through his body, but he did take heed to the once subtle, but now strong vibrations of his new blades.

"Come, Protector," El'Rathiem growled through clenched teeth. "Let me show you how to die."

"Sorry." Elijah grinned wickedly as he walked to meet the man. "I've already taken that class."

El'Rathiem howled and charged at him, his arms reaching for his throat. In a flash, Elijah had the twin blades out and working. Then he was behind El'Rathiem looking at the demon patiently. El'Rathiem looked down stupidly at the bloody stumps that were once his arms.

"No! Protector! You must say the words!" the priest yelled weakly.

Elijah turned to the prone priest and glared at him. "What words, old man?"

"If you kill the beast as he is now, you will only be killing the human he infests; you must bring him into his physical form. Then, and only then, will your weapons strike to kill," the priest explained.

Elijah looked back at the man. His arms had nearly regenerated.

"But be warned, Protector, once the demon is in his physical form, his true power will accompany him," the priest added.

"Say the words, old man!" Elijah urged the priest.

The demon's hands were slowly forming. If he could bring the demon into its physical form while its hands were gone, he would have a great advantage.

"Say the words!" he shouted as the possessed man turned on them.

"*Anel nathrak doth dien dienve!*" the priest shouted.

Suddenly, the man fell to his knees and the demon howled out in pain as its spirit was torn from the man's body. A form began to appear where the man once stood. Slowly at first, but then before Elijah could blink three times, it was there, in all of its terrible glory. It stood fully seven feet tall and was as wide as a Volkswagen. Its reddish-black skin glistened in the candle light, and its huge muscled, elongated arms promised Elijah a nice pounding. Its tree trunk legs ended in hooves, and its gigantic canine head, complete with horns, swung to glare at Elijah with eyes as black as its heart.

Elijah shot the priest a woeful look. "Are you sure you said the right words?"

"Remember the words, Protector, and strike for the heart, or take its head from its body," the priest instructed.

Elijah looked back to the demon and its broad powerful neck. "There has to be an easier way to do this," he whispered.

"Fool! Now you shall feel my power!" El'Rathiem bellowed, rearing back and letting out a howl that shook the very foundation of the sanctuary.

The demon's pompous roar turned into a yelp of pain. It looked down curiously, clutching at the holes that were now spilling his black blood onto the floor of the church. Elijah smiled as he approached again, this time from the other side. His swords found the demon's skin repeatedly, poking holes in its thigh and waist. The demon howled again as it spun around in vain, trying to catch this bothersome pest that agitated him.

Elijah stalked the demon, skipping just out of its reach, waiting for an opening. But El'Rathiem was on guard now. He had felt the sting of those terrible blades, and they seemed to suck away at his very soul.

The demon slammed its fist into the floor with enough strength to fell a small building. The floor shook violently, and Elijah stumbled awkwardly, trying to keep his footing. Incredibly fast, El'Rathiem closed the distance between them. Elijah knew he was in trouble as he staggered this way and that, trying to retain his balance. But the floor splintered and cracked, his foot falling into a knee-deep hole.

He felt the air rushing out of his lungs as El'Rathiem slammed a giant fist into his chest. Elijah flew backward through the air, crashing into and through the first, second, and, finally, the third row of pews.

"Muthafucka," Elijah whispered slowly, feeling the pain in

his back. "You didn't even have to hit me like that, man," he complained.

He rolled to the side as a pew crashed into the spot where he had landed. He had no idea how he was going to get close enough to even strike at the demon now, let alone decapitate it. Another pew flew at him. This time Elijah braced himself and went with the blow as it knocked him backwards into another row of pews. He lay completely still. El'Rathiem, seeing the missile connect with its target, howled in triumph.

He stalked over to the Protector, who lay face down among the splintered woodpiles. The demon reached down, chuckling as he pulled the limp body over. Elijah's blade drew another smile of its own—across the demon's neck. The demon grabbed at his throat as the dark blood spilled forth. El'Rathiem turned and searched about frantically for a way out.

The Protector was on him then, stabbing and slicing away with those horrible blades. El'Rathiem felt his soul weakening with each attack as the blades sucked the very life from him. Elijah felt the hum of the swords increase with every blow; he felt the strength they pumped into him as they stole the demon's life force.

The demon howled in pain and launched a desperate backhand, trying to sweep the Protector and those terrible blades away so he could escape. His arm returned to him minus a hand.

The Protector, now completely absorbed in the battle lust, stalked forward fearlessly. His expression grim, he leapt into the demon's chest, blades leading. The demon howled in pain again as the blades drove into its upper body. Then El'Rathiem fell forward, seeking to crush the Protector underneath his own weight. But the Protector was too quick for such a move. With blinding speed, Elijah snatched his swords from the demon's massive chest and threw his arms around its neck, swinging to land on El'Rathiem's back as they crashed to the floor.

Father Holbrook watched it all in amazement. He had seen so many Protectors come and go, but none of them were like this one. He stared in disbelief at the speed and fluidity of his movements; the blades he had selected seemed to be one with him. It was truly a sight to behold. A smile slowly found its way to the old priest's face as he watched the demon fall. If he would have blinked his eyes, he knew he would have missed the killing blow, so fast was this Protector. Then the Protector stood, looking down at the headless body of the demon.

Elijah watched as the body shuddered and slowly began to degenerate into dust. In moments, the body was gone, leaving only a pile of dust as evidence of its existence.

"Amazing," Father Holbrook whispered, coming to stand next to the Protector.

Elijah reluctantly let the battle lust fall away. He welcomed the power and satisfaction from the fight. It reminded him of the times when he would dream, when he would give back all the pain and suffering he had endured. "Are you okay, old man?" he asked the priest, sliding his blades into their sheaths at his sides.

"Me? Oh yes . . . I'm fine. I'm fine," the priest replied, glancing over his shoulder. "But it appears I will be quite busy for some time," he added, referring to the destruction the two combatants had wrought.

"My apologies, good priest," Elijah offered, his gaze following that of the priest.

"Apologies? Nonsense, no need. I would gladly wield a hammer and nails for the rest of my days to witness such grace and beauty in battle," Father Holbrook answered, offering a smile. Then he inhaled deeply. "It would seem that already you have garnered the full attention of the dark realm." He stared at Elijah seriously. "This was no minor fiend or imp. . . . This was a true demon."

"Good Priest—"

"Holbrook. My name is Father Holbrook. Now you must be on your way; there are demons awaiting your sword!" Father Holbrook said, ushering Elijah toward the back of the church.

"But I thought you were supposed to teach me something," Elijah commented as Father Holbrook hurried him to the front doors.

The priest stopped then and his expression grew stern. "Protector," he began quietly.

"Elijah. My name is Elijah," Elijah interrupted him, looking at the priest's suddenly stern visage curiously.

"Protector," Father Holbrook began again, ignoring Elijah's words. "You have taught me more in these few moments than I could ever teach anyone. Go now, for there is nothing more I can give you except my prayers. Now please, go," he finished, pushing Elijah through the door and closing it quickly with a loud boom.

Father Holbrook leaned back against the door, his heart heavy. He had not felt such feelings in a long time. He had spent all of his adult life behind these doors, devoting his life to his God. He could not remember the last time he had laughed so. This Protector was indeed special. Father Holbrook found himself wanting to go with the Protector, to adventure out in the wide world at his side. To laugh and smile, and behold the amazing dance of those blades.

"Ahhh, the musings of an old man," Father Holbrook whispered to himself as he sighed heavily and turned to walk back into the church.

Elijah stood outside the door, one eyebrow raised in confusion.

"Strange one, he is," he muttered, turning around, his

thoughts on getting back home now. He looked down at his waist. Then he spun and yelled at the doors. "Hey! How in the hell am I supposed to get these things on a plane?"

Ebonee groaned and slowly opened her eyes. She looked around to see where she was. She tried to sit up and felt pain shoot through her arm. She winced and fell back down onto the couch where she lay. She could hear voices in the background.

"The tape," she said to herself, remembering what had happened. Fighting the pain away, she sat up.

" 'Bout time you woke up."

Ebonee looked up to see Kenyatta looking down at her.

"How do you feel?" she asked, handing her a glass of water.

Ebonee took the water and swallowed a few sips. "I'll be okay. Thank you."

Kenyatta sat down in the chair across from her. "So who was those guys shootin' at you?"

"I'm not sure," Ebonee answered. "Where is my jacket?" She looked around the small, comfortable room.

"It's in the closet . . . over there." Kenyatta pointed to a door in the corner next to the front door.

Ebonee forced herself to her feet, pausing to fight away the dizziness.

"You a tough little somethin', ain't you?" Kenyatta remarked as Ebonee walked to the closet and retrieved her jacket.

She fished through the pockets and pulled out the tape. Sighing in relief, she walked back to the couch. "Got to be," she answered absently, checking for her gun.

"I have a box of bullets in the kitchen if you need some," Kenyatta offered, walking into the kitchen and coming back with a small box, which she sat on the table.

Ebonee looked at her curiously.

"Living in the projects you have to take certain precautions," Kenyatta explained.

"No doubt, I know what you mean." Ebonee came up in the projects herself in Chicago, so she knew how it was. "So how did you happen to be at the airport?"

Kenyatta shifted uncomfortably. "My brother left us a note. He came by here that same night."

"You knew he was coming here, didn't you?" Ebonee looked at Kenyatta suspiciously.

"I had an idea."

"You know he's wanted for another murder now, right?"

"Murder?" Kenyatta muttered, looking at her doubtfully.

"He killed a cop at the airport—at least that's how it appears. I have my doubts, though," she added, walking over to look at some pictures hanging on the lavender-colored wall.

"Please, my brother ain't never killed nobody, 'cept hisself, and he didn't do that right!" Kenyatta said, chuckling to herself.

"Is this your brother?" Ebonee pointed to a picture of a man holding a little girl in his arms.

"Yeah, that's him and my daughter."

Ebonee stared at the picture for a moment. She felt that she knew this person. There was something about those eyes.

"So do you think he did it?" Kenyatta asked.

"I'm not too sure. But I'm beginning to think that whether he did it or not is the least of his problems," Ebonee reflected, recalling the conversation between Parks and the regional director.

"How you figure?"

Ebonee sighed deeply, finally turning away from the picture. She didn't know who she could trust now. Her director may quite possibly be dead, and he was the only one who knew of her undercover status. The local authorities would be no help; she had no idea how deep this organization ran. Her options seemed very limited indeed. And suddenly she felt very small. Her badge would do her no good now. She looked back at the picture, back into those beautiful brown eyes. She had reviewed his record. His rap sheet was virtually spotless. He had served in the military for almost ten years, receiving numerous awards and commendations. He had a good job making decent money. What would drive him to kill himself?

"Kenyatta, why did your brother try to kill himself?" she asked, still looking at the picture.

"You mean, why *did* he kill himself?" Kenyatta corrected. "I don't know; we never got a chance to talk about it. But it was probably over some chickenhead."

"A girl? How do you know?"

"Because he was always stressin' over some chick or another. I ain't never seen somebody fall in love as much as he did," Kenyatta replied.

Ebonee let out a little snort; she had been in love before, and had received nothing but a broken heart in return. She had even contemplated suicide, but she found she didn't have the courage.

"Love can do that to you," she said quietly, returning her gaze to the picture, and those eyes.

Kenyatta walked over to the front window. "Sounds like you're speaking from experience."

"Somethin' like that," Ebonee said, pulling herself from the picture and walking over to pick up the box of bullets.

"He got that shit from my mom. She's the same fuckin' way, all emotional and shit," Kenyatta said, staring out through the lavender curtains at the strange car that was now parked in the parking lot.

"What about you? Haven't you ever been in love before?" Ebonee asked, finding herself liking this straight-up young lady. She reminded her of herself in a small way, an independent, no nonsense type of girl—just not as brazen.

"Hell no. I don't love shit but myself and my daughter. I

don't need no man. If I can't get it by myself, then I don't need it," Kenyatta said, frowning up her face as she spoke.

"I wish it were that easy," Ebonee replied, wishing for a moment that she could be as strong as Kenyatta when it came to dealings of the heart. But she knew that was impossible. The last five years had been rough for her; she had caught her fiancé in the bed with another woman. It had devastated her. If it were not for the bureau keeping her busy, she didn't know what she would have done. She had only recently let go of the past, and had gone out with a handsome young man she had known from the academy. She hadn't really felt anything as far as love was concerned, but she was so tired of being alone.

"You seeing anyone special?" Kenyatta asked.

"Not anymore," she answered with a sarcastic snicker.

"Why not? What did he do?"

"He tried to kill me," Ebonee answered flatly, drawing a confused look from Kenyatta. They sat for a moment looking at each other, and then they both erupted in a bit of laughter.

"That's a good fuckin' reason not to see him anymore."

"I didn't like his corny ass no way."

Kenyatta sucked her teeth. "Man, these muthafuckas think niggas is so stupid," she said, still looking out of the window. "They think nobody don't see their asses sittin' there in their jump-out."

"Jump-out?"

"Girl, you been out of the ghetto too long. You don't know what a jump-out is?" Kenyatta looked back at Ebonee curiously.

"No, what is it?" She got up to walk over to the window.

"It's a car the cops use when they're undercover. They call it a jump-out because when they pull up, they jump out and they just got yo' ass!" Kenyatta explained, smiling.

But Ebonee's smile was gone now as she peeped out of the

curtain at the car. "How long have they been out here?" she asked seriously.

"They just pulled up while we were talking. Why? They friends of yours?"

Ebonee was about to answer when her cell phone rang. She glanced back at the car to make sure they weren't making any moves. Then she walked over to the couch and pulled the phone from her short black blazer.

"Hello?"

"Agent Lane?"

"This is Agent Lane," she replied, looking at Kenyatta.

"Agent Lane, what's going on down there? I just got a call from Director Scott. He said you were missing," the voice said, sounding concerned.

"Director Moss?" Ebonee asked, confused.

"Yes. You sound surprised. Why haven't you reported?"

"W-w-well, they told me you were on vacation," she answered, stuttering as she tried to figure out what was going on.

"Vacation? That's nonsense. I haven't been out of the office all day. Who did you talk to?"

"Assistant Director Glenn."

"Glenn?"

"Sir, does Director Glenn know my status?" Ebonee inquired.

"Well, he has access to our files, just like I have access to his. But there should be no reason for him to—" He paused. "Are you implying what I think you are, Agent Lane?"

"Sir, he knew it was me before I had a chance to speak. It was as if he was waiting for the call," she explained.

"That doesn't mean he's linked to—"

"Sir, they just tried to kill me!" Ebonee exclaimed, interrupting him in mid sentence.

"What? Where are you now?"

"I'm safe . . . for the moment. But this thing is big, sir. The

Deputy Assistant Director is a part of it also, along with Parks and Richards," she explained.

"Do you have any proof?"

"Yes. I have a recorded conversation between Parks and Scott."

"Do you have it with you?"

Ebonee paused for a moment. How could she be sure she could trust him? She decided that she didn't have any choice.

"No. I left it someplace safe," she lied.

"Okay . . . Look, I'm on my way there. Get the tape and I'll call you when I get there to let you know where to meet me."

"But what about the case?" Ebonee asked.

"What about it? I'll get some men down there to take care of it. We'll get him."

"But sir, that's another thing. I think they're setting this guy up. I don't know why yet, but I'm pretty sure."

"Okay. I'll inform them of that. But the important thing for you is to get the tape and stay out of their way. I'll contact you soon."

Agent Lane stared at the phone for a moment, her mind frantically working.

"What's up?" Kenyatta asked, looking at her.

"I'm going to try and help your brother as best I can. I don't believe he did what they're accusing him of."

"So what's our next move?"

Ebonee's eyebrows went up. "Our?"

"What? Do you think I'm going to let you do this by yourself? This is about my brother. I want to help," Kenyatta said, walking to the kitchen.

"It's too dangerous. And you'd just get in the way."

"Get in the way? I ain't hear you complaining when I saved your ass back in that parking lot!" Kenyatta exclaimed, walking back into the living room with her nine millimeter, slapping a clip in it with a sharp snap. "And as far as it being dangerous . . . shit, it's dangerous walking to the fuckin' Chinese store in these projects. And besides, I can handle myself." Kenyatta slid her nine millimeter into her waist and stared at Ebonee with a look that told her it would be useless to argue. "Now, like I was sayin' . . . what's our next move?"

Ebonee stared at Kenyatta for a moment. She couldn't help but smile as she remembered how she herself was once the same way.

"Okay. But for the record, my answer is no. But I can't force you to not follow me around," she replied, smiling. "Now, I've got to get back to the airport, but first we have to get rid of the 'jump- out.'" Ebonee smiled as she referred to the undercover feds out in the car.

"No problem. I'll fix their fuckin' asses." A grin came to Kenyatta's lips as she walked over and picked up the phone.

Ebonee walked back over to the picture on the wall, and stared again into those beautiful eyes. What was it about those eyes? Why did she get the feeling that she knew those eyes from somewhere? But from where? She had never met Elijah before in her life. She was sure of that.

"All right, come on. Let's get ready. You need a disguise," Kenyatta said after hanging up the phone.

"What about the jump-out?" Ebonee asked curiously, following Kenyatta up the stairs.

"Don't worry about them. It's all good. Now come on, I have a couple of wigs you can try on," she said, leading Ebonee to her bedroom. She pulled out about three or four wigs, tossing them onto the bed. Ebonee chuckled to herself as another wig flew onto the bed.

"What? You ain't never wear a wig before?"

Ebonee picked up one of the wigs and looked at it curiously. "Well . . . actually, no."

"Well, it ain't difficult. Now pick one." Ebonee picked out a brown wig that was styled in micro braids that would hang down well past her shoulders. "This one," she decided, smiling as she held it up. She had wanted to let her hair grow, but being in the service had prevented her from doing so.

"Bitch. I knew you were going to pick that one. That's my favorite. I want my shit back, too," Kenyatta muttered, causing Ebonee to laugh.

Kenyatta tossed her a stocking cap. "Put this on. And pull the wig on over it."

Ebonee followed her directions and walked over to the mirror sitting on top of the old oak dresser. She smiled widely at her reflection in the mirror. Then Kenyatta walked out of the room and returned with a black mini skirt and a short cut-off T-shirt, with the word 'flirt' written across the front.

"What am I supposed to do with this?" Ebonee asked, looking at Kenyatta suspiciously.

"You can't wear what you've got on. And they will never guess you to be dressed like this."

"I guess you're right," Ebonee agreed, sliding out of her bloodstained suit and into the clothes that Kenyatta had given her. When she looked in the mirror again, she couldn't believe her eyes.

"I look like a hoochie!" she exclaimed as Kenyatta walked over to put her wig back into a ponytail.

"There, now you look like a respectable hood rat," Kenyatta said, and they both fell into a fit of laughter.

Kenyatta walked over to the upstairs window and peeped out. "All right, come on. They're here," she said excitedly, leading Ebonee out of the room and down to the back door.

"Kenyatta, the keys," Ebonee said, stopping short of the door and holding out her hand.

"What? I can drive," Kenyatta said, her tone sounding as if her feelings were hurt.

"We've been down that road before—the wrong way! Remember?" Ebonee said with a smile. "Keys!" she insisted, thrusting her hand out forcefully.

"All right, here!" Kenyatta sucked her teeth as she tossed Ebonee the keys to her mother's Sebring. They walked through the back of the house and got in the car.

"You sure they're ready?" Ebonee started the car.

"Let's find out." Kenyatta turned on the radio to blast some hip-hop.

Ebonee looked at Kenyatta and shook her head, smiling as she pulled the car around the side of the building.

One of the men sitting in the car looked over as Ebonee and Kenyatta cruised past.

"Hey! That's them! Tail them!" he shouted, slapping the driver of the car on the arm.

"What the hell?" the driver stated, slamming on the brakes as he stared out of the front windshield in disbelief.

"What? Why are you stop . . ." His voice trailed off into nothing as he looked out at the road ahead. At least twenty brothas, all packin' various firearms, surrounded the car.

The driver put the car in park and raised his hands, looking over helplessly to his partner, whose hands were also in the air.

"I hate the ghetto."

Kenyatta bounced to the beat as they drove along, her hands waving in the air as she sang the words of the song. Ebonee looked at her out of the corner of her eye. Kenyatta didn't have a care in the world. Her buoyant spirit infected Ebonee, and she couldn't stop smiling.

"Come on, girl! I know you still got some ghetto in you! Let the top down!" Kenyatta shouted over the music. Then she reached over and hit the switch for the convertible top to pull back, since Ebonee couldn't seem to find it. It was early October and still kind of warm out.

"Come on, girl! I know you feel that beat! Roll wit' it, girl!" Kenyatta shouted, swaying from side to side.

Ebonee's smile seemed to stretch her face past its limits.

She looked over at Kenyatta and slowly joined her in her rhythmic bounce.

"Yeah! That's it. You got it, girl!" Kenyatta grinned as Ebonee fell into the groove. She threw her hands up into the night air, still grooving.

"Kenyatta in the house! Ebonee in the house!" Ebonee shouted into the night. She got caught up in the moment, squealed happily, and threw her hands up into the air, her thigh accidentally bumping the steering wheel and causing the car to swerve. She snatched her hands back down and corrected the vehicle, just missing a parked car.

"Let's not get carried away, Thelma," Kenyatta said, looking at Ebonee apprehensively.

Ebonee giggled and put her hand to her mouth. "Sorry, Louise!" They both shared a good laugh.

Chapter Nine
UnWanted Passions

Elijah dialed the numbers on the small piece of paper from a payphone in the hotel lobby. Terry had given him this number just in case he wanted to stop by before the return flight took off.

"Hello, Terry?" he said, hearing her pick up.

"Hi, Elijah! You coming up?"

"Ummm, how did you know it was me?" Elijah said, stalling. He really didn't want to go up to her room.

"Just come on up, silly! It's room 319. Bye!"

Elijah sighed deeply and hung up the phone. The hilt of one of the blades poked through the front of his trench coat, as if to remind him of why he was there. He glanced around cautiously, tucking it back in. Then with another sigh, he headed across the shining marble floor and to the elevator.

The door swung open before he could knock, and Terry pulled him into the room, slamming the door behind him.

"You owe me, mister!" She pushed Elijah's back up against the door, her lips gently touching his chin.

"Terry! Slow down!" Elijah exclaimed, holding her at arms' length.

She pushed his arms down and leaned back in hungrily, kissing at him, her hands touching him all over. "We don't have time. I can't wait!" she gasped, reaching for Elijah's belt. Her hand found the handle of one of his blades instead. Her eyes opened wide, and she looked at Elijah incredulously.

"I need your help," Elijah said, opening his coat to reveal the blades. "Can you get these onto the plane for me?" he asked, pulling away from her a bit.

Terry sighed and her shoulders slumped. Then she grinned wickedly and stepped back into his arms. "Maybe," she teased, running her fingers across his chest.

"Terry, I'm serious," Elijah said, grabbing her hands and holding them down on both sides of her body.

"So am I," she whispered, pulling her hands free. She reached up and put her arms around his neck, clicking off the light in the process. "So am I."

Elijah leaned his head up against the small window and watched the ground fly by beneath him. He tried desperately to fight back the emotions that now assaulted his mind. He had succumbed to Terry's advances, but as he felt her lips gently gliding across his and her hands gently touching him in sensual places, memories had flooded into his mind.

Memories of that night.

His eyes were closed, and she was just about to say the words. He could still taste her wonderful full lips. Elijah squinted, reliving those precious, yet painful moments again. He heard the loud bang over and over again. He saw the tears in her eyes as she shuddered in his arms, blood flowing out onto the street. Then she whispered, with her dying breath, for Elijah to kiss her. Then she was gone. Just like that.

Elijah remembered the rage; he felt it flowing through him as the picture of his soul mate lying dead in the street flashed inside of his mind.

"Elijah! Wake up. . . . Elijah!"

Elijah sat forward in the seat violently, his breathing heavy.

"You okay?" Terry asked, sitting down in the seat next to him. "Wow. That must have been some nightmare," she stated, looking down at the armrest, which was twisted and crushed.

Elijah looked over at her, his breathing returning to normal. "You have no idea," he whispered, looking away. "Terry, I'm sorry about—"

"No. I told you already I understand. I'm sorry for trying to force you to do something. I mean, I had no idea what had happened to you," Terry replied, looking at Elijah sympathetically. Then she smiled wide. "Besides, that just means you owe me triple!" she exclaimed, bringing a smile to Elijah's face.

"I'll meet you in the baggage claim area when we land and give you your . . . your . . . your whatever they are," she finished, rising with a smile and walking happily back into the coach section. Elijah leaned back, and his smile soon disappeared as his thoughts went back to Taysia.

Dalfien stalked angrily up to the old white man wearing the suit. He had felt the telepathic link between himself and El'Rathiem break a short while ago. It was a link that all greater demons possessed that allowed them to communicate with each other by sending thoughts across their own plane of existence. Dalfien had seen the images of the Protector—had even felt the horrible bite of those damnable blades. Dalfien had then felt the fear in El'Rathiem as the Protector sliced a line across his brother's throat.

El'Rathiem was an unthinking fool. And that was where he had made his mistake—always relying on his fists. But Dalfien would not make that mistake.

"Bring two of your men to me at once—two that are loyal to our master. The Protector will be here soon, and your men will need help," he growled.

"To what master do you refer?" Director Scott asked, looking at Charles curiously.

"Just bring them!" Dalfien shouted angrily, spraying the words into Scott's face.

The director wiped the moisture from his cheek calmly. "Charles, there are other matters we must take care of. Why is this man so important?" he asked, not intimidated in the least.

Dalfien forced himself to calm down. He wanted nothing more than to bite into this fool's head and taste of his brain, but he couldn't do that—not yet, at least. He needed them.

"He is a threat to The Order, and he must be dealt with," Dalfien said after a moment.

"He is not the only threat to The Order, Charles. Although you are the only one who seems to think that he is. No one else has ever heard of this man before. But more importantly, we must do something about the girl. She knows too much," Scott explained.

"Then kill her and be done with it!" Dalfien shouted impatiently.

"I'm afraid it's not that simple; she has a tape."

"So? Kill her and find the tape!" Dalfien was growing tired of this world and its rules.

"You don't get out much do you, Charles?" Scott asked, staring at Charles suspiciously. "She is on to us. She escaped one attempt on her life—God knows how. So she obviously has hidden the tape somewhere. Hence, we cannot kill her."

"Then find her and bring her to me. I will get the information you seek from her mind," Dalfien replied, grinning wickedly.

"Hopefully it will not come to that. Assistant Director Moss is on his way here with Director Glenn. Moss is the only one she trusts."

"Is Moss with us?" Dalfien asked.

"No, but Glenn is. Glenn has been monitoring their activities," Scott stated.

Dalfien looked at him curiously. "So why have you wasted my time? Telling me of things you supposedly have taken care of?" he asked callously, walking toward the director, his eyes cold and full of evil intentions.

Scott balked at the gaze now fixed upon him. All of his bluster was gone. "Y-y-you s-s-said you wanted two men?" he stuttered, backing away.

A wicked grin found its way to Dalfien's lips as an idea came to his demonic mind. "No," he began, coming to stand uncomfortably close to the director, "only one."

The director backed away, fumbling in his pocket for his two-way radio. "Get Boyd down here now."

"Yes, sir, he's on his way."

"What's going on, Charles?" he asked, fearfully.

"You will find out soon enough," Dalfien responded, holding the director's gaze with his own.

A huge metal door slid open, and Agent Boyd walked into the room. They were in an old abandoned factory about two miles away from the airport.

"Yes, sir?" Agent Boyd joined the two men.

"Agent Boyd! In whom do you place your faith?" Dalfien shouted at the man.

"In the Dark Lord, sir!" Boyd shouted, coming to attention.

Then Dalfien turned to Director Scott with an evil grin. "And you, Director?" He moved closer to the man, his evil grin inches from his face. "In whom do you place your faith?" The words slid from his lips like venom.

"In the Dark Lord," Scott replied weakly, fear spreading through his body. It was now blatantly apparent to Scott that the darker side of the sect had expanded beyond any of the council members' control.

Dalfien stepped back then, his cruel grin not diminishing. He fell back into himself, seeking his home plane. Before he stepped through the portal in his mind, however, he paid Charles a little visit. He found Charles's consciousness huddled in a deep corner of his mind.

Dalfien chuckled as he sent images of horrible tortures and promises of immense pain into the human's mind. Charles screamed and huddled into a little ball, covering his head fearfully. Satisfied, Dalfien moved through the portal and into the demonic plane. His corporal form passed through the lower levels without a thought. Imps looked up at his passing, hoping they would be called on to bring torture to some human in the worldly plane. Dalfien knew they would not be enough.

He slowed as he approached the creatures he sought—fiends. Fiends were lower level demons, just a step above the imps. Smarter and much nastier creatures, they were much more difficult to control than an imp. It was not uncommon for a demon of lesser mental prowess as Dalfien to summon a fiend to perform a task and have it run rampant on the earth killing anything it came across, only to eventually have its host be killed and its vile, sentient form sent back to the demonic plane.

Dalfien had supreme confidence in his abilities, for he was not only attempting to summon one, but two of the creatures. He focused his mental energies on the many creatures, picking out two of the strongest and most devious of the lot. He sent images of Director Scott and of Agent Boyd into their minds.

The fiends departed without haste, flying through the demonic plane with all speed. Dalfien returned to the worldly plane first. He watched as Agent Boyd's body began to tremble and his eyes rolled back into his head.

Scott looked on in horror. Then he, too, felt the burning in his flesh as the fiend took over his mind and body. The director let out a horrible howl of pain, falling to his knees under the torment of the invading fiend. Then as quickly as it had begun, it was over. The two stood before Dalfien, patiently awaiting his orders. They seemed docile and obedient enough, but Dalfien knew that if his mental hold slipped in any way, they would run rampant.

He grinned evilly as he implanted images of the Protector, images of the fiends bringing him to Dalfien. They nodded their comprehension and turned to leave.

"No!" Dalfien sent the mental command into their minds, accompanied by promises of tortures so horrible that the fiends fell to their knees, groveling their apologies. "I have not given you permission to leave!" he thundered, commanding their respect. He waited a moment to be sure they had understood the results of disobedience.

"Go!" he shouted, turning to walk back into the empty room. The fiends complied, walking swiftly out of the door.

Elijah felt the tiny chill bumps rolling along his skin as soon as he set foot off the airplane. But they were three times as eerie as when El'Rathiem had attacked him. Something, or some things, was about. Something very evil.

Elijah's eyes darted around the airport as he walked down the ramps, following the signs for the baggage claim area. The chills ran through him again when he noticed two men approaching directly in front of him. They were pale as ghosts, one older with salt and pepper colored hair, the other decidedly younger, but both with ill intentions. Elijah knew that they were not the only ones following him. He had picked up the other two suits when he had walked off the plane. But he got no ill vibes from them, so he ignored them.

This was a setup, plain and simple. They had been obviously waiting for him. He knew the two approaching from the front were indeed some type of demons. He also knew that he couldn't fight them here, with so many people around. And, most importantly, he needed his blades.

Elijah played it cool as they approached, pretending to be ignorant of their intent. The fiends stopped abruptly when they confronted the Protector, looking to each other in confusion. Dalfien had only instructed them to bring the Protector back to him alive. One of the fiends, Boyd's, scratched at its head curiously. It had never received an order like that before.

Elijah cocked his head to the side curiously as the two fiends stood stupidly in front of him. He realized then that the vibes he was getting from these two was nowhere near comparable to the vibe he had received when he had first stepped off the plane. That vibe was more comparable to the demon he had fought in the church. He understood then. These two were messengers of some sort—lackeys, probably sent by some greater entity to bring Elijah to him.

Elijah decided he would find out, but not until he felt the comforting hum of his twin blades at his waist. He sensed the other suits approaching from behind.

He waited until the last minute.

"Mr. Garland, FBI, come with us, please," one of the suits announced, flashing a badge and reaching out for Elijah's arm.

He led Elijah in the direction of the baggage claim area. The two fiends looked at each other curiously again and turned to follow. Elijah didn't act; as long as they were heading in the direction of the baggage claim, he would wait.

"I'm a friend. When we get outside, make a run for the

black car. I'll cover you," Agent Parks whispered to Elijah as he led the way toward the baggage claim area.

"What?" Elijah asked, confused.

"Get in the car and the driver will take you someplace safe. You can trust me. I know you didn't kill that cop, but we don't know why they want you," Parks explained.

"Who? Who wants me?"

"Don't worry about it now. The driver will explain everything once you're safe," Parks said, looking around nervously.

Elijah shrugged. "Whatever," he replied, not really interested in the man's good gestures. He was more concerned with getting to his blades. "Wait, I have to get my bags," he added, hoping the generous man, who claimed to be his friend, would let him.

"No time, we'll have someone pick them up for you later," Parks replied, as they made their way to the exit.

Elijah searched frantically for Terry and his blades. He didn't see her anywhere among the travelers in the crowded area.

As the exit doors opened up, Elijah spotted Terry standing alone buy the baggage chute. He pulled free of Parks and ran. Immediately, the two fiends were on his heels.

"Terry!" Elijah shouted, causing the woman to look up.

He could feel the fiends at his back, and he knew he wouldn't have time to discuss the situation with the surprised woman. He had to find a way to slow them down without killing their human hosts.

Maybe he could just incapacitate them. He stopped suddenly and did a 180, kicking one of the fiends in the kneecap, bending it back with a loud snap. Without hesitation, he grabbed the other surprised fiend by the arm and slung him around before letting go. The fiend flew across the floor and slid all the way into the hard metal of the baggage machine, leaving a huge dent.

Elijah ran on.

"Terry, where are they?" Elijah yelled as he ran up to the wide- eyed woman.

He looked back at the fiend who he had kicked in the knee. It stood there stupidly, looking down at its sickly twisted knee. Without a thought, it reached down and snapped the knee back into place and resumed its pursuit.

"I-I-It hasn't come down yet," she stuttered, looking at Elijah curiously. "What's going on?"

"No time to explain," he answered, glancing over to the other fiend, who was back on its feet now, shaking the cobwebs away.

"Freeze! FBI!" Agent Parks yelled, drawing his weapon as he neared Elijah. "Everyone get down!" he added, shouting at the top of his lungs.

"Elijah, what did you do?" Terry asked with a smile, ignoring the order.

The fiends were both up and ready again, but they paused, as Agent Parks seemed to have the situation under control.

"What are they in?" Elijah asked quickly.

"They're in a green army duffel bag."

"I said get down!" Agent Parks yelled again.

People in the area looked at each other curiously, wondering what was going on. Elijah needed a diversion. And he knew just the word that would give it to him.

"Bomb!" he yelled out, watching as the green duffel bag slid out of the chute.

Chaos followed.

Travelers stampeded for the exits. The fiends jumped into action, shoving their way through the panicking mob.

Elijah jumped onto the metal conveyer and scooped up the bag. "I'll see you around, Terry! Thanks!" he yelled back over his shoulder.

"You better! You owe me triple!" Terry yelled, and then she was gone, lost in the panicking crowd.

Elijah pulled his belt out of the bag and clasped it around his waist as he ran. He felt the soothing hum of the blades and smiled. In almost no time at all, the area was empty except for Elijah, the two fiends, and three other FBI agents.

"Freeze! Throw the weapons down!" Parks yelled at Elijah.

Elijah laughed and jumped down off the machine, feeling the hum of the blades increase as the fiends slowly approached.

"Director Scott! Get back!" Parks yelled, watching the director and Boyd close in on Elijah. They hadn't even drawn their weapons!

"Director Scott!" he yelled again.

"They can't hear you. They're possessed," Elijah explained to Parks.

"You shut up! And put the weapons down!" he shouted at Elijah again.

"Sorry, can't do that," Elijah replied, eyeing the fiends.

"Don't make me shoot you!"

"Ooooh, I'm scared now." Elijah spun the blades around in his hands so that their tips were pointing behind him and the edge of the blades ran next to his forearms.

Parks looked at Director Scott and Agent Boyd, both of whom seemed to be in some kind of daze. They completely ignored him, and still, they stalked toward Elijah with their weapons sitting uselessly in their holsters. He didn't know what to make of it.

Elijah backed away a step and began the chant that would bring the creatures out of their hosts. "Anal nutcracker—" Elijah paused, confused. He had forgotten the words! "Ummm, just a minute, guys," he added, backing away another step.

"Shut up! Another word out of you and I'll shoot!" Parks shouted nervously.

"Anal . . . no . . . Anel, yeah that's it," Elijah mumbled to himself, wondering if this fool would really shoot him.

He would have to find out.

"What the hell is going on in there?" Ebonee exclaimed when they pulled up to the baggage claim area.

People were running everywhere.

"Looks like somebody shouted 'bomb' in that muthafucka," Kenyatta replied, chuckling. Then she thought about it and her smile left. "You don't think there's really—"

"What's the matter? They don't set off bombs in the projects, Kenyatta? You look worried!"

Ebonee pulled as close as she could to the front of the entrance and parked. "Stay here, I'm going to go check it—"

"Okay," Kenyatta replied before Ebonee's last word was out.

Ebonee proceeded to walk the rest of the way to the entrance. She came to an abrupt halt as she neared the electronic glass doors. Glass exploded everywhere and she looked down curiously at Scott, who growled in anger after crashing through the door and then stumbled back to his feet, only to be buried again by the form of Agent Boyd, who flew out next.

Agent Parks stood completely still, his gun trained on the suspect. He watched in confusion as Scott and Agent Boyd threw themselves at Elijah again. The other three agents stood around waiting for Parks to make a move, but as Parks watched the scene unfold, something about Scott and Boyd unnerved him. The beating they were taking at the hands of the suspect seemed way too much for a normal man to take. Yet they kept getting up, kept charging in. Parks looked to the other agents, an idea coming to mind.

"Don't just stand there, help the director!" he shouted, following the melee to the exit doors.

Elijah searched his mind frantically for the words to bring the demons into their physical form. He wasn't sure how much more damage the men's bodies could take, and he felt himself tiring.

As he launched Boyd's body into the air to land on top of Scott, he felt the other suits closing in on him. He charged out behind Boyd, jumping over their scrambling bodies and almost knocking down the woman who had walked up and now stood staring at him. He looked up into the woman's face and froze. His mouth dropped open, and he felt his knees weaken. Ebonee, too, found herself paralyzed, locked in the grip of those eyes, those beautiful, light brown eyes.

Kenyatta watched the two of them standing there, looking at each other stupidly. She slammed on the horn, screaming out for them to come on. Either they were deaf or stupid, because they paid her no mind at all. They just stood there, gawking at each other. That is, until she saw the two men leap onto Elijah's back. She started the car and slammed on the gas.

"Taysia?" Elijah whispered, almost pleadingly, his eyes searching Ebonee's for some hint of affirmation. The world seemed to stop for him; there was only her lovely face, the face of the only woman in this world that he had truly loved. The woman who had been taken away from him so cruelly. Could it truly be? But he had held her dying body in his arms, had tasted her kiss on her dying breath. How could this be? Suddenly he saw the ground rushing up to him as the fiends forced him down, pinning him to the ground, one on each arm, their knees in his back.

Ebonee snapped out of her delirium and pulled out her gun, just as the other agents ran out.

"Don't move, Agent Lane!" one of them shouted, pointing his weapon in her direction.

The other agents followed suit. Seeing the suspect down and pinned, they focused their attention on Ebonee. She lowered her gun, seeing that she had no way out of this situation. Her eyes went to the suspect, who was still struggling against the two men.

"Get down on your knees! And drop the weapon!" another agent instructed, walking slowly around and behind her.

Ebonee complied, slowly dropping to her knees and bringing her hands up to place them behind her head. The agent kicked her gun away and looked to the other agents for instructions.

"Kill her," one of them said, nodding at the agent standing behind her.

Rage filled the Protector when he heard the words. Scenes of that night flashed into his mind: her dying body lying on the cold sidewalk, her lifeless eyes staring into space, the blood trickling from her lips.

"*Anel nathrak doth dien dienve,*" he whispered through clenched teeth, the words seeming to find his lips on their own accord.

Elijah felt the weight of the demons lessen as their spirits were dragged out of their hosts' bodies. In a flash, he was up, blades drawn and ready.

A shot rang out, and Elijah turned and watched the agent behind Ebonee clutch at his chest in confusion, falling to the ground dead. Kenyatta, her gun smoking, screamed out for them to get in the car.

Another shot rang out, this one coming from somewhere inside of the terminal. Another agent fell. Ebonee scrambled for her gun, and the remaining agent ran for cover. Elijah watched the fiends taking form in front of him.

They were humanoid in shape with elongated arms that ended in wicked claws. Their heads were devoid of any facial features, except for a huge maw filled with rows of wickedly sharp teeth. Before the creatures could blink, or whatever it was that creatures with no eyes would do, one of them felt a sharp pain in its neck. It looked to its partner in confusion before its head slowly fell from its body.

Ebonee looked on in shock as the demon's head slowly rolled to come to a stop at her feet. She looked back to Elijah, who was now stalking the other fiend.

"What the fuck?" Kenyatta whispered, gawking at her brother battling the demon.

The demon backed away, its courage depleted with the loss of its companion. The Protector closed in quickly, the rage flowing through him. He felt the bullet tear into his back, but he paid it no mind.

Ebonee saw the bullet hit Elijah, and it spurred her into action. She traced the bullet's trajectory and found its source: the remaining agent. She let off a couple of rounds in his direction, pinning him behind the wall.

The fiend, its back bumping into the wall of the terminal, howled in rage. Having no place to run, it leaped forward, claws threatening to tear the Protector's heart from his body. Ebonee watched in amazement as the Protector, his movements a blur, rendered the demon clawless and minus a leg in what seemed to her to be one fluid movement. The fiend fell to the ground, writhing about until the Protector's blade found its heart, silencing it forever.

Ebonee heard the sirens as the local authorities approached. She heard the horn and Kenyatta screaming for them to get into the car. Elijah heard nothing; the rage still held him.

Ebonee ran to him, grabbing him by the arm. "Come on!" she yelled, attempting to pull him to the car.

Elijah spun on her, his sword stopping at her throat. She froze as their eyes locked again. The rage was gone as fast as it had come. Again Elijah found himself looking into the eyes of his beloved. And again, he found he could not move.

Ebonee found her voice, as the sirens grew louder. "I'm here to help," she said, her heart racing with his sword floating near her throat. But that wasn't the reason her heart was beating out of control. She saw the longing in his eyes; she could feel the pain, the confusion, and the love. "We have to go . . . please," she said softly, reaching up to gently push the blade down. Elijah felt his own heart racing as he looked into her beautiful eyes, as he listened to her wonderful voice.

"Elijah . . . come with me . . . please."

Elijah slammed his eyes shut after the words left her lips.

"Elijah . . . kiss me . . . please."

The words exploded in his mind.

He shook his head violently, trying to dislodge the memories. Ebonee wanted to grab him and chase away whatever demons he faced in his head. She wanted to comfort him, to bring a smile to that handsome face. The sirens grew louder, and she could see them approaching now.

"Elijah!" She took his face in her hands. "We have to go! Now! Come on!" she exclaimed, pulling his arm forcefully.

Elijah opened his eyes at the touch of her hands on his face; he heard the intensity and the urgency in her voice. He pushed the memories out of his mind and forced himself to act. Ebonee smiled lightly, seeing that she had finally gotten through to him.

Then her world exploded.

Blood splattered her face and she blinked her eyes, her mouth open in a silent scream. She watched Elijah grab at his torn throat, falling to his knees. The world seemed to be moving in slow motion. Ebonee fell to her knees, grabbing desperately at Elijah, the blood spurting from his neck in gushes. Stubbornly, he tried to force himself up, pushing Ebonee away, his eyes wide, not understanding his fate. Ebonee cupped her hands over her mouth, watching in disbelief. Elijah staggered a few feet and then fell, dropping to his knees and still clutching at his throat.

Ebonee heard the shouts and yells as the local authorities

arrived on the scene, and then she heard Kenyatta's screams as she fought against the policemen, trying to get to her fallen brother's side. But her eyes never left the now still form of the man lying a few feet away from her.

The world seemed a blur to her. She felt arms on her, trying to pull her to her feet. It was as if she were watching it all from a distant far off place. She saw the paramedics wheel a stretcher over to Elijah's body, lifting him up onto it and rolling him toward the ambulance. The hands pulled her to her feet; they were asking her something.

The paramedics hoisted the stretcher up and into the ambulance. And then they were gone.

"Who are you, miss?" the officer asked again, unsure of what to make of the woman.

Ebonee absently reached into the tight back pocket of her miniskirt and held her badge out for the officer to inspect. Her eyes never left the ambulance making its way through the traffic.

"Agent Ebonee Lane," the officer said, looking up from the badge. "Are you okay?"

Ebonee looked at the man blankly for a moment.

"Do you need medical attention?"

Ebonee blinked rapidly, looking away as she came back to reality. She shook her head negatively, looking around at the policemen taping off the area.

"Quite a mess you guys made here," the officer stated, following her eyes. "Well at least you got your man. Too bad he took out three of your guys in the process."

"What?" Ebonee asked, suddenly alert.

"Yeah, your buddy there," he nodded in the direction of the last agent, the agent who had taken the last shot. "He explained everything."

Ebonee watched Agent Parks as he talked to another officer, then his eyes glanced her way. He stared at her for a moment, causing her to quickly look away.

"What about the girl?" Ebonee asked, remembering the tape.

"We're going to take her downtown for questioning," the officer replied. "If that's okay with you."

"No. I'll take her," she said quickly. "Where is she?"

"Hold on, I'll get her for you," the officer replied, turning to call one of his colleagues. "Hey, Tom! Release the girl into Agent Lane here's custody."

"Thank you. I'll take her downtown," Ebonee said, walking toward the black convertible. Then she turned back. "What about the suspect?"

"We've got two men escorting the ambulance to the hospital, where they'll probably take him straight to the morgue from the looks of it." He chuckled dryly. Ebonee walked on.

"Get the fuck off of me!"

Ebonee heard Kenyatta's shouts as she approached the car, escorted by an officer.

"It's okay, officer. I'll take her from here."

"My pleasure!" the officer replied, shoving Kenyatta roughly in her direction.

"Pussy!" she yelled, tears still in her eyes as she looked back in the officer's direction.

"Come on, get in the car," Ebonee stated, opening the door of the car.

"Where are we going? Where did they take my brother?" Kenyatta asked, standing with her hand on the door handle.

"Hey! Where are they going? Stop them!" the agent yelled, running toward them.

"Get in!" Ebonee yelled.

Kenyatta jumped over the door and into the passenger seat. Ebonee slammed on the gas and left the agent standing there, fuming.

"How's his heart rate?" one of the paramedics asked, looking over at his partner.

"This is crazy. There must be something wrong with this thing," he replied, tapping on the machinery in the back of the ambulance.

"Why? What does it say?" the first paramedic asked curiously, his hand applying pressure to the wound on Elijah's throat.

"It reads normal."

"What the hell?" The paramedic looked down at Elijah's wound in amazement.

"What? What's wrong?" the second man asked as the first paramedic looked down at his hand.

"The bleeding's stopped," he said, looking up at him curiously.

"Did you get a clamp on it?"

"No, I didn't do anything! It just stopped!"

"Move your hand, let me see," he instructed. "Holy shit! Did you see that?" the second man exclaimed, looking at the first in amazement. The first man sat back, not at all sure of what to make out of what he had just seen.

"I'm not sure what I just saw," he said quietly.

"What's going on back there?" an officer asked, peering at the two paramedics from the front of the ambulance.

"Ummm, we're not exactly sure," the second paramedic answered, still staring down at the wound—the wound that was closing right before his very eyes.

"Is he dead yet?" another officer asked, sitting next to the window, not too concerned.

"Doesn't matter, we'll turn him over to the feds when we get to the hospital," the other officer replied.

"Hey," the ambulance driver began, nodding at the officer sitting next to the door, "could you do me a favor?"

"What is it?" the officer replied.

"Could you empty this out the door for me?" He handed him a cup. The cup was filled with tobacco spit.

"That's disgusting. Empty it yourself!" he replied, turning his head in repugnance.

"I would, but it would be kind of hard to do while I'm driving. And if I don't empty it, it will probably spill," he said, again handing the cup across the officer sitting in the middle.

"God, that shit stinks! Empty it already, will ya?" The middle man elbowed the officer next to the window.

"For Christ sake, gimme the damn thing!"

He turned to the side and cracked the door open. The driver of the ambulance slammed on the gas then, and veered the ambulance sharply to the left. The officer sitting closest to the door fell, screaming as he tumbled down the street. The second officer caught a hold of the handle just above the door on the roof of the ambulance and held on for dear life.

"What the hell?" he exclaimed, trying to keep his grip.

Then he looked over at the driver, and found the barrel of a gun staring back at him.

"What's going on up there!" one of the paramedics shouted, holding on frantically. Then he heard a gunshot. The driver quickly righted the ambulance and turned off onto a side street.

"Hey! What happened?" the paramedic asked, leaning up through the seats.

Another gunshot.

The second paramedic bolted for the back door when the ambulance came to a stop in a vacant alley. He opened the door and stepped out, just in time to see a black sedan slam into the back of the ambulance, crushing him. The ambulance driver walked to the back of the vehicle and motioned for the driver of the sedan to back up.

He pushed the paramedic's body to the side and hopped up into the back of the ambulance. Taking the gun, he placed it in Elijah's hand. He then donned a pair of rubber gloves and tossed the gun on the floor.

Then he walked back to the back door and motioned for the other driver to come and assist him. He released the shackles that had been placed on Elijah's arms and attempted to lift him to the door. His eyes popped open wide as Elijah's hand found his throat.

Elijah slammed the man into the wall of the ambulance, dislodging machinery and rendering the man senseless.

Comforted by the gentle hum of his blades, still at his sides, he waited for the driver of the sedan to get closer. When the man stepped up to the back of the ambulance, Elijah snatched him inside, slamming him roughly up against the wall of the ambulance.

The man struggled, going for his gun. Elijah thrust his forearm into the man's throat, pinning him to the wall of the ambulance and then grabbed his other hand, which now held a gun. He slowly squeezed, crushing the man's hand around the cold steel of the weapon.

The man screamed out in pain, and the gun fell from his deformed fingers. Elijah pushed his forearm in harder, stifling the screams. "Who are you?" Elijah growled, his lips inches from the man's terrorized face.

The man's eyes bulged in his head and he gasped for air. Elijah, realizing that the man couldn't breathe, let alone speak, lessened the pressure on his throat. "Who sent you?"

The man's eyes closed as he sucked in some air. "The FBI," he croaked, bringing another thrust from Elijah's forearm. The man winced and gasped, clawing at Elijah's arm desperately.

"The FBI doesn't kill innocent civilians," Elijah replied quietly. Reaching down with his free hand, he produced one of his blades. Bringing it up, he let the tip rest on his forearm, drawing a slow line of blood on the man's windpipe.

"Now, who sent you?" he asked again, once more releasing the pressure from the man's neck.

"Okay . . . okay, I'll talk. Just don't kill me."

"I'm waiting," Elijah replied, letting his blade slide a bit further across the man's neck.

"I work for the FBI! I swear! My badge is in my pocket. You can check it if you don't believe me!"

Elijah shifted the hilt of his blade downward ever so slightly, forcing the tip up into the man's neck.

"All right! All right already!" the man squealed, trying to inch his back up against the wall as the blade dug into his neck.

Elijah relented enough to let the man continue.

"All I know is that Charles wants you!" he confessed, swallowing hard.

"Who?"

"Charles . . . Charles Kreicker. He's the leader of a secret organization called The Order of the Rose!"

"What kind of organization?" Elijah asked curiously.

"White supremacists, Satanists . . . They have eyes and ears everywhere, from the House of Representatives to the grocery store your mother used to shop at," the man explained, sounding cocky as he told of his powerful organization.

"What do they want from me?" Elijah asked, ignoring the man's boldness.

"I don't know. I just follow orders. Whatever information you have, or whatever it is you did to piss him off . . . I only know he wants you badly, so badly that he has the whole organization looking for you," the man finished, glowering at Elijah.

"Where is this Charles man at?" Elijah asked, again digging the tip of his blade into the man's neck, stealing the smirk from his face.

"I don't know! I told you, I only follow orders!" he gasped.

"And what were your orders after you had picked me up?" Elijah growled, twisting his blade deeper into his neck.

"I was supposed to take you to an old abandoned warehouse down by the stadium!" he confessed. "Building fourteen!" he added, anticipating another twist of the blade.

Elijah looked at the man for a second and then a wicked grin found his lips. "So . . . which are you?" he asked quietly, his grin deepening as he leaned in closer to the man.

"Wh-what are you t-t-talking about?"

"A Satanist . . . or a white supremacist?" Elijah finished, feeling the nasty desire to kill the fool where he stood. Before the man could respond, Elijah's sword pommel smashed into his temple, sending him into darkness.

Elijah stepped out of the ambulance and looked around. It was nearing dark. He recognized the area immediately; it was not far from the apartment he had shared with his friend, Darryl. He decided to make a stop there, and maybe call and see if he could locate his sister. He started to walk away, and then turned to gaze at the black sedan.

He parked the sedan a few feet away from the front of the apartment building in a no parking zone. He stepped out and glanced in the direction of the apartment, and then after a moment turned and walked in the opposite direction. He began to feel uneasy, as people walking by stared at him, some of them turning and following him with their eyes. He pulled the hood of his trench over his head, finding comfort in its shadows. He made his way quickly to the waterfront. Soon he was standing alone with the chill night air blowing in off of the water.

He looked down as the memories once again returned to him. Maybe it was in his mind, but he thought he could still see the stain in the sidewalk.

This was where she had died.

He heard the calls of a street peddler then, walking along carrying a bucket filled with roses. He walked over to the man and purchased one of the roses. Then he walked back to the spot.

Kneeling, he looked out onto the water as the moon lazily began its rise. The scene brought with it the memories of that night. How bright and so full of life the moon seemed to be that night, so warm and inviting. But now it seemed cold and lifeless to Elijah.

He laid the rose down onto the spot, absently wiping away the tear that had found his cheek. Then he stood, forcing the memories away. He stared out onto the dark water, the wind whipping the tail of his trench coat about. One thought guided him then.

"It's time we meet, Charles."

"Director Scott, can you hear me?" The voice sounded like it was far away. "Director Scott!" Parks said again, louder. He stood next to the hospital bed, looking down at the Deputy Assistant Director.

"W-w-where? W-what happened?" Director Scott moaned lowly.

"Sir? Can you hear me?"

"Where am I?" Director Scott asked again, his senses returning slowly. "Parks?" he added, bringing the visitor into focus.

"Yes, sir," Parks answered, fighting back the urge to interrogate the director. He had a million and one questions.

"Last thing I remember is talking to Charles," Scott said slowly, trying to remember what had happened after that encounter.

Parks looked at him curiously. "Sir, you mean you don't remember what just happened at the airport?"

"Airport? No. I remember we were about to attempt to apprehend the fugitive, and Charles asked me . . . He asked me . . ." His voice trailed off. "What about Agent Lane? Was she dealt with?" He tried to sit up in the bed.

"She escaped, but we did manage to bring in the fugitive. But there is one problem."

"What?" The director asked, deciding it wasn't such a good idea to try and sit up.

"The evidence shows that our man was clearly defending himself when the officer attacked him. If this gets out to the press . . ."

"That's no problem. Issue a statement that the fugitive was taken to our field house here and detained. Then tell them that when the evidence came out he was innocent; he was released on his own recognizance. That should clear us," the director replied smoothly.

"And Agent Lane?"

"Find her and kill her!" Scott replied harshly.

"Is that an order, sir?"

The director looked at Parks, his demeanor calm. "For the sake of your career and mine, it is a suggestion. She knows too much," he said, his gaze holding Agent Parks in place.

"Understood," Parks replied. He turned and walked out of the room.

A shadowy figure turned and crept into the small, dark alley. He wore only a dark sweat suit, its hood pulled up over his head, hiding his face in the shadows. Walking to the rear of the ambulance, he tapped on the doors. The doors swung open. The ambulance driver and the driver of the sedan sat waiting.

"Where is the gun?" a cold intimidating voice came from the shadows of the hood.

"Right here, sir," the ambulance driver replied, bending over to hand the weapon to the man.

The man reached out a gloved hand, accepting the weapon.

"What should we do now?" the driver of the sedan asked,

wincing slightly, as the cuts on his neck from the Protector's blades stung.

The hooded figure paused and considered the question.

The driver of the sedan had no time to react. The bullet exploded into his head, dropping him dead where he sat. The ambulance driver froze, paralyzed with fear. There was a second shot. Then he, too, lay dead on the floor of the ambulance. The hooded figure slipped the gun into his pocket and walked out of the alley unseen.

Director Scott glanced over at the sleeping form of Agent Boyd lying in the bed next to his own. He tried to remember what had happened after his encounter with Charles. But it was no use. The door to the room opened then, and the light went off.

"Who's that?" he asked, staring at the figure approaching his bed. "Oh, I wasn't expecting to see you . . ." his voice trailed off and a look of bewilderment came to his swollen face.

A muffled shot rang out. The figure walked over to the other bed and there was another muffled shot. Then he was gone.

Ebonee dropped Kenyatta off at her mother's house against her will, and with some persuasive pleading, she talked Eva into letting her borrow her car. Then she was off to the hospital.

The look in Elijah's eyes kept playing over and over again in her head. She felt a sense of urgency, thought that those eyes had called out to her, and only to her. She shook her head. She had to stay focused. There was too much going on for her to let her heart govern her actions. She was brought back to the moment when her cell phone rang.

"Agent Lane," she answered.

"Where are you?" the voice asked.

"Director Moss?"

"Yes. Come to the hospital on Eighth and Spruce,"

"I'll be there in five," she replied, hanging up the phone.

She walked into the lobby of the hospital, and police were everywhere. She walked up to an officer whose arm was in a sling. "Excuse me," she said, pulling out her badge and showing it to the officer. "Agent Lane, FBI. What's going on here?"

"Two of your guys got offed upstairs. Your buddies are up there now. Fifth floor," he answered, looking at her with more than a bit of curiosity. "Need me to show you the way? Come on," he added, smiling.

"That's okay. I'll find it."

"Okay. But if you need anything, just ask for Officer Jones. I'll be glad to assist you in any way you need," he said, his eyes admiring the view from behind.

Ebonee got off the elevator and looked around.

"Agent Lane," a voice came from down the hall. It was Director Moss.

She made her way to the room, avoiding the crime scene detectives as they went about their business.

"What happened?"

"Double homicide. Someone put a bullet in Director Scott's head, and Agent Boyd's," Moss said, looking at her curiously. "Nice outfit," he added, his eyes looking around the hall.

Ebonee pulled at the hem of the short skirt, embarrassed. "Do we have any leads?"

"They found the murder weapon in a dumpster outside. They're checking it for prints as we speak."

"What about the tape?"

"It's useless now. Scott is dead."

"What about Parks?"

"Don't worry about Parks. I'll handle that," Moss said, his cell phone ringing. "Excuse me."

Things were getting more and more confusing to Ebonee as she thought about it all. Where was Parks? And who was it that shot the agents at the airport? The shots had come from inside of the terminal.

Now someone had executed the Deputy Assistant Director and another agent. But why?

Charles Kreicker.

The name came to her as she remembered the conversation between Parks and Scott. Whoever this Charles Kreicker was, she felt he had something to do with it all. Director Moss hung up his phone and turned back to Ebonee.

"Well, looks like we've got some more bodies on our hands," he began, looking to be deep in thought. "They just found the ambulance they were transporting your man in, along with five more corpses."

Ebonee's eyes lit up at the mention of Elijah. "What about Elijah?"

"You mean the fugitive?" Director Moss asked, looking at her curiously.

"Yes, the fugitive," Ebonee corrected herself, blushing.

"No sign of him. He disappeared," he said, a thoughtful expression on his face.

"You don't think that he—"

"I don't think anything. I'll know something when the weapon tests come back. Apparently the fatal wounds on all of the men in the ambulance were made by the same weapon that was used to kill our friends here." Again they were interrupted by his cell phone. "Excuse me."

Ebonee could see it coming a mile away. This was a setup if ever she had seen one. She knew the prints on the weapon would come back as Elijah's. And again that name came back to her— Charles Kreicker.

"That was the lab," Moss said, turning back to Ebonee. "The prints belong to our fugitive."

"Sir, this is a setup!" Ebonee exclaimed, looking at him earnestly. "You have to know that!"

"Agent Lane, I know I have bodies piling up, all of them killed with the same weapon—a weapon that has your fugitive's fingerprints all over it. As far as I'm concerned, he's our man. If you can prove otherwise, I suggest you do so, quickly. Do you have anything to go on?"

"On the tape, they spoke of a man named Charles Kreicker. Something about him being here and that he wanted Elijah." Her eyes blankly stared at a wall as she thought.

"Charles Kreicker. He's a cult leader in Eastern Pennsylvania. We've been watching him for some time. You think he has something to do with this?"

"I know it. Sir, I looked into the fugitive's eyes. There is no homicidal maniac there. I know he didn't do this."

"Agent Lane, do you think a jury is going to care about what you saw in his eyes? They are going to see the same thing I see: dead bodies, a smoking gun, and his fingerprints all over it. I trust your judgment, Agent Lane, but you know I need proof to do anything. Now if you think this Charles fellow has something to do with all of this, then you shouldn't be here wasting your time chatting with me. You should be out there trying to find evidence. Besides, isn't that what I pay you to do anyway?" Moss said, his stern expression softening. "So go ahead, get out of here. If you need any backup, let me know. And by the way, if you find out anything new about this Elijah Garland, let me know immediately. I've got some friends in Maryland looking over his blood samples."

"Friends?" Ebonee asked, raising an eyebrow.

"Yeah, they specialize in this sort of thing."

"What do you mean, this sort of thing?"

"The paranormal, the unexplained," he said, looking at her seriously. "That is what this is, unless you can explain to me how a man who attempts to blow his brains out of the back of his own head gets up and walks out of the hospital in three days without a scratch. And from the police reports that were taken at the airport, apparently he took two more bullets, one in the neck and one in the back."

"I know. I saw it with my own eyes," Ebonee replied, wondering what kind of impact this would have on her being assigned to this case.

"Don't worry. This is your case. They have their hands full anyway, something about super soldiers. Anyway, you better get going. I'll be in touch." He turned and walked back into the room. Ebonee headed for the elevator, pondering her first move. She decided to check out Elijah's apartment first.

Chapter Ten
By the Skin of His Teeth

Dalfien paced in front of the long warehouse window, but not in anger. Not this time. This time his pace was filled with fear, an emotion with which he had little acquaintance. This Protector seemed to be more dangerous than Dalfien had anticipated. He had destroyed not only one, but two fiends in only a matter of minutes. Dalfien had felt the fear in the fiends just before their mental link to him was terminated by the Protector and those wicked blades.

He took no comfort in the security of the dozen or so members that he had sent for; all of them were well armed and trained by the best, but he knew they would not be able to stop the Protector. Even worse, he had not heard from Charles's contacts from the FBI.

"Excuse me, sir," a man said approaching the open doorway. "A call for you," he added, indicating the cell phone he held in his hand.

"Who is it?" Dalfien asked, hoping that it was his contacts from the FBI.

"They wouldn't say. They only said that they were a friend."

"Bah! Bring it to me!" he said angrily. He snatched the phone from the man and waved him away. "Who is this?"

"Charles, I suggest you go back to your compound in Eastern Pennsylvania. The Order will no longer support you in your personal affairs," the voice said.

Dalfien did not know how to reply. He had never been threatened by a human.

"You have brought enough attention to us as it is. I've cleaned up your mess. And I've arranged for this person you're after to be dealt with. Charles, I warn you, go back to your compound. If you do anything to bring further attention to The Order, you will be dealt with also," the voice finished, and then Dalfien was listening to a dial tone.

He chuckled to himself; a human had just threatened his life. His smile faded soon enough. The man had said that the Protector would be taken care of. He wondered if he should rely on them to take care of his problem. Could they succeed? He decided that he would rather find out than face the Protector himself.

But not without leaving a little gift.

He walked to the open doorway and motioned for the guard. "Bring the girl," he instructed the man. "And inform everyone that we will be going back to the compound within the hour." A wicked grin came to his face as he walked back into the room.

Ebonee arrived at Elijah's apartment shortly after midnight. The streets were crowded with shoppers and partygoers: punk rockers with spiked Mohawks, couples strolling, teenagers drifting from storefront to storefront, browsing all the wares the shop owners presented. It was a normal sight on the popular Central Philadelphia street. She pulled up behind the black sedan parked a few doors down from Elijah's apartment in a no parking zone. Noticing the government license plate, she decided to check it out. She walked up to the door of the car, carefully dodging the many people traversing the crowded sidewalk. It was open. She sat down inside and began to rummage through the glove compartment.

Finding nothing, she slammed the compartment closed. Then she looked down at the armrest. She opened it to find a small notepad, a pen, and a two-way radio. The pad was blank, but she ripped the first page off and put it in her pocket along with the phone. Finding nothing else, she opened the car door and swung her feet out. Something caught her attention. She examined the headrest and found a single strand of curly, white hair.

"Elijah," she whispered to herself, looking toward the apartment.

She got out and headed for the apartment, daring to hope that he was there. The lights were on; she could see them from the street. She passed two black men wearing white cook outfits at the entrance of the alley, taking a smoke break from their jobs in the restaurant on the other side of the alley. She continued down the half-lit corridor, her face contorted in a painful grimace as the pungent aroma of old urine clashed with the sweet smells coming from the loud blowing kitchen vents. She hurried to Elijah's door and pushed it open. She walked up the steps to the apartment door and paused, listening. Someone was definitely inside, whom though, she didn't know. She decided to knock.

She heard footsteps and then the door cracked slightly. A short black man stuck his head out of the door.

"Yes?" he asked, looking at her curiously.

"Hello, I'm Agent Ebonee Lane—FBI. You are?" she said, showing him her badge.

"Oh. Hello, my name's Darryl. Elijah isn't here if that's why you're here. I've been here all day, and I haven't seen him," he replied, opening the door and leaning against the doorjamb.

"Do you mind if I look around?" Ebonee asked, smiling.

"Uh, no, no. Come on in. His room is the same way it was when he left it," Darryl said, walking into the living room. "I saw on the news that they're looking for him. I guess you guys haven't found him yet." He clicked off the video game he had been playing.

"No, we haven't," Ebonee replied, looking around the apartment.

"You want a drink or something? Orange juice, beer, soda, wine, or milk?"

"Yeah . . . yeah, I would," she answered. "What kind of beer do you have?"

"I have . . . let me see . . . Bud, Bud Light, and Coors."

"No Heineken?" she asked, smiling. Heineken was her favorite beer—that's when she got a chance to have one—and after the day's events, she could sure use one, even if she was technically on the job.

"Wait. I think Elijah still has a few in here. I don't like them myself. But he does," he said, pulling one out for her. He opened it and handed her a glass. "Do you want lemon?"

"How did you know?" she asked, smiling.

"I just guessed. That's the way Elijah always drank his. I figured it was a Heineken thing," he replied, shrugging as he handed her a slice of lemon. Ebonee sat down on the couch, her smile wide as she thought that she and Elijah, so far, had some things in common.

"So how long have you known Elijah?" she asked Darryl.

"Long enough to know he didn't do what they're saying he did. His sister maybe, but not Elijah," he replied, grinning.

Ebonee had to laugh at that one.

"So you know Kenyatta?"

"I take it you've met her, too," he answered, noticing her laughter.

"Yeah, she is a trip."

"I've known Elijah and Kenyatta for almost five years now," Darryl said.

"So what makes you so sure he didn't do what their accusing him of?"

"I don't know, it just doesn't fit him. He was too happy to do something like that."

"Too happy? What do you mean?"

"I mean, he was always laughing, and always trying to make everyone else laugh. I don't think there was anyone who didn't like Elijah. I mean, I could be in the foulest mood ever in my life, and he would notice and do something stupid just to get me to laugh. And it didn't matter what was going on in his personal life. He always hid that. He never let that show. I guess that's why he ended up doing what he did," Darryl said, smiling as he remembered some of the dippy things Elijah would do.

"Do you mind if I have a look at his room?"

"No, no. It's the room at the top of the steps to the right," he responded, taking a sip from his own beer.

Ebonee walked up the steps, eyeing the broken banister with a bit of suspicion. "What happened to the banister?"

"Actually, I have no idea," Darryl shouted up the steps. "There was a fire a few days after Elijah shot himself. Well, there was a fire *reported*. I rushed home to find the fire department inside. They didn't know how the banister was broken either. But there was no fire."

Ebonee continued into Elijah's room. The room was neat and well kept. A small collection of CD's sat on the window sill. They were all Prince CD's, she noticed with a smile. They had something else in common.

She walked over to the computer that sat on a desk in the corner of the room. But it wasn't hooked up. Next to the computer was a stack of notebooks. She picked one up and flipped through it.

Poetry. She picked up another to find it was the same. They were all filled with poetry. She walked over to the bed and sat down on its edge, opening one of the books to the first page and reading it aloud.

"The Greatest Fool"
There will never be a greater fool than me,
loving completely, giving my heart blindly.
Ignoring the voices in my mind,
their prophecy of pain coming to pass each time.
No greater fool will you find,.
the greatest fool of all time.
4ever trying.
4ever crying.
Thoughts of dying.
Hoping happiness will come to pass,
knowing that if it does, it won't last.
The greatest fool there ever will be,
The greatest fool you ever will see.
Happiness, joy, love and peace,
turn their backs and laugh at me.
Wasted tears fall from my eyes,
always believing every lie.
Oh look! A fool that cries!
That's what they say when they see me.
The greatest fool there ever will be.

"Wow. Aren't you Mr. Right," she whispered, flipping through the notebook. "Of course it's my luck, I finally meet someone that I know I could fall in love with and they're a wanted killer." She chuckled dryly to herself, praying that she was wrong.

She was pulled from her contemplations by the doorbell. Picking up the books, she headed back downstairs.

"What's up, man? We was in the neighborhood and decided to stop by. You want to go get a drink with us?" Eric said to Darryl, walking into the living room with Troy.

"Naw, I'm chillin'. You guys want a cold one?" Darryl asked.

"Yeah, yeah. That's what's up," Troy replied.

"Yo, you got company?" Eric asked, seeing Ebonee's open Heineken on the table.

"Oh. That's the FBI lady's. She's upstairs looking through Elijah's stuff."

"Oh. That means they didn't catch him yet—good," Eric said, accepting a beer from Darryl.

"He better not let them catch him. You know they gonna hang his ass. Shit, they still mad about OJ," Troy threw in, causing the three of them to burst into laughter. "And he done supposedly killed, what, six, seven white folks? Man, ain't even gonna be no trial. They just gonna catch his ass and take him straight to the electric chair. They ain't gonna take no chances with no jury!" he added, fueling the laughter even more.

"Man, you know Elijah ain't do that shit," Eric said, still smiling.

"I don't know, man. Elijah is cool and shit and I know I don't know him as well as y'all do," Troy began, motioning at Eric, "but damn, his prints is all over the gun, man!"

"You right, you don't know him as good as we do. And we're telling you he didn't do no crazy shit like that. Will you tell this crazy nigga something, D?" Eric exclaimed, taking a gulp of his beer.

Darryl sat back in his seat on the couch. "Even if he did do it, I bet there is a valid reason for it. That's if he did it,"

Then all conversation ceased as Ebonee Lane made her way down the steps. She had not found time to change her clothes, so she knew she was going to hear it from the guys in the room.

"Gotdamm!" Troy exclaimed under his breath as Ebonee walked over to the couch.

"Hello, gentlemen."

"How you doing, baby?" Eric greeted her as smooth as he could.

"Oh. Ebonee, this is Eric and Troy. He's known Elijah all his life, so maybe he could answer your questions better than me," Darryl said, nodding at Eric.

"You're in the FBI?" Troy asked excitedly.

"Oh shit!" Eric suddenly exclaimed, staring Ebonee in the face. "Troy, who she look like?" He looked at Troy. "Think about it. Look at her, and think about Elijah," he added, trying to jog Troy's memory.

Troy's face contorted in deep thought. "Oh shit! Delicious!" he finally exclaimed.

"Delicious?" Ebonee asked curiously.

"Umm, that's just what we called her, a little nickname," Eric said quickly, and then he turned to Troy. "What was her real name again? Elijah told me but I forgot," he said, slapping his hand on his knee repeatedly, trying to remember.

"Taysia?" Ebonee asked softly, remembering the name Elijah had said when he had first seen her.

"Yeah! That's it. Hey, how did you know?" Eric asked.

"I heard it someplace before," Ebonee replied.

So that explained why Elijah looked so surprised when they had first met.

Ebonee continued. "Was she his girlfriend?"

"I don't think so. But Elijah wanted her to be. I think he and her were going to be. That is, until that night," Eric said.

Things began to clear up for Ebonee. "The girl that was killed on the waterfront?"

"Yeah, that was her. You look just like her," Eric said.

Ebonee sighed lightly and turned to Darryl. "Do you have a pencil or a crayon?" she asked, glancing at her watch.

"I think there's something in the drawer in the kitchen," he replied, getting up to look. She followed him into the kitchen.

"Here you go." He handed her a blue crayon. "Don't ask me where it came from, because I have no idea." He smiled.

"Thank you." Reaching into her pocket, Ebonee pulled out the piece of paper she had taken from the car outside. "Oh, by the way, I want to take these in for evidence if you don't mind." She indicated the stack of notebooks.

"No. I don't care. Take whatever you need."

Ebonee peeled the crayon and laid it flat on the piece of paper, then slid it across the surface lightly.

"So you're investigating his case?" Troy asked from the living room.

"Yes I am," she answered, reading the words on the paper: *Stadium district. Building fourteen.*

She put the paper back into her pocket and walked back into the living room.

"So what's the word? Do you think he did it?" Troy asked.

"Honestly, no I don't. Now if you guys will excuse me, I have to go," she said, picking up the notebooks.

"Can you take me with you?" Troy asked, smiling. "Arrest me, anything, just take me with you!" he cried, causing Eric and Darryl to laugh and shake their heads.

"No, sorry, but thanks for the compliment. And thanks for your time," she said to Darryl as she headed for the door.

"I've got a pound of weed in my pocket! Come on! Take me downtown!" Troy exclaimed.

Ebonee shook her head.

"You have to excuse him; he doesn't know how to treat a beautiful lady," Darryl apologized for Troy as Ebonee walked out of the door.

"That's okay. I'll let him slide because he's Elijah's friend and because I'm dressed like a hood rat. Here." She handed him a card. "If you talk to Elijah, or remember anything that might help me, give me a call."

She headed back to the car and took off for the stadium district. It wasn't far. It actually would have been about a ten-minute drive on the expressway, maybe less. But there was some kind of event at one of the three huge arenas in the area and traffic was almost at a standstill.

She sighed heavily as she sat in the traffic jam. Then she looked at her pocket curiously. She thought she had heard a voice. Then she remembered the two-way cell phone. She pulled it out and waited.

"Mike, you there?" came a voice through the static.

She turned up the radio in the car and quickly flipped the stations until she found a man's voice talking. She held the radio up to a speaker in the car and pressed on the transmitter repeatedly, making it sound as though her transmission was breaking up. Then she waited again.

"Mike, you're breaking up. Listen, we're pulling out. Heading back to the compound in Eastern Pennsylvania. Something's got Charles spooked. He was rambling something about leaving someone a gift. He hasn't stopped laughing about it since we left. Well anyway, I'll see you back at the compound." The transmission ended.

Ebonee's heartbeat quickened. *A gift?*

"Elijah, it's a trap!" she exclaimed, slamming her foot on the gas and veering into the emergency lane.

Elijah felt the chill bumps again as he approached the back of the warehouse. He crept silently along, staying in the shadows. He didn't know how many of them were waiting for him. The subtle hum of his blades told him the demon was there, and that was all that mattered.

He completed a circuit of the first floor and found not a soul. But someone had definitely been here recently; the nu-

merous cigarette butts told him that much. He found his way
to the stairs and cautiously made his way up.

Still no signs of life. He paused, hearing something coming from a doorway on the other side of the building. It
sounded like the muffled cries of a woman. Elijah approached
the doorway silently. He peered around the corner and into
the room. There standing chained to the wall, was a woman.
She was completely naked, and sweat glistened in the moonlight on her hourglass-shaped body.

Elijah raised an eyebrow curiously. He *was* still half man.

He made his way over to her. Her mouth was covered with
a piece of masking tape, and her hands and feet were secured with heavy chains. Her blue eyes pleaded with him
from behind the straying strands of blond hair that hung
over her face. Still, he felt the eerie chill bumps along his
skin. His blades, too, seemed to hum with more intensity.

He looked around again, confused. Wherever the demon
was hiding, he was doing a good job at it. He looked back at
the woman. Her breasts were heaving as she sucked in air
through her nose. He reached up and snatched the tape
from her mouth, punishment for making him think per-
verted thoughts.

"Please, untie me quickly. He'll be back soon, and he's
going to kill me!" she cried, her mouth pouting sweetly.

"Who's going to kill you?"

"The demon . . . Dalfien," the woman replied, wiggling fu-
tilely against the chains, causing her other body parts to jig-
gle seductively.

"Dalfien . . ." Elijah echoed the name.

"Yes, now please, hurry and untie me!"

Elijah slid one of his blades back into its sheath at his side,
then reached up and began to unchain one of her hands.
Images of the beautiful woman shackled to the wall before
him began to flitter into his mind.

He was naked, the woman on her knees in front of him,

her head moving in a back and forth motion, her mouth slurping hungrily at his manhood.

Elijah shook his head violently, fighting the scene away. One of the woman's hands was free.

He reached for the second, and the images returned. This time he was on his back. The woman was on top of him, riding him, her head thrown backward in bliss as he slammed up into her. He could feel the velvety soft tightness of her vagina as her perfectly-shaped breasts bounced rhythmically.

Again, he shook his head violently, chasing away the images. He realized then, as the woman's other hand fell free of the chains, their origin.

Before he could act, the woman's left hand found his throat and her right hand dug into his chest, her fingers searching for his heart. If not for his natural reflexes, he would have already been dead.

Pain like no other he had ever felt in his life coursed through his body. He held the woman's wrist with his left hand, struggling to keep it at bay. The woman howled in glee as her fingers brushed over the beating organ.

"*Anel . . . nath*—" Elijah tried to say the words to bring the demon into its true physical form, but the pain was too great.

He dropped his blade to the floor, and his right hand found the woman's neck and slammed her head back against the wall. But the woman paid it no mind. She howled madly as her left hand reached around Elijah's neck and pulled him in closer. Again, Elijah felt the fingers brush against his heart. He screamed in agony.

Ebonee hit the exit doing about eighty-five miles per hour. The car careened to the left as she fought to maintain control of it. Her heart raced as the car slammed into the guardrail, throwing up sparks. She growled and pressed on. Finally she reached her destination, and without hesitating, she crashed through the gate that was marked Building fourteen.

She brought the car to a screeching halt in front of the building. Jumping out, her weapon in hand, she ran head first into whatever danger lay inside of the dark building. She heard the scream and knew it was Elijah. Was she too late? She searched the floor for stairs. Finding them, she hurried up.

Another scream.

"Elijah, please . . . hold on!" she murmured to herself, running for the open doorway.

The demon's strength was unstoppable, but Elijah's resolve was unyielding. The woman's arm was neither. It snapped like a twig from the pressure. Elijah fell to the ground, clutching at the hole in his chest. He looked up in time to see Ebonee running into the room, her weapon raised and aimed at the woman.

"No! Don't shoot!" he managed to yell.

Ebonee froze in her tracks, unsure of how to proceed.

"Freeze! Don't move!" she yelled at the woman.

Elijah rolled to the side, forcing the excruciating pain to the back of his mind. He scooped up his blade just as the woman pulled herself free of the chains.

"I said freeze!" Ebonee yelled again, firing a warning shot into the air.

The woman turned to regard her almost curiously, her broken arm dangling sickly at her side.

"*Anel nathrak doth del dienve!*" Elijah recited the words through clenched teeth.

Ebonee watched the woman's body suddenly stiffen and then fall to the ground. In her place stood a beast that should not have been. It was something out of a child's nightmare she thought, as the seven-foot behemoth roared in front of her.

Elijah rolled and came to his feet, waiting for the demon

to charge. But it didn't. It had been warned by Dalfien of those horrible blades.

The demon instead reached up into the ceiling, tearing a section of drainpipe down. Elijah watched and waited. He didn't care what the demon used; the outcome would be the same in the end. The demon would die.

Thinking itself very clever, the demon slammed the pipe downward in an attempt to crush the Protector where he stood. Elijah jumped to the side, avoiding the attack easily, even grinning a bit when the cast iron pipe exploded into tiny pieces. The demon looked at the remaining piece of pipe he held in his hand curiously.

He felt the bite of the Protector's blades then, digging into his side, sucking at his very soul. Elijah did not feel the pain in his chest any longer, but he knew it was there, waiting for the rage to subside. He stepped around to the back of the howling demon, his blades cutting into the creature's back repeatedly. The demon stumbled forward, seeking to escape the terrible pain that the blades were unleashing.

Ebonee's eyes never left the Protector. She watched in awe at the way he moved. Every muscle seemed to compliment the other without a wasted step. It was perfection.

The demon threw itself forward into a roll, which looked rather awkward to Elijah, given the creature's size. But it bought the demon some time. The Protector took a step in the demon's direction and the beast returned to its feet to face him.

Suddenly, Elijah felt the demon in his mind again. Sultry images of the woman flashed across his consciousness, naked, voluptuous, and longing to please him. But The Protector would have none of it now. He knew the demon's tricks. He focused on the pain, bringing images of the demon's fingers brushing against his heart to force the mental attack away.

Then he rushed in, blades leading. The demon searched

frantically for some sort of weapon with which to defend it-self. Instinctively, the demon raised its arm in defense, as one of the blades sliced it free of its body at the forearm. The demon howled in anger and pain, charging forward.

The Protector fell backward to the ground, his blades playing a wicked tune of pain as they sliced at the demon's belly and hips. The demon ran over and beyond him, seeking only to be away from this tormentor of souls.

The Protector jumped to his feet, following the beast as it ran for the open doorway. The demon could feel the hungry blades at his back, longing to taste of his soul. It paid no attention to the woman standing in its path, her gun pointing its way.

Ebonee snapped out of her trance when she saw that the demon was heading her way. She opened fire. Bullets ripped into and through the demon's abdomen, but the demon only howled in rage and kept coming.

Elijah felt a bullet pass through his shoulder. He ignored it. He had to get to the beast before it got to Taysia.

Ebonee emptied the clip, but still the demon closed. She froze in fear as the demon howled out, now only a few feet away from her. Then the creature's eyes went wide and it stopped running to stare down at the tip of the thrown blade now protruding from its massive chest.

The Protector caught up. With his remaining blade, Elijah chopped downward at the creature's leg, severing it at the knee. The creature toppled, still with the look of surprise on its ugly maw. Then its head rolled cleanly from its shoulders.

The Protector, standing over the headless body, which had begun to disintegrate, looked up at Taysia. Then his pain returned. He fell to his knees, growling and clutching at his chest.

"Elijah!" Ebonee shouted, running over to kneel next to him.

Elijah looked up at her, the darkness forcing its way into his mind. "Taysia," he whispered, wincing from the pain, "I . . . love you." His voice trailed off into the darkness and unconsciousness took him away from the pain.

Ebonee held him in her arms, her eyes full of tears. She listened to the words and wished they were meant for her.

She cradled Elijah's head close to her chest, looking out of the far window into the night sky. A tear escaped her eye and she gently slid her cheek across Elijah's forehead. *If only they were meant for me.*

"Director Moss? Yes, this is Agent Lane," Ebonee said into the phone. She had managed, with some difficulty, to get Elijah out of the building and into the car. She had then left the city, driving along the turnpike until she stopped at a small motel.

"What do you have, Lane?" Moss asked.

"There is an abandoned warehouse in the stadium district. It's number fourteen. I just left there a few minutes ago. There is a girl there who I believe can shed some light on our friend, Mr. Kreicker."

"What about our fugitive?"

Ebonee sighed and took a deep breath, looking over at the sleeping form on the bed. "He's with me."

"He's with you? Agent Lane, I don't have to inform you of the consequences of aiding a wanted man. Now I suggest you bring him in right now," Moss replied, lowering his voice so that no one could hear his conversation.

"Sir, I can't do that. The girl will be able to tell you everything. They set a trap for him at the building. . . . Kreicker was there. Get the girl and question her. I'm going after Charles Kreicker. Please, sir. Just give me forty-eight hours and I will get you all the evidence you need."

"I'm going to pretend we never had this conversation, Agent Lane. Now you've got twenty-four hours to get him back here. If you're not back by then, your picture will go up next to his on the wanted posters. Do you understand?" he whispered fervently. "You seem to be forgetting that this is not my jurisdiction. I don't know where Director Glenn is, but I'm sure he'll pop up sooner or later. And when he does, it's his show. . . . You've got twenty-four, Lane. Goodbye."

Ebonee hung up the phone and turned around to find Elijah standing in front of her.

"Oh, you're up," she said, looking away as his eyes studied her intently. "How do you feel?" she added, walking over to sit down on the bed.

Elijah didn't reply; he just stared at her—at her eyes. He couldn't believe how much she resembled Taysia. Could this be what Gabriel had meant when Elijah had questioned him about Taysia? He had told him that he would find out and the resemblance was too close for mere coincidence. But the eyes—they held him the same way that Taysia's eyes had once held him. Her body, her lips, everything. Everything was just like Taysia.

"Oh, I'm sorry. I know we've been running into each other, but we haven't had the chance to be properly introduced," Ebonee said, trying to avoid looking into his eyes. "My name is Ebonee—Ebonee Lane." She stood and extended her hand.

"Ebonee," Elijah replied in a whisper.

His eyes seemed so sad. He looked at her outstretched hand, and then back at her eyes. He felt the urge to pull her close and taste of those lips again.

Again?

"Elijah," Ebonee began softly, seeing the sadness in his eyes. "I know who you think—"

"Don't assume to think you know anything about what I feel or think," he began angrily, fighting the emotions of his past away. He turned around, ashamed to face her. "I'm sorry. I didn't mean—"

"It's okay. I understand," Ebonee said softly, walking over to place a hand on Elijah's shoulder.

"You couldn't possibly begin to understand," Elijah whispered, turning to look at her, his eyes about to overflow with tears.

Ebonee's heart raced; they were so close. She felt herself wondering, wondering what it would be like to be held in his strong embrace.

"I don't understand," he said, closing his eyes as the first tear escaped.

Ebonee's hands shook. Never had she felt so much emotion from any one man in all her life.

"It's okay. . . ." Ebonee placed her hand gently on Elijah's cheek.

Elijah felt himself melting from the touch. It was just as he remembered, so soft and gentle. "I don't understand. Why me?" Elijah whispered through the tears.

All of the emotions he had blocked out caught up to him. Ebonee felt the overpowering pain in Elijah's heart—she could almost touch it. His skin was smooth and warm to the touch. She closed her eyes, imagining their lips connecting for the first time. Gently, she pulled his head down to hers, her heart racing as their lips drew close. Elijah felt the pain disappear; all thoughts vanished from his mind. All thoughts except happiness. It was the same feeling he had when they were alone on the waterfront, right before—

Elijah's head stopped moving downward, and he opened his eyes, a confused expression on his face. Ebonee looked into his eyes, waiting.

"You're not Taysia," he whispered, sounding as though he had just found understanding.

Ebonee sighed softly and closed her eyes as she turned away.

"No, Elijah, I'm not," she whispered, looking deeply into

his eyes once more. "I'm Ebonee," she said sadly, gently pulling away from him.

Elijah felt her sadness, and he reached out a hand to gently turn her back around.

"No, please don't—" he began, searching for what to say. "I know you're not Taysia. I know Taysia is gone—"

"She will always exist in your heart," Ebonee said, looking away. She couldn't compete with this Taysia.

Elijah reached a hand out and gently touched her cheek, guiding her eyes back to his. "Ebonee . . . When Taysia died, my love died with her. Any hopes of happiness, I gave up when she ceased to be. I truly thought I would never feel that way ever again." He paused, sadness in his voice. "I don't know who you are, and I don't know why you are here. But there is one thing I do know—one thing I could never forget. I've known love once. That feeling is something you can't forget." Again he paused as the emotions ran through him. "When you placed your hand on my cheek—" He stopped, his emotions overwhelming him.

Ebonee searched his eyes and found only what he claimed—love.

Again her hand gently found his cheek.

"Shhh, don't say any more," she whispered. Closing her eyes, she leaned in close.

Bringing his head down to hers, she felt it too, then, as their lips softly touched. For that brief moment, Ebonee forgot about the world. There was no FBI. There were no fugitives, no directors, no white supremacists, and no demons. There was only happiness.

"Wow! I am so good!"

Elijah and Ebonee looked up simultaneously at the sudden interruption. Elijah, upon seeing the man dressed in a long, tan trench coat with white hair flowing about his shoulders, couldn't help but smile. Ebonee, on the other hand, went for her gun.

"Who are you!" she yelled, forcing herself in front of Elijah, her gun on the intruder. "And how the hell did you get in here?"

Gabriel looked at Elijah curiously. Elijah smiled and shrugged.

"What? You mean he hasn't told you about me?" Gabriel asked, sounding as though his feelings were hurt.

Ebonee glanced back at Elijah. Seeing the smile on his face, she relaxed a bit. "You know him?"

"Yes, Ebonee. You can put the gun away. He's an . . . *old* friend," Elijah replied.

"Actually, Elijah and I are a bit more than *old* friends," Gabriel said, walking over to the two of them. "We're family! Isn't that right, Elijah?" He threw his arm around Elijah's shoulder with a smile.

"Don't you have a war to fight or something?" Elijah asked, moving away from him.

"Ummm . . . excuse me . . . but . . . how did you get in here?" Ebonee asked, her eyebrows raised, looking from Elijah back to Gabriel.

Elijah let out a short sigh. It didn't make any sense to keep her in the dark and he didn't have time to sugarcoat anything. "Ebonee, Gabriel is an angel,"

"Archangel, son!" Gabriel interrupted.

Elijah smiled, shook his head, and then he continued. "You see, apparently there's this war or something going on in heaven—"

"An angel . . . You're telling me this man here is an angel?" Ebonee interrupted doubtfully.

"Archangel!" Gabriel threw in. Now it was his turn to shake his head.

"If you'll listen, I'll explain it all. Do you want to hear?" Elijah asked, looking at Ebonee questioningly.

"Be my guest," Ebonee replied, taking a seat on the bed, a smirk on her face. But then she remembered the demon and all the other crazy things that had been happening, and her smirk disappeared.

Elijah, seeing that she was now listening intently, continued. "Look, we don't have a lot of time, so I'll give you the short and sweet version." Elijah looked over at Gabriel for approval.

Gabriel nodded with a huge smile. Elijah took a deep breath and started his story. "Okay . . . like I said, there is a war of some kind in heaven. Between the angels or something, I don't know. . . ." Gabriel frowned and Elijah shrugged his shoulders. "Anyway, Gabriel here is one of the good guys. Now the good angels can't fight the war in heaven and battle Satan and his demons here on earth at the same time." He paused again, taking another deep breath. "So Pops here—"

"Pops?" Ebonee asked, interrupting again.

"What? Didn't he tell you? I told you we were family!" Gabriel said, walking over to put his arm around Elijah again. "Can't you see the family resemblance?" he added, looking at Elijah with a smile.

"You mean to tell me he's your father?" Ebonee asked, standing to inspect the two.

Before Elijah or Gabriel could respond, she was talking again.

"That would mean that you're—"

"Half angel," the two of them said in unison.

"A Nephilim, to put it biblically," Gabriel added.

"That would explain the accelerated healing and the inhuman strength," Ebonee continued, putting it together.

"Correct. So Pops decided to take matters into his own hands and make his own little group of demon hunters, or whatever, to help keep Satan from overrunning the earth while they battled in heaven. And . . . I guess that's about it," Elijah finished.

Ebonee sat down on the bed, shaking her head once more. "I need an aspirin."

Elijah looked over at Gabriel, and shrugged again. "So what are you doing down here?"

"Just checking up on you. Oh, by the way, nice selection," he said, indicating Elijah's blades. "I saw what you did to the church. Father Holbrook seems to be a changed man since your visit," he added, walking to stand in front of Elijah. "So how many bad guys have you bagged?"

"I think five. Two big ones and three little ones," Elijah replied, a smile finding his lips.

"That's all? You're slacking; you should be up to at least ten by now," Gabriel grinned.

"Sorry to disappoint you. I'll try harder from now on," Elijah said sarcastically.

"You do that. Well, things seem to be okay here. I'm going to go back now. Keep up the good work," Gabriel said, and then he looked over at Ebonee, who was still lying back on the bed with her hand over her face.

He didn't say a word though, as he looked back at Elijah, his grin spreading. He opened the door to the motel room and headed out.

"Hey, Gabriel!" Elijah shouted after him.

Gabriel looked back over his shoulder.

"Thanks," Elijah said, sounding very serious.

Gabriel sighed deeply as the night air whipped his white hair about his head. "I owe you that much. I'm not as uncaring as you may have thought. Good luck, Protector."

And then he was gone.

Ebonee sat up when he was gone and the door was closed once more. She looked over to Elijah, who had not moved.

"So what was that last little exchange about?" she asked curiously.

Elijah smiled and walked to the bed, sitting down next to her.

"I was just thanking him for a gift. Nothing important," he

replied, looking her in the eye, knowing that it was actually the most important gift he had ever received.

Ebonee slid over closer to him, forcing the interruption from her mind. She didn't care about Gabriel or his demons or anything else, for that matter. The only thing she cared about at that moment was the feeling she got when their lips had touched and they had held each other. She had spent her life waiting for that moment when Mr. Right would come along and sweep her off her feet. And Elijah seemed to be holding a vacuum. There was no way she would deny the feelings that enveloped her at his touch. There were no doubts, no questions.

It was right.

Elijah felt her hand on his as she slid over to him. He, too, longed to have that feeling return to him again. And he knew that Ebonee was the only one who could give it to him. Again their lips touched, and the love washed over them both. Her lips were as soft as fine silk.

Elijah's breathing came in short, uncontrolled gasps as the passion quickly returned to him. His hands shook as he reached up to gently stroke her smooth beautiful face. Ebonee leaned into Elijah, forcing him back down onto the bed, her tongue tasting the sweetness of his lips and reveling in their softness. She could barely remember the last time she had been with a man, and the desire burned in her now.

Ebonee sat back, straddling Elijah's lap, her hands resting softly on his chest. She pulled Elijah's hands up to her face, placing one on each cheek. Her eyes closed when she felt his touch, his hands gliding softly down to her neck.

Elijah felt his arousal then, as he marveled at her physical beauty. He watched as she guided his hands down further to her breasts.

Knock . . . knock . . . knock . . .

Ebonee opened her eyes and stared down at Elijah in disbelief. Elijah could only smile.

"That's it. I don't care who it is this time; friend of yours or not, they're getting a bullet!" Ebonee exclaimed. Jumping up, she pulled out her gun and walked to the door.

Elijah beat her there, swinging the door open. There, standing in his white robe, was Father Holbrook.

"Father Holbrook?" Elijah said, surprised.

"I've found you!" the old man exclaimed, his smile wide. Elijah looked over at Ebonee and shrugged.

"Father?" Ebonee repeated, at a loss for words. Then she shrugged and threw her hands up in the air, walking away. "First angels, now a priest! What's next? A choir?" she ranted, flopping down onto the bed.

Elijah smiled and turned back to Father Holbrook.

"You're a long way from home, Father. How did you find me, anyway?" he asked, waving the priest in.

"I have my ways, young Protector," he answered, walking in and dropping his bags to the floor, his eyes lingering on the scantily dressed female. "I'm sorry if I have disturbed you. I didn't know you—"

"What brings you here, priest?" Elijah interjected, cutting to the point. But Father Holbrook didn't reply.

"Priest?" Elijah said, as the priest continued to stare at Ebonee curiously.

"Priest!" Elijah said again, more forcefully, pulling the priest from whatever contemplations he was having.

"Hmmm? Oh . . . y-yes, yes," he stuttered, turning to look at Elijah. "What were you saying, young Protector?"

Elijah sighed heavily, looking over to Ebonee for help. Ebonee rolled her eyes and looked away, offering none.

"Why are you here?" Elijah repeated slowly.

"Oh! Yes, I can answer that for you. I have decided to do something with the remaining years of my life. I have been cooped up in that church for over fifty years now. It is time I got out and experienced the world. And what better way to do so than at the side of a Protector! And what better way to serve my God, than to be out in the world vanquishing Satan's foul children!" he exclaimed happily. "That is, of course, with your help," he added with a wink.

"With my help," Elijah repeated sarcastically, shaking his head in disbelief.

"Well, I mean . . . of course . . . Not exactly." The priest stumbled over his words, causing Elijah to smile weakly. "That is, if it's okay with you."

Elijah dropped his head, smiling. He couldn't deny the father his chance to see the world. And he kind of liked the crazy old man anyway.

"Fine with me, old man. Just stay out of my way when the time comes for the killing," Elijah replied. Then he looked the priest up and down and added, "And please . . . find something to wear other than that,"

"You can't be serious," Ebonee said, looking at Elijah. "It's way too dangerous, and he'll just slow us down."

"I'll have you know I was the fastest alter boy in my day! No one could light those candles quicker than Thaddeus Holbrook! No one!" Father Holbrook exclaimed, shaking a wrinkled finger at Ebonee.

Ebonee let out a deep sigh and looked at Elijah, who had sat down next to her on the bed once again, his hands covering his mouth to hide his smile.

"I guess he told you," he whispered, drawing a quick punch in the arm from Ebonee, who couldn't help but smile.

"Hmmph! Kids!" Father Holbrook mumbled to himself as Ebonee and Elijah giggled like little children.

"So, have you named them yet?" he said loudly, drawing their attention from one another as he stepped closer, dropping his bag to stare at the twin blades.

"Named what, old man?" Elijah smiled, looking up at Father Holbrook.

"The blades, of course. You must name them," he said, looking at Elijah as if he should have known better.

"The thought never occurred to me," Elijah admitted.

"They are not properly yours until you have given them names. They are merely lifeless pieces of steel without a name. Give them life, Protector! Name them!"

Elijah stood up and pulled out the blades, admiring their deadly beauty. He sat one of them down on the bed and examined the other closely. It hummed softly at his touch, its ebony blade outlined by a silver cutting edge along its slightly curved length on one side. He ran his fingers along the flat part of the blade, studying the intricate engravings there. "Soul Seeker," he said, looking to Father Holbrook, who nodded his acceptance.

Then Elijah exchanged the blades. Again, he felt the calming hum as he ran his fingertips along the flat part of the blade. His eyes went to Ebonee, who was sitting there looking at the two of them like they were crazy. "Enobe (pronounced eh-no-bay)," he said after a moment.

"Enobe?" Father Holbrook asked curiously.

Elijah cut an eye over to Ebonee.

"Ahhh . . . *Enobe*," the priest said, understanding. "Well, it's your blade; name it what you will," he added, raising his eyebrows.

Ebonee stood up then and shoved her gun in between the two.

"Smith and Wesson," she said dryly, before walking over to gather her things. "Now if you two are finished playing with your toys, we have to be going." She headed for the door.

Father Holbrook glanced at Elijah curiously. "Is she always this demanding?"

Ebonee glared at him, one eyebrow raised, awaiting his response.

"Only when it's hot," Elijah began, smiling as he put on

his black leather trench coat, moving to follow Father Holbrook out of the door, "in hell!" he added as he walked by Ebonee, who laughed and gave him another swift punch in the arm. Elijah laughed, too, and for the second time in his life, he felt he had found happiness.

Chapter Eleven
DEMONS, IMPS, FIENDS . . . AND LOVE?

Director Moss pulled his car up to the scene. The front of the building was alive with the flashing lights of police cars and the chatter of radio communication. To the average person it would seem to demand their attention. But Director Moss was used to it. He walked past the ambulance and entered into the warehouse.

"Where's the girl?" he asked an officer coming out.

"Who are you?" the policeman asked, looking him up and down. He knew who he was from the suit, but he figured he'd give him a hard time anyway.

Director Moss sighed and pulled out his ID.

"Director Moss, FBI. Now where is the girl?" His patience was wearing thin.

The officer looked long and hard at the ID. Then he looked at Moss. "She's upstairs. They've got her stabilized and coherent," he replied flatly, turning to walk away.

Director Moss made his way up to the second floor. He found some of his people working on the scene.

"Agent Divasek," he called to one of them. "Is that her?"

he asked, motioning toward the woman huddled in a blanket.

"Yeah. That's her," Divasek replied, walking to stand next to Moss.

"What happened?" Moss asked, his eyes studying the woman's body.

"Well, from what we have so far, I don't really know," Divasek admitted. "We collected a couple of sets of finger prints off of the chains—"

"Chains?"

"Yeah, apparently someone chained her to the wall . . . over there. Whoever it was left in a hurry. There are tracks outside, and footprints. Now the interesting thing is, we found two sets of prints on the chains. My guess is someone came in after they had gone and was trying to rescue the woman," Divasek explained.

"Tried?" Moss asked curiously.

"Yeah. Tried." Divasek led Moss over to the wall and the chains. "Looks like our little princess may not have wanted to be rescued. These footprints are the freshest, they show a struggle. Looks like the rescuer got one of her hands free, and to show her appreciation, she attacked him. My guess is she was choking him, or whoever. Then the rescuer grabbed her arm with his left hand and tried to keep it off his neck. This leads to even more interesting facts," Divasek said.

"What's that?"

"Well, in the process of trying to keep from being throttled by our little princess here, the rescuer only used one hand, his left hand. We know this because of the bruises on her wrist." Divasek continued.

"What's so interesting about that?"

"The woman's forearm was broken in half like a twig. Do you know how much pressure it would take to break a human bone in half like that, given the angle and the circumstances here? It's impossible," Divasek said.

"So what are you telling me? That we're dealing with mutants with superhuman strength?" Moss asked, his eyes still on the woman.

"That's exactly what I'm telling you. Whoever the rescuer was had to be at least as strong as she is, or possibly stronger. And she did this while getting her head bashed into the wall!" Divasek exclaimed, pointing to the blood on the wall. "And that's not all." He grinned as he led Moss over to another set of prints on the floor.

"I save the best for last," he said, shining his flashlight down onto the floor. "You tell me what that is," he said, kneeling next to the director.

Moss stared at the prints in confusion. "They look like . . . like hoof prints," he said quietly, not fully understanding what he was looking at.

"That's exactly what they are. Someone apparently has a gigantic two-legged goat running around fighting with mutants." Divasek chuckled.

"Is that blood?" Moss asked, his eyes finding the red stains on the floor.

"Yep, and a lot of it. I've already sent a sample to the lab, along with the prints."

Director Moss reached into his trench coat and pulled out a rubber glove and a plastic baggie. He scooped up a sample of his own and placed it in his pocket. Then he stood up and looked at Divasek. "You said she was strong. Strong enough to break the chains?" he asked.

"The human bone is hard to break. So yes. Yes, she could have broken the chains," Divasek answered.

"Then why did she wait?" Moss thought out loud.

"Hey, my job is to tell you what happened. *Why* it happened? I leave that up to you guys."

Director Moss paused and looked back at the woman. "Is she talking?"

"Talking? No. *Can* she talk? Yes. But she won't say a word to anyone,"

Moss figured he knew why. "Let me know when you get the results back from the lab." He headed toward the woman.

"Why? Are you taking over the case?" Divasek asked curiously.

"No, not yet at least. But if things keep happening the way they are, I may be."

He approached the woman and kneeled down next to her, glancing around to see if anyone was paying them any attention. Then he spoke to her. "It's okay. I'm a friend," he said to her, placing his hand on hers.

The woman looked up at him suspiciously. "A friend?"

"The Order," Moss said, playing a hunch.

Her eyes softened at the mention of The Order.

"Now, what happened here?"

"I-I-I don't really remember. Charles sent for me, and I can't remember what happened after that," she whispered.

"Why were you here in the first place?"

"You don't know?" she asked suspiciously.

"I've been on vacation; I haven't spoken to Charles since I got back," he lied.

The woman stared at him for a moment and then exhaled heavily. "All I know is that Charles came here looking for a man. I don't know who. But I know he wants him dead," the woman explained. "Charles said that your guys pulled out and left him on his own, so he sent for us."

"Did you happen to hear the names of the people he said pulled out on him?" Moss asked.

"I did overhear him saying something about a man named—"

"Well, well, well. If it isn't Director Moss," a voice called out from behind them.

Director Moss turned to see Assistant Director Glenn.

"I haven't seen any little green men running around the streets of Philadelphia," he said sarcastically. "What brings you into my neck of the woods, Director?"

"Little green men," Moss echoed, sighing softly as Glenn continued to speak

"Or should I say, paranormal activity, the unexplained phenomena—it's all a bunch of crap, anyway." He paused and thought about something. "Or am I or someone under my command under investigation?" he asked, looking at Moss curiously.

"Director Glenn, while you've been off doing whatever it is you do, there have been several homicides in your jurisdiction."

"I know what's been going on in my jurisdiction. And I don't need your help to figure it out. And since no one under my supervision is being investigated by Internal Affairs and there is nothing supernatural about this case, I suggest you leave my crime scene," Director Glenn said quietly, almost threateningly.

Director Moss studied the man intently. Moss was in his mid forties, but the years had been good to him; he was tall and solid with only a hint of gray showing in his dark hair. He had never trusted Glenn, and when Agent Lane had suggested that he was a part of the attempt on her life, he got the strong feeling that it was true. But he couldn't prove anything—yet.

"Director Glenn, unless you consider a man blowing half his brains out into a bathtub, only to walk out of a hospital three days later without a scratch, normal, or the fact that two of your men attacked this same man at the airport and had no recollection of it at all, not to mention the fact that you're standing on hoof prints made by some kind of animal that's stalking mutants in your city, I don't think there is anything normal about this case at all. Shall I continue? Because I can," Moss said, growing angrier with each word. He really didn't like Glenn.

"What are you babbling about . . . hoof prints?" Glenn asked, trying to keep his voice down. His anger, too, was growing by the second.

Director Moss pointed down to the floor.

"Can I please just go home?" the girl cried.

Moss wanted to finish questioning her; he had an idea of the name she was about to say, but he couldn't afford to guess.

"Where is Agent Lane?" Glenn asked director Moss, ignoring the girl.

"Don't you know? She's *your* agent. Why are you asking me?" Moss asked, his suspicions growing deeper with every word out of Glenn's mouth.

Glenn's nostrils flared in anger, but he fought it back. "You seem to be so interested in this case, I thought you may have contacted her, that's all." Glenn sounded somewhat shaken.

"Well, why don't you call her?"

Glenn shook his head and turned to walk away. "Yes . . . I'll do that. I'll call her from my cell phone. I left it in the car."

"No, Director. Here, you can use mine." Director Moss pulled his cell phone from his pocket, his eyes boring into Glenn.

"I don't have the num—"

"That's okay. I locked it in my phone when I got it from your now deceased deputy assistant. Here," Moss said, pushing a button and holding the phone out to Glenn. He watched the director's eyes intently; he could see the nervousness in them as he took the phone from his hand.

"Agent Lane."

"Agent Lane, this is Director Glenn." He turned his back on Moss as he spoke into the phone, to the dial tone.

Ebonee had hung up as soon as he had said his name.

"What's your status, Lane?" he continued, pretending to be talking to her. "Okay. Keep me informed. I'll contact you later," he said, hanging up the phone and tossing it back to Moss.

"Well? What's her status?"

"That's not your business, Director. If I need your assistance, I'll ask for it," he said angrily, and then he walked over to the girl, ignoring Moss.

Moss looked down at his cell phone. He clicked through the menu and found the call duration selection. He selected it, and the numbers came up for the last call: 00:02. He looked back at Glenn, who was now questioning the woman. Then the woman pointed to him and Glenn looked up at him, his eyes full of hatred.

Moss decided it was time for him to call in some backup. He walked out of the building and to his car. There was no doubt in his mind that Glenn had tried to have Agent Lane killed. And he knew for a fact that he was somehow connected to The Order of the Rose. There was just one piece of the puzzle missing, and that was this Charles Kreicker fellow.

Agent Lane seemed to be on the right track. Moss headed for his hotel room, trying to put the pieces together. When he pulled up to the hotel he still hadn't quite figured it out. He proceeded to his room and slid the electronic card key through the lock. The door opened and he walked into the darkness. He flipped on the light as the door closed behind him. There, sitting in a chair by the bed, was Agent Parks, holding a gun with a silencer attached. Moss froze where he stood as he heard the hammer cock.

*   *   *

"I don't believe that no good son-of-a-bitch had the nerve to call me," Ebonee exclaimed, tossing the phone into the back seat. "I know he had something to do with trying to have me killed!"

"Who was that?" Elijah asked, his eyes on the road ahead.

It was not yet daybreak, and Father Holbrook was snoring loudly in the back. They didn't know the exact location of the cult's compound, but Ebonee had a general idea where to look.

Ebonee leaned her head back onto the headrest. "My boss, Director Glenn."

"Your boss tried to have you killed? Why?" he asked, looking over at her briefly.

"I work for Internal Affairs. I investigate the investigators. I was put on assignment here because the bureau had suspicions that some of our operatives were members of a radical group based in Eastern Pennsylvania. Director Glenn, the head of operations here, and also the man who I believe tried to have me killed, is one of the ringleaders. Or at least that's what I intend to prove."

"So my case just happened to come up while you were doing that."

"Well, basically, yes. Aside from the fact that you walked out of the hospital without a scratch after blowing out half your brains, which falls under the title of 'unexplainable,' which is part of the same branch that I work for. So I probably would have been assigned to your case anyway. But since the same people that are after you are the same people I'm trying to catch, it works out pretty nicely. By the way, do you have any idea why they're after you anyway?"

"I know why—and it's not a 'they'—it's an 'it,'" Elijah replied.

"An it?"

"Yeah, a demon, remember? Gabriel? Father Holbrook back there . . . the blades and stuff?" Elijah asked, smiling.

"How could I forget?" Ebonee said with a hint of sarcasm. "So you think that this demon is somehow controlling The Order?"

"The Order?"

"Yeah, The Order of the Rose. That's what they call themselves."

"Well, I don't know anything about The Order, but this Charles fellow is not what he appears to be."

"So you're saying he's a demon," Ebonee conjectured, looking at Elijah curiously.

"That's exactly what I'm saying. And I intend to kill him."

"You can't kill him. I believe he's our link to the deputy assistant director I've been investigating," Ebonee said.

"Not kill him, kill the demon. The demon possesses your man's body. You see, they can't come into this world in their physical form. Only their spirit can infest a human host. The only way to bring them out is by saying the words the old man told me to say . . . or something like that." Elijah shrugged his shoulders.

"Oh. I see," Ebonee said quietly, remembering the girl back at the warehouse. "So once you say the words, it makes them solid, living beings in our world . . . so you can kill them."

"You got it," Elijah said, winking at her.

"But once they leave the person's body, what happens to them? Do they know what's going on while the demon is in control?"

"Ebonee, all I do is say the words and kill them. Ask the old man back there, he should know."

"Please, he's unconscious. I haven't heard anyone snore that loud in years," Ebonee replied, smiling.

"Can I ask you a question, Ebonee? I'm curious."

"Sure, what is it?"

"How in the hell did you get my mom to let you take her car?" Elijah stared at her in wonder.

Ebonee smiled wider. "Easy, I just asked her," she lied.

"Just like that? You just asked her and she said yes?"

"Yeah, why?"

"I couldn't get her to let me drive it to the corner store if my life depended on it!"

Ebonee grinned. "It sounds like somebody is jealous to me."

"Damn right, I'm jel! All the times I let her drive my car! Even after she borrowed it once and brought me back a crumpled up license plate which was all that was left after she totaled the car! And she never let me use her car! And here you come, a complete stranger, and she just tosses you the keys?" Elijah complained, trying to hide his smile.

"Yeah, but it was only because I told her I was trying to help you," Ebonee answered, placing her hand on Elijah's leg.

"Yeah, right. I bet. Don't give me that," Elijah said, his attention drawn to the rearview mirror. There was a set of headlights behind them, and they had been there for quite a while.

Ebonee sensed his anxiety. "What's wrong?"

"There's a car behind us. It hasn't moved at all. I speed up and it still stays the same distance away. I slow down, they slow down. I think were being followed."

Ebonee glanced back, and then she looked at Elijah.

Elijah smirked. "Friends of yours?"

"I don't know, let's find out," she answered, checking her weapon.

Elijah took the next exit and watched as the car behind them slowed but continued on by. After pulling into the parking lot of a twenty-four-hour diner with no signs of a pursuer, Ebonee finally relaxed and put her gun away. She looked over at Elijah as they sat quietly in the night. Here was a man she had only known for half a day, and she was head over heels in love with him. Her mind went back to the motel room and the moment they had shared a kiss and a little bit more. Her body quivered as the emotions of that moment went through her again.

"There will never be a greater fool than me . . . loving completely, giving my heart blindly . . ." Ebonee whispered the words, breaking the silence.

Elijah looked at her; he knew those words all too well.

"Ignoring the voices in my mind, their prophecy of pain coming to pass each time . . ." He recited the second verse of the poem.

Ebonee turned sideways in her seat, resting her head against the headrest, her eyes staring softly into Elijah's.

"Elijah," she began, her eyes wandering away from his gaze, "I've never been in love before," she said softly, her voice barely a whisper. "When I first saw your picture over your sister's house, I found myself unable to stop looking at it. I couldn't stop looking at your eyes. I don't know why, but I just couldn't. And when I went to your apartment and found your poetry . . ." She paused, collecting herself as she tried to find the words she wanted to say. "I don't know. I started reading them and I just couldn't stop. You know, I think I was already in love with you by then." Her eyes once again found Elijah's.

Elijah reached out a hand and gently caressed her cheek. Ebonee felt the tears then, and she smiled, bringing her hand up to hold Elijah's in place.

"This is crazy. Falling in love with someone that easy," Ebonee quickly added, closing her eyes as her first tear fell.

Elijah sighed softly and swallowed hard, feeling his own tears calling. "What's not crazy when it comes to love?" he asked, his voice soft and sexy to Ebonee's ears. "I told you, when Taysia died, I swore I would never again love another. Then when I saw you at the airport, my world shattered." He took a breath. "You see, I had decided to be someone else. Someone cold and uncaring, devoid of emotion. I decided that I would live out the rest of my days alone, not opening up my heart to anyone ever again. But then you came along," he said, a smile escaping his lips, "and brought all those feelings back to me. Desire, passion . . . lust . . ." He stopped to gaze into her eyes. "*Love,*" he added softly, leaning in close, his face only a few inches from hers.

The sun peeked over the horizon as dawn approached.

"Elijah," Ebonee began with hestiation. She looked at him blankly, her mind trying to figure out whether or not these feelings she was feeling were the truth. Finally after a moment, her eyes lit up as she decided to accept the facts. "I love you," she whispered, her head reclining on the headrest, a warm smile on her face.

"I love you, too . . . Ebonee," Elijah replied, emphasizing her name.

He leaned in to gently place a kiss on her cheek. Ebonee tilted her head to the side at the last minute to bring their lips together once more. Elijah felt the passion burning inside of him once again as they shared a kiss. Ebonee savored every second their lips were together, her tongue exploring every inch of Elijah's soft lips. If they could have known the hell that lay only a few moments into the future, they would have held that kiss just a bit longer. Elijah sat back suddenly, a silly grin on his face.

"So . . . where did you say you were from?" he asked, drawing a laugh from Ebonee, and another quick punch in the arm.

"You are so stupid!" She laughed and leaned over to lay her head in his lap. Elijah smiled and gently stroked the side of her face. "I'm from Atlanta, by way of Chicago, if you must know," she added, turning to lie on her back so she could look up into Elijah's eyes.

"Well, you know everything about me. You know my sister, my mother, you've even read my poetry, which, by the way, not many people have."

"Well, I'm not many people. And I love your poetry. Now what do you want to know about me?" she asked, snuggling close to him.

"Okay, let's start with, ummm . . . your parents." He smiled down at her.

"They live in Atlanta. I'm an only child, so I'm very spoiled. Next question."

"How old are you?"

She grinned widely. "Old enough."

"Okay, when is your birthday?"

"August first, nineteen wouldn't ya like ta know," she replied, her grin spreading further.

"For real? Mine is July thirty-first! Come on, what year?" he asked excitedly.

"Okay. But you can't tell anyone. Sixty-nine," she confessed.

"Are you kidding? That means we were born a day apart!"

"That means sixty-nine was definitely a good year!" Ebonee laughed.

"Okay. Let me see . . ." Elijah said, leaning his head back to think of some more questions.

"*Crystal Ball*," Ebonee said before Elijah could think of his next question.

He gave her a suspicious glance. "What do you know about that?"

"More than you think," she replied. Grinning mischievously, she lifted her shirt to reveal a tattoo around her belly-button in the shape of the symbol that adorned the front of the CD cover of Elijah's favorite musician.

"Freak!" Elijah exclaimed, smiling wide.

"Like you," Ebonee returned, licking her lips seductively.

"What's your favorite movie?" Elijah asked.

"I don't know," she said, looking up at the roof of the car, in thought. "I have a lot of favorite movies. Let's see . . . *Scarface*," she began naming them off.

"Loved it." Elijah smiled.

"*Evil Dead 2*," she continued.

"Awww man, did he go through hell in that movie or what?" Elijah laughed, remembering it. "I must have watched it a hundred times."

"I liked when his girlfriend's head bit his hand. He must have knocked that thing up against every wall in the place!" she exclaimed as they both shared a good laugh.

"Nooo, how about when dude jumped on him and had him pinned down on the ground, and he was still whippin' his ass!" Elijah added, fueling their laughter.

Suddenly Ebonee's eyes filled with tears, and she tried to speak, but couldn't find her voice through the sudden sobs.

"What, baby? What's wrong?" Elijah asked softly, stroking the side of her face tenderly.

Ebonee caught her breath somewhat and looked into Elijah's eyes. "I don't ever want to lose this feeling, Elijah," she cried, wrapping her arms around him at the waist and burying her face into his belly. "I don't ever want to lose you! I've never felt this way about anyone ever before."

Elijah closed his eyes and fought away his own tears. He truly had believed he would never feel this way ever again. Surely not a week later. But here he was, in love again. Elijah looked down at her and a smile found his lips.

"Cherry pie," he said, smiling.

Ebonee wiped her tears away at the words, and a smile then found its way to her lips.

"Apple kisses," she replied, remembering the words to the song on their favorite Prince album. Then they both finished together. "Everything is cool!"

"Hey, did someone say apple pie? I'm starving!"

They both looked back at Father Holbrook, sitting up and rubbing his belly. They laughed out loud at the sight of him.

"What? Priests eat too!" he exclaimed.

"No doubt about that!" Ebonee said, glancing at the priest's round belly.

Elijah laughed heartily. "I think he took the phrase 'Our Daily Bread' to heart!"

"Are you two implying that I'm obese?" Father Holbrook asked, looking at them incredulously.

"Why, heavens no, Father, we would never say something like that about you," Ebonee said, trying to hide her smile. "Would you like to go inside and get something to eat?" she asked, cutting her eyes at Elijah.

"Can we?" he asked quickly, sitting forward hopefully.

Ebonee and Elijah exploded into laughter once more.

"Crazy children!" Father Holbrook muttered, watching them disdainfully.

Elijah opened the car door. "Come on, let's feed the old man before he has a baby."

They walked into the restaurant and found a booth. Elijah and Ebonee paid no attention to the stares they got from the few people inside. Father Holbrook on the other hand, still dressed in his robes, got a little flustered.

"What? Haven't you people ever seen a priest before?" he shouted, looking around at the staring eyes curiously.

"I told you to change your clothes," Elijah said when they had sat down.

"I don't think that's why they're staring at us," Ebonee remarked, glancing around the restaurant at all the faces—all the white faces.

"Now that you mention it, I do feel a little out of place," Elijah replied, glancing around.

"Would the two of you excuse me? I have to go to the bathroom. If the waitress comes, I want eggs, bacon, and potatoes with a side of white toast. Oh, and a large glass of OJ," Father Holbrook instructed, getting up to find the bathroom.

Alone once more, they returned their thoughts to each other.

"You are so beautiful," Elijah said, staring at her apprecia-tively. Ebonee blushed and returned the stare.

"No, you are," she replied, sighing heavily. "I just hope nothing ever changes," she added, sounding afraid. Elijah could see the fear in her eyes, and he only wanted to make it go away.

"Ebonee, I promise you." He leaned close over the table, taking her hand in his. "I promise that I will never ever change. I will protect your heart with my very life. I'll never let anything come between us. I promise you this," he said softly, and he meant every word of it. Ebonee felt the sincer-ity in those words and she was comforted.

"Can I take your order, please?"

Elijah and Ebonee looked up at the skinny, redheaded waitress.

"Just coffee for now," Ebonee replied, looking over at Eli-jah. "You want me to order for the priest?" she asked. Elijah nodded and she rolled her eyes. "And two eggs, bacon, and potatoes, and a large orange juice for our friend."

"And you?" The woman turned to Elijah

"A cup of coffee . . . for now," Elijah replied. For the first time since he had been out of the hospital, he could wait to eat. Ebonee's company was all he needed.

"You're not hungry?" Ebonee asked curiously.

"Actually, I'm starving, but I'm not too sure if I want to eat here," Elijah said. Still, he felt the stares on him. "What about you?"

"Well, I'm going to eat. I just don't know what I want yet." She picked up the menu.

Suddenly Elijah went stiff, feeling goose bumps pass over his skin.

"What is it?" Ebonee asked, sensing his alertness.

Elijah scanned the restaurant and his eyes locked with those of a man, standing behind the door of the kitchen, looking through the small round window.

"Wait right here," Elijah instructed her, getting up to head for the door.

"What? What is it?" she asked, standing to follow him.

"I'll be right back. Wait here. It's probably nothing," Elijah stopped and said to her. He refused to put her in danger again. "Please, just wait here for the old man. I'll be right back." Then he was off for the door.

Ebonee sat back down slowly, her eyes following him. Something told her to go after him. She had survived this long in the service on her instincts, and right now her instincts told her that something was not right. But she would not go against his wishes. She knew he was only trying to look out for her. So it was with great reluctance that she sat and watched him disappear into the kitchen.

Elijah ignored the shouts of the staff and walked right through the kitchen door. He saw the man disappear through another door. He knew it was probably a trap, but he would rather go to it than have it come to them, and endanger Ebonee.

He didn't hesitate. Throwing the door open wide, he ran into the room with blades drawn. The single man stood at the back of the stock room, apparently alone. He stood there, not making a move.

Why didn't he attack? Something was up. Elijah had faced the demons a couple of times before, and each time they had attacked without delay, no matter the time or place. Then why was this one waiting?

A distraction.

Elijah realized his mistake too late. He heard the screams back in the restaurant, and turned to run back, only to be confronted by a second man. Now the man behind him sprung into action. Elijah dodged to the side, avoiding the man's lunge.

"Anel Nathrak doth del dienve!" He chanted the words to bring the demons into their physical form. The men stiffened as the trespassing spirits left their bodies.

Elijah was now confronted by two of the same type of fiends that he had encountered at the airport. He waited for their wild attack. But it never came. One of the fiends reached out to the metal storage racks and ripped a section of it off to use as a weapon. The second followed suit.

They're getting smarter, Elijah mused to himself. *Not good.* Still, they made no move to attack. They just stood there, glaring at Elijah evilly and guarding the open door.

Elijah heard more shouts from the dining room. He knew Ebonee was in trouble. The Protector rushed into action, charging the creatures with Soul Seeker and Enobe leading the rush. He stabbed at the first creature's face, a simple attack. The creature batted Soul Seeker away easily, but it was Enobe that drew first blood, stabbing at the creature's neck, even as the second creature's clubbing swing from behind was deflected by the impossibly fast return of Soul Seeker.

The demons howled in rage as Enobe and Soul Seeker weaved and sliced lines of blood on their bodies. The Protector grunted angrily. Each second he spent battling these two was a second too long. Ebonee needed him. He had to finish these two quickly. He was fully on the offensive now, scoring hit after hit at will, but they were minor wounds, and he knew that only decapitation or striking at the hearts of the fiends would end this battle.

He sent Enobe into a straight thrust, directly at one of the demon's hearts, forcing it back, and then he turned both blades on the other demon. Enobe sliced in low, while Soul Seeker worked the creature's defenses high. Then the creature howled in pain when Enobe sliced through its knee, dropping it to the floor. Soul Seeker found the creature's exposed neck a second later, ending its life.

The Protector jumped to the side, accepting the glancing blow to his shoulder as the remaining fiend rushed at his back. Alone, the fiend posed little threat. Elijah walked right up to it, Soul Seeker batting away the wild swing of the metal pipe and Enobe finding the fiend's heart a split second later. The Protector violently kicked the dying form from his blade and ran out into the kitchen, leaping over the dazed and confused body of one of the formerly possessed men. The screams had subsided, and his fear grew as he busted through the door and into the dining room.

Ebonee was gone.

He saw the people gathered at the window in the front of the dining room, staring out into the bright sunrise. He ran as fast his legs could carry him, crashing through the wooden door without even attempting to touch the knob, just in time to see a black van speeding off down the highway. He cursed to himself for being so damned brickheaded. He was the one who had told her to stay there. He had put her in more danger by trying to keep her out of it. He stormed back into the restaurant, heading for the kitchen once again, and the two men.

Father Holbrook stepped gingerly out of the bathroom, wiping his hands on his white robe, looking around at the confusion. He spotted the Protector stalking toward him, an angry glare in his eye.

"Eh? Did I miss something?" he muttered to himself. The intense look on the Protector's face warned him to keep his comments to himself. He followed him into the kitchen.

Elijah found the men right where he had left them. One of them was sitting up now, shaking his head groggily. The Protector wasted no time. Walking right up to him, he grabbed the man around the neck with one hand, lifting him clear off the floor and slamming him violently into a wall.

"Where!" the Protector demanded, his eyes afire with anger and rage. The man's eyes bulged as he struggled to breathe, his feet kicking wildly at the air. "Where!" the Protector demanded again, pulling the man forward and slamming him into the wall once more.

"Calm yourself, Protector," Father Holbrook said after a moment, gathering himself. He had never seen such rage in a man before, and it had shaken him somewhat. "A dead man tells no tales," he added, returning the angry look that the Protector flashed at him with one of calmness.

Elijah's body virtually shook with rage, but the calm visage of the old man helped bring him back. He released his grip on the man's throat just enough to allow him to breathe.

"I suggest you tell him what he wishes to know, before your luck turns," Father Holbrook instructed the man, but his warning wasn't necessary.

"R . . . R . . . Rosy Acres . . ." the man gasped, fighting for every breath.

The Protector, satisfied with the answer, pulled the man forward once more and slammed him back into the wall again, knocking him senseless. Then he let him fall to the ground. Father Holbrook winced when the man hit the floor. Then he watched the Protector stroll past him to the dining room. He hurried to catch up.

"I assume they have taken the young lady," he said, skipping along behind the Protector, his little legs almost at a run.

If the Protector heard him, he would not have been able to answer anyway. For as they stepped through the shattered front door, police cars came screeching to a halt directly in front of them. Elijah stopped, as six patrol cars surrounded him.

"Freeze! Don't move!" came the shouts as the officers drew their weapons, taking cover behind the cars.

The Protector's mind raced. He had no time to deal with these fools now. He glanced back at the old man and in one swift, fluid motion, drew Enobe and twisted around, pulling the priest in close, with the blade to his throat.

"Drop your fuckin' guns right the fuck now!" Elijah screamed, turning the priest back and forth. "Drop them or I'll kill this muthafucka right now!" he screamed.

The officers looked around to the head trooper, unsure of how to proceed.

"You think I'm fuckin' playin?" Elijah shouted, seeing the officer's hesitation. He twisted the priest's neck up and back, exposing his neck to Enobe. "Relax, old man. Just play the game," he whispered to Father Holbrook.

"Please! He means it! He's killed before!" Father Holbrook shouted, glad to be of assistance. The lead cop motioned for the officers to drop their weapons and back away. "I've seen him do it! Hundreds of times!" Father Holbrook shouted, determined to make the policemen believe his act. "Why, once in London—"

"That's enough, old man!" Elijah whispered fiercely into the priest's ear, as he made his way to his mother's car.

"What? I was only going to say—"

"The old man is with him!" came a shout from the restaurant.

Elijah froze when he heard the words, standing completely still in front of the open door of his mother's car. The officers froze, too, unsure of how to react.

Then all hell broke loose.

"Shoot him!" the lead officer yelled out, running for his weapon.

"Get down!" Elijah shouted to Father Holbrook, shoving him inside the car as gunfire erupted.

Elijah felt the searing pain as bullets tore through his body. He dove into the car and started it, leaning over as he slammed it into gear and hit the gas.

"Pray, old man, pray!"

Bullets shattered the windshield. He peeked up just enough to guide the car out of the lot and onto the highway, the other cars fast in pursuit. Elijah floored it, sending the black sports car down the highway at a blur.

"Maybe if we talked to them and explained everything," Father Holbrook said shakily, his head pressed back into the seat's headrest, eyes wide.

"Maybe if I were not America's most wanted, and maybe if we were not in bum-fuck Egypt surrounded by rednecks, and maybe if I were a couple of shades lighter . . ." Elijah said sarcastically, veering around and through traffic. He looked into the rearview mirror; the cops were still with him. He had to lose them and lose them quick. Ebonee needed him.

Elijah searched the area ahead and saw an eighteen-wheeler cruising along in the right hand lane. Up ahead, an exit branched off of the highway to the right. He had a plan. He slowed as he came up next to the eighteen-wheeler, the cops gaining ground; they were right behind him.

"Old man," Elijah said, looking over to Father Holbrook, "pray."

He judged it perfectly, swerving in front of the trailer; he came out on the other side, hitting the exit at full speed. The car slammed into the guardrail as he fought to keep it on the road. Only two patrol cars had been able to make the exit, and they were closing fast.

The exit took them to a long dusty road, which traveled in the same direction that they had been heading in on the highway.

"Fuck!" Elijah exclaimed, his eyes glued to the road ahead.

"What? What is it?" Father Holbrook asked, straining to see ahead of them.

He was old and his vision was not as good as the Protector's, so he couldn't see the railroad crossing ahead, and the flashing lights that warned of an approaching train. Elijah gripped the steering wheel tightly and floored it. The train was not yet at the crossing; maybe they could make it.

Maybe not.

Chapter Twelve
INTO THE DARKNESS

"Well howdy do, Director." Agent Parks grinned, placing the red aiming dot of the silenced weapon on Director Moss's forehead.

Director Moss sighed deeply and relaxed a bit. "What are you doing here?" he asked, trying to ignore the fact that the red dot was hovering on his forehead.

"Someone wants you dead," Parks replied, his grin still holding his lips.

"Someone wants me dead?" Moss repeated, slipping off his coat nonchalantly.

Parks sighed at the question. "Yes, someone wants you dead. And that's my final answer," he said sarcastically.

"Let me guess. Is it the same person who wants Agent Lane dead?"

"Hey, you're pretty good at this. Can you figure out who?" Parks sat forward in the chair, the red dot still marking a spot on Moss's head.

"Glenn," Moss replied calmly, tossing his coat onto the bed.

"Is that your final answer?" Parks asked cynically, his grin spreading.

"So Glenn gave you the order to kill Agent Lane, and now he's sent you after me?" Moss asked, ignoring his humor.

"Not quite, I had nothing to do with the attempt on Lane's life. He called in Richards and Boyd for that. I just happened to be there at the time, so I had to play along."

"Richards?" Moss asked, his face twisted up in a look of surprise.

"Yeah, can you believe it? Surprised me, too, boss. It's amazing what some people will do for a buck these days, isn't it?" Parks replied, laughing.

"Do you have it all documented?" Director Moss asked, turning his back on Parks.

"Of course I do, sir. That's why you sent me in, right?" Parks laughed again, the red dot still never leaving its mark.

"Good, then all we have to do is present the evidence to the board and file charges. What about the fugitive?" Moss asked.

"Garland? Damnest thing I ever seen in my life. I put a bullet through his neck myself! Just won't die, I tell you! Shame he killed all them people in the ambulance, cause he was an innocent man up until he went and did something stupid like that."

"You think he did it?" Moss came back.

"Between you and me," he began, looking at the director as if he were amused, "no, I think we both know who killed those men, which brings me back to Richards." He paused as he guided the red dot down to the director's heart. "It must have taken an awful lot of money to make a man turn his back on his own people. I mean, what do you think it would take? Four? Maybe five hundred thousand dollars?" he asked, rising to his feet. Moss remained silent; he knew where this was going. His mind raced as Parks kept talking.

"How about eight hundred and fifty thousand dollars? Yeah, that's about what it would take—for me, at least. Excuse me, won't you?" Parks pulled his cell phone out of his pocket, never taking his eyes—or the red dot—off of Director Moss. "Parks here. Oh? That's a delightful surprise. Saves me the bother of finding her myself. Is she dead yet? Why not? Garland? Okay. I'll get there as soon as I wrap up our loose ends here. Yes, sir, I'll make sure she doesn't walk out of there alive. . . . All of them? Hey, if that's what you want, you got it. Hey, I'll see you in Cancun."

Parks hung up the phone and a smile spread across his face.

"Well, Director, looks like I've got to cut our little conversation short," he said, taking a step toward Moss and raising the gun. "It's a shame really. You really are a good listener. Maybe in your next life you could be a shrink or something." He laughed, his finger tightening on the trigger.

Moss closed his eyes just as he heard the knock at the door.

"Gun!" he yelled, dropping to the floor as the distracted Parks pulled the trigger.

The bullet grazed his temple as the FBI agents kicked in the door. Parks took the first one down with a second shot that went right through the man's eye. Then he crashed through the balcony doors as the other two opened fire. He looked over the side of the balcony to the parking lot below. They were two stories up. He picked a spot and leaped over the rail, relaxing every muscle in his body as he landed on his back on top of a car, shattering the windows.

"Shit, that's gonna leave a bruise." He groaned as he rolled off of the car and landed on his feet, stumbling into a run.

"How is he?" one of the agents asked.

"He's breathing. Looks like the bullet just grazed him.

Better get an ambulance." The other agent kneeled over Moss and began checking him.

"Did you get a look at the intruder?" the kneeling agent asked, getting up to go and check on the other fallen agent.

"Yeah, it was Agent Parks," he answered, returning the man's surprised look with a grim expression.

"I guess that explains why Moss called us in," he said, looking down at his dead associate—his dead friend.

Ebonee groaned. She was semi-conscious. She could hear voices.

"E-E-Elijah," she whispered weakly. But she got no answer.

She was lying down; she could tell that much. She opened her eyes slowly, but could see nothing. Her vision was still blurred. It was dark, that much she could tell. Slowly, she was coming back to the world of the conscious. She remembered watching Elijah walk into the kitchen of the restaurant, and then the men who had come in through the front. She had made them out for trouble when she first saw them, and had even managed to pull her weapon. But then she had felt a sting in her neck, and then things had gone black.

She turned her head to the side, trying to make out the blurry figures in the darkness, trying to understand the whispers she heard all around her. She felt the cold and realized she was naked. She forced her head up only to realize that she was tied down. Her arms were outstretched, and her feet were together. She was tied at the wrists and ankles.

She struggled at the binds for a moment, and then gave up. She sighed deeply and then inhaled a deep breath. She tried to focus on her surroundings—the sounds and the smells. From the darkness and the cold, she figured she had to be somewhere underground. And the smell, she smelled wax burning. Candles maybe, and smoke.

"She's awake," she heard a voice to her right say. Then she

felt a hand on her head as her eyelid was raised open. Still she could only vaguely make out the shape of a face.

"Good, then she won't miss the ceremony," she heard another voice say. "Has the drug worn off yet?"

"Let's see." She heard the man rambling around for a moment, looking for something.

"Aaaggghhh!" Ebonee screamed out as she felt the pain in her hand.

"She can feel," the voice said, dropping the knife to a table.

"Good. Bring the stakes."

Ebonee forced the pain away and opened her eyes, trying desperately to focus on the blurry images around her. Her strength slowly returning, she struggled against the restraints once more. Then she felt his cold touch. On her leg. Moving up higher. She felt the evil in that touch. She thrashed about wildly, trying to remove the unwanted contact.

An evil smile spread across Dalfien's lips as he watched her body twist about at his touch. He leaned in close to her, his lips inches from her face.

"You smell of the Protector," he whispered evilly.

Ebonee could feel the hatred in his cold voice. She turned her head to the side, trying to block him out, but his icy hand grabbed her jaw and held it firmly.

"Are you prepared to die for him?" Dalfien asked, his voice still a whisper.

"Fuck you!" Ebonee shouted, her chest heaving in fear.

Dalfien let his eyes roam down the length of her body. Then he slid his hand from her jaw, slowly tracing a line down her neck, and to her chest. He paused in between her round breasts.

Ebonee's eyes opened wide and her jaw fell open in a silent scream as the vision entered her mind. The huge demon was on top of her, a vile and ugly creature, sweat rolling off its massive shoulders and falling into her eyes, stinging them.

She felt her legs open up, as the creature forced himself into her, tearing her apart.

"Aaaggghh!"

Ebonee's scream echoed through the vast underground complex, causing its inhabitants to look up in wonder.

"That is just the beginning of your torment, my sweet," Dalfien whispered, once again his mouth inches from her quivering lips.

Tears found their way to Ebonee's smooth skin; the vision had been all too real. She tried to force the resonating images and the pain away. She took her mind back to the motel room when Elijah had first held her in his arms. She envisioned herself there, safe within his protective embrace. Her body went perfectly still as she concentrated. She knew Elijah; she knew the Protector would come for her. He would save her from this foul beast.

"Yes, I am counting on that," Dalfien whispered into her ear, reading her thoughts as if she had spoken them plainly.

Her heart shuddered at the words. She realized then, that this was not about her at all. It was a trap. A trap for Elijah.

She heard another person approach, dropping something heavy on the table. She ignored the voices again, going back to her image of Elijah's embrace. She paid no attention to them as they opened her hand and held it open.

Then her world shattered.

"Aaaggghh!" she screamed out in pain as the stake punctured the palm of her hand. She watched in horror as the hand wielding a large mallet went up into the air once more.

"Aaaggghh!" she screamed again, sobbing as the heavy mallet glanced off the top of the stake, crushing two of her fingers. Her mind phased in and out of consciousness as the pain rived through her body. Again, she felt Elijah's loving embrace around her, as the mallet came down again and again. Then there was only the darkness.

* * *

The front end of the train poked onto the road as they drew closer.

"Oh my," Father Holbrook whispered as the train came into his field of vision. The patrol cars eased up a bit, thinking they had him trapped. But Elijah had other ideas.

"Old man, you have a very good head on your shoulders. I suggest you duck if you want to keep it there," the Protector said to the priest, a sinister grin on his lips. The priest looked at him, confused. Then he looked back to the road ahead, and noticed that they were not slowing in the least.

"You're not thinking to—" the old man began, realizing what the Protector was planning to do. "Excellent!" the old man shouted in glee, crawling down onto the floor.

Elijah looked at the old man curiously, not knowing what to make of his gleeful shout. He turned his attention back to the train, slowing a bit to time it just right. When he saw the flat car, he slammed onto the gas pedal, hurdling the sports car at the train at over ninety miles an hour. He dropped his head down at the last moment as glass exploded around them. He felt the excruciating pain in his left shoulder as the bottom of the train tore the windshield and the top of the headrests off of the car.

He ignored the pain and forced himself up. Looking back at the train and the empty road behind him, he laughed. Then he looked forward again to where the windshield used to be, his expression turning grim.

"My mom is going to kill me."

Elijah and Father Holbrook drove for about an hour, hoping to see some sort of sign or indication that they were heading in the right direction. It was almost noon, and Elijah's urgency to save Ebonee was eating away at his patience. There seemed to be no end to this road they were on, and there was nothing as far as the eye could see except green grass and pastures, cows, horses, and the occasional barn.

Elijah was still cruising at about ninety when the right

front tire blew out. The car swerved off the road into the dirt, sending up a cloud of dust. When they finally came to a stop, Father Holbrook, waving his hand in the air as the dust settled around them, was the first to make the discovery.

"Oh my, how convenient," he announced, looking to his right, at the signpost the car had slid up to.

It read: *ROSY ACRES 5 miles.*

Elijah jumped out of the car and winced as he hit the ground. His shoulder had not yet completely healed. Grunting the pain away, he made his way around to the front of the car to inspect the tire. There was hardly any tire left to inspect, though. He walked back to the trunk and opened it with the key. Then he slammed the trunk down angrily, remembering that he had borrowed his mother's jack and tools to fix his own car a while back, but he had not gotten a chance to return them.

"Let's go, old man," he said, walking away from the car.

"Oh, yes, yes . . . coming," the priest said, shaking the dust from his robes as he climbed out of the car, only to trip and fall into the dirt. Elijah sighed deeply and shook his head as the old man clambered back to his feet.

"No need to fret over me; I'll be quite fine. Just a little slip, that's all," Father Holbrook explained, hurrying to catch up to the Protector.

A few yards behind the sign was a road that led up and over a grassy hill, disappearing into the trees. They made their way along the road, the old man huffing along, trying to keep pace with the Protector.

"I take it you have a plan, young Protector?" Father Holbrook managed to say between gasps of air, drawing no response from Elijah.

Elijah's mind was deep in thought. He wondered if Ebonee was okay, if she was being tortured at the hands of the evil demon, if she was even still alive. He shook his head violently at the thought. He had to believe she was still alive.

It was his only motivation at the moment. Father Holbrook noticed the gesture, and stopped abruptly.

"You are not the only one who seeks to help the girl, young one!" he exclaimed to the Protector's back. "You are not alone!" he shouted after him.

The words seemed to have some effect on Elijah.

Alone.

He had thought himself that for a very long time. He had spent most of his life feeling just that way. Alone. After the death of his grandmother, he had gone into a shell, never revealing any of his emotions to anyone and keeping all his fears and worries to himself. Then he had met Taysia, and she opened up his heart, only to be ripped from him by fate.

Now, there was Ebonee, a second chance at a once in a lifetime find. He was determined not to lose that chance. He did not respond to Father Holbrook's words, but Father Holbrook realized with a smile that he did slow down a bit.

"You love her," Father Holbrook commented out of nowhere as they approached the tree line. Elijah tried to ignore the words, but he found them overwhelming.

"What do you know of love, old man?" he answered, trying to fight back his tears.

"Do not be fooled by my age and these dusty robes, young one," he began, feeling that he had opened up some sort of communication with the distant Protector, "for I was not always so. Do you think I came out of my mother's womb with a Bible in my hand, reciting the twenty-third Psalm? No, no, I was once young and free of heart as you are now, my friend." He paused, his mind going back to those times, times of fun and irresponsibility. His tone lowered and his expression saddened. "And yes, I have known love."

Elijah looked over at the man for the first time since they had begun walking, hearing the sadness behind his words.

"You see, there was a young lady by the name of Marybelle. The most beautiful lady I had ever laid eyes upon," he began, pausing to look up at the trees as he remembered her lovely smile. "And charming, too. The sweetest woman you could have known was my Marybelle. I remember the feeling I would get when I would hold her close to me and she would proclaim her deepest love for me." He took a deep breath, sighing as he did so. "We were to be married; I recall the moment I proposed to her. She had accepted without hesitation, the happiness in her smile and in her voice— it was what I lived for." He smiled, seeing her face once more in his mind's eye.

"Well?" Elijah asked after a moment, bringing the priest from his daze.

"Well, what?" the priest replied, at a loss for a moment.

"Did you marry her?" Elijah asked eagerly, caught up in the story of love the old man was telling.

"Oh, yes. That," Father Holbrook replied, his memory returning to him. "Alas, no, we would never be married, my Marybelle and I." He sighed, staring off into space.

"Well why not? You both loved each other, right?" Elijah asked, not understanding.

"Oh, yes! Yes, we did indeed. But I soon came to realize that love was not meant for me; my Marybelle was killed in a terrorist bombing in Southern Ireland a week before we were to be wed."

"That is why you joined the church," Elijah offered, understanding the old man's pain.

"Yes. I hid myself behind those huge doors, afraid—afraid of life and the pain it brought with it. I knew I would never find another to replace my Marybelle," Father Holbrook said, coming to stand next to the Protector.

Elijah closed his eyes slowly and came to a stop, his guilt weighing him down as he thought of Taysia. He, too, had known the same. He could not deny his love for Ebonee. But how could he have let himself think of even replacing Taysia in the first place? How could he allow himself to fall in love again, and so completely?

"But I was wrong, so wrong. For forty some odd years, I hid away in that church, thinking that I would never find someone to replace my Marybelle. It took me forty years to figure out what you have solved in a mere three days, Protector." Father Holbrook stared up into Elijah's eyes intently.

Elijah looked at him, confused. Yet he felt the emotion welling up in him, felt the tears.

"I-I-I don't understand." Elijah looked away from the Father's intense gaze.

"My Marybelle is gone. Just as your Taysia is gone." He whispered the last words. "Yet you had the courage to move on. You realized what I did not: that you're not *replacing* Taysia. Nothing will ever replace her memory, but it does not stop you from building new memories to go with your memories of her. I know now that my Marybelle would have wanted me to do the same. I envy you, young Protector. I wish I would have had the courage and wisdom that you now possess when I was your age."

Elijah lowered his head in shame, wiping away the tear that had found its way to his face. If only the old man knew. Then a warm smile found its way to his lips. Maybe he did know.

"Thank you, old man," Elijah said softly, his guilt gone as he swallowed back the rest of his tears. Father Holbrook returned his warm smile with one of his own.

"Enough of that! Now, we had better hurry. We have a damsel to rescue!" Father Holbrook exclaimed, rushing forward only to trip on his own robes, sprawling out onto the grass.

"Oh my, I seem to have misstepped again," he mumbled to himself. This time Elijah laughed as he watched the old man scramble to his feet, waving Elijah's helping hand away.

"You don't walk much, do you, Father?"

Elijah smiled as Father Holbrook glared at the ground as though it were a mortal enemy. His reply came out in a rush of air, as Elijah shoved the old man back to the ground; a car had sped past them. If they had been seen, then it was not apparent. Father Holbrook reached out and grabbed a broken tree limb and used it to help pull himself up. Elijah's eyes followed the car until it disappeared over the hill not too far ahead. He looked back to the priest and chuckled.

"That stick is almost taller than you, old man," he quipped.

"It will help keep me out of the dirt." Then he looked at Elijah with a smirk. "And perhaps keep you from shoving me into it as well!" he exclaimed, shaking the stick at him menacingly.

They proceeded along, following the road just inside of the tree line. When they came to the hill they stopped once more. Ahead of them there was a gate about eight feet high and topped with barbed wire. On the road there were sentries armed with automatic rifles, guarding the entry to the compound, which stood maybe a half mile from the gate. It was a monstrous building that resembled a small mansion. Other smaller buildings dotted the area around it. Elijah approached the gate cautiously. A low hum reverberated from it as he neared.

"Electricity," he commented to himself.

"Now would be a good time for that plan I asked you about," Father Holbrook sneered, leaning on his walking staff.

"What good will a plan do us? He knows I'm here. Just as I know he's in there . . . with Ebonee," Elijah replied, turning as he spoke the words. "Shhh, listen," he said suddenly, hearing a sound. "Come on!" Elijah pulled the Father along hurriedly. They ran back over the hill to see a truck slowly rumbling up the road.

"Get out there and stop the truck, old man," Elijah said to the priest, who looked at him like he was crazy.

The Father began to protest. "How do you sugg—"

"I don't care how you do it! You wanted a plan, this is it. Now stop the truck!"

Father Holbrook threw his hands out wide and looked up to the sky, and then made his way to the side of the road, just inside of the trees. He waited until the slow moving vehicle pulled up to where he was hiding, and then he ran out, deceptively fast. As the truck moved past, he slammed his stick into it, then sprawled out behind it on the road, something he had become quite good at recently, Elijah noted.

The truck skidded to a halt and two men jumped out and walked back to investigate.

"What the hell was that?"

Elijah could hear them as he waited to make his move.

"Oh shit! You hit a priest!" one of the men exclaimed, laughing.

"Hey! Father! Are you okay?" the driver asked, standing over Father Holbrook. "What the hell are you doing out—" The rest of his words came out in a high pitched squeal as Father Holbrook's walking stick found the man's groin.

"What the he—" the other man began to say, but his words, too, were lost in unconsciousness as the Protector grabbed him by the neck from behind, slamming his head forward into the back of the truck. Father Holbrook winced as the man's head clanged loudly off the metal.

"Is such violence always necessary?" Father Holbrook asked, calmly whacking the remaining man over the back of the head with his walking stick.

"Only when I'm fighting," Elijah said, grinning as he dragged the man's body over to the trees.

"Do you know how to drive, old man?" Elijah asked the priest.

"Yes, but it's been a while." Father Holbrook eyed the truck curiously.

Elijah dumped the other unconscious man's body off the road and walked back to the truck, opening up the back door. It was a laundry truck. He walked to the front and grabbed an extra uniform that was hanging up on a rack. Walking back to the rear of the truck, he tossed the clothes to the priest.

"Put these on."

"What about you?" the priest asked, catching the clothes.

"Just get the truck to the building, and then we'll go from there," Elijah said, helping the old man into the truck.

Father Holbrook donned the clothes and then walked to the front of the truck. Sitting down in the driver's seat, he waited for Elijah to give him the go-ahead. Elijah found an empty laundry bin and swung a leg over the edge.

"Let's go, old man," he shouted to the front of the truck.

Father Holbrook took a deep breath and then put the truck into first gear, grinding the clutch as he pushed the gearshift forward. He winced at the loud sound and pressed down on the clutch harder. Finally he got it in gear. Sighing heavily again, he eased his foot up. The truck lurched forward sharply, unceremoniously dumping Elijah onto the floor in the back.

"Ouch!" Elijah exclaimed, as the truck moved forward.

Father Holbrook smiled as he heard the Protector hit the floor. "That serves you right! Push me into the dirt, will you!" he muttered under his breath, enjoying the moment.

"What was that, old man?" Elijah asked, climbing back into the bin.

"Nothing!" the priest said quickly, trying to contain his smile.

The truck crawled to a stop as they approached the closed gate. One of the sentries walked over to the driver's side and looked at the driver curiously.

"Hey, I've never seen you on this route before. Where's Fred?" he asked, looking at Father Holbrook suspiciously.

"Oh, yes. Fred, he's . . . home sick I'm afraid," he answered somewhat shakily.

"Sick, huh?" the guard said skeptically. "He seemed just fine yesterday," he added, motioning another guard to check the truck out.

"Well, between you and I, I think he called out just to piss off our manager. He's a real pain in the ass," Father Holbrook said, trying his best to sound like an American working class man.

The guard chuckled. "He's okay, Sam," he shouted to the other guard, who was already inside of the truck and eyeing the laundry bin. Elijah held his breath as he heard him approaching.

"I know what you mean. Sounds like something Fred would do," the guard said, handing the old man a clipboard. "Here you go, sign in."

The guard in the back of the truck turned as he heard the other guard say it was okay. But then he decided to check the bin anyway. Elijah heard the man turn, and relaxed a bit, then tensed up once more as he heard his footsteps return.

"You know where you're going?" the guard asked, taking the clipboard back from Father Holbrook.

"Actually, a little guidance would help," he said, glancing nervously back over his shoulder, as the guard inside had not yet exited.

"Take it around to the back of the building. There's a ramp and a set of double doors. You can't miss it. Inside, just take the hallway to the right, and the laundry room is the first door on your left," he instructed, walking to open the gate.

The guard inside of the truck threw back the dirty laundry, and his eyes went wide. Elijah grabbed the man by the throat and pulled him into the bin. The guard struggled and tried to scream out, but Elijah slipped his arm around his neck and gripped him tightly in a chokehold, cutting off his air supply.

Father Holbrook stepped onto the gas and drove the truck through the open gate.

"Thank you, I'll see you on my way out," he shouted to the guard as he passed, waving a stubby hand out of the window. The guard watched as the truck drove past, waving back as he closed the gate.

"Sam, grab me some coffee, will ya?" he shouted back over his shoulder. "Sam?" he said again, turning about curiously. "Now where in the hell has he run off to now!" he added angrily, stalking to the guard booth to get his own coffee, muttering something about incompetence.

Elijah held the man in the chokehold until he felt him stop moving. When the truck came to a stop he released him and climbed out of the bin, checking his pulse.

"Alive?" Father Holbrook asked as he walked to the rear of the truck.

"Yes. It would be so much easier if I could just kill them all," Elijah muttered to himself as he looked out of the back window.

The rear of the building was alive with activity. Men were moving about, carrying boxes out of the building to another truck, loading it up. A third truck was being unloaded at the same time.

"What do you think it is they're loading?" Father Holbrook asked, moving to stand next to Elijah.

"I don't know, but I can guess that it's not Girl Scout cookies," Elijah replied, catching a glimpse of a black man who had walked out of the building and was now instructing some of the men on how to load the truck.

"That's strange," Elijah observed. "A chocolate chip cookie

in vanilla wafer land." He wondered what the man could be doing here. "Come on, old man." Elijah returned his thoughts to the business at hand.

He pulled the unconscious man out of the bin and tied his hands behind his back. Then he gagged him and secured him to a metal tie-down loop in the wall of the truck near the floor, tossing some dirty laundry on top of him. He climbed back into the bin and looked at the priest.

"Get me inside," he said, pulling the dirty linen over his head.

Father Holbrook looked around the truck and found the clean uniforms that were meant to be delivered, hanging on a rack. He laid them over the top of the bin and threw the door open. He stepped down from the truck and pulled the bin to the edge. Bracing himself, he pulled the wheels over the edge. The weight of the bin shifted forward, threatening to tip the bin over as Father Holbrook struggled to keep it upright.

"Here you go." One of the men stopped and helped the old man pull the bin from the truck.

"Thank you, son. Thank you," Father Holbrook said quickly, hurrying the bin along.

He made it inside without further incident. Following the guard's directions he made his way to the laundry room. Once inside, he closed the door and locked it.

"Okay. We're in," he said to Elijah.

Elijah pushed the linen aside and climbed out of the bin, ignoring the chill bumps that ran along his skin. He walked past Father Holbrook and cracked the door open, only to pull it closed quickly as two armed men stepped out of a door farther down the hall. He thought for a moment that he would be able to get around easier if he used one of the uniforms, but he quickly dismissed the idea, remembering the color of his skin. He waited until the footsteps passed and peeked back out into the hall. Seeing the way clear, he looked back to the priest.

"Stay here as long as you can. I'll meet you in a while," he said, ducking out of the room before the old man could protest.

"But—" Father Holbrook began as the door closed. He shook his head, swallowing the rest of his words. Then he looked back to the bin, and an idea came to mind. He quickly emptied the bin of its contents and pushed it back into the hall. He made his way back to the double doors, watching the men carrying the boxes to a door further down the hall in the opposite direction. He waited until the last of the men entered the room and quickly made his way to the door opposite the door the men had entered.

He ducked inside quickly, praying that the room was unoccupied. His prayers were answered. He looked around the large storeroom and then cracked the door open once more. The men had come back out and the last one had just disappeared through the double doors. He took a deep breath and ran across the hall, stepping into the room just as the next set of workers came into the hall carrying more boxes. He looked around nervously at the huge room. Boxes were stacked on tables and in corners as workers unloaded and reloaded the boxes on tables in the center of the room. He slipped into a corner and pulled one of the boxes down. Kneeling, he opened the box carefully.

"Oh my," he whispered to himself, reaching into the box to pull out what appeared to him to be small chunks of soap.

Dalfien knew the Protector was close; he could feel his presence.

"You really take this cult stuff seriously, don't you?" Agent Parks asked as he looked up at Ebonee.

The candlelight reflected off of her creamy brown skin, as

she hung from the large cross erected over the sacrificial altar in the center of the underground chamber. Blood dripped from her hands and feet, which had been staked into the wood. Her head hung down, her chin in her chest.

Dalfien ignored the man's words as the four men, who had volunteered to receive a 'special gift' from their dark master, entered the chamber from the north entrance. He would be ready for the Protector when he came.

"Why don't you just let me put a bullet in her head?" Parks asked, walking up to stand next to Charles.

"You can do with the girl whatever you please—after she has served her purpose," Dalfien answered, looking over the four men and preparing himself to make the mental trip to his own plane of existence.

Agent Parks looked back up at Ebonee as he thought about Dalfien's words. His eyes followed a path slowly up her legs, to her shapely hips, then up farther to her bare, voluptuous breasts. "Whatever I please?" he whispered to himself, a wicked grin finding his lips. Then he turned back to Charles just as Dalfien was returning from his mental journey. "How can you be sure he will come?" he asked, looking at the four men curiously as they walked away. He thought he saw their eyes glowing a dim red. He shook the thought from his head and looked back at Charles.

"He is already here," Dalfien said absently, motioning for his servant to come over.

Agent Parks raised an eyebrow. He was just about to ask him how in the hell he knew that, but decided to let it go.

"There is an intruder in the complex. See to it that he finds his way here," Dalfien instructed the servant.

Agent Parks shrugged and turned to walk away.

"Where are you going?" Dalfien asked him, his eyes burning into Agent Parks.

"I-I-I was going to find someplace to . . . ummm . . ." Parks stammered under the evil gaze.

"Stay," Dalfien replied, an idea forming in his dark mind.

Agent Parks swallowed hard, unable to resist Charles's command.

"You may be of use to me," Dalfien hissed.

Elijah found his way to a set of steps leading down. Somehow, he had avoided being spotted. He didn't buy that for a second. He could feel that the demon was closer now. And he could tell by the way the guards would always seem to appear behind him or in front of him at certain points, not acknowledging him, yet always there, seemingly directing him along. Herding him like a sheep being led to the slaughter.

"Let's see how sharp your shears are, fiend," the Protector whispered to himself as he made it to the bottom of the steps.

He glanced around the corner, seeing no one. He noted that there were no windows in this hallway, and from the distance of it, it had to run past the walls of the building itself, underground. There were no doors along the length of it, at least none that he could see.

He was heading in the right direction; he could tell by the increase of the chill bumps running along his skin and the subtle vibration of the twin blades at his waist. He glanced once again down the long hallway. He would be exposed for too long a period of time once he started down the hall.

Voices from the top of the steps spurred him on. He broke into a run near the middle of the hall, glancing over his shoulder to see if there was any pursuit. There wasn't. They were definitely directing him, but as long as the feelings kept getting stronger, he didn't care. He slowed as he neared the end of the hallway, approaching what appeared to be a dead end.

He walked up to the far wall, searching it for some kind of switch or anything that would give him a clue on how to proceed. Finding nothing, he stepped back, looking back down the hall curiously. Four guards watched his every move, but they made no move toward him.

The Protector inhaled deeply, an angry scowl finding his face. He was growing tired of these games. He decided to take his anger out on the guards. He took one step toward them and froze. The far wall of the hall began to move, turning like a revolving door, revealing a dark passage beyond.

Elijah didn't hesitate for a moment. He stepped through the opening and headed down the passage. Torches flickered in sconces along the stone walls of the tunnel as the wind blew in from the now closing passage. Elijah walked along the tunnel cautiously, having to stoop in some sections of the passage as the roof lowered and then rose again. It was about wide enough for two people to walk side by side with their elbows tightly at their sides.

He walked for what seemed to be an eternity for him, longing to see his Ebonee again. Finally he could see light flickering from an opening up ahead. He proceeded carefully. Then he heard a scream. A woman's scream.

Ebonee's scream.

Bringing Soul Seeker and Enobe to the front, he charged blindly into the dimly lit chamber.

Chapter Thirteen
ONE LITTLE, TWO LITTLE, THREE LITTLE DEMONS

Father Holbrook pushed the door open and peeked inside. The room was empty. He walked inside; it seemed to be some sort of records room. He didn't know what it was he was looking for, but he began searching through the shelves and in the drawers. He made his way over to a large desk in the center of the room. He walked behind it, rummaging through the drawers and found a notebook that had the letters *NP* written across the front. Digging deeper, he found several more, each with initials of its own. Opening one of them, he found a list of names, monetary amounts, dates, and what appeared to be weight measurements.

"Oh my. I do believe this may be important," he mumbled to himself, stuffing the pads into his laundry bag.

He rummaged some more, finding a map of the complex. His heart stopped as the door knob to the room turned. A man entered the room, flicking on the light. He paused. Did he hear something move? His eyes looked around the room suspiciously. Seeing nothing, he shrugged.

"I need to get some sleep," he mumbled to himself as he walked over to the desk. He was just about to open the drawer to retrieve the notebook to record his newest entries when the door opened.

"Hey, Jimmy. Your wife's out front—says she needs the keys or something," a guard informed him. Father Holbrook was still holding his breath, curled up tightly under the desk.

"Damn that woman! It's always something with her!" he shouted, heading back to the door briskly.

Father Holbrook wasted no time; as soon as the door closed, he scrambled up and ran over to it. He waited a moment to make sure the man was gone, and then he stepped back into the hall, throwing his sack over his shoulder and walking back the way he came.

He found the hallway he had originally come in through and noticed that the men were no longer working. He walked to the double doors and jumped back as he saw the men gathered around the truck. Then he saw the men who had originally been driving the truck, standing and rubbing their heads as the guard was helped down out of the truck.

"Oh my. Looks like our plan has a few snags," he muttered to himself, rushing back to the storeroom where he had hidden the laundry bin.

He leaned back up against the door, wondering what exactly he should do now. He knew it would only be a matter of time before the whole complex was on alert and looking for them. Well, whatever happened, he decided that he would rather be by the Protector's side than alone when it did.

He reached inside of his laundry sack and pulled out the detailed map of the complex. He figured that since they were dealing with demons, the most natural direction to go in search of one would be down.

He located his storeroom on the map and charted his course to the large chamber underneath the complex. Then he folded the map up and stuck it in his back pocket, sighing deeply. He said a quick prayer and cracked open the door. The guards had not yet begun their search. He darted out of the room and made his way toward the stairs that would lead him to the lower levels of the complex.

Dalfien tensed himself as he felt the Protector approaching. He stood atop the altar next to the hanging form of Ebonee Lane.

Agent Parks slipped to the side and behind the upraised platform, seeing Dalfien's attention off of him. Ebonee rolled her head to the side. She couldn't feel the pain any more from her hands and her feet. The ropes around her wrist had cut off the circulation, causing her hands to go numb. She felt the dagger's tip against her side, though, as Dalfien ran its cold edge down to her hip. Blood flowed down her leg from the newest wound the dagger had created.

"Scream out for him," Dalfien hissed into her ear, bringing the dagger's tip back up to the wound in her side.

Ebonee's vision had returned, but she had chosen to keep her eyes closed tightly. Tears still managed to escape her closed eyelids, though, as the pain from the wound and the evil in Dalfien's voice tore at her. She shook her head violently, trying to deny his commands. She would die before she let Elijah fall into this evil one's trap. She focused her mind on that place again, in Elijah's arms. She felt his soft hands upon her face.

"Aaaggghhh!"

Her scream echoed throughout the chamber and down the four tunnels again as the dagger dug into her flesh. Her face contorted in pain and suddenly her eyes were open, staring into those of her torturer. She saw the pure evil in those cold eyes, the hatred. But she neither flinched nor turned her gaze. Nor did she scream out anymore. She was beyond pain, beyond any torture that the demon could devise.

She returned that hateful look with one of her own. One

born out of pain, despair, and rage. Dalfien flinched at the woman's sudden glare. He pushed the dagger in deeper, their eyes still locked in a test of wills. He soon realized that she was beyond physical pain. The cold look in her eyes told him that much.

Ebonee's body shook from the sheer hatred she held for this demon at that moment. Dalfien chuckled awkwardly and tried another approach. Ebonee felt the demon then, trying to force his way into her mind. But she knew the truth of the beast now, and Dalfien found he could not find a way through the wall of hatred and rage she had built in her mind.

Scowling angrily, he slapped the insolent woman across the face with the back of his hand. Ebonee's head jerked to the side from the force of the slap, her eyes closed. Suddenly the rage and hatred were gone, replaced by a sadness that brought tears flowing from her now open eyes, eyes that watched as Elijah charged into the chamber with his blades gleaming in the light of the torches and candles as he charged into the trap.

Elijah ran into the chamber, ignoring the man standing next to the opening. He stopped cold in his tracks as his eyes found the altar and what was on top of it. His hands shook visibly as his eyes took in the sight.

A strange calmness fell over him as he looked at her. Blood dripped from her feet, which were staked to the cross she hung upon. Her hands, too, dripped blood from the holes driven into them by more stakes. And her eyes, he saw in them sadness as she gazed at him, her tears falling unabated. She looked as though her will had been crushed. Elijah saw only hopelessness in those beautiful brown eyes, a hopelessness that seemed so out of place. Then his eyes fell upon the wound in Ebonee's side, Charles, and the dagger he held in his hand, still dripping with Ebonee's blood.

Their eyes met then, and the world seemed to not exist any longer. Dalfien knew then that there would be no trap, no surrendering, no bargaining for the woman's life as he looked into hatred and rage much deeper than his own. He brought the dagger up to rest underneath the girl's chin.

"Stop where you are!" he commanded, drawing a drop of blood from Ebonee's neck.

But if the Protector even heard the words, they would not have stopped him. If he would have taken a moment to think, Elijah probably would have stopped at the command, fearing for Ebonee's life. But he was no longer in the realm of logical thought. The rage was too much, and the pain and hatred would not be denied its release. He only felt the soft hum of the blades. He only felt the desire to kill. To hurt.

"Kill him!" Dalfien shouted out, seeing that there would be no talking.

He looked around frantically for something. Finding it scrambling about in the shadows, he jumped down and grabbed Agent Parks roughly by the neck.

A single purpose drove the Protector as he stalked toward the altar and the source of his pain. He sensed the man approaching him from behind. Without a thought, he dropped down low, causing the man to flip over his kneeling form and land roughly on his buttocks. A second later his head was rolling away into the shadows of the chamber.

"Elijah . . . no," Ebonee whispered weakly, seeing the hate and rage in his eyes. There was no compassion there, no mercy. Only hate and rage. These were not the eyes that had captured her heart. No, these eyes did not belong to her Elijah. She had to bring him back; she had to find her Elijah. She refused to let it end like this. She would not lose him— not now, not ever.

"Elijah . . . please, come back. I need you!" she cried out through her tears. But Elijah neither slowed nor even acknowledged her words. His eyes stayed the same, cold and uncaring. Hope drained from her expression and she lowered her head in submission.

"Elijah . . . I love you," she whispered, closing her eyes. Elijah was right beneath her now, and the words found their way home,to his heart.

He paused and looked back to the decapitated body. Then he looked up to Ebonee, the warmth and love returning to his gaze, as the three other men closed in on him.

Father Holbrook heard the screams from the chamber as he made his way down the southern tunnel. He knew the screams belonged to Ebonee. He picked up his pace, moving his tired old legs along as fast as they would carry him. What he would do when he got there, he didn't know.

Suddenly, the tunnel dead-ended, and the Father skidded to a halt. He looked at the wall in confusion and pulled out the map.

"The chamber should be right here," he whispered, looking back to the wall.

Suddenly the wall shifted and began to turn, revealing the long, eerie tunnel beyond. Father Holbrook was then knocked from his feet as Agent Parks crashed into him and continued down the tunnel. Father Holbrook looked after the man curiously until the door once again started to shift. He crawled through the opening just as it slid to a close with a loud thud, as did the rest of the exits, trapping them all beneath the complex.

The Protector, regaining control over the rage, was at a loss as the three men fell upon him. He was forced down to the ground. He felt his ribs crack as the men pounded their fists into him. He fought them desperately, struggling to regain his feet.

He had to say the words.

An arm found its way around his neck and he felt the ligaments there tearing. On his hands and knees now, still with Soul Seeker and Enobe in his hands, he kicked out at one of the men, catching him in the chest, sending him flying backward. He tried to say the words, but found he could not draw any air. He twisted and turned frantically, grabbing at the man's arm, dropping his blades.

Still, the blows from the other man came in, sending flashing lights exploding into his vision. One of the men paused as he saw Soul Seeker lying on the ground; he picked it up, only to howl out in pain, dropping the suddenly red-hot weapon back to the stone floor.

Elijah felt the darkness closing in on him as he gasped for air. His struggling slowed, and he tried his best to cover up from the pounding the two men were giving him. *So this is how it ends.* His eyes found the altar and the cross above. His only thought was to look upon Ebonee one last time before he died.

Ebonee watched as the three men tackled Elijah to the ground; she thought for a moment that she had seen the light return to his eyes. She dared to hope that somehow they would make it out of this horrible place, but then she saw the man choking Elijah, and the others beating him unmercifully. She saw Elijah's movements slowly lessen. Then she saw his eyes as their gazes locked. She saw resignation there, and more so, she saw the love that had captured her heart. But there was no fight left in that gaze. No hope.

"Elijah! Nooo!" Ebonee screamed out, her tears falling freely. She shook at the ropes and stakes holding her to the cross violently in desperation, ignoring the pain that ran through her body from the action.

"Fight them, Elijah!" she cried though her tears. "Get up! Don't you give up on me!" Her chest heaved as she sobbed. "Please, please, Elijah . . . get up!" Her last words came out in a whispered cry, as she realized that he could no longer hear her.

Elijah felt the darkness closing in on him, as he heard Ebonee's frantic pleas. But he could not find the strength to go to her. He felt a tear on his own cheek, a tear that was quickly knocked away by a hammering fist. As the darkness closed around him, he thought for a moment that he heard another voice, a familiar one, shouting something into the darkness of the chamber.

"*Anal nathrak doth dien dienve!*" Father Holbrook shouted, walking into the light of the torches.

Hope returned to Ebonee's eyes as the old man came into view. She watched as the three men suddenly stood and began to jerk violently, dropping Elijah to the stone floor. She found her voice again as the demons began to assume their true forms.

"Elijah! Get up, damn you!" she screamed with an urgency fueled by love, hope, and fear. "You made a promise to me! A promise I expect you to keep!" she cried out, trying to force her will into him. "Get up, Elijah! Don't you die on me!" Her hope increased tenfold when she saw his body stir.

"Elijah! I know you can hear me! Please, you have to get up!" Her voice failed her, the words were no more than a mere heavy rasp drowned in her sobs, as the demons were now standing over Elijah's prone body.

Ebonee shook at her restraints again, causing the ropes holding one side of the cross up to give, sending the cross lurching forward and twisting to the right, snapping to a halt at a weird angle. Ebonee cried out in pain as the force of the snap sent waves of pain from her staked hands into her head.

Elijah heard that cry.

He forced himself to breathe deeply and roll over onto his hands and knees to regain his strength. But the demons were upon him then. Great and terrible they were. Their dark red skin glistened in the torch light. All were seven footers with muscles that bulged as if they were trying to escape the confines of their skin. But there was something different about these demons.

They were armed.

One wielded a huge flaming sword, another a club-like weapon, and the last carried a chain with a spiked ball dangling from its end.

"Nooo!" Ebonee cried out as the demon with the sword raised its hand into the air, ready to split Elijah in half.

Ebonee slammed her eyes shut as she saw the demon's arm descend. Then she heard the old man again, shouting out. She couldn't understand the words he was saying; it sounded like another language. But the demons understood it all too well. Their huge hands went to their ears as they howled out in pain. They turned about frantically, searching for the source of their torment.

The demon carrying the club reacted first, hurling its weapon blindly in the direction of the voice. It flew harmlessly above the priest, striking the low, sloping ceiling and dislodging a huge stone that fell directly on top of the old man's head.

Father Holbrook collapsed as the stone rendered him unconscious. With the voice silenced, the demons turned their attention back to the Protector. But he was gone. They looked around curiously, trying to find the half-dead human. But the Protector was anything but half-dead.

He watched them from the shadows of the altar that he had scrambled behind when the old man had diverted their attention. He only needed to catch his breath. He prayed that the old man was okay. His eyes went up to the drooping form of Ebonee, hanging with her tear-filled eyes closed. But she was still breathing, he noted, seeing the rise and fall of her chest.

He intently watched the three huge creatures stalking about, searching the shadows for him. His eyes caught something else as he looked around the chamber. A human form huddled in the shadows. The man's blonde hair gave him away.

It was Charles. But something was wrong. He no longer felt the emanations of power that he had felt upon entering. He felt the three demons now present, but none of them fit the power of the beast he sought. These were lesser demons. He would have to deal with that later. Right now, he had to get Ebonee down. But he couldn't do it with three angry and very large weapon-carrying demons in the chamber. He would have to kill them.

All of them.

He took a deep breath to steady himself, letting the soft hum of Soul Seeker and Enobe comfort him. One of the demons howled out, as it found the body of the old man. It raised its club into the air, intending to make sure the human did not rise and utter those blasphemous words again. Another howl filled the chamber, a howl of pain, as Soul Seeker sliced through the darkness and embedded itself up to the hilt in the demon's chest.

The Protector came in right behind it, Enobe stabbing at the demon's heart unmercifully. The demon had never felt such pain before, as Soul Seeker sucked at its very soul. The other two demons howled in rage and charged toward their fallen brother. The Protector snatched Soul Seeker up from the lifeless body of the demon, as its last vision—a white-haired demon with fire in his eyes—filled the other demons' minds with rage. He stepped over the already decomposing body and waited.

The sword-wielding demon arrived first, its sword slamming down into the stone floor where the Protector had once stood, sending chunks of stone and sparks flying from the force of the swing. Its eyes went wide as dark blood seemed to appear out of nowhere along its outstretched arm. Enobe and Soul Seeker struck repeatedly from the demon's side as it howled in rage, feeling the bite of those terrible blades.

The Protector dove into a roll as the spiked ball sailed over him and bounced heavily off one of the stone columns that supported the ceiling. Dust and debris fell from the ceiling in complaint. The Protector came up on his feet out of the roll behind the first demon, his blades stabbing at the creature's exposed backside. The demon howled again as the blades bit at him, swinging its arm around in a powerful backhand attack. At the same time, the ball came back in again, seeking the Protector's back. He knew immediately that he wouldn't be able to dodge them both.

He braced himself as best he could and accepted the backhand, which sent him flying to the side and into the stone column, bringing more dust and debris down on top of them. The Protector winced in pain as he slid down the stone column, and closed his eyes for a brief second.

When he opened them, he saw a flaming sword slicing in, aiming to decapitate him. He ducked away at the last moment, fighting the pain away as the entire column exploded into dust.

He worked his way in between the two demons, an idea forming in his mind. He faced off with the sword-wielding creature, stabbing at it repeatedly until he heard the rustle of the chain as it uncoiled. He thrust Soul Seeker and Enobe ahead low, dropping his body to the ground flat in anticipation. The demon, thinking itself to have a clean shot to split the Protector's head open, raised its sword up high, just as the spiked ball slammed into its face, crushing bone.

The Protector slipped Soul Seeker back into its sheath and reached out for the chain, grabbing it just as the demon pulled it back in. He went for the ride, enjoying the demon's confused look as Enobe slashed across its throat, sending its headless body falling to the ground to land with a thud that

shook the entire chamber. But the chamber didn't stop
shaking, as more dust and debris began to fall from above.

Large sections of stone fell to the ground, as the weight of
the ceiling, no longer supported by the smashed column,
began to fall down upon them.

Father Holbrook groaned and rolled over onto his back.
He opened his eyes just in time to see a huge boulder fall
from the ceiling directly above his head. He froze in fear,
closing his eyes, praying like never before. His prayers were
answered as Enobe shattered the boulder into dust. Father
Holbrook opened his eyes to see the Protector staring down
at him.

"Haven't you slept enough today, old man?" Elijah asked,
offering the priest a hand. "Get her down," the Protector instructed, handing the priest Enobe. Then he remembered
the demon, howling as it had attempted to pick up Soul
Seeker. But the priest took the weapon without concern and
headed over to the altar as the ceiling threatened to smash
down upon them all.

Elijah stalked back toward the dazed remaining demon,
its canine maw horribly disfigured by the spiked ball. The
Protector walked in calmly, knowing that this battle was already over, which further fueled the rage of the beast. Its
angry howl came out gurgled as it raised its flaming sword
into the air with both hands. Still the Protector moved in
calmly, showing no hint of fear, as the sword came down. A
quick step to the side and a downward slash from Soul
Seeker left the demon's eyes wide, staring at the bloody
stumps it used to call hands. A simple twist of the blade, and
another slash left the creature headless.

Father Holbrook winced as he pulled Ebonee's hands
from the stakes. He looked about awkwardly as the room
shook beneath him and debris crashed down around him.
He could not let her body fall to the ground, but the way the

cross was hanging, if he cut the last rope around her wrist, that's exactly what would happen. He sighed heavily as the room continued to fall apart all about him.

"Cut the rope, old man!" the Protector shouted, looking up at him.

Father Holbrook let out another sigh, this one of relief as he cut the remaining rope. Elijah caught Ebonee's body and tenderly laid her down, cradling her in his arms. He looked up at the old man, who was now crawling down from the top of the altar.

"The roof will collapse and bury the three of us if we don't get out of here," Elijah announced, looking back to the exit from where he had come.

"It's sealed," the priest replied, looking around frantically. Then his eyes opened wide as he remembered something.

"The map! Oh my . . . yes, the map! There was something about this room I saw on the map. Wait!" the old man stated excitedly, pulling a piece of paper from his pocket. He stumbled over to a torch and began studying it.

"Hurry, old man, we don't have much time!" Elijah shouted after him. Then he looked down to his precious Ebonee. Her eyes were still closed and her breathing was slow—almost non-existent. "Hold on," he whispered.

Charles watched them from the shadows, watched them as they destroyed his sanctuary. He had felt the demon leave him, taking its great power with it. He was happy when at last he found himself back. Back in his sanctuary to lead his followers once more. But now they had destroyed it. This group of fools had destroyed his beautiful sanctuary. He squeezed the handle of the dagger tightly. Someone would pay for this.

He stood up, ignoring the crumbling ceiling as large rocks and dirt fell all around him. His eyes found the kneeling form of the Protector, his back to him facing the altar.

Yes. He would pay for their sins. He charged forward, raising the dagger into the air.

The Protector stroked Ebonee's cheek softly, leaning over her to protect her from the falling debris. He saw a rock skip past him. One thing alerted him to the danger from behind.

Falling rocks didn't skip.

He reached around at the last moment and swept the dagger wide as it descended. Still, it managed to slice at his shoulder. He grabbed the man by the throat and pulled him in sharply, slamming his own head forward to meet his. The man fell to the ground, unconscious. Elijah closed one eye and shook his head vigorously.

"I knew that was going to hurt," he mumbled, shaking away the sting of the head butt.

A larger boulder fell and another column collapsed.

"Old man!" Elijah shouted into the chaos. "Hurry!" he added, pulling off his trench coat, and wrapping Ebonee's naked body in it.

Father Holbrook came running back then.

"The altar, Protector!" he shouted over the chaos as the place shook violently. "Under the altar!" he yelled, pointing at the huge, solid, stone altar.

The Protector stared at the huge piece of stone and then motioned for the priest to take care of Ebonee. Then he walked up to the altar and placed his shoulder up against it.

"There must be a switch or something!" Father Holbrook shouted, realizing that the block of stone had to weigh at least a thousand pounds, maybe more.

Elijah's feet slid out from under him, as he leaned into the altar, pushing with all his strength.

If he could just get a little leverage.

A large chunk of ceiling crashed directly onto the Protector's straining back. He growled out in pain, but he didn't stop pushing. Father Holbrook watched him in complete awe. So full of life was this Protector!

The chaos grew as the Protector struggled against the stone altar, and more and more of the ceiling crashed down all around them. Father Holbrook heard a loud, shifting noise above the confusion, as though boulders were being rubbed together. He looked up to see the entire section above them split in two, the one column supporting its weight and trembling under the multiplied weight due to the loss of the other two columns.

"Oh my," Father Holbrook whispered, then looked back at the Protector. The stone altar had not moved more than a few inches. He sighed heavily and bowed his head, praying fervently once more.

But it wasn't prayers that the Protector needed; it was leverage, which was exactly what he got when he felt the altar slide forward another inch, revealing an opening underneath. Elijah could smell the fresh air wafting in up through the hole.

Leverage.

He reached his hands down into the small crack, grasping the base of the altar at its bottom, and heaved.

He growled angrily as every muscle in his body strained and pulled. The altar flipped over onto its side, exploding as it landed. The Protector motioned the old man into the hole, and then he gently lowered Ebonee's body down to him. The room shook violently once more as Elijah grabbed Charles by the scruff of the neck. He tossed the unconscious man into the hole and looked up just as the ceiling caved in.

Father Holbrook stumbled into the tunnel, which was about as wide as he was tall, and its height was about the same. He staggered awkwardly as the ground shook beneath him, falling back against the wall of the tunnel. He looked down at the woman he cradled in his arms, and then back to the dark hole he had entered through. He saw a man's form drop heavily onto the floor, followed by the Protector.

"Keep moving!" Elijah shouted at the old man, grabbing Charles by the shoulder and dragging him forward.

Elijah feared that this tunnel, too, would collapse in on itself as the tremors continued. They could see a light at the end of the long tunnel, and made for it. The tremors slowly subsided as the dirt settled above them.

Father Holbrook stumbled and nearly fell; he had almost forgotten his age in all of the excitement. But now his body was refreshing his memory. Elijah saw the old man's movements and called him to a halt.

"Rest here; we should be safe now," he said to the old man, dropping Charles to the ground and walking over to take Ebonee's body from the old man's embrace. Father Holbrook leaned up against the smooth wall of the tunnel and slid down to a sitting position, completely exhausted. Elijah did the same against the opposite wall, cradling Ebonee close to him. He looked down at her lovely face, which was a bit dirty except for the tracks that her tears had left.

"Ebonee," he whispered softly, bringing his hand up to gently stroke her cheek. He leaned his cheek down to her mouth and felt her breath upon his skin. Leaning back once more, he stroked her face lovingly. "Don't you give up on me," he whispered, remembering her words to him.

Ebonee heard the voice calling to her, reaching through to pull her away from the darkness. She heard the voice of the man she had come to love. She fought the darkness away and forced her eyes open. Straining to focus, his face came into view. Again she felt the warm tears rolling down her cheeks. Elijah smiled softly as he saw her eyes flutter and open. His own tears fell, too, as she licked the dryness from her cracked lips.

"Cherry pie," she whispered weakly, a smile coming to her lips.

Elijah's own smile nearly stretched around his head at the words.

"Apple kisses," he whispered the appropriate reply, his heart full of love for this strong woman he had come to adore, as they completed the saying together.

"Everything is cool."

Chapter Fourteen
IF AT FIRST YOU DON'T SUCCEED . . .

Elijah maneuvered the black motorcycle through the heavy Atlanta traffic with ease. The bike was magnificent, the best he had ever ridden. He looked down at the console on the handlebars as he stopped at a light. There were so many buttons and gadgets. He still didn't know what half of them did.

His attention was drawn to the red sports car that pulled up next to him as its horn tooted. He turned to see two young beautiful sistahs smiling at him as they admired his bike. He reached up and pushed a button on the side of his helmet, and the smoke colored visor faded, revealing his handsome face. The driver of the car lowered the passenger window, smiling wide.

"Nice bike," she said, elbowing her girlfriend as she pushed at her arm, telling her to ask him his name.

"Thank you," Elijah smiled, turning his head back to look at the light.

"When can you take me for a ride?" she asked, licking her lips seductively.

Elijah swore he had never seen a light that took this long

to change in his life. He was just about to ask her to repeat the question when another bike, just like his own, came to a stop in between him and the car.

Ebonee reached up and tapped the button on her own helmet and her face slowly came into view. She glanced at the two women briefly and smiled, winking. Then she turned to Elijah as the light changed and gave him a playful slap on the rear.

"Race you home, baby!" she shouted, and took off across the intersection.

Elijah heard the woman in the car mutter something about a bitch, but he was well into the intersection after that. Ebonee flew through the traffic with Elijah right behind her. Angry drivers honked their horns as the two of them swerved and darted through the maze of cars.

Ebonee hung a right at the next corner down a long, empty alley. She slowed a bit to let Elijah catch up. She pushed a button on her console and a garage door at the end of the alley screeched as it began to open. Elijah pulled up next to her as they sped down the alley, throttle wide open. He smiled, knowing that the best she could do in this race was a tie. Her digital image appeared suddenly on the face of his visor, grinning cunningly.

"See you at the finish line, flirt!" she exclaimed, pushing yet another button on her console.

Elijah's mouth fell open at the image of her sexy leather-covered backside leaning over as she shot ahead of him, leaving him in the dust.

She was already off her bike and pulling her helmet off when Elijah pulled into the garage.

"What was that all about?" Elijah shouted, pulling off his own helmet.

"What was what about, loser?" Ebonee asked, looking at him with a smirk.

"How did you do that?" he asked, walking over to follow her up the stairs.

"How did I do what? Catch you flirting? Or smoke you back here?" she asked, stopping at the top of the steps.

Elijah stopped and stared into her wonderful smile. It had been at least four weeks since the cave-in at the compound. Ebonee had spent half of that time in the hospital recovering from her injuries. The other half she had spent here in her home, with her mother keeping guard, that is, taking care of her. Elijah had stayed by her side the entire time, having been vindicated of any wrongdoing by the FBI. It was actually Director Moss who gave the order.

They were still searching for Director Glenn; he had disappeared shortly after the attempt on Moss's life. Gone, too, was Agent Parks, who Elijah believed was possessed by the demon he was still after. Charles Kreicker was charged and sentenced to prison on a number of different charges. Moss did not believe that Kreicker was responsible for the deaths of the men in the alley. Rather, it was his hunch that Glenn had a lot to do with it.

"What do you mean caught me flirting?" Elijah replied, looking at her with his face frowned up. "I wasn't flirting!"

She smiled and took off her black leather riding jacket. "You were too! I saw the way that girl was looking at you!" she said, turning on him and walking into his chest, looking in his eyes accusingly. "But that's okay." Her warm smile returned as she threw her arms around his neck. "It just lets me know that I have the bestest man in the world," she finished, bringing his head down to hers for a passionate kiss.

Elijah relaxed and enjoyed the moment, savoring every second of their kiss. It had been a long time since they had so much as hugged. Today was the first day they had actually gotten time to be alone. Ebonee had been under the watchful eye of Mother Lane. That's what Elijah called her. She was old fashioned and believed wholeheartedly that a man and woman should be married before engaging in any lewd activities. She and Father Holbrook had gotten along wonderfully.

"Maybe I should flirt more often if this is how you react," Elijah teased, smiling as he looked down into her eyes.

"Try it and I'll break your nose," she replied, cutting her smile short to let him know she was serious.

She kissed him again and pushed herself away, walking into the kitchen. Ebonee's pad was cool. It had to have been some kind of garage or automotive repair shop before it was converted into a home. It was simply a huge repair bay. A set of wide steps dominated the first floor, sitting just beyond the garage doors. The stairs led up to the second level, which was a balcony that stretched around the entire room. At the top of the steps was a carpeted landing, and to the left was the kitchen, den, and storage area. To the right were the master bedroom, a training area, and a hot tub. Downstairs there were two rooms in the back of the garage underneath the balcony. She used these rooms as bedrooms for guests.

"So how did you get this place, anyway?" Elijah asked, taking a seat on one of the four stools along the counter in the kitchen.

"Oh, I forgot to tell you," she said, pulling a box of Frosted Flakes out of a cabinet. "My daddy owns a string of auto repair stores. This one was going to be one of those, but I talked him into letting me have it," she explained, opening up the fridge to get some milk. "Want some?"

"Nah, I'm cool. Did you tell your boss I said thanks for the bike?"

"My boss? You can tell him yourself; he's your boss now, too," she said, smiling through a mouthful of Frosted Flakes.

"Whatever. I don't believe that crap for a minute. First, I'm America's most wanted and now they're going to make me an FBI agent? Tell me another one," Elijah said, rolling his eyes.

"It's true," Ebonee said, wiping a drop of milk from her chin. "If you don't believe me, you can ask him yourself. He's coming by later," she finished, picking up the remote control and clicking on the flat screen TV that hung on the wall.

"Who says I want to be an FBI agent, anyway?" Elijah asked, standing up to take off his leather trench.

"Hey! What are you doing?" Ebonee asked, seeing him take off his coat.

"What?"

"Did I tell you to take that coat off?" she asked, walking toward him as she sat her bowl of cereal down.

"I didn't know I needed permission," Elijah replied, raising an eyebrow as she stepped into his face.

"Maybe I like you with it on," she whispered, looking up into his eyes mischievously.

"Is that so?" he replied, smiling.

"Maybe I want you to carry me into the bedroom with that coat on, Protector," she whispered seductively, reaching around Elijah to place her hands on his behind.

"Is that so?"

"Well?" Ebonee said, bulging her eyes out as if to say, 'Let's go.'

Without another word, Elijah swept Ebonee up off her feet, spinning her playfully around in a complete circle. She giggled happily as he made his way around the balcony to the bedroom.

"Wait!" Ebonee exclaimed, reaching out to the dresser for another remote control. Elijah leaned her over so she could grab it, and then spun her body around so that her legs were wrapped around him as he held her up. "*Crystal Ball.*" She smiled as she clicked a button and the CD player started.

Elijah knelt down and sat her lightly on the bed, his lips kissing at her neck. His hands found the bottom of her shirt and gently pulled it up and off. Their lips met softly at first, as Elijah's hands gently slid down her sides to her waist. He nudged her back down onto the bed.

Still on his knees, he leaned over her, running his lips along her smooth, flat belly, kissing her lightly up to her breasts, softly licking around her nipples. Ebonee moaned softly and her back arched in anticipation. Elijah felt the desire return to him then; he felt the passion he thought was lost. His only thought then was her pleasure.

His lips traced their way down to her navel and the tattoo. Ebonee closed her eyes as she felt his lips exploring her curvaceous body. They were so smooth and soft. She felt her arousal growing and she knew she was already dripping wet. She moaned again, her body flexing as his tongue found her hip. Then she felt his hands unbutton her leather pants, and down went the zipper. Her body nearly melted as she felt his lips kissing at her lower belly. Her body was exquisite; a goddess would be jealous, Elijah knew. He felt the hypnotic beat of the music as he slowly slid her pants down. . . .

"Hello! Ebonee? Elijah?" Father Holbrook shouted as he entered the garage carrying some grocery bags.

Elijah's heart melted as he dropped his head into Ebonee's lap. "Why, Why, Why!" he cried into her smooth skin.

Ebonee giggled and sat up, pulling her shirt back on and sliding her pants back up. She gently reached down and cupped Elijah's face in her hands, smiling. "Cherry pie," she said, grinning.

Elijah frowned and pouted. "Apple kisses," he offered reluctantly.

"Everything is cool," she finished for them both, knowing that Elijah didn't think anything was *cool* at that moment.

"We're up here, Father Holbrook," Ebonee sighed, and stood up clicking off the stereo. "We'll be right down," she added, looking back to Elijah, who hadn't moved from his knees.

"You coming?" she asked, smiling.

"No!" Elijah said sarcastically.

She laughed. "I meant are you coming downstairs, crazy."

"Yeah, I'll be down in a couple of minutes," Elijah replied, crawling onto the bed.

"Why a couple of minutes?"

"Because I can't go down there like this," he answered.

"Like what?"

Elijah stood up and showed her like what. Ebonee giggled and put her hand up to her mouth. "Oh, I see. Well, I'll see you when you come . . . down," she laughed, walking to the steps, leaving Elijah in his rather stiff predicament.

She walked downstairs to find Father Holbrook standing with Director Moss.

"Good afternoon, Miss Lane," Father Holbrook said as Ebonee approached them. "You have a visitor." He nodded to Director Moss.

"Agent Lane, how are you feeling?" Moss asked as Father Holbrook proceeded up the stairs with his grocery bags.

"Afternoon, Director, I feel just fine," Ebonee replied politely.

"So how do you like the bikes?" he asked with a smile, looking over at the two motorcycles. "They were just finished, and needed to be tested."

"They're excellent. Can we keep them?"

"Well, as long as they're being tested I don't see a problem with them being here," he said with a wink. "Now where is your new partner?" He grinned.

"So you were serious about bringing him in?" Ebonee asked, her eyes going up to the kitchen where Elijah and Father Holbrook were now talking.

"Agent Garland," Director Moss called up to Elijah.

Elijah looked around curiously. "Who the hell is he talking to?" he asked Father Holbrook.

"I believe he is talking to you, young Protector," Father Holbrook replied, glancing down the steps.

"You with this Protector stuff, and now this one with this agent crap!" Elijah grumbled, throwing his hands up into the air as he made his way down the steps. "I'm sorry, were you talking to me?" he asked the director as he stopped at the bottom of the stairs.

"Your name is Elijah Garland, isn't it?"

"Oh, yeah it is. I thought I heard you say something about *Agent* Garland or something. My mistake," Elijah said, walking to stand next to Ebonee.

"I did say that. I said that because you are now a member of the FBI, courtesy of me. Here." He pulled out a badge and a nine-millimeter handgun and pushed them in Elijah's direction.

Elijah took the badge and inspected it. "How did you get my picture?" he asked, looking at the photo curiously.

"You have a driver's license, don't you?" Moss asked in return.

"Yeah . . . but how did you—"

"FBI. We can do whatever we please . . . if it's worth the doing," he interrupted Elijah.

"Well . . . thanks, but no thanks," Elijah said, handing the badge and gun back to Director Moss. "I'm not very good at taking orders," he finished, turning to walk over to the large desk and the computer in the center of the back of the garage.

Director Moss glanced over to Ebonee for assistance, who only shrugged and smiled.

"I'll put it this way, Agent Garland," the director began. He had hoped it wouldn't have come to this. "This case is not over. We still haven't found Director Glenn or Agent Parks. And until we do, all we have is a gun with your fingerprints on it and five dead bodies. All killed with that weapon. Now, the way I see it, you can do one of two things: you can take this badge and this gun and work with us. Or you can sit in a jail cell until we find the real killers. I know you didn't do it. Ebonee knows you didn't do it. But a jury might not see it that way. Now, it's your call," he finished, pushing the badge and weapon back toward Elijah.

Elijah looked at him and then at Ebonee. He knew he could have walked out at any time he chose. But that would only put the FBI back on him. And he didn't want that. He couldn't do that to Ebonee.

"Fine then," he replied after a moment, snatching the badge from the director. "But don't expect me to wear one of those stupid suits!" he added, frowning.

Ebonee laughed and walked over to him, taking the badge to inspect it.

"Don't forget this," the Director said, tossing the gun to Elijah. Elijah caught it and looked at it, then tossed it back.

"No thanks. I hate guns."

"You sure? You never know, you might need it," Director Moss said.

Ebonee looked down at Elijah's waist at the twin blades and looked back at the director. "He doesn't need it," she insured the director, who put the gun on the desk.

"Well, I'll leave it here anyway. Now, about the case," he said, walking over to the computer. He pulled out a CD and laid it on the table. "Now we know that both of them are still in the country. We have all the airlines covered. We think they're probably still somewhere on the east coast. Whether or not they're working together, we don't know."

"What's on the CD?" Ebonee asked, picking it up.

"A list of private contacts that Director Glenn made on the east coast."

"If they're private, why do you have them?" Ebonee asked.

"Agent Parks provided us with this information before he turned to the highest bidder."

"You mean Parks was actually working for you?" Ebonee asked, looking at Director Moss suspiciously.

"Yes."

"Why didn't you tell me?" she asked.

"Why should I have told you?" he returned flatly.

Ebonee raised her eyebrows and tilted her head to the side. "Good point," she finally said.

"Anyway, it's all we have to go on now, and you two try not to destroy the evidence this time. If it were not for Father Holbrook up there and his laundry sack, we wouldn't have been able to shut down The Order of the Rose."

"Well, I don't need your disk to find this Agent Parks guy," Elijah said, walking away from the desk.

"Why? Do you know something we don't?" Moss asked, looking at Ebonee suspiciously.

"No. What he means is we'll check the places on the disk and let you know what we find," Ebonee said quickly, not wanting to get into the demon matter.

"No. If he knows something, I want to know what it is. We're supposed to be a team now," he said, looking at Elijah as he walked away.

"Okay. He wants to know," Elijah replied, turning back to them. Ebonee sighed and sat heavily into the seat behind the desk.

"I believe that this Agent Parks—or whatever his name is—is playing host to an old friend of mine," Elijah began.

"Playing host?" Director Moss asked, glancing at Ebonee curiously. Ebonee shrugged and turned away, offering no help.

"Yes, playing host. Your friend, Charles Kreicker, was originally possessed by a demon. That's the reason I went there. To kill the demon."

"A demon?" Moss asked skeptically.

"Well as you probably already know, I'm not your average brotha," Elijah said.

Director Moss raised an eyebrow at the statement. He did know that Elijah was not the average man. That much was evident. The blood samples he had taken from the warehouse proved that. They were still running tests on those samples now. But he decided to let him continue, pretending to be ignorant of the facts.

"Well, let's see . . ." Elijah paused, looking over at Ebonee. "Should I give him the short and simple version?"

"Oh, by all means," Ebonee replied, not believing that the director would buy any of it anyway.

"Okay, here goes," Elijah said, taking a deep breath as he looked Moss in the eye. "I am a demon hunter. My father is an angel, and I've been chosen to hunt and kill demons. I don't know how I know when a demon is around—I just do. I find them, I say the words to make them assume their physical form, and they come out of whoever they are possessing at the time. And I kill them."

"That would explain the hoof prints at the warehouse," Moss muttered to himself.

"What?" Elijah asked.

"Nothing. So you're saying that Charles was a demon?"

"No. I'm saying Charles was possessed by a demon. But somehow the demon managed to escape the compound. Agent Parks was the only one there at the time that got out. So my guess is that this demon transferred into Parks' body before I could get to him."

"Oh. I see. And you can sense when these demons are close?" Moss asked curiously.

Ebonee sat up and stared at the director. "You believe him?"

"I'm not saying I believe or disbelieve anything, Agent Lane. But I have seen a lot of stranger things working with the Unexplained Phenomena Department."

"Did he just call me a freak?" Elijah asked, looking at the director suspiciously and drawing a laugh from Ebonee.

"I'm not calling you anything, Agent Garland. All I'm saying is that I have no reason to dispute your claims. If you are what you say you are, then so be it. Whether or not I believe you or not is of no importance," Moss said, looking Elijah in the eye. Then he turned to Agent Lane. "What about you? Do you believe him?"

"Yes," she responded without hesitating. "The things I saw in that chamber—"

"Agent Lane, you said they drugged you in the chamber, right?" Moss interrupted.

Ebonee returned the curious look with one of her own. "Are you saying that I imagined all of it?"

"I'm just stating the possibilities. The remnants of the drugs in your system showed traces of hallucinogens," Moss replied.

"I know what I saw, and I wasn't hallucinating either!" Ebonee said defensively.

"Calm down, Agent Lane. I'm not saying that you were. Just stating the possibilities . . . like I said," Moss replied, although his instincts said that she wasn't lying.

"Well, in any case, we'll look at your disk and check the places out," Elijah said, interrupting the bantering.

"Do that. And let me know if you get any leads," Moss said, turning to leave.

As Moss walked out of the door, he wondered if what Elijah claimed was true. This was the main reason he had made him a part of the bureau. He knew that Elijah wouldn't go along with any tests or experiments that the bureau would want to run if they knew the truth. And he couldn't let Elijah get away. So he decided to find out for himself what the truth really was. He had already destroyed the evidence that the original doctor from the hospital had collected. He had reported the doctor's findings unsubstantial. This was easy enough to do, considering the implications. So he had to keep Elijah in check until he could get enough information to verify his claim. But what if he were telling the truth? What if this demon-possession phenomenon was actually the truth?

"Oh well, I guess I'll find out soon enough," he whispered to himself as he drove off.

"Well?" Ebonee asked, after the door had closed. "Should we take a look at it now?"

"Why not? Since we're not going to be doing anything else!" he shouted, glaring up at Father Holbrook. Ebonee laughed and slipped in the disk.

"I beg your pardon? Was someone talking to me?" Father Holbrook shouted down, leaning over the railing of the balcony.

"No, Father Holbrook," Ebonee sang in her best Catholic-school-little-girl-answering-the-teacher voice. "I don't know where you got him from," she said softly to Elijah, smiling.

"Same place you got your boss from. They had a two-for-one sale."

"Our boss," she corrected, looking over the list with a smirk.

"Don't remind me," he answered, walking over to look at the screen with her. "So what do you have here?"

"It's a list of places Glenn has either contacted or been to in person," she explained.

"So what do you think? Start from the top?" Elijah asked, turning away from the computer screen.

"I don't think so. If we did that, we would have to go all the way to New York. There are a couple of places on the list here in Atlanta. I figure we can start here and work our way north."

"What is this? A camera?" he asked, pointing to the little round eye on the top of the screen.

"Yep. If the person you're talking to has one, you can see each other. It's a video phone. I've never used it, though."

"Yeah, I'm sure you haven't—Ebonee's Exotic Web cam, $2.95 per minute," Elijah teased, laughing as he walked toward the steps.

"If I did, you'd be on it twenty-four seven!" she laughed.

"Damn right!" Elijah returned, laughing with her.

"I guess we can get some rest and start out first thing in the morning," Ebonee said, clicking the computer off.

"Fine by me," Elijah replied, heading up the steps with Ebonee behind him.

"Father Holbrook. Did my mother say when she was coming back?" Ebonee asked as they reached the top of the steps.

"Yes, she said she was not going to sit around while you two frolicked around in the streets like a couple of school kids," he replied, as Elijah looked at him with his brow crinkled up.

"Okay, did she say when she was coming back?" Ebonee asked slowly, raising her eyebrow curiously.

"Oh, yes. She said to call her if you needed her for anything," Father Holbrook said, squirming under Elijah's curious gaze.

"Thank you," Ebonee said, looking at Elijah as he continued to stare at the priest. "What's wrong with you?" she asked him.

Elijah stared at the priest for a few seconds more. "I think I liked you better in your robes," he said to Father Holbrook, causing him to look down at his outfit. Ebonee, who hadn't really paid him any mind, looked again.

"Oh, my God," she said in disbelief.

"What? What's wrong with this?" Father Holbrook asked, looking down at his wardrobe.

"Where did you find that get-up?" Ebonee asked, slapping Elijah on the arm as he giggled away.

"Why? What's wrong with it?" the priest asked, raising his chin with pride. "I picked it up this morning while the two of you were out doing God knows what," he added, turning sideways and checking himself out.

"What's wrong with it? What's right with it?" Elijah exclaimed between laughs. "You look like Santa Claus!" he added, bending over with laughter.

Ebonee tried to contain her smile, but Elijah was right. He did look like Santa Claus with his gray hair and beard.

He wore a white button-down shirt, a pair of brown trousers, and some red suspenders.

"Father Holbrook," Ebonee began, elbowing Elijah in the ribs to quiet his giggling, "just because you're old and from England, you don't have to dress like it—no offense. I bet you're probably kind of cute under all of that hair," Ebonee added, trying to spare the old man's feelings.

"Oh, my. You may be right. Well, what do you suggest I do?" he asked, blushing.

Ebonee looked at Elijah, who was still cracking up. "I suggest that you go with Elijah and let him pick you out some clothes," Ebonee said. Seeing Elijah's frown she added, "And take you to the barber shop for a trim."

Elijah frowned some more and muttered something under his breath about being stuck with the old man.

"And a shampoo. Anything else you think I'm leaving out, Elijah?" she asked sarcastically, grinning wickedly.

"No! That's enough!" Elijah exclaimed, turning his back to roll his eyes.

"And a manicure!" Ebonee shouted, knowing he was making a face. Elijah slumped his shoulders and shook his head, smiling.

"How does that sound to you, Father Holbrook?" Ebonee asked, smiling at the old man, who leaned in close to her.

"Can I get one of those massages too?" he whispered, catching on to her little game. Elijah heard him and turned to glare at them both.

"Of course you can! Isn't that right, Elijah?" she asked, turning to Elijah, her lips turned up in a smirk.

"What? Right now?"

"I don't see why not. We're not going anywhere until the morning, so why not?" Ebonee asked.

"Yeah. Why not, young Protector?" Father Holbrook chimed in, standing behind Ebonee.

"Old man, don't push—" Elijah began, but then he caught the angry glare that Ebonee sent his way. "Come on then!" he finished, stomping down the steps, Father Holbrook on his heels. Then he turned and let Father Holbrook pass. He looked up at Ebonee with her ear-wide grin.

"I'm gonna get you back. You know that, right?" he announced, causing her grin to spread wider.

"Hurry back, now. And don't forget his manicure," Ebonee replied sweetly with a wink.

"Okay. You got that. Just don't be mad when I get you back," Elijah said, turning to catch up to Father Holbrook.

"Cherry pie!" He heard Ebonee shout out from the rail.

"Apple kisses!" he shouted back, grudgingly.

"Everything is cool!" he heard Ebonee finish, and he didn't have to look back to see the silly smile that was sure to be on her face. He turned his attention back to the old man, who was moving rather quickly for the door.

"Slow down, old man, before you trip and—" Elijah swallowed the rest of the words as Father Holbrook went sprawling across the floor, "fall," Elijah finished, shaking his head in disbelief.

"Oh, my, has anyone seen my walking stick?" Father Holbrook asked, sitting up and looking around curiously. Elijah looked back up at Ebonee, who was enjoying every second of his discomfort and rolled his eyes, causing her to laugh out loud.

She watched Elijah help the priest up and walk out of the door. She laughed all the way to the bedroom and flopped down on the bed, thinking of how happy she was now that Elijah was in her life. She stretched out on the bed and yawned.

"Cherry pie," she whispered to herself, staring up at the ceiling, smiling.

She had always wanted to play those little love games with someone. With someone that truly loved her. She closed her eyes as she thought of Elijah. She knew without a doubt that he loved her. She saw him in her mind, fighting those demons again, all for her. Risking his life for her. He was everything she had ever wanted in a man, and so much more. And he was so sexy! Smart, compassionate, polite, and sexy! Those four things never came all together in just one man! Either they were sexy and so full of themselves it was ridiculous, or they were polite and compassionate but ugly to the bone! And here was Elijah, all of the above, and he acted like he didn't even know it!

She pictured his face in her mind. Those soft, light brown bedroom eyes, eyes that had captured her heart when she first looked upon them. And those full, sexy lips that he seemed to lick every time she was watching. She couldn't stop seeing them in her mind. She moaned in protest as she slid out of her pants and pulled the sheet over her.

She remembered Elijah's lips on her. Kissing her own lips, her neck. She opened her mouth and licked her tongue across her lips, remembering his taste. She felt his hands on her waist, their smooth touch intoxicating. She felt them sliding down her pants. She brought her hand up to her breast, touching it softly, imagining that it was his soft caress. She slid her hand gently down to her belly, shaking as his lips kissed at her softness. Her fingers made their way under the top of her panties. She closed her eyes tight and bit her bottom lip as Elijah's tongue found her love.

"Ebonee," the shrill voice called out to her as she lay in her bed.

It was dark outside, and Father Holbrook and Elijah had

yet to return. She rubbed at her weary eyes, trying to focus on the flashing lights that came from the darkness.

"Ebonee," the whisper came again, bringing an icy clamminess to her skin.

Chills ran through her bones as she looked around the garage fearfully. There it was again. The flashing blue light, disturbing the suddenly not-so-peaceful darkness. Ebonee pulled the covers around her naked body. Naked? She thought she had fallen asleep in her underwear and shirt.

"Ebonee," came the voice once more, beckoning to her, pulling at her very soul.

A strange but familiar smell filled her nostrils. An odor that brought to her mind memories of her visit to a Catholic church.

The smoke. The smoke the priests would carry along in that metal container hanging from a chain, swinging it back and forth.

"Ebonee!" the shrill voice exclaimed again, jolting through her like a bolt of lightning.

Ebonee followed the source of the flashing light to the back of the garage. It was the computer; she could see it from where she sat on the bed. She got up off the bed and walked over to the railing. Her naked body flashed blue in the eerie darkness as she shrugged the chills and the eerie smell away, thinking herself foolish to be afraid in her own home.

She walked to the stairs, holding the railing tightly as the blue light continued its eerie play in the darkness. She swore that she had cut the thing off, but maybe not. She walked down the steps slowly, looking at the staircase curiously. With each step she took, the bottom of the staircase seemed to get farther away. Down and down she went, until she was running, running as fast as her legs could carry her, but still the end of the staircase eluded her. She stumbled and fell, landing on the stone floor hard, scraping her knee.

The flickering blue light disappeared, leaving her in darkness so complete she thought her breath would be stolen away. She sat there in the darkness, terrified to move. She huddled her knees into her chest as a chill so cold ran through her very bones. Her heart seemed to be trying to escape her chest, trying to flee the thick, overbearing darkness.

"Ebonee," the voice whispered again, echoing over and over in her mind.

Her eyes tried frantically to find some small sliver of anything, anything to hold onto in the darkness. But she could not find her hand in front of her face for the thickness of it. Suddenly, a candle flickered far to her right, and another far to her left. She watched as the dull, yellowish glow spread along each wall, revealing the stone and stained glass windows of a church. Two more candles flickered to life, these two next to the first on each side of the room. Then two more, and two more, all moving toward the front of the enormous room.

She watched as the candles lit up, finally stopping what seemed like a city block away.

The darkness seemed to bite at the annoying light; she could feel its hatred of the light as it spread, revealing a large sanctuary. Rows upon rows of pews, all empty. The darkness seemed to gather at the front of the sanctuary as if it were trying to blot out something there. Ebonee strained her eyes, trying to make out the scene ahead of her. Were they crosses?

She stood and took a step in the direction of the darkness, then another step. Soon she was walking with speed toward the empty void that lay ahead of her. Slowly, she could make out the forms. Two small crosses stood to the left and the right of a larger cross. She strained her eyes again. There was a body on the cross in the center.

A sudden sense of urgency ran through her veins, and she

knew exactly who was on that cross. She was running then, as fast as her feet would take her. She could see his white hair, hanging wildly about his beaten and bloodied face.

"Elijah!" she screamed out, fear building in her soul.

Blood covered his naked ebony body, giving his skin a golden-red hue. Darker blotches of blood poured from the many gashes in his torn torso. His lips moved and she could hear him whispering her name, calling to her, as if he were right next to her. She pushed her naked body to run faster, trying to get to the man that held her heart, wanting to help.

She saw the demon then.

A wicked, vile creature, its clawed, crimson hand floated next to Elijah's heart. Its ugly canine maw spread wide in a wicked grin, revealing rows upon rows of razor-sharp teeth.

"Nooo!" she screamed out as the aisle she was running down began to lengthen with each stride she took.

The demon sneered and roared, digging his black claws into Elijah's chest, drawing blood. A feeling of utter hopelessness and despair filled Ebonee then, for she knew she would never make it in time. Tears fell from her eyes as the demon pushed his hand in deeper, clutching at Elijah's beating heart.

"Elijahhh!" Ebonee screamed out, falling to her knees as the demon ripped Elijah's beating heart from his chest. "Nooo . . . Elijahhh!" Her screams echoed all around her as her tears fell to the cold floor of the sanctuary. "Elijah!" she screamed again and again.

Elijah heard her shouts as he entered the garage.

"Ebonee!" he called out to her, running in the darkness to the stairs. He saw her form lying in the bed, writhing and screaming.

"Stay here," he instructed Father Holbrook as he took the stairs, three at a time.

His heart raced as he ran to the side of the bed. The sheets were soaking wet with perspiration and she continued to twist and writhe, screaming out his name. He touched the lamp beside her bed to turn on the light, and then he grabbed her shoulders.

"Ebonee! Wake up!" he said firmly, shaking her lightly. "Ebonee!" he shouted again, louder this time as she grasped at him. Ebonee's eyes opened, and when she saw Elijah she quickly threw her arms around him, sobbing heavily.

"Elijah! I'm sorry! I tried to get to you, but I just couldn't!" she cried, squeezing him tightly.

Elijah held her and gently stroked her back. "Baby, it's okay. I'm here," he whispered.

"But he had you, Elijah! He killed you! I watched him do it! And there was nothing I could do to stop him!" she cried, her tears falling on Elijah's shoulder. "You were calling out for me to help you and I couldn't! I ran as fast as I could, but you just kept getting farther and farther away!"

"Ebonee, it's okay. It was just a bad dream—"

"No! It wasn't a dream! It was real! I saw you, I was there!" she screamed, rocking back and forth in his arms as she remembered.

"Baby, it was not real. I'm right here," Elijah said, leaning her forward so he could look into her teary eyes. "No one killed me—see?" He gently touched the side of her face with the palm of his hand.

Her eyes seemed to open for the first time as she realized he was sitting right in front of her. She threw her arms around him again and squeezed him tightly. Elijah thought his eyes would pop out from the force of her embrace.

"Elijah!" she exclaimed, kissing at his face frantically. "I'm so sorry I made you take Father Holbrook out alone!" she added, talking rapidly.

"Calm down, baby. It was just a dream," Elijah said again, smiling as he held her by her shoulders, looking into her eyes.

"But it was so real!" she exclaimed, wiping at the tears.

"I know; some dreams can feel very real. Believe me, I know." Elijah seemed to drift away in his memories for a moment. He rested a hand on her knee.

"Ouch!" Ebonee complained, pulling his hand away from her knee quickly. She pulled back the covers curiously to find smeared blood and a fresh scrape on her knee.

"How did you do that?" Elijah asked, looking at the wound.

Ebonee's heart almost stopped as she remembered. She stared at Elijah, a fearful look in her eyes.

"What? What's wrong?" he asked, seeing her disturbed expression. Her gaze seemed to be distant then, as though she were looking directly through Elijah.

"In the dream," she began after a long moment of silence, "I fell."

Agent Parks lounged lazily in a large leather chair. A small desk lamp provided the only light in the room. He picked up the telephone and dialed a number.

"Director Moss," came the answer on the other end.

"How's the head, old pal?" Parks asked, grinning.

As soon as Director Moss realized who he was talking to, he pushed a button on his desk to begin a trace.

"Where are you?" Moss demanded.

"Come on, that's all you have to say to an old friend?" Parks teased.

"Turn yourself in now, and maybe the board will go light on you," Moss said.

"The board? What a joke. You're a funny guy, Moss. Real funny. Now if you're done with your silly humor, I'd like to tell you the reason for this call," Parks replied, his tone serious now.

"I'm listening," Moss replied, trying to keep him on the line long enough to get the trace.

"I can give you Glenn," he said flatly.

"In exchange for what? Your freedom?"

"That . . . and a few other requests," Parks replied, smiling as he observed the second hand on his watch.

"We'll find Glenn sooner or later without your help. And do you really think I'd work out a deal with you?" Moss asked.

"If you want Glenn you will," Parks said confidently. Then he chuckled. "So did you get it?"

"Get what?" Moss asked as an agent walked into the room to hand him a piece of paper with the results of the trace on it.

"The trace. Pretty long list, I bet," Parks announced, smiling as he looked at the blocking device he had installed on the telephone. Moss balled the paper up and waved the agent out. "You won't find Glenn without my help. You know that as well as I do, and as far as you and I are concerned, it was business—nothing personal. I was only following orders. Orders from Glenn. I know you're not the type to hold a grudge. And I know you want Glenn. The only way you're going to get him is to work out a deal with me."

"Father, everyone is gone now," a voice said from the door of the room. Parks quickly put his hand over the phone as he sat up, glaring at the nun who had walked in.

"Get out!" he whispered angrily, waving frantically at the door. The nun dipped her head in apology and left the room.

Moss overheard the woman's words but decided not to let Parks know that. "Hello? Are you still there?" he asked curiously.

"If you want Glenn, I can give him to you. You have twenty-four hours to think about it. I'll be in touch," Parks said angrily, slamming down the phone. He looked over to the figure sitting in the large chair behind the desk, his face covered by the shadows. He could barely make out the man's eyes as they fluttered open. He did see the white teeth as a wicked smile came to the man's face.

Dalfien was satisfied.

It had taken him a while to find the path, but he had located it without too much trouble. He had been there before, torturing the woman as she had hung upon the cross in the underground chamber. There had been no resistance this time; perhaps she had been asleep. Nevertheless, he had accomplished his goal and implanted the visions of the church in her mind. It was only a matter of time now.

He looked over at Agent Parks. He had freed the man soon after leaving the compound, seeing that the man's heart was as black as his own. Dalfien knew that he would be of greater assistance to him without a demon's presence in his mind. Agent Parks had realized the possible benefits of working with Dalfien immediately, and did not pass up the opportunity.

"So how come you can come in this place, anyway? I thought you couldn't come on holy ground or whatever it's called," Parks stated after a moment, tired of looking at the silly grin on Dalfien's face.

"Holy? Bah. There is more evil in some churches than in the entire world," Dalfien replied, snorting at the idea. "Take our priest here." He indicated the body he now possessed. "He has a strange affection for small children. His followers suspect him, but they are too caught up in their own sin to point a finger."

"But isn't this supposed to be the house of God?"

Dalfien frowned at the mention of the word. "It is a place where sin gathers and nothing more! A place where foolish men come to confess their sins and seek forgiveness, only to leave with more thoughts of sin on their minds," he said, lifting up the small cross that hung from a chain around his neck and glaring at it with a sneer.

Parks was just about to ask another question when his words were stolen from his lips. The air seemed to evaporate from the room as the door slowly creaked open. Parks stood up sharply at the intrusion, thinking it was another nun coming to report.

He opened his mouth once again to rebuke the insolent nun, but found he could hardly breathe, let alone speak, as an evil so pure—so malevolent—filled the room. Parks clutched at his chest as the figure walked slowly into the dimly lit room. Each step he took brought with it hatred and malice. Parks found himself huddling in a dark corner, afraid to even lay eyes on the evil that he knew to be present.

Dalfien knew at once who this visitor was. Still, his eyes went wide and he dropped his gaze to the desk in front of him, his heart racing as the figure approached.

He was beautiful.

His jet black hair hung down to his shoulders and his face was angelic in appearance. A simple brown leather trench coat flowed as he walked.

"Have you finished the task I set forth for you, Dalfien?" the beautiful man asked, his voice as sweet as honeydew.

"Master . . . I have not," Dalfien replied, his gaze never leaving the desk in front of him.

The beautiful man walked past the desk and stopped at the window, staring out into the darkness. "Could it be that the task is too great?" the melodic voice came again.

"Master, no task that you can give would be too great for me to accomplish in your name," Dalfien replied reverently.

"Then why is the task not completed?" Lucifer asked, turning to stand behind Dalfien.

Dalfien felt his master's eyes on him. Felt him in his mind. He knew that any answer he provided would be foolish. He could not admit his fear of the Protector outright. Yet to deny it would be to lie, and to lie would be useless.

"Is he so powerful? Ahhh, I see," Lucifer whispered, leaning down so that his lips were next to Dalfien's ear. "It is the blades you fear?" he continued, walking through Dalfien's thoughts as if they were an open meadow. "Very well. This will aid you," he said as Dalfien's eyes went wide.

Before him on the desk, the shaft of a seven foot spear appeared. At the end of the spear was a short, flat blade that glowed red in the dim light. Dalfien dared to touch it. His fingers paused as they passed over it, afraid that it would be snatched away from him.

"The Spear of Suffering," Dalfien whispered in awe as his fingers felt the warm metal. How many angels had fallen to this dreadful weapon, wielded by The Master himself? His eyes followed its shaft to the glowing red blade at its end. It was said that the mere touch of the enchanted blade was enough to drive any being mad.

"Be done with your task, Dalfien," Lucifer whispered, standing straight and walking back to the window. "I leave you now. There is a rather amusing war going on; my brothers seem intent upon killing one another. I don't want to miss any of the action." A grin creeped across his face.

Then he unlatched the window and pulled it open wide. He paused and gave Dalfien a final glance. "Do not fail me, Dalfien."

The words floated upon the air as if they were a string of butterflies, so light and beautiful. But Dalfien felt the weight of them upon his black heart as the figure exploded into a hundred black crows, shrieking as they dispersed into the night.

"Is everything okay, young Protector?" Father Holbrook asked, walking along the rail of the balcony toward the bedroom.

"I don't know," Elijah replied, his eyes on the scrape on Ebonee's knee.

"What happened?" the priest asked, coming to stand at the foot of the bed.

Ebonee retold the dream to the priest, who listened intently. He put a hand to his now clean shaven chin, meaning to stroke his beard. His eyebrow rose as he remembered that his beard was now gone.

"Child, when you faced the demon in the chamber, did he enter your mind?" Father Holbrook asked after a moment of thought.

Ebonee shifted uncomfortably on the bed as she recalled the horrible account. "Yes," she replied.

Father Holbrook gave a deep sigh and looked at Elijah. "It was no dream, Protector. Once the demon has been in your mind, he can easily return. No, this was a vision. A vision put into her mind for a purpose," the priest explained.

"What purpose?" Elijah asked curiously, his face stern.

"That, I am afraid, remains to be seen." Father Holbrook looked back at the shaken Ebonee. "All we can do is wait." He turned to walk back the way he had come.

Elijah watched him leave, then his gaze returned to Ebonee. Anger filled his heart as he looked upon her shaken form. It was him the demon wanted. He cursed himself for letting his heart fall to this beautiful woman. His gaze fell to his waist and the hilts of his blades, vibrating now, as they felt his rage simmering. She had been taken because of him, and now she was being tormented because of him. If he were to leave, then maybe the demon would leave her alone.

"No. Elijah, please, don't think that way," Ebonee said softly, seeing Elijah's thoughts clearly upon his face.

He looked up into her eyes as she brought her hand to his cheek. He saw the strength return to those eyes as her hand gently stroked his face.

"It is because of me that you are in danger," he whispered, his eyes leaving hers as he spoke.

"I would rather face danger by your side than be safe without you," she replied softly.

Elijah closed his eyes for a moment, then sighing deeply he turned to her. "Ebonee, I could not bear the weight of losing you because of my love for you," he began, as images of the past flitted through his mind. Images of Taysia, lying in his arms, her blood flowing onto the ground as she died—died because of him.

"Then you must see to it that you don't, Elijah. Because I will not let you leave me. I can't." She turned his head softly so that their eyes reconnected.

He heard the voices then.

The voices in his mind, telling him to leave, trying to guard his heart from the pain that would surely come if he lost her. But it was too late now. His heart was lost. Lost in her beauty and compassion. He would not leave her. He could not.

Ebonee watched as his eyes softened and his resolve melted away. The fear that had come to her with the dream was gone now, chased away by his mere presence. There was no danger great enough to keep her from him. This she knew without doubt. She leaned forward and gently placed a kiss upon his soft lips. "I love you," she whispered, sitting back to look into his eyes as she said the words with a warm smile on her face.

"And I love you." Her soft lips left him helpless. He smiled warmly as her kiss infected him.

"Cherry pie," Ebonee said, causing his smile to spread even more as he shook his head.

"Apple kisses," he replied, chuckling softly as she embraced him.

"Everything is cool," they said together as they enjoyed each other's embrace.

"Let's go for a ride," Ebonee said suddenly, sitting back with a smile on her face.

"Now?" Elijah asked curiously. It wasn't that late, but after what had just happened he didn't think she would be up for such a thing.

"Yeah, why not? It's nice out and we probably won't get any more time to spend just relaxing and having fun after tonight. And besides," she said, getting up to find her leather pants. "I am in no hurry to get back to sleep!" she proclaimed, causing Elijah to smile.

"Okay. Where are we going?" Elijah asked, giving in.

"Well, do you like to dance? I know a nice club we can go to. I think we could use a little loosening up," she replied, sliding into her tight black pants.

"Sounds good to me." Elijah got up from the bed to join her as she walked to the stairs.

Father Holbrook heard the garage door open and ran out to see what was going on. He stared out of the open garage door at the two figures, speeding down the alley side by side.

"Do be careful, young Protector," he said, smiling as he turned to walk back to the comfort of his bed. "Young people . . . so full of li—" His words were cut short as he tripped over the hem of his long robe and went sprawling onto the garage floor. "Oh my, I do believe I am getting a bit clumsy in my old age," he muttered as the garage door closed.

Chapter Fifteen
FLIGHT

Elijah brought his bike to a halt alongside of Ebonee's as they stopped at a traffic light. The bright moon glinted off the shiny black helmets and caused their leather trench coats to glow with a bright bluish color. "Where are we going?" he asked, touching the side of his helmet so that the smoke-colored visor faded into a transparent shield.

Ebonee did the same, looking over at Elijah with a smile on her face. It was a very nice night; a light breeze blew lazily through the streets, a hint of winter in its scent. But the warm air seemed to be fighting it away. "Do you remember where Main Street is?" Ebonee asked.

"Yes," Elijah replied, flipping open the storage bin in front of him to put a CD into the CD player.

"Well, we're going to go to Main Street and make a left. Take it all the way to its end, and the club will be on the right. You can't miss it—you'll see my bike parked out front!" she teased, tapping the side of her helmet once more to return the smoked appearance. "By the way, I hope you like the view." She chuckled lightly.

"What view?" Elijah asked into his helmet, opening up the two-way communicator.

"The view of my behind when I smoke you!" she exclaimed, tearing off into the intersection before the light changed.

Elijah smiled and shook his head. God, how he loved this woman! He watched as the single red taillight on the back of Ebonee's motorcycle shot off down the street as the high horsepower engine screamed into the night.

Ebonee had a good head start and was already a full block ahead of Elijah as he turned onto Main Street. He hit the throttle as he turned the corner onto the large three-lane thoroughfare. Traffic was heavy as the city's nightlife began.

Elijah's black trench coat whipped in the air behind him as he weaved in and out of traffic. To his right he could see the expressway running parallel to the large street.

His eyes drifted down to the console and the buttons by his left thumb. Turbo would be the only way he could hope to catch her. He just hoped that she didn't hit hers first. His eyes went back up to the street ahead, seeing Ebonee about a block ahead with heavy traffic in front of her. He figured she wouldn't be able to hit the turbo until she was past the congestion. But he was in the same predicament. He continued weaving in and out of traffic, trying to get a clear lane so he could hit the turbo button.

Ebonee was weaving and ducking in between cars, trying to reach the front of the pack so that she, too, could hit her turbo button. It became obvious to Elijah that Ebonee would reach a clear point first when he saw the traffic ahead of her thinning.

Elijah blew through an intersection, the loud hip-hop music blaring in his helmet, urging him on. But still he wasn't gaining any ground on Ebonee. He focused on the traffic directly ahead of him, trying to plot a path that would allow him to hit the turbo and pass the congestion without killing himself in the process.

Ebonee smiled as she stared up ahead, her thumb hovering over the turbo button as the traffic slowly disappeared behind her. She glanced into her rearview mirror and saw Elijah weaving in and out of traffic on her left about a block behind. Her smile widened, knowing that he would never clear the traffic in time to catch her with his turbo boost; that's if he even knew where it was.

Elijah shook his head in disbelief. He couldn't believe he was about to do what he was about to do. His eyes focused on the car in the center lane in front of him as he swiftly approached. His left thumb hovered over the black switch as he waited for the car next to it to slow just a bit, just enough to give him a break.

He braced himself as he flipped the switch, and was very surprised when he saw the glowing, red, targeting crosshairs appear on his visor along with an intermittent beep. He glanced down to see two rockets extend from the bottom of the bike's frame.

"Oh, shit! Wrong switch!" he whispered excitedly, flipping the switch back up. He sighed deeply in relief as the targeting cross- hairs disappeared and the rockets retracted.

He stared down at the many buttons and switches again. This time he placed his left thumb over a different button, again bracing himself for the speed.

His heart raced as his thumb came down on the turbo button and the bike shot forward. He leaned hard to the right, narrowly missing the rear of the car in front of him as the loud horn blared from the car he had just swerved in front of. He growled in determination, his leg brushing against the guardrail as he quickly shifted his weight back to the left, veering in front of the car he had just passed. He felt the rush of adrenaline flowing through him as he guided the bike back to the guardrail, passing the traffic as if it were standing still.

Ebonee veered her bike over to the right lane, passing the car in the center lane. In front of her was wide, open road. She glanced to her left, searching for Elijah in her mirror as her thumb came down on the turbo button. Her heart nearly jumped out of her chest as Elijah flew by her on her right, dangerously close, the roar of the bike's engine a mere memory as she watched him pull away. A loud jubilating scream echoed in her helmet.

"Fucking lunatic!" Ebonee screamed, smiling as she leaned forward in the seat.

Elijah leaned casually up against the motorcycle in the parking lot across the street from the club as Ebonee slowly pulled her bike up next to his. She noticed the shit-eating grin on his face immediately as she pulled off her helmet and dismounted the bike.

"There is something seriously wrong with you," she said, walking up to stand in front of him. She tried to hide her smile.

"One word—" Elijah smirked, his arms crossed in front of his chest, "loser." He laughed, fending off the series of light slaps Ebonee came in at him with as she joined in his laughter.

"You're crazy!" Ebonee exclaimed, relaxing comfortably in his arms as he smiled down at her.

They shared a kiss, Elijah feeling the happiness he had longed to feel for so many years. It was a happiness he had thought was lost to him forever.

"Come on, silly," Ebonee finally said, pulling Elijah by the hand through the parking lot.

"Wait." Elijah glanced down to the hilts of the blades protruding from the front of his black trench. "I can't take these in there."

"Leave them on the bike," Ebonee offered.

Elijah sighed and walked back over to his motorcycle, removing the blades as he searched for a place to store them.

He did not want to leave them. They had become a part of him, and he felt totally naked without them.

He wedged them into a small area between the large muffler and the body of the bike, trying to make them look like part of the bike itself.

"I don't feel very comfortable leaving them out here like this," Elijah commented, referring to the motorcycles.

"Don't worry, they're perfectly safe—watch," Ebonee replied, extending her hand that held the key to her bike.

She clicked a button and the bike gave off a small beep.

"Try it," she said to Elijah. Elijah did the same, pulling the key out and pushing the button.

"That doesn't comfort me much," Elijah said.

Ebonee sighed lightly and stepped over to Elijah's bike. She waved a hand over the seat, and Elijah stared down at his hand that held the vibrating key.

"Cool," Elijah stated, placing the key in his pocket as Ebonee stepped back over to him.

"Feel better? It's state of the art. If anyone touches the bikes or the blades, we'll know. Now let's go."

Elijah, feeling better, placed his arm around Ebonee's shoulder and walked next to her across the parking lot. They noticed the row of motorcycles parked on the sidewalk next to the entrance of the club.

"Nice bikes," one of the riders said as they stepped up the stairs leading to the front door.

"Thank you." Ebonee smiled as they came to a stop on the steps, waiting in line to be searched.

Elijah could hear the loud music as he stepped through the front door. He raised his arms, letting the large bouncer frisk him. Ebonee waited just beyond the doorway, smiling as Elijah held up his arms. Elijah smiled as he stepped up to her, wanting nothing more than to have a good time tonight and forget all about their other issues.

Ebonee noticed the stares immediately as scantily dressed

women whispered and nodded toward Elijah. She frowned and turned to him, placing a serious expression on her face.

"No flirting," she said, staring into Elijah's brown eyes.

"Who? Me?" Elijah replied, trying to look innocent.

Ebonee's serious expression turned into a long laugh, as she admired the handsome man standing before her. His cornrowed white hair accented his smooth, flawless, brown skin. *Damn, he is so fucking sexy!*

"Come on! Let's get a drink," Ebonee announced, pulling her man by the hand into the main room of the club.

The place was packed with men and women dancing and drinking, talking and having fun. They made their way to the bar near the rear of the club on the other side of the dance floor. There were no empty seats, so they stopped and stood next to the wall, observing the people around them.

"I'll get the drinks. What do you want?" Elijah offered, talking loud so that he could be heard over the blaring music.

"Same thing you're drinking," Ebonee answered, eyeing the two women sitting at the bar staring at Elijah.

"Heineken?" Elijah asked, trying his best to ignore the three black guys whispering and staring at Ebonee from the edge of the dance floor.

"Yep." Ebonee turned to the side and placed her hand on Elijah's ass, making sure that the two girls could see. She smiled as they rolled their eyes and turned their attention elsewhere.

"Okay, I'll be right back," Elijah said, turning to walk to the bar.

Ebonee gazed after him until he was at the bar, admiring his smooth, confident stride. Her attention was drawn to the dance floor as a smoky haze began to waft out onto the floor and a well known hip-hop tune began to blast. She waved the smoke away as couples moved to the dance floor. Her head began to nod to the beat and she felt the rhythm moving her. She glanced back to the bar to find Elijah, but the crowd had grown and she couldn't make him out.

"Excuse me."

Ebonee turned to see one of the men that had been staring at her from the edge of the dance floor smiling in her face.

"Wanna dance, baby?" he asked.

Ebonee sighed deeply, smelling the cheap cologne that reminded her of soap. "No, not right now," she replied, trying to be polite.

The man stood there, still smiling.

"Then can I buy you a drink?" he asked, leaning close to yell in her ear.

Ebonee cut her eyes to the other two men he was with. Seeing them whispering and staring, she rolled her eyes. "No thank you, I'm with someone," she said, stepping back a bit.

"Damn, you are so fine, baby. My name is Roy. I'm a lawyer. Came down here tonight to have some fun with my boys. You sure you don't want to dance?" he persisted, his lips uncomfortably close to Ebonee's ear once again.

Ebonee frowned as the alcohol and bad cologne filled her nostrils. "I said no thank you," she reiterated, turning her head to look for Elijah. She frowned again as she spotted him; one of the girls that had been staring at him was all up in his ear as he leaned over the bar waiting for his drinks. She could see the forced smile upon his face as he shook his head negatively at the chubby woman.

"Well, maybe later, baby," Roy announced, seeing her attention elsewhere.

Ebonee breathed a sigh of relief as he walked away, staring back at her with a grin. *Was that supposed to be seductive?* She shook her head in disbelief.

Elijah sighed as he picked the drinks up off of the bar. He

already felt completely naked without his blades, and now he could feel the chubby girl next to him undressing him with her eyes. "Maybe later," he said, smiling down at the short woman.

He had no intention of dancing with her. Not that he wasn't flattered, but he intended to devote his entire evening— not to mention his life—to Ebonee. Besides, he had promised her no flirting.

Elijah frowned as he turned and walked away, realizing what he had just done. He hadn't done it on purpose; it was just in his nature. And it was a habit. He cut his eye back to the chubby girl and saw her wide grin. Sighing heavily, he made a mental note to keep his tongue in his mouth for the rest of the night.

Ebonee crossed her arms as she watched him approach, a silly smirk on his face.

"I told you no flirting," she chastised, holding her stern expression for a moment before her smile slowly eased back into place.

"Sorry?" Elijah sheepishly smiled back as he handed her the beer.

"I got your sorry right here, mister!" she laughed, giving him a playful punch in the stomach.

Elijah laughed and threw his arms around her, giving her a tight squeeze. He snorted and shook his head as he noticed the three men staring at them from the edge of the dance floor.

"Every night I gotsta fight ta prove mah love," he whispered in his *Five Heartbeats* imitation.

"What?" Ebonee asked, smiling as she sipped at the beer from her straw.

"Nothing." Elijah watched the people moving and grooving on the dance floor.

"Roy, she checking you out, man," Paul said to his friend, Roy, as they all gawked at Ebonee.

Roy stared at her, figuring she wouldn't look back at him because she was with that skinny little chump.

"Damn, she fine as shit, Roy. I don't think you got it in you. You can't handle that," Mark added, shaking his head as he smirked at Roy.

"Why she wit' that nut, anyway? Lucky li'l muthafucka," Paul continued.

"She won't be by the time tha night is over," Roy commented absently, still staring at Ebonee.

"She ain't gonna be with you!" Paul laughed.

"I got twenty say he pull dat ho," Mark shouted above the music, pulling out a roll of money. "Dis nigga smooth, boy."

"Das a bet," Paul said, pulling out his own roll.

"Go pull dat ho, Roy! Show this nut-ass nigga what a true playa is!" Mark shouted as Roy continued to stare at Ebonee.

Elijah watched them closely, knowing there was about to be trouble. He watched as the stocky man staring at Ebonee swelled up, flexing his muscles in his tight, short-sleeve black shirt.

"Go on, Roy!" Mark shouted, as Roy stepped away toward Ebonee and Elijah.

Elijah sighed as he watched the man approaching. He didn't want any trouble. He decided to let Ebonee handle it, knowing that the man and his friends were no threat to him. Hopefully he would take his rejection like a man and calmly walk back to his friends.

"Excuse me."

Elijah felt a tug on his leather coat sleeve. He turned to see the chubby girl smiling up at him.

Ebonee blinked her eyes closed slowly, shaking her head in disbelief as the chubby girl smiled away.

"You ready, baby?"

It was Ebonee's turn to look and see Roy standing right up on her, smiling just as happily as the chubby girl in the dim light of the club.

"My cousin wants to know if you want to dance," the chubby girl announced loudly over the music, rolling her eyes at Ebonee as she motioned back to the bar where a slim sistah sat, smiling at Elijah.

"Come on, let's go," Roy said firmly, reaching down to grab Ebonee's hand to lead her to the dance floor.

Elijah glanced back to see Roy reaching for Ebonee's hand, a cocky look in his eye as he stared at Elijah. Before Elijah could react, Ebonee stepped by him.

"You okay?" she asked the chubby girl, her eyebrows raised curiously.

"You got a problem, bruh?" Elijah asked as Roy stepped closer, still reaching for Ebonee's hand.

Elijah knew there was no easy way out of this now. As he watched the stocky man ball up his fists, he also took note of the other two men stepping closer.

"Bitch, is *you* okay?" the chubby girl shouted, her neck twisting as she scowled at Ebonee.

Ebonee could feel all eyes beginning to stare as the confrontation heated up.

"*You* got a fuckin' problem?" Roy shouted back at Elijah, stepping forward.

Elijah exhaled deeply, twisting his lips up in a smirk. Roy was at least fifty pounds heavier than Elijah and looked as though he spent all of his time in the gym, the way his muscles bulged out of his tight shirt.

There was a brief moment of loud silence.

Then all hell broke loose.

Roy came in with an overhand right, swinging hard enough to dent a car. Ebonee's quick jab caught the big girl in the nose, snapping her head back, allowing Ebonee a chance to glance over at Elijah. She smiled as he winked his eye at her, holding Roy's huge fist in his left hand.

Roy's eyes grew to ten times their normal size, as the skinny guy raised an eyebrow, staring at him curiously, with his fist in the palm of his hand. Before Roy could react, and before his two friends could step in to help, he was sliding backwards across the slippery dance floor.

"Idiot," Elijah muttered, as he felt the man's friends closing in.

"Bitch, you hit my cousin!"

Ebonee slipped to the right as the slim woman charged her, lifting her left knee to drive it into the girl's ribs, just as her big cousin shook off Ebonee's first punch. Then she rushed in.

Elijah spun to his left, dropping down as he kicked out his left foot, sweeping Mark from his feet. Mark hit the ground on his back hard, just as a chair slammed across Elijah's back.

Elijah glanced around the club, ignoring Paul as he dropped what remained of the chair and threw his arms around Elijah, trying to wrestle him to the ground. Elijah smiled. The club was in complete chaos. Everyone was running and fighting. He caught Ebonee's eye as she dropped the big girl yet again. She smiled at him, shrugging her shoulders.

"Cherry pie!" he yelled, swinging Paul off of his back, and into the approaching bouncer.

"Apple kisses!" Ebonee shouted back, kicking the big girl in the head as she tried to get up again.

"Everything is cool!" they shouted in unison as the lights came on and the music screeched to a halt.

Bodies were flying everywhere; Elijah didn't think there was a single person in the club not hitting or being hit. He had to force himself to concentrate, not wanting to hurt anyone too badly.

He laughed as another chair smashed across his back, but when he turned to deal with the idiot, his smile disappeared.

Chill bumps ran eerily across his skin and he shivered involuntarily. His hands went instinctively to his hips, searching for the blades he knew were not there.

A fear he had never felt before gripped him, holding him paralyzed as Roy found another chair to hit him with.

Ebonee glanced over to her man and she, too, paused, watching as Roy swung away with yet another chair. She saw the fear in Elijah's eyes as he accepted the blow with no acknowledgement at all.

Elijah's eyes scanned the chaos filled room nervously, his heartbeat tripling as he pondered this strange dread that had fallen over him. Then he saw him.

The beautiful man was standing across the dance floor, his jet black hair lying gently upon the shoulders of his long, brown, trench coat. He stood there, staring at Elijah. The chaos seemed to avoid him, seemed to halt whenever anyone came close to him.

"Elijah! What is it?" Ebonee saw the fear in Elijah's eyes spilling over into her own heart as she ducked a punch and ran toward him. She followed his line of sight to see what he was staring at.

"Elijah, what—" The words fell from Ebonee's open mouth as she stared at the most beautiful being she had ever seen. His face was angelic, so smooth and clear, without blemish. She froze.

Elijah felt his chest rising and falling as he forced himself to breathe. He pushed the fear into the back of his mind and turned to search for Ebonee.

"Ebonee!" he yelled, watching as the man took a step in his direction.

Ebonee snapped out of her daze and glanced at Elijah. "Right here!" she shouted, kicking a would-be attacker away without a thought as she fought her way to Elijah's side.

"Come on!" Elijah exclaimed, grabbing her by the hand as soon as she was close.

Elijah turned for the exit and his heart froze again. Lucifer was there, a wicked grin on his lips.

Ebonee felt her hands go numb as she stared into Lucifer's cold gaze. She stood paralyzed behind the Protector, unable to look away from the devil himself.

Elijah suddenly felt very small, very helpless, and weak. His shoulders slumped under the wicked gaze of Satan. Then he felt the small hand in his own, squeezing tightly. That grip was all Ebonee could focus on as the fear flowed through her.

Elijah took a deep breath, forcing his eyes closed, telling himself that the fear was just a trick of the devil. He concentrated on his memories, the memories of Ebonee's bloody body hanging upon that cross in the underground chamber, using the rage that vision inspired in him to fight the fear away.

Lucifer smiled and cocked his head to the side curiously as Elijah's fear slowly turned into a simmering rage. Ebonee felt Elijah's hand let go of hers then.

"Ebonee, run," the Protector instructed, an eerie calmness in his voice as he glanced down at her.

Ebonee wanted to refuse, wanted to stand by his side and fight. But the look in his eye and the tone of his voice left no room for argument. She ran as fast as she could into the chaos around them. As she made her way to the exit, her eyes darted back to the two forms staring each other down.

Elijah followed her for a moment with his eyes. Then he stared back at the figure before him. He had to buy Ebonee some time so she could escape. He closed his eyes, succumbing to his memories and feeling the rage build as he stood before the creature responsible for all of his pain, all of his heartache.

Elijah's fists clenched, longing to hold Enobe and Soul Seeker in his palms as the rage continued to build.

But it was not rage or hatred that forced Elijah into action. It was common sense.

He knew that with or without the blades, there was no fighting this one.

Elijah ran, only to come to a skidding halt once more as Lucifer stood before him yet again, cutting off his flight. Fear once again filled his mind as he felt his body go weightless and drift slowly up into the air. He then watched as the wall suddenly rushed at him, closing his eyes right before he slammed into it. Plaster and wood exploded out from the impact. Before he could hit the floor and let the pain register, he was weightless again, floating back away from the smashed wall.

Again he slammed into another wall, this time shattering glass as his body bounced off of the mirrored wall. He fell heavily this time, groaning as he tried to force himself up.

"I probably should have went to church this morning," he muttered, looking up to see the devil slowly approaching.

With a deep grunt, Elijah stormed forward, having no place left to run. He growled angrily as he once again felt the weightlessness. Once more he slammed into the wall, shattering more glass as the chaos continued around them. A few stopped to watch the spectacle, but most were still wrapped up in their own personal battles.

Elijah didn't fall to the ground this time; instead, he felt his arms stretch out and his head being forced back against the wall, his feet crossing as they were also pinned to the wall. He strained every muscle in his body, desperately trying to free himself from the hold.

But it was useless.

His heart raced as he hung there, completely helpless. Large shards of glass from the broken mirrors suddenly drifted up off the floor, daggers aimed at the Protector's heart. They hung there, motionless for what seemed to be an eternity to Elijah. Elijah then watched as the shards of glass hurled toward his heart.

Elijah closed his eyes, accepting his fate, just as the large bouncer grabbed the dark figure from behind in a bear hug. Elijah heard the glass shards shatter as they fell to the ground beneath him, just as he, too, fell to the floor.

He did not wait to see the huge bouncer go flying backwards through the air as Lucifer mentally disposed of the human. Elijah ran as fast as his legs could carry him. The bouncer bounced heavily off of a table and lay motionless. Lucifer turned back to the Protector, only to find him gone.

Elijah approached the exit at a dead run, ignoring the chaos that still dominated the club. He never looked back. As he approached the door his eyes caught the slight movement as the cigarette machine to the right of the exit began to shake. Elijah growled angrily as the machine slid into his path, blocking the exit door. Lowering his shoulder, Elijah barreled into the heavy metal machine.

Ebonee sat atop her bike, her eyes glued to the front door of the club. Her heart raced as she watched the cigarette machine explode through the double doors, with Elijah tumbling behind it. She let out her breath as Elijah rolled to his feet, ignoring the burning pain in his right shoulder.

"Go!" he yelled as he ran up and jumped on the bike next to her. But Ebonee was already moving.

Elijah glanced back over his shoulder as he gunned the throttle, just in time to see the front doors of the club explode outward. He ducked reflexively as one of the doors sliced through the air directly above him. Not needing any more incentive, Elijah hauled ass, throwing the front wheel of the bike into the air as he sped away behind Ebonee.

The dark figure stepped out and glanced around at the shaken people standing outside, staring dumbfounded at the club entrance. Four riders, standing next to their bikes by the entrance, caught the figure's attention. In a moment, their eyes were rolling back in their heads and their consciousness was lost, as four fiends answered their master's call.

Lucifer then stepped off of the top step, vanishing before his foot could touch down. A large black raven flapped its mighty wings as it climbed high into the night sky, in pursuit of the Protector.

Elijah heard the roar of the other four motorcycles as he turned a corner. Then he felt the chill bumps run along his skin once more.

"Ebonee," Elijah began, tapping the side of the jet black helmet to open up communications with her. Her image appeared a second later. "We have company: four riders behind us," he announced as he swerved between two cars as they sped along Main Street.

He did a double-take as he glanced at the driver in the car he was passing. The man's head snapped around violently as the fiend entered his mind.

Elijah hit the brakes hard, almost sending himself over the handlebars as the bike came to a skidding halt, just as the car swerved to the left in an attempt to smash him into a parked car.

Elijah hit the gas and veered around the vehicle as it slammed into the parked car along the side of the street.

"Elijah? You okay?" Ebonee asked, glancing into her rearview mirror at the large fireball behind her.

"I'm fine!" Elijah replied, swerving in the nick of time as the second of the two cars swerved to hit him, narrowly missing the back of his bike.

Elijah wondered just how many drivers he would have to avoid as he looked ahead to the crowded street. He swerved again, hitting the throttle as a car slammed into the guardrail behind him and sent sparks flying. Elijah's thumb hov-

ered over the turbo button, but it did not fall as he glanced
up to the traffic and busy intersections.

"Elijah, we have to make it to the freeway! We can lose
them with the turbo there!" Ebonee exclaimed, her voice
ringing into Elijah's helmet.

"How far?" Elijah asked, glancing over his shoulder repeatedly to keep an eye on the estranged driver. He sighed
heavily as he watched two of the motorcycle mounted fiends
zoom past the car.

"There's an on ramp up ahead. About five miles," Ebonee
said.

"I think we lost two of them," Elijah commented as he passed
another intersection. "Maybe not," he added as he watched
the other two riders swoop onto Main Street as he passed the
intersection. They were on his tail.

"Keep moving. I'm going to try and slow them down," Elijah said, falling back.

Ebonee stared ahead; there were four intersections left
before the entrance to the freeway.

Two of the riders shot past Elijah in pursuit of Ebonee as
he slowed down, thinking they were only after him.

"Shit! Ebonee, two of them are on your tail!" Elijah shouted,
just as one of the remaining two riders behind him pulled
up alongside him swinging a heavy chain. Elijah winced as
the chain fell across his back repeatedly.

"Son-of-a-bitch!" Elijah growled as the chain connected
once more, almost causing him to lose control of his bike.

Ebonee glanced over her shoulder just as the two riders
closed on her. She focused her attention on the intersection
ahead as the traffic light turned red. She saw the big rig
speeding across the intersecting street at the last moment.

One of the riders was right behind her now, close enough
to spit on. She gunned the throttle, leaning down into the
wind as the bike shot forward. She swooped in front of the

rig, her back tire missing its fender by inches. The rider behind her wasn't as lucky.

Ebonee turned her head to look back and saw the riderless bike sliding along behind her, sparks flying up into the night.

"Ouch," Ebonee muttered, returning her eyes to the road ahead. Only three more intersections to go, and the other rider was closing fast.

Elijah growled in anger once more as he felt the metal thump across his back. His heart skipped a beat as he swerved quickly, narrowly avoiding the wrecked bike lying in the middle of the three-lane street, almost losing control himself. He watched the chain-swinging fiend as he winded up for another attack.

Elijah timed it perfectly, swinging out his left arm and allowing the chain to wrap around it. He jerked his arm back sharply, pulling the rider from his bike and watching him tumble and slide down the street behind him.

"Mmmm, that's gotta hurt," Elijah murmured, and then he winced as he watched a car run over the rider's body.

"Two more intersections and we're home free!" Ebonee announced, the street lights streaking along her black helmeted image in Elijah's visor.

"Next time you decide to leave your garbage in the street, let me know!" Elijah joked, looking back as the second rider drew close.

Ebonee flew through the next intersection with the rider on her heels. He pulled up next to her, brandishing a long lead pipe. Ebonee snatched her left hand off of the handlebar just in time as the pipe whooshed through the air. Her front wheel wobbled as she fought to keep control of the speeding bike with one hand.

She regained control and swerved close to the rider, kicking at him with her left foot, making him swerve away. She cursed to herself as the rider managed to maneuver his way around the slower moving car in the center lane, and then pull closer to her again, ready for another swipe.

Elijah saw the light change to red at the coming intersection just as the rider pulled up even with him, his eyes trained on Elijah and not the road ahead. Elijah chuckled softly and waved at the rider, getting a silly, perplexed gaze in return.

Elijah slammed on the brakes, bracing himself as the bike stopped on a dime. He shook his head and sighed, watching as the crossing bus picked up another passenger in the middle of the intersection.

Elijah hit his throttle again as he heard the collision and loud blaring horns behind him. He saw the possessed driver in his rearview mirror smashing his way through the traffic behind him.

Ebonee swerved away from the rider to avoid another swing from the heavy lead pipe. She could see the on ramp up ahead, on the other side of the last intersection. "I can't seem to get rid of this pest," Ebonee said, her image appearing in Elijah's helmet again at the sound of her voice.

Elijah could see them now, just ahead, a block away. He hit the black button on his right, bringing up the targeting crosshairs.

"Ebonee, when I tell you, I want you to veer away from him as quickly as you can, okay?"

Elijah waited as the crosshairs tracked the rider's bike, attempting to get a lock. His thumb was ready to hit the button a second time, to hopefully launch a rocket.

"Why? What are you going to do?" Ebonee asked anxiously, kicking at the rider as he once again pulled in close.

"Just do it!" Elijah yelled as the targeting system locked on the rider's bike, turning from red to green as the intermittent beep changed to a single, steady tone. Elijah's thumb hit the button. He closed his eyes as a bright flash of light came from the front of his bike and the rocket tore down the street, leaving a winding, smoky trail as it closed in on Ebonee and the rider.

"Now!" Elijah shouted, as he watched the rocket closing in on the two speeding bikes.

Ebony kicked at the rider one last time, forcing him to swerve to the left, just as the explosion sent him airborne in flames. Ebonee's eyes went wide as she stared back at the huge ball of flames.

"What the hell? Elijah, are you crazy?" she exclaimed as she hit the on ramp.

Elijah smiled as he passed the burning debris, his eyes looking over to the expressway running parallel to Main Street. He could see Ebonee ahead as she slowed down to wait for him. Something on the expressway caught his eye, and he stared in disbelief as an eighteen-wheeler suddenly swerved, slamming a passing car into the guardrail. Elijah was still almost a block away from the freeway entrance as Ebonee pulled over on the shoulder.

"Oh, shit."

"What's wrong?" Ebonee asked, turning to stare back at the on ramp just as the eighteen-wheeler jackknifed. She watched as the rear of the tanker skidded around and off the road, flipping as it did so. Flames and sparks shot up into the sky as the tanker rolled across the ground in a wide arc, coming to a stop on the on ramp.

Elijah heard the horns behind him again, and he knew the possessed driver was still pursuing him. He slowed down and stared back at the wreckage on the on ramp.

"What are you going to do?" Ebonee asked worriedly.

"Good question," Elijah replied as he felt the chill bumps crawl across his skin. Lucifer was still on their trail.

His mind raced as he glanced back to see how close the possessed driver had come.

"Fuck!" he exclaimed, as the driver shot out from behind another car and quickly closed in on him.

Letting out an exasperated sigh, Elijah ducked his head down and gunned the throttle, hurtling forward directly toward the wrecked tanker.

"Hey, Ebonee, this thing wouldn't happen to come with a fire extinguisher, would it?" he joked, as he approached the burning silver cylinder.

"Elijah . . ." Ebonee's words trailed off in a sigh as she figured at that moment that Kenyatta was absolutely right about her brother: He was too fucking crazy to die.

Elijah hit the black button as soon as he heard the single tone, sending the remaining rocket screaming toward the burning cylinder. He held on for dear life then, as he hit the turbo button right behind it.

Ebonee guided her bike onto the expressway, looking over her shoulder as a second explosion rocked the area and an enormous fireball filled the skyline.

Elijah's bike exploded through the flames and twisted metal, emerging on the other side as a bright orange streak. The flames seemed to rage higher in protest as the turbo kicked in.

Ebonee hit her own turbo as she watched the red streak come flying through the ball of fire, a wild cry of ecstasy filling her helmet as Elijah screamed through the wreckage.

"Hell yeah! I love this thing!" Elijah exclaimed as Ebonee steered her bike in behind his.

"You need help," Ebonee said flatly, lowering her head as the cars and red taillights became a blur.

Elijah could only laugh and smile as he felt the evil presence fade away behind them.

Chapter Sixteen
NEEDLE IN A HAYSTACK

"Yeah . . . they just walked in. Okay . . . I'll see you when you get here." Director Moss hung up the phone and looked up as Ebonee and Elijah stepped into his office. His eyes lingered on Agent Garland for a moment. "I thought you wouldn't wear one of those ridiculous suits," he commented, his brow raised curiously.

Elijah shifted uncomfortably as he frowned. Ebonee had gotten him to try the suit. Ebonee smiled as she noticed his awkwardness, knowing the suit wouldn't last long. He did look sexy in it, though.

"Don't worry, I have a change of clothes in my bag," Elijah commented sourly, cutting an eye at Ebonee, who smiled.

"So, how was your flight?" Moss asked as he reached into his desk drawer to pull out a file.

"What are we here for?" Agent Lane asked, crossing her arms over her chest. "We were just about to start on the list—"

"Forget about the list for now," Moss interrupted her, leaning back in his soft, comfortable leather chair to regard them both.

"So how is the nightlife down in Atlanta?" he asked, his arms crossing his chest as he waited for an answer.

"Nightlife?" Ebonee repeated curiously.

"Yeah. Life? At night?" Moss said smartly. "Seems that there were a number of accidents last night in Atlanta. Along with a few explosions—an overturned tractor trailer—you two wouldn't know anything about this, though, would you?" Moss finished sarcastically.

Elijah suddenly found the pictures on the wall very interesting as he stared to his right, pretending to not hear Moss's question.

"Accidents?" Ebonee repeated, trying to look surprised. "What accidents?" She brought her hand up to scratch her head and stared at the director with a dumbfounded expression.

"Who fired the rocket?" Moss sighed.

"Rocket?" Ebonee glanced at Elijah. "What rocket? I don't know anything about any rockets, do you?"

"Noooo, no. Somebody was firing rockets?" Elijah strained to keep the surprised expression on his face. "Imagine that."

"It was you, wasn't it?" Moss said evenly, staring at Elijah. "You fired a rocket at an overturned tractor trailer—a trailer carrying gasoline of all things!" Moss exclaimed. "The explosion was heard for miles! Hell, you could see the fireball from Macon!"

"But it was already on fire! It was gonna blow up any—" Elijah said catching himself too late, "way," he finished sheepishly.

Ebonee shook her head and chuckled as Elijah shut his eyes tight, frowning as he dropped his head.

"Stupid!" Ebonee muttered under her breath.

Moss shook his head and stared at the two of them incredulously. "I gave the two of you those bikes for a reason. They are for FBI business only, not your personal enjoyment. You can't just go around blowing things up!" he chided.

"I swear, it was already on fire. It was gonna blow up anyway," Elijah said, shaking his head. "I hit the button by accident! I ain't even know the rockets was there!" he continued, talking fast. "Did you tell me the rockets was on the bike?" he asked, staring at Moss with his eyebrows raised. "No, you didn't. Was there a little sticker on the button, sayin' 'rockets' or something? Damn! I ain't know!" He looked back and forth from the director to Ebonee, his shoulders hunched up in a helpless position.

Ebonee laughed and shook her head.

"Enough about that," Moss said, shooting Elijah a disdainful look and picking up a folder from his desk. "I called you here because I have some new information on our friend, Parks. He seems to have an idea that he can work out a deal for information on Glenn's location. He called me yesterday. We tried to trace the call, but he had a trace block," Moss explained as he reached into the folder.

Elijah sighed heavily as he stared at the pictures on the wall, thoroughly bored.

"Then what's the information?" Ebonee asked, her smile disappearing.

"For everything we make, we make something to counter it. We were able to narrow it down to a somewhat exact location," Moss replied.

Ebonee crossed her arms in front of her chest, narrowing her brown eyes at the director as Elijah rolled his eyes and looked away. "Somewhat?" she asked.

"We know he's in the 718 area code," Moss said evenly, drawing a raised brow from Ebonee as she waited for him to finish. "That's it."

Elijah laughed, pulling at the constricting black tie to loosen it up.

"That's it? You know he's in New York City? That's a big help," Ebonee sighed.

"There was one other thing I overheard in the background while we were talking. I believe he is in a church." Moss sat forward in the chair.

"Oh, that narrows it down," Elijah muttered with a smirk, as he returned his gaze to the pictures on the wall.

"Director, do you know how many churches there are in New York?" Ebonee asked.

"Actually," Moss shot them a smirk of his own as he extended his hand holding a stack of papers out for Ebonee, "I do. Here, this is a list of them."

Ebonee accepted the papers with a chagrined expression.

"You can't be serious," she breathed, flipping through the list.

"Oh, I'm very serious. This is why we pay you." He pulled open a drawer in his desk to retrieve another folder. "Here are your plane tickets. You can pick up a rental when you get to New York."

"Director Moss, there are two agents here to see you."

Moss stared down at the intercom on his desk, adjusting his wireframed glasses.

"Send them in, Ms. Jones," he announced, pushing a button as he looked up to Ebonee and Elijah. "I suggest you get going. And Garland, aren't you glad you bought that suit?" he teased as the door opened.

"Ha, ha. You're a comedian now," Elijah muttered as he frowned, turning for the door behind Ebonee just as a short, red-headed woman accompanied by a slender white guy with short, brown hair stepped in.

Elijah cocked his head to the side curiously as they passed, trying to figure out why they were staring at him.

"What? Am I an alien or something?" he asked, just as Ebonee grabbed him by the arm and pulled him from the office.

"What? She was all up in my mouth!" Elijah complained in defense to the accusing look Ebonee was giving him.

"You have no idea who they are, do you?" she asked, her expression shifting to amusement. "Oh, forget it. Let's get you out of that suit," she finished, turning as he followed her out.

They wasted no time getting down to business. Elijah called Father Holbrook and instructed him to meet them at the airport in New York. They both then boarded a plane and made the trip to New York to begin their search.

After about two weeks of church-hopping and interviewing pastors and congregation members, they began to get bored.

They sat outside of an old Baptist church in the Bronx. It was getting late in the evening, and neither of them really wanted to go in. They sat outside for a moment, both of them staring at the front door of the church dejectedly.

"Come on," Ebonee finally said with a sigh, pushing open her door halfheartedly.

"No," Elijah returned flatly, crossing his arms over his chest in defiance.

Ebonee stared at him curiously. "What do you mean no? You can't say no," she said, frowning.

"No," Elijah repeated, staring blankly ahead. "I refuse to go into any more black churches."

Ebonee's face twisted up in confusion as she gazed at him. The sun was just dipping below the skyline. "What?"

"You heard me. I refuse to go—"

"Why?" Ebonee interrupted him, her face still contorted as she stared at him.

"I refuse to be saved again. And again. And again," he answered, nodding his head with each repetition of the word.

Ebonee sighed heavily as she watched Elijah's white cornrowed head bob up and down. Slowly, the car was filled with her snickering until she was laughing out of control. Elijah stared at her with one brow raised, thinking that the woman had finally lost her marbles.

They had been searching for almost two weeks now, and had not come up with anything. Father Holbrook had been very enthusiastic about the mission at first, wanting to experience his faith in other environments, he had said. But after the twentieth church, even he had lost his vigor and had requested to be dropped off at the hotel.

Elijah waited a moment for Ebonee to catch her breath before he continued. "And besides, half of them are more full of shit than a septic tank in the suburbs," he said, his eyes going outside to the front of the rental car. "Look at that Benz right there." He pointed at the brand new Mercedes parked in front of them. "I bet you that's the pastor's! I'll bet you all the money I've got. How much you willin' to lose?" he finished, staring at her questioningly.

Ebonee continued to laugh, shaking her head in denial as Elijah kept talking.

"See? Look. What's the license plate say?" he asked, pointing again.

"Jesus," Ebonee managed to breathe through her laughter.

"Jesus my ass. It should say 'collection plate' on that muthafucka!" Elijah exclaimed, his ire rising as he thought more about it.

Ebonee was in tears now, leaning over with her head resting on the steering wheel as she cried. Her stomach was beginning to cramp from laughing. "Get out of the car!" she finally screamed, pushing her door open and stepping out.

She laughed all the way to the red wooden front door. The paint was old and peeling, and the large church looked as though it could use a makeover. Ebonee sighed, wiping the wetness of her tears from her face. Her short, black hair shimmered in the fading sunlight as Elijah continued to mutter obscenities about the corruption of churches in the black neighborhoods.

She knocked lightly on the door just as her cell phone rang and the door to the church swung open slowly.

"Go ahead, I'm going to take this," Ebonee said to Elijah as she backed away from the door and his growing frown.

"You know you ain't right. That's cool, though. You got out of this one. Give me the damned pictures," Elijah said, feigning anger as Ebonee smiled and handed him the pictures.

Elijah turned his attention to the bosomy young woman who had answered the door. She wasn't the prettiest girl in the choir, but the pastor probably figured she would do. Elijah sighed, shaking the bad thoughts from his mind as he asked the woman if the pastor was in.

He was then led into the large building through the sanctuary. He stared around at all the audio and video equipment positioned in the chapel itself. Large screen televisions, huge speakers, reel-to-reel machines . . . They had everything.

He followed the woman into a long hallway, ignoring her as she stared over her shoulder at his white hair. She stopped outside of a door that held a small plaque that read *PASTOR*.

She knocked lightly, and a bellowing voice shouted for them to come in. Elijah stepped into the plush carpeted room behind the woman and walked up to the large, shiny, black wooden desk. Behind the desk sat a young handsome black man. His teeth were almost too white and his suit was expensive. Elijah tried his best to suppress a frown as the man stood and extended a brightly glittering hand in greeting.

"Agent Garland," Elijah announced weakly, as he wrestled with his new badge, attempting to flip it open like Ebonee. "F.B.I." He finally got the blasted thing open to present to the pastor.

Then Elijah accepted the pastor's offered hand, wondering why every black preacher had to squeeze your hand as if they were trying to break it.

"God bless you, Agent Garland. I'm Pastor Trevose. Welcome to our humble church. How may I help you?" the pastor asked, his voice loud enough to be heard three doors down.

Elijah blinked his eyes slowly, trying to keep his contempt to himself. He also fought the urge to ask him why in the hell he was screaming. "Well, uhhh—" Elijah began, staring down at his hand, which had begun to go numb, "you could start by giving me back my hand." He wondered to himself just why the pastor had to squeeze his hand so damned hard. Was he trying to prove something? Because, if so, then he should have crushed every bone in the dark-skinned pastor's sweaty hand.

"Oh yes, forgive me. Please, have a seat," Pastor Trevose returned, gesturing to one of the two soft, black leather chairs sitting in front of his desk.

"No. That won't be necessary. I just want to ask you if you've ever seen this man before," Elijah replied, handing him a picture of Agent Parks.

Pastor Trevose took the picture and examined it for a moment, handing it back to Elijah.

"Don't get too many white folks in here."

"Okay, thank you," Elijah returned, quickly turning for the door.

"Wait!" the pastor bellowed, stepping out from behind his desk to follow Elijah to the door.

Elijah sighed deeply and his shoulders sagged as he waited for the pastor to catch up. "Yes?" he asked dejectedly.

"Our church is having a revival tonight. I just wanted to extend an invitation. If you're going to be in town, you should stop by," the pastor said, smiling wide.

"Okay," Elijah replied flatly, turning for the door once again.

"Are you saved?"

Elijah fought back his frown and smiled as the pastor stood in front of him, his hand on the door knob, but not turning it. "Yes, yes I am," he responded, smiling as he looked at the short man.

"Well, praise the Lord! Praise the Lord. Glad to hear it. Do you have a church home?"

"Look, I'm sorry, Pastor, but I'm on official F.B.I. business, remember? So I really must go." Elijah was on the verge of exploding. He figured that the man only wanted another hand to feed the collection plate.

"Oh, yes, yes. I understand. Well remember, our door is always open," the pastor replied, opening the door finally and extending his hand. Elijah accepted his hand and squeezed real hard.

"Ow! Ow!" the Pastor whispered, leaning over as Elijah applied a little more pressure.

"Oh, I'm sorry. Forget my own strength sometimes. Well, take care!" Elijah smiled sincerely for the first time as he stepped out of the office.

He met up with Ebonee back in the car

"What are you cheesing about?" Ebonee asked, turning the key to start the car as she stared at Elijah's smile in the dim glow of the streetlights.

"Nothing, man. Nothing." Elijah laughed lightly, shaking his head. "Can I ask you a question?"

"Of course. What is it?" Ebonee's smile slowly eased onto her lips as Elijah's never faded.

"I just want to get a second opinion. Because . . . I just want to make sure it isn't me. Maybe I'm seeing things fucked up, but—" He paused, his teeth gleaming in the light as he smiled. "Churches are supposed to be the house of the

Lord, right?" he asked, awaiting her reply as she pulled the car out of the space.

"Uhhh, yeah. I guess," Ebonee answered slowly, almost afraid of where this was going.

"And the house of the Lord is for the people, right?" He paused again, waiting.

"Yeah."

"Then why the doors locked? To keep the people out?" Elijah asked, a thoughtful expression upon his face.

Ebonee opened her mouth to answer but was too late.

"Then why are the doors locked? Why I gots to knock on my Father's door? A door that is always supposed to be open to the people. I'm the people! You're the people! Hell, we all the people!" Elijah exclaimed, his voice rising as he began to speak faster.

Ebonee laughed lightly and tried to get a word in. "But people steal—"

"So they lock the doors to keep the people that steal out? Hell, those the ones need ta be in there!" Elijah exclaimed.

"But they can't just let all that expensive equipment get stolen," Ebonee said between breaths, laughing.

"That's another thing. Why they need all that stuff anyway? Did Jesus have a big screen TV? Did he have a microphone? Nawww!" he exclaimed, shaking his head vehemently. Seeing Ebonee in tears again only spurred him on. "He ain't have none of that shit, yet he spoke to the multitudes! He ain't have no radio station, no TV program that only comes on when the infomercials go off. Naw, he didn't need that shit! Man, they so full of—" Elijah's voice trailed off as Ebonee put a hand over her mouth, shaking her head as she laughed.

"Are you finished?" she asked lightly, still giggling. "Because that was Moss that called."

"Oh? Are the crusades coming to an end?" Elijah asked sarcastically.

"God, I hope so," Ebonee sighed, leaning her head back against the headrest and closing her eyes. "I could care less if I ever set foot inside of another church again."

"Well, I guess we better pick up the priest," Elijah said as Ebonee turned a corner. "So we have to meet your boss somewhere?"

"Our boss you mean?" Ebonee replied, cutting her eye at him.

"Whatever."

"Yes. I don't know the details as of yet, but I guess he'll fill us in when we get there," Ebonee explained as she pulled the car into the hotel parking lot.

"The guy we are after is the guy who tried to kill you, right?" Elijah asked as they both stepped out of the car. Elijah's eyes found Ebonee's backside as she walked in front of him and he sighed, wishing that they could have a few moments alone.

"Glenn," she said over her shoulder, snorting derisively. "He's a real piece of work."

"I can kill him, right?" Elijah asked, smiling as Ebonee turned to regard him.

"If you can beat me to it," she replied, a grin on her full, red lips. "I just hope he gives me a reason to," she finished as they walked through the sliding doors.

"Trying to kill you isn't enough?" Elijah asked absently, turning to observe himself in the large mirrors on the wall of the lobby.

Ebonee stopped and turned around, her hands on her hips.

"Why is it that you have to stare at your own reflection in every mirror you see?" she asked, cocking her head to the side as she awaited his response.

Elijah's brow went up as he returned her curious gaze. "I don't." He paused and considered the question. "Do I?" he asked, gazing back at the mirror.

"Ummm, yes, you do," Ebonee said, a smile forming on her lips. She never figured Elijah to be the conceited type, and he actually did not really act like it. But she had noticed his intense love of reflective surfaces.

"Well, I never really noticed," Elijah answered, grinning as he continued to admire himself in the wall length mirror, adjusting his black leather trench coat.

"How old were you when you first lost your virginity?" Ebonee asked, reaching out a hand to pull the long, white braids out from behind his coat collar.

"What? Where did that come from?" he replied, looking surprised.

Elijah realized then just how little the two of them actually knew about each other.

"Just answer the question," Ebonee said, smiling as they finally reached the elevator. They stepped on and Ebonee sighed, seeing more mirrors.

"Okay, okay. I think I was eighteen or nineteen. I got raped," Elijah said, shrugging as he looked at her through the mirror's reflection. "God, you are so beautiful."

"You got raped?" Ebonee exclaimed.

Elijah shrugged again as his eyes went to Ebonee's. "Oh, no. That was the second time. The first time I was about the same age," he clarified, remembering.

Ebonee's mouth was still twisted up in doubt. She was still stuck on the rape issue. "You were raped?" she asked, giving him a doubtful look as the doors opened up.

"Yeah," Elijah answered flatly.

"Men don't get raped; you can't rape the willing."

"Well I was far from willing," Elijah said as they stepped down the hall.

"Yeah, right. I bet you weren't," Ebonee said, turning up her lip.

Elijah laughed lightly as they came to their door. "She was ugly, old, and had like seven kids," he explained.

"What were you doing with her in the first place?"

"She stole my jacket out of my locker at this fast food place I was working at. She told me if I wanted it back, I would have to come over her house and get it." Elijah pushed open the door to the sound of snoring.

"And she raped you when you got there?" Ebonee asked as she stepped by him into the room.

"That's about the size of it. She told me that if I wanted the jacket, I had to give her what she wanted. Next thing I knew I was getting stripped. And that was that." Elijah shrugged once again, smiling into Ebonee's eyes as he un-ceremoniously woke Father Holbrook from his slumber. Ebonee shook her head and smiled.

They informed Father Holbrook of their plans and were soon on their way to Valley Stream. They met Director Moss at a small shopping center a few blocks away from a large mall.

Ebonee pulled the rental car into the lot and shut off the engine, nodding to the black SUV parked directly across from them. Elijah nodded his understanding and stepped out of the rental with Ebonee, leaving Father Holbrook in the car alone.

The few shoppers going about their business all took note of the strange black man with stark white hair as he passed, his head low and collar up. Elijah took comfort in the low hum of the twin blades at his sides, tucked away out of sight under his black trench coat.

Ebonee's eyes gave the dark parking lot a quick once over, looking for anything out of the ordinary. But other than the curious stares, nothing was out of place. She pulled her own brown trench coat closer around her as she felt a breeze blow in. Her eyes went to the cloudy sky, almost expecting the rain to fall upon her skyward gaze. She could smell the rain in the air. She paused, inhaling the refreshing scent deeply before opening the rear door of the black SUV and climbing inside.

"Glad you could make it."

Elijah adjusted his blades as he entered the vehicle from the other side. He, too, could smell the rain coming.

"Here."

Moss handed both of them a pair of wire-rimmed glasses with a tiny earpiece attached to the arm.

"These will keep you in touch with us and each other. Parks says he wants the two of you to meet him in the food court," he explained, his eyes darting around the parking lot and then staring at the both of them, one at a time.

"So what is this going to be? You making a deal with him or what?" Ebonee asked, as she placed the glasses on her face.

"Hardly. As soon as you make contact, make the arrest," Moss informed her, his gaze holding her so she would be clear on that point.

"You really think he'll show up?" Elijah asked, resting his head gently on his finger as he leaned against the back door as if he were bored.

"Well, that's what we're here to find out."

Elijah sighed lightly and slipped the glasses on, letting them rest on the tip of his nose. He gazed out the window over the rim of them. He ran a hand over the hilt of Enobe as he sat there; somehow he knew his blades would be needed very soon.

"You with us?" Ebonee asked Elijah. She, too, had her glasses tilted downward and was peering over the rim at Elijah. She could sense his apprehension.

"Yeah, yeah," Elijah replied, glancing up at Ebonee from his ponderings.

"And Ebonee?"

Ebonee turned to regard Moss as he spoke, pausing to be sure he had her attention.

"We want him alive; if he can lead us to Glenn, then he's no use to us dead. Understand?"

"Yes," Ebonee replied blankly.

Elijah continued to stare into her eyes as she spoke the word, and he knew she would kill Parks if he so much as blinked.

"Good. Then let's get this over with. We have three units, one at each entrance of the mall. They will stay put, out of sight until contact is made. Okay, let's move," Moss ordered.

Ebonee and Elijah exited the SUV and quickly walked back to the rental.

"No glasses for me?" Father Holbrook asked as Ebonee started the car and slowly pulled out of the parking lot.

"Father Holbrook, I want you to stay in the car and leave it running. Do you know how to drive?" Ebonee asked as she pulled up to a stoplight.

"Of course I do."

"Good, here." Ebonee handed Father Holbrook a two-way radio. "If we need you, we'll call you on this," she explained, her eyes going over to Elijah.

Elijah sat with his left hand resting comfortably on the hilt of one of the blades, his light brown eyes staring out at the dark sky as the storm clouds slowly drifted in. He focused on the remaining stars as they flickered brightly above.

"So, any funny feelings?" Ebonee asked.

"No, not yet," Elijah replied absently, his eyes never leaving the stars.

"You will tell me, right?"

"Yes."

But Elijah had no intention of telling her. He would not put her at risk again. He sighed deeply, shifting in his seat as he felt Ebonee staring at him. "Come on," he quickly said, feeling guilty as Ebonee's brown eyes sought out the truth behind his own. He stepped out of the car just as Ebonee put the rental in park. He waited in front of the car, his eyes still on the remaining stars as a few mall goers passed by, staring at him.

His hands rested on each hilt of the blades under his trench coat, letting the comforting hum soothe him.

"Good hunting, Protector," Father Holbrook shouted behind them from the car window as they made their way to the mall's entrance.

Ebonee frowned at the statement. She knew Elijah wouldn't tell her if the demons showed up. She sighed as she glanced at him as he held the door open for her, knowing he was only trying to protect her. They proceeded to the food court in silence, Elijah ignoring the many stares he received from the shoppers going about their business.

They arrived at the food court, chose a table, and sat down.

"Well? What now?" Elijah asked.

"We wait," Ebonee answered, her eyes darting around the food court suspiciously.

"We should split up," Elijah stated, turning to stare into her eyes over the rim of his glasses.

"No," Ebonee replied almost too quickly. "I mean, we should stay together. He might get spooked if he sees one of us and not the other."

"Okay."

Elijah turned around in the seat as people mulled about, carrying their bags or food trays around them. Some stared openly at Elijah, while others did so less conspicuously. Ebonee also stared at Elijah, her eyes glued to his over the rim of her glasses.

They sat in silence for a while; the only time either of them spoke was to tell Moss the situation. Ebonee kept her eyes on Elijah the entire time, waiting for him to act. She had no intention of letting him run off alone to do battle, and she knew without a doubt that was what he would do.

"Ebonee," Elijah began, his eyes never leaving the newspaper on the table.

"Yes?"

"Why are you staring at me instead of keeping an eye out for Parks?" he asked, a smile slowly spreading on his lips.

"I'm not. . . ."

Ebonee let the words die on her lips, seeing the smirk on Elijah's face; she knew it didn't make any sense to lie. She sighed deeply and looked away.

"Ebonee, look. I'm not hiding anything from you. I haven't felt anything since we've been here."

"Yeah, but will you tell me if you do?" she asked, her eyes searching his once again.

It was Elijah's turn to sigh deeply now, as he felt the love in her eyes as she stared at him. His smile disappeared.

"Look, I can't help what I am now, and I refuse to put you in any danger. I can't let anything happen to you. Can't you understand that?"

"Can't you understand that I—" she paused, remembering that Moss was listening to every word they said.

Elijah knew what she was about to say and he took his glasses off, motioning for her to do the same.

"Listen. These demons are not your everyday bad guys. You know that first hand. They will do anything and everything within their power to see me dead. If that means using you to get to me, then that's what they'll do. You know all this already. I didn't ask to be this way, Ebonee, but I am. I'm as far from normal as you can get. I have been given a gift to deal with these creatures. You haven't—"

"No, but—" Ebonee tried to interject.

"But nothing, Ebonee. You can't do anything to help me when it comes to them. I'm sorry, but it's true. You know this. Remember the underground chamber?"

Ebonee lowered her gaze as she listened to Elijah's words.

She knew he spoke the truth. She sighed sadly, nodding her head in affirmation slowly.

"Listen, I know you only want to help, but I would die if anything happened to you because of me, so let's make a deal," he said, smiling as she glanced up curiously.

"A deal?"

"Yeah. You leave the demons to me, and I'll leave the common criminals to you."

"Wow, that sounds really fair."

Ebonee frowned as she said the words, unable to hide her sarcasm. But she couldn't deny the common sense of his offer.

"Okay," she sighed regretfully.

Elijah felt a sudden pang of guilt as he saw the sadness cross her expression. He ignored it, looking away. It was something that had to be done.

He blamed himself for Taysia's death; after all, it was his past that had brought about the incident. The jealous husband's bullet was meant for him and him alone. He refused to lose Ebonee. Slowly, he pushed his glasses back up onto his face and they sat in silence.

"We're here, sir," Ebonee said as she listened to Moss's voice in her ear. He was inquiring about the long moment of silence. She glanced over at Elijah, who was looking the other way. She shook her head and smiled as she followed his eyes over to the table across from them, and the two scantily dressed, young black women there, staring at Elijah and whispering.

Elijah felt Ebonee looking at him and shot her a glance. Ebonee frowned playfully, her brow rising as she looked over to the table and then back at Elijah. Elijah smiled and shook his head, shrugging helplessly.

Elijah let his gaze lift upward to the large glass dome above the food court and to the remaining stars poking out between the advancing storm clouds. For a brief moment, Elijah forgot about the demons. He forgot about the blades at his sides. He forgot about all the pain and the tears. He forgot about it all.

Ebonee saw the odd, serene look in his eyes and she, too, glanced upward to the night sky. *What do you see with those beautiful eyes of yours?* Ebonee thought as she watched the bright stars flicker between the darkness of the storm clouds.

Elijah blinked slowly, a single tear falling from his eye. For a moment he was a child again, back in Wisconsin where he and his grandmother would visit each year. Things were so simple then. His only worry was what kind of trouble he could get himself into that would outdo his cousins' mischief. He opened his eyes slowly, his memories fading away as the storm clouds rolled in swiftly.

Too swiftly.

Elijah blinked his eyes rapidly, tilting his head in confusion. Lightning flashed across the sky, followed by a deafening boom as the thunder followed.

Ebonee jumped, shaken from her contemplations by the loud sound. All around them, people stared up at the now black sky, pointing and whispering.

Elijah stared up at the darkness as others around them began to gather their things and began running for the exit, wanting to get to their cars before the rain came. His jaws grinded in anticipation and his breathing became shallow. His nostrils flared as he felt the first subtle vibrations in the blades at his waste.

"Elijah, what is it?" Ebonee asked, her eyes fearful as she stared at him. Her words were drowned out by another loud boom.

Elijah's gaze never left the large dome. He squinted, attempting to make out the tiny black dot he thought he saw floating in the sea of blackness. Slowly, the huge crow came into focus, as it alighted itself on the dome, just as the rain began.

Elijah kept his eyes on the bird; somehow he knew that the bird's tiny black eyes were focused on him.

"Excuse me, is your name Ebonee?"

Ebonee tore her gaze away from Elijah to regard the drenched woman standing next to her. She held a white envelope in her hand.

Ebonee stared at the woman, at a loss. Then her eyes went to the scattering crowd, searching frantically.

"Y-yes. Why?"

"Someone asked me to give this to you."

She turned to see the woman extending her hand out to her with the sealed envelope in it.

"Who asked you to give this to me?" Ebonee asked quickly, her voice filled with urgency as she took the letter from the woman.

"Some guy outside," the woman replied, shrugging as another flash of lightning caused both of them to flinch in fear. "Can you believe this weather? The news didn't say anything about a storm tonight," the woman commented, staring upward as Ebonee opened the envelope.

"Thank you." Ebonee pulled a small note from the envelope.

"No problem," the woman answered, her eyes lingering on the dome and the dark sky above as she turned and walked away.

Ebonee unfolded the note and read the words. "It says to meet him outside in five minutes," she said, glancing up at Elijah, but his gaze never faltered from the dark sky above.

"Elijah?"

Elijah felt Ebonee's hand on his own as he continued to stare up at the small black creature.

"Elijah, we have to—"

Ebonee's words were again drowned out as another frightening crackle of lightning and boom of thunder exploded above them. Her heart almost stopped beating as she felt Elijah's skin grow cold to the touch and felt the tiny chill bumps run under her fingers and up Elijah's arm.

Ebonee froze, knowing what that meant.

Abruptly, Elijah stood. He watched the crow as it spread its wings and flew off into the swirling darkness of the storm. He felt the hum at his waist then, stronger than before.

His nostrils flared in contempt as he dropped his gaze to the two forms standing to his right in front of a service corridor between Popeye's and KFC. They watched him also.

Ebonee's heartbeat doubled as she followed Elijah's gaze to the two men.

"Get Parks," Elijah said, his voice cold and icy.

Ebonee knew there was no room or time for an argument as she watched Elijah step off toward the two individuals. She fought the desire to follow him and turned to head for the exit, her eyes over her shoulder as the two men disappeared into the corridor. She looked away as Elijah gave chase.

"I'm going outside," she announced into the transmitter, glancing at the corridor one last time just as Elijah disappeared into it.

Elijah paused as the lightning and thunder roared above him. The two figures stood at the end of the corridor now, near the exit, waiting, watching.

His black leather trench coat flew up behind him as he broke into a run. The men disappeared through the door and out into the raging storm. Elijah exploded through the door a moment later, coming to a stop in the drenching rain. His eyes searched the dark parking lot, now crowded with cars as they honked their horns angrily at each other, wanting to be home out of the storm.

He found them a second later, standing across the lot in the rain, waiting. Elijah slowly began walking toward them, ignoring the blaring horns as he stepped out into traffic, the water running down his face as he gripped Enobe and Soul Seeker.

He broke into a trot as a bus pulled up in front of the two figures, cutting off his line of sight. He growled angrily as the bus moved on, and he found the figures gone. They were on the bus.

Elijah took off after the bus, leaping clear over the hood of a passing car as he angled to intercept it. The rain seemed to beat down in anger because it could not understand why it could not fall on the impossibly fast moving man.

"What the hell?"

Moss did a double-take as Elijah flew past the black Ford Explorer.

"Where the hell is he going? Agent Lane, where are you?" Moss exclaimed.

"I'm outside the south entrance," Ebonee replied.

"Why is Garland over here?" Moss asked, watching as Elijah caught up to the bus. "Smith, get around here and follow that bus! Garland is on it!"

Elijah stepped onto the crowded bus, his eyes going to the back and the two figures staring at him.

"A dollar fifty," the driver announced.

Elijah glanced at the driver, and then back to the crowd of people staring at him. He searched his pockets and quickly deposited two dollars into the machine, his eyes going over the passengers thoughtfully as he grabbed the silver bar overhead.

The bus lurched forward then, as the many passengers returned their minds to whatever it was they had been on, forgetting Elijah and his stark white locks as they talked among each other. The two possessed men grinned evilly at Elijah from the back of the bus as it slowed and came to a stop once more.

More people crowded onto the hot bus, forcing Elijah to

take a step closer to the demons. They sneered at him—mockingly almost—as they held their positions at the rear of the bus next to the back door.

Elijah forced himself to breathe through his nose, trying to placate the rage and desire in his heart to cut the fiends down where they stood. Enobe and Soul Seeker vibrated lividly at his sides, longing for him to do the same.

"Ouch! Could you watch it, please?"

Elijah glanced down into the frown of an elderly woman sitting in an aisle seat in front of him. Her eyes went to the hilt of Enobe as it poked out of Elijah's trench coat. He snarled at the woman and shifted his weight sideways, turning to stand facing the back of the bus, one hand on each silver rail on either side of the roof of the bus.

A young black woman with three children stood in front of him now. All three children stared up at the stranger, smiling widely as their mother pulled them closer to her, her eyes flashing suspiciously to the hilt of the blade.

Elijah inhaled deeply through his nose as he pulled the leather trench coat closed securely, returning his gaze to the fiends. Again the bus stopped, and more passengers crowded on, dripping wet and cursing the foul weather, forcing Elijah and everyone else closer to the rear of the bus.

Elijah's grip on the silver bar tightened as he went over the words in his mind—the words that would bring the demons' true forms forth. *Not here. Not with so many innocent people in the way.*

Once again, the bus came to a lurching stop, sending one of the children—the smallest of the three—falling into Elijah's legs. Elijah tore his eyes from the fiends and gently held out a hand to help the little girl regain her balance, just as the rear door opened up.

"Say thank you, Taysia."

Elijah felt the lump growing in his throat as he heard the child's mother call her name.

For a moment, the fiends no longer existed. The storm didn't either, and there was only the priceless, angelic, toothless smile of the small girl as she stared up at the Protector.

"T'ank you, mister," the child grinned, her large brown eyes sparkling as her mother's protective arms pulled her close. Elijah sighed heavily, letting his grim expression slip for only a moment to return the child's smile.

"You're welcome . . . Taysia," he said softly, memories flashing through his mind at the mention of her name. He glanced up at the mother and found a grateful smile upon her face as she nodded her thanks.

"Please move to the rear of the bus so that other passengers may board."

The bus driver's loud voice brought Elijah back to the situation at hand, as more soaking wet passengers pushed onto the crowded, rolling sauna.

His eyes went back to the fiends as he moved ever closer to them. Only the woman and her children separated them now. Elijah's heart raced as he stared them down, waiting for one of them to make a move so he could say the words and be done with them.

A thought occurred to him as he felt the bus slowing again to make another stop: Why hadn't they attacked him?

He had no time to think about it as the back door of the bus swung open and the woman and her three children stepped toward the door.

"Bye-bye, mister!" Taysia cried happily, waving as she followed her mother to the steps. Again Elijah found a smile on his face as he brought up a hand to wave goodbye to the precious child.

A low snarl was the only warning Elijah received as the fiends suddenly sprang to action. Elijah threw his arms out wide, catching the woman and her three children as they were shoved back into him. The fiends jumped off the bus at a run.

Elijah quickly righted the woman and her children as she cursed the two men for every cent they were worth and made his way to the back door just as it was closing. He stepped down and shoved his foot forward in between the closing doors, forcing it back open. He growled at the delay as he leaped from the bus into the drenching rain.

He stared around the empty street corner until he saw them standing in front of a subway entrance, waiting. He thought nothing of it as they disappeared down the wet, dimly lit stairs, taking up the chase once again. Elijah didn't see the black Explorer come skidding to a halt on the wet asphalt above, nor would he have cared if he had.

The fiends jumped the tollgate and ran down the platform, drawing a curious stare from the homeless man lying on one of the benches in the foul smelling subway stop.

Elijah leaped over the tollgate without slowing just as the middle aged, graying toll taker awoke from his sleep to see the running figures charging down the platform. He yawned heavily, stretching his arms out, and then, shrugging, put his head down to get some more sleep.

Elijah heard the rumble as a train roared down the tracks on the other side of the station. He watched the fiends pause at the end of the platform, looking back. Again, they were waiting. The lights flickered on and off as the train sped through the station. Elijah wasted no time jumping down onto the tracks, disappearing into the dark tunnel behind the two fiends.

He had to concentrate in the darkness, his eyes focusing on the uneven slats and loose rocks on the floor of the tunnel as he ran on. Another low rumbling began, slowly drowning out the incessant sound of cascading water. Elijah glanced up from the floor of the tunnel just as the lights of the speeding train rounded the bend ahead. He heard the deafening hoot of the train's fog horn sound as he dove to the side, hitting the ground hard against the wall of the tunnel.

The wind buffeted him as he lay still in the smelly stream of water, his hands covering his ears as the train screamed by. After a moment, the train was gone, and Elijah rose to his feet and glanced back down the tunnel as the lights of the train disappeared into the darkness. His eyes went down, checking to ensure that he still retained all of his necessary body parts.

As his heartbeat returned to normal, Elijah took off in pursuit again.

Up ahead he could see the lights of the platform in the distance. As he closed on the platform, he felt the rumbling in the wet ground once again. The deafening roar of the train filled the tunnel just as Elijah leaped onto the platform. He rolled to his feet and glanced at the train as it sped by on the other side of the station. He stood up then, his hands going to the hilt of the blades as he scanned the platform. Trash littered the old abandoned rail stop, and the smell of old urine caused his nose to twitch.

The sound of running water dominated the area as Elijah's eyes found the fiends. They stood at the other end of the platform, once again, waiting.

"*Anel nathrak doth dien dienve.*"

Enobe and Soul Seeker flashed their ebony shine as Elijah drew them from his sides, whispering the words to bring the fiends forth into their own form as he slowly stalked toward them. He watched as the two men fell to the ground, unconscious, as the fiends took shape where they had once stood.

The fiends immediately went for weapons. One snatched a section of piping from the tiled wall of the station, and the other tore a bench from its moorings in the dim, flickering light.

Elijah snorted derisively—the weapons would do them no

good. He closed to within six feet of the creatures and paused, staring at their huge tooth-filled snarls as another train roared by on the other side of the station. Elijah's eyes darted around the empty station suspiciously as the chill bumps ran along his skin. *Good . . . Dalfien is here.*

Elijah's hands gripped the hilt of the blades tightly, his knuckles turning pale as he felt the larger demon's presence. He lowered his stare to the two fiends waiting in front of him, his eyes filled with hate for the one who had put Ebonee on that cross in the chamber, for the one who had tortured her, hurt her.

Another train rushed by, the wind blowing Elijah's leather trench coat into the air behind him as the fiends charged. Enobe and Soul Seeker flashed into action, dancing out in front of the Protector as if they were an extension of Elijah's thoughts. The lead pipe clanged harmlessly off of the blade's defensive perimeter, as Elijah dodged the downward slam of the bench. The bench broke into pieces on the floor of the station and the fiend howled out in pain as Soul Seeker dug nasty holes into its eyeless face.

Elijah felt the rumble as another train approached. He positioned himself with his back to the tracks and the edge of the platform, his blades swatting away the lead pipe as the weaponless fiend howled in anger, charging directly for the Protector and ignoring the biting as Enobe sliced at its ribs as it passed. Elijah spun in a circle, the hilt of Soul Seeker slamming into the back of the creature's head, sending it staggering forward into the side of the speeding train. Its body flipped awkwardly in midair, as the train's momentum lifted it from the platform. It landed on the cold, steel tracks a second later—headless and very dead.

The second fiend backed away from the Protector slowly, realizing its fate. It had no desire to feel the cold bite of those blades anymore. Elijah set his determined gaze on the single remaining fiend as he stepped forward. Then he froze in his tracks as a feeling of undeniable dread caused his body to tremble visibly. Only his gut reflexes kept his head upon his shoulders.

Elijah ducked and dropped into a roll just as the flat blade of the spear cleaved through the air where his neck had been. The fiend was upon him then, its lead pipe swinging down at him with renewed vigor. Elijah parried the blows easily, regaining his footing as he looked at the newcomer. Enobe danced out to his left, keeping the fiend at bay as Elijah locked gazes with a thin, elderly white man dressed as a priest, holding a huge spear comfortably in his hands, with a wide grin spread out upon his lips.

"*Anel nat—*"

The words died on Elijah's lips as the huge spear suddenly shot forward at his midsection. Elijah somehow managed to turn to the side and avoid the man's deceivingly fast attack, bringing Soul Seeker down to swat the spear to the side.

Elijah recognized the feint for what it was—too late. Dalfien reversed the swing of the blade, bringing the spear back in. Elijah twisted again, thinking to accept the glancing blow to his hip and to return with a counter. The flat of the blade bounced harmlessly off of Elijah's side, yet Dalfien continued to grin, bringing the blade back to lean upon it easily.

Elijah's eyes then went wide, as waves upon waves of despair filled his mind. Agony tore at Elijah's body, sending him to his knees. Fear ripped into his heart, coursing through his veins, snatching away his will to fight.

Another train roared past.

It took every ounce of willpower in Elijah's body to force the terror away as he looked up into Dalfien's evil grin. His eye then went to the flat blade of the spear and its dim reddish glow. He knew then the source of the unspeakable terror.

Elijah then felt a sharp pain in the back of his head, a pain that quickly spread down to the base of his neck, burning its way through the vertebrae of his spine. He remembered the fiend at his back too late, and he heard the loud clatter of Enobe and Soul Seeker falling to the floor of the station.

His last vision was of the old white priest, a wicked smile dancing across his face as he stared down at the unconscious Protector.

Chapter Seventeen
VENGEANCE

Ebonee jumped from the black Explorer before it could come to a complete stop in the pouring rain behind the first black truck that had followed Elijah to the subway entrance.

Her heart pounded in her chest as her worst fears began to take shape in her mind—images of Elijah hanging limply from a cross.

"Next stop!"

Ebonee skidded to a halt in the pouring rain as an agent stepped up from the subway, shouting, running for the first black Explorer. She turned and ran back to her ride and they proceeded to the closed subway stop. Parks hadn't shown up. If he did, then he was probably spooked by the sudden turn of events. At least that's what Ebonee thought.

She bolted out of the SUV as it again stopped. She pushed the agent aside as he fumbled with the lock on the gate of the entrance. Pulling out her gun, she took aim and blasted the lock off, running down the steps at full speed. Ebonee slowed down, her soaking wet clothes clinging to her shapely body as she approached the scene. Another agent was there, waiting.

"This is all we found," he said, holding the two blades and the pair of sunglasses up as Director Moss ran up behind the silent Ebonee.

Ebonee stared at the blades, her fears coming to pass. Again, the images filled her mind, blood pouring from the many wounds on Elijah's beaten and torn body, as he hung there upon the cross.

"And him."

Moss stared over at the groggy man leaning up against the wall of the platform in a daze. Ebonee recognized him as one of the men Elijah had taken off after.

"What does he know?" Moss asked.

"He doesn't know anything."

Moss and the agent stared at Ebonee curiously as her eyes lingered on the prone man.

"He was possessed," she added blankly.

"Possessed?" Moss repeated, staring at her skeptically.

Suddenly Ebonee's brown eyes lit up, and she ran over to the man, leaving Moss alone with the agent.

"Any signs of where they went?" he asked, his eyes following Ebonee.

"There's a trail of blood leading over to where we found him unconscious. Then it disappears," the agent replied, pointing over to the man Ebonee was approaching.

"Think, dammit!"

Moss ran over to Ebonee as she grabbed the man by the collar, shaking him violently as she questioned him.

"What's the last thing you remember?" Ebonee shouted.

"Relax. I don't think he'll be able to answer you with his tongue rattling around in his head like that," Moss said, placing a firm hand on Ebonee's shoulder. Ebonee let the man go reluctantly, fearing what his answer would finally be.

"What's your name?" Moss asked the man softly.

"M . . . Michael . . . Michael Grant," the man said weakly, his blue eyes batting rapidly as he tried to focus.

Moss turned as a train roared by, causing the lights to flicker. Then he turned back to the man. "What's the last thing you remember, Michael?"

Ebonee stared intently at the man, holding her breath as Moss questioned him. She knew that every second they wasted was a second closer to Elijah's possible death. Moss eyed her suspiciously; she looked as though she was ready to reach into the man's mouth and force his tongue to move.

"W-where am I?" the man whispered hoarsely, bringing his hand up to the side of his head.

Ebonee let out a low growl as the breath she held escaped her lungs.

"Michael, listen to me very carefully. My name is Director Moss. I'm with the F.B.I. You were—"

"What's the last fucking thing you remember?" Ebonee exploded, cutting Moss off as he sighed in resignation, watching as Ebonee shook the man roughly once more.

"I-I-I was in church," the man stuttered, each word bouncing out of his mouth with every shake Ebonee gave him.

Tears began to fall from Ebonee's eyes as she continued to shake the man.

Candles—two rows of them, leading down into the darkness.

"Where?" Ebonee screamed, the man's head glancing off the wall as Moss tried to pry her away from the man. Her tears were hidden by the trickling drops of water falling from her damp hair down upon her face, but Moss knew they were there. "Where, damn you?"

"Saint Gabriel!" the man finally shouted fearfully.

Ebonee released the man and stood up straight.

"Where is that?" she shouted, as Moss stared at her incredulously—he had never seen her like this before.

"On Fitzwater and Fifth!" the man answered, cringing in fear.

Ebonee darted off, snatching up the blades as she did so. She froze in her tracks, feeling the low hum as the blades vibrated in her grasp. She saw an image in her mind of Elijah holding the blades in his hands. They wanted her to take them to him.

Director Moss quickly informed the remaining agents to wrap things up and to take care of the man. Then he ran up the steps behind Ebonee Lane.

"Come on," Moss shouted at Ebonee, motioning her toward the lead vehicle. He stared up at the sky curiously as they jumped into the truck. There was no sign of the storm at all. The moon was shining brightly and there was not a cloud in the sky. The only remnants of the storm were the wet ground and soaked clothes they were wearing.

"Follow me," Moss instructed another agent, who ran to the second truck.

"Hurry!" Ebonee yelled, feeling the low hum of the blades in her lap.

Moss slammed on the gas and spun the truck around, the large tires spinning along the wet asphalt as they tried to get a grip.

The truck flew through an intersection, its siren blaring and red and blue lights flashing.

"Okay, which way? This is Fifth," Moss announced as he slowed at the light.

"Right!" Ebonee yelled, unsure. She felt the vibrations in the blade diminish as the vehicle tore down the wet street.

"No! The other way!" she shouted. Moss slammed on the brakes and whipped the truck in a 180, cursing as the tires fought to grip the slick road.

Ebonee felt the vibrations intensify as they crossed the intersection where they had turned right.

"Are you sure?" Moss asked, glancing at Ebonee. "How do you know?"

"I just do," Ebonee replied simply, chilling images of candles popping into her mind as she stared out at the street ahead.

She prayed she was not too late.

Elijah slowly felt his consciousness return to him. He inhaled deeply through his nose, taking in the scents around him. He pictured a church in his mind as the aroma of the frankincense and myrrh thickly filled the air. He felt the dull pain in his neck from where the fiend had landed a clean blow with the lead pipe.

He knew he was hanging—on a cross most likely—from the way his arms were outstretched. The pain in the palms of his hands didn't bother him, neither did the pain in his feet. But what did bother the Protector was the absence of the soothing hum of Enobe and Soul Seeker at his waist. Elijah opened his eyes then, ignoring his surroundings as his eyes went to his waist and the empty sheaths that hung there. The blades were gone, along with his shirt, trench coat, and boots.

Sweat glistened on his naked, ebony body—the heat was stifling. His awareness expanded to the area surrounding him as he looked up at his arms. Thick, steel chains secured them to the horizontal section of the cross and shackles bound his wrists in place. In front of him hung a thick, black curtain, stretching across the front of what he presumed was the stage in the front of a large church. He heard low whispers on the other side of the curtain just as an organ began to play its holy tune. Candles were the only source of light that he could make out through the thickness of the curtain.

"Good, you are awake," the voice said from below him off to his side. Elijah lowered his gaze to the slim, elderly priest as the man stepped into his line of sight, carrying the long spear with the reddish, glowing blade.

Dalfien.

Elijah felt his hatred and rage building once more as he

recognized the goose bumps rolling across his skin. He jerked wildly at the chains binding his arms, growling in anger. The chains rattled in protest and the wood of the cross creaked, but they held him fast.

Dalfien chuckled, further enraging the Protector.

Elijah's breathing came in short, measured rasps as his nostrils flared with each breath, his teeth grinding together with enough force to shatter his jawbone.

"*Anel nathrak—*"

Elijah's words were cut short as the spear's blade shot forward. His eyes rolled to the back of his head, and his mouth fell open in a silent cry of misery as terror filled his soul. Never had the Protector felt such pain in his life. Tears fell from his closed eyes, as the sorrow filled his heart.

His heart felt as though it would explode.

Elijah panicked. His only desire was to get away from the sorrow and the terror. The chains shook and rattled once again as his body reacted to his natural instincts of survival.

Dalfien chuckled once more as he slowly drew a line of blood across the Protector's muscular chest with the tip of the spear's flat blade, enjoying Elijah's torment. Then he pulled the spear back, hearing the splintering of wood. As soon as the spear was removed, Elijah's body went limp. His head slumped, his breathing barely evident; there was no more fight left in him.

"That is better," Dalfien whispered, stepping closer to the cross. "I will enjoy killing you," he began softly, grinning wickedly as he spoke, "but there is something I want you to see first."

Elijah could hear the words, but they sounded distant, far away.

"Were you aware that this particular church has over four hundred followers?" Dalfien smirked. "All gathering tonight for a midnight mass." His smile stretched out farther. "Can you imagine the chaos when I summon one hundred fiends

into their midst?" Dalfien laughed hoarsely, the sound sending chills up through Elijah's spine. "It will be a massacre!
The doors will be locked and none will escape!" he exclaimed.
"And then," he added softly, his head slowly cocking to the
side as he stared up at the Protector, "then, I get to watch
you die."

Dalfien paused as he stared up at the Protector, his smile
never fading. Then his eyes squinted up, as though he had
remembered something.

"You know, someone else once hung upon a cross as you
do now." Dalfien paused as he watched Elijah's light brown
eyes slowly open and stare down at him, his anger rising
again. "No, no. Not her," Dalfien added softly. "I care nothing of the girl. No, this was a much longer time ago," Dalfien
explained, his eyes holding Elijah's. "How long, Protector?
How long before you give up your spirit as he did? It didn't
take long to break him; he was weak."

Dalfien chuckled loudly as his attention was drawn to the
curtain and the loud voice now speaking.

Elijah heard the voice as his eyes went to the thick, black
curtain. He envisioned a church filled with people, all with
their rosary beads and bowed heads, giving homage to their
god on the other side of the curtain.

"It seems the festivities have begun. I must leave you for a
moment, but rest assured, I will return very shortly." Dalfien
smiled up at the Protector and then nodded to someone off
to the side. "Gag him," he instructed, and then he disappeared through the curtain.

Elijah closed his eyes as the man climbed up behind him,
slipping a gag into his mouth and tying it tightly. Elijah's
chest rose and fell rhythmically as he focused on the voice
on the other side of the curtain.

"As they were going out, they met a man from Cyrene,
named Simon, and they forced him to carry the cross. They
came to a place called Golgotha—the Place of the Skull.

There they offered him wine to drink, mixed with gall; but after tasting it, he refused to drink it. When they had crucified him, they divided up his clothes by casting lots. And sitting down, they kept watch over him there. Above his head they placed the written charge against him: This is Jesus, The King of the Jews. Two robbers were crucified with him, one on his right, and one on his left. Those who passed by hurled insults at him, shaking their heads and saying, 'You who are going to destroy the temple and rebuild it in three days, save yourself! Come down from the cross, if you are the Son of God!'"

Elijah recognized the scripture as the crucifixion. His eyes went up the chains as the reader read on. He pulled hard, his sculpted muscles bulging as he strained. He heard the wood splinter, but it did not give. His body slumped from the exertion and he listened to the man's voice again.

"From the sixth hour until the ninth hour darkness came over all the land. About the ninth hour Jesus cried out in a loud voice, 'Eloi, Eloi, lama sabachthani?' which means, 'My God, my God, why have you forsaken me?' When some of those standing near him heard this, they said, 'He's calling Elijah.'"

Elijah's ebony skin glistened in the dim light as his chest began to rise and fall faster, as Dalfien's words returned to him. He pictured his Savior upon the cross, blood dripping from the wound in his side. Elijah had never been the overly religious kind. Although his grandmother had led him by the ear into church every Sunday faithfully up until the day she had died, Elijah still had his questions about faith and religion on a whole. In the end he had decided that it would be safer to believe than to not believe, than be cursed and spend an eternity in hell.

He flexed again. The wood splintered once more and the chains bent, but still, they held him fast.

"Immediately one of them ran and got a sponge. He filled it with wine vinegar, put it on a stick, and offered it to Jesus to drink. But the rest said, 'Leave him alone. Let's see if Elijah comes to save him.' And when Jesus cried out again in a loud voice, he gave up his spirit. At that moment, the curtain of the temple was torn in two, from top to bottom. The earth shook and the rocks split. The tombs broke open and the bodies of many holy people who had died were raised to life."

Elijah could hear another voice now. It was Dalfien's, but his words were gibberish.

Suddenly the curtain in front of Elijah fell, and he gazed into the shocked and horrified expressions of the crowd.

A woman screamed.

Dalfien turned his back to the people and faced the Protector, smiling wickedly as he finished the chant.

Another scream erupted from the crowd.

Elijah stared in the direction of this latest shout and watched as fiends and imps possessed the weaker members of the church.

Then there was chaos.

One man's throat was ripped out, and another had his bowels removed as the demons viciously tore into the mass of human flesh. Bodies flew everywhere; some were trampled in the aisles of the church as they tried to reach the gigantic doors—doors that were locked tightly.

Elijah watched in silent horror as the anger began to build in him once more, until it was a boiling rage. His ebony body trembled as he felt the anger burning in his soul.

Dalfien's smile lessened as he stared at the Protector, and he quickly scooped up the spear and stalked forward. Somewhere in the back of the church Elijah heard the breaking of glass. He thought he saw figures climbing in through the windows, but he couldn't make them out in the candlelight and through the anger that had now begun to blur his vision.

Gunshots rang out into the chaos, and Elijah knew immediately that Ebonee had arrived. A low growl began from deep within the Protector's belly, as he thought of Ebonee, once again in danger because of him. His muscles twitched uncontrollably as his gaze settled on the approaching Dalfien.

Ebonee let off another shot as she made her way to the front of the church, hitting one of the possessed men in the leg, dropping him. Her eyes went to the long walls of the church and the large stained glass windows, with scenes of angels and other images from the Bible—and the candles.

Moss ran behind Ebonee, a confused expression etched upon his stern face as he gazed at the chaos around him. He let off a round, hitting a crazed woman who charged at him madly. Ebonee ran with a fear so intense that she quickly left Moss behind as she stared down the aisle to the cross—and the dark figure hanging upon it. Her heart raced as she ran, expecting the cross to fade further out of view with each step she took—just like in the dream.

She fired another shot when another fiend charged at her, hitting the man in the shoulder and dropping him momentarily as she ran on. The cross did not fade away, and she could see the slender priest approaching Elijah now—the glowing spear reaching out for Elijah's heart.

Elijah could see her now, running in all haste to the front of the church to save him. His eyes fell upon the blades tucked into her belt. Dalfien's eyes followed Elijah's gaze to the running girl and he looked back at Elijah with a wicked grin, hoisting the spear up and turning for the approaching woman.

"Nooo!"

Elijah's scream reverberated throughout the large church

as his anger and pain released. Hate sent a burst of energy into the corded muscles of his arms, and he flexed. The wood splintered again, and the chains stretched taught. Elijah's body trembled in fury as tears ran down his face, mixing with the sweat and blood.

Again he screamed, and again the wood splintered, giving way to the power of his rage and splitting on each side as he brought his arms forward with a cry of desperation. Pain shot through the Protector as he plummeted to the hard stone floor, his hands ripping free of the stakes.

"Anel nathrak doth dien dienve!"

Elijah stared up to see Father Holbrook standing behind the podium, reciting the words to bring the demons into their physical form and release the human captives. Dalfien froze as he heard the words, and so did every other fiend and imp as they were torn from their astral plain and into this plane of existence.

"Elijah! Catch!" Ebonee shouted as she tossed the blades to the Protector.

Enobe and Soul Seeker fell short, clanging to the ground a few feet away from the prone Protector. Elijah tried to crawl forward, but his feet were still staked and chained to the lower portion of the cross. A deafening roar reverberated through the church and Elijah looked up to see Dalfien, all seven feet of him, his muscles rippling in his true form. Ram-like horns protruded from his head. His massive legs were like those of a goat, down to the hooves. The demon's black eyes fell upon Elijah. The spear in its grasp seemed tiny as the blade glowed a brighter red. The demon's gaze then went back to Ebonee, who was firing at will now, sending bullets blasting through demon brains.

Dalfien took a huge step in the woman's direction, and rage once again filled the Protector. Elijah reached down and grabbed the wooden cross around its broken base, his muscles going taut as he strained with every ounce of his energy. The wood splintered again, giving way as the cross was ripped from the floor. Dalfien stared back at the Protector, just as Enobe and Soul Seeker sliced through the chains and Elijah grunted, ripping his feet off of the stake. The Protector was free.

Dalfien howled in anger as he rushed toward the Protector, his spear held high. A fiend charged in at Elijah, howling angrily until its head fell from its body, rolling across the floor.

"We can't let these things get out!" Ebonee shouted as she backed up to where Moss was standing, reloading her nine millimeter.

"They won't die!" Moss yelled, sweat trickling down his balding head as he fired off shot after shot, one catching a fiend in the head, dropping it momentarily. But it was back up and charging forward no sooner than Moss had dropped another.

"Here!"

Moss turned and caught the magazine that Ebonee had tossed his way.

"They're hollow tips—aim for the heart!" she instructed.

Moss fumbled with the magazine briefly as another fiend closed in on him. He slammed the clip into the nine millimeter just as it reached a clawed hand for his throat. He fired the remaining bullet out of the chamber, hitting the creature in the forehead. The fiend's head snapped back violently, but snapped back forward, and it snarled angrily. Another shot was fired, this one leaving a gaping hole in the fiend's chest, taking with it a chunk of the fiend's black heart. This time the fiend did fall—dead. Moss watched in amazement as the body dissipated into nothingness before his very eyes. He stared down at the spot until another fiend lunged out of the crowd for him.

Enobe pulsed vibrantly as it sucked the strength from the fiend's heart. Elijah absently kicked the creature away with his naked foot, his eyes locked with the approaching giants. He swung Soul Seeker out in a low arc, spinning in a complete circle, severing the fiend's legs at the knees as it stalked him from behind.

He kept moving.

Determination was etched into his face. This would end now. One way—or another.

Dalfien roared as he hefted the spear over his horned head, meaning to split the bothersome Protector in half. Elijah crossed Enobe and Soul Seeker above his head, catching the spear as it drove downward. The force of the blow sent Elijah to his knees, sending cracks through the cement where his knees had impacted. Dalfien chuckled—a disgusting sound coming from his grotesque maw—as his muscles bulged.

Elijah felt the sweat rolling from his face as he strained to keep the spear up, still on his knees. Closer the spear came, the creature's strength slowly overpowering the Protector. Elijah remembered the terror that the spear had invoked in him from only a mere touch. He dove to the side, just as the spear chipped into the cement, sending sparks flying where Elijah had been kneeling. Elijah came to his feet and leapt into the air, flipping sideways as the spear swung about in a sweeping arc. Over the spear he went, Enobe and Soul Seeker crossing once more as he pushed downward at the spear in midair. The spear sliced through the podium and Elijah almost laughed as he caught a glimpse of Father Holbrook.

Father Holbrook wore the Protector's long, black, leather trench coat and brandished a short silver mace, crushing any fiend's skull that ventured close—all the while quoting the scriptures.

Elijah darted in before Dalfien could adjust from his mighty swing. Soul Seeker and Enobe sliced into the demon's massive shoulder and neck, bringing a roar of anger from the gigantic demon. Dalfien turned the spear back the other way, attempting to sweep the Protector and those stinging blades away. But Elijah followed the demon's movements, staying behind him and moving with him, his blades stabbing at the demon's neck and shoulder hungrily.

Suddenly, Dalfien reversed his movements, swinging out with his left hand. Elijah got Enobe up to deflect the blow—but too high. The back of Dalfien's huge fist slammed into him, sending him flying into the air and through two rows of thick wooden pews. Elijah felt the jagged edges of the wood tearing into his flesh. Blood and sweat glistened on his back and arms as he stood once more, ignoring the intense burning from his broken ribs. He waited as Dalfien stalked through the splintered wood.

Down came the spear again in an angled slash. Elijah waited until the last moment and dove forward into a roll, the tip of the spear tearing into his arm. He felt the terror as he completed his roll. Dalfien stared down in surprise as Soul Seeker plunged into his belly up to the hilt. He howled out in pain as the blade sucked at his life force. Elijah wobbled on his knees as the effect of the spear rocked him to the bone. Dalfien kicked out with a hoofed foot, catching the dazed Protector square in the chest, sending him flying back once again. He reached down and snatched Soul Seeker from his stomach, hurling it behind him angrily.

Elijah felt the air leave his lungs as he smashed through three more rows of pews, landing in a heap among the splintered wood.

He could barely move. Pain assaulted him with every attempt to do so, as the spear's effect lingered. He felt sorrow forcing the darkness upon him, and he felt the sudden urge to just close his eyes and go to sleep. He lay completely still, his eyes closing as he accepted the coming darkness. Only the strong vibrations of Enobe kept the darkness at bay. Somehow he forced himself to his hands and knees, focusing on the vibration in his right hand as Dalfien stalked on.

Ebonee saw the blade land a few feet away from her. She blasted a hole in the chest of the nearest fiend and made her way over to it. She scooped it up with her left hand and immediately felt its violent vibrations. Her eyes scanned the church for Elijah. *No . . . let him handle the demon. I'll only get in the way.* Her thoughts were interrupted as she heard a howl at her back. She swung around and saw Soul Seeker whistling through the air as it decapitated an angry demon. Ebonee paused a moment, feeling the strength flowing into her from the vibrating blade. But she had little time to ponder the sensation as she blasted another demon as it reached for Moss's unprotected back. She felt a sharp pain in her shoulder blade as a fiend clubbed at her with its closed fists. Ebonee fell into a roll, her gun dropping to the floor. She gripped Soul Seeker in both hands, just as the creature hurled itself upon her. She propped the hilt of the blade against the floor and let the creature impale itself. She fought free of the demon as it died, getting to her feet.

She swung Soul Seeker out in an arc as another creature approached her. She was amazed at how light the blade seemed now, with the vibrations emanating from it, sending strength into her—energizing her as she tore into the demons with a renewed vigor.

Moss stared at her in amazement as she cut the remaining fiends near her down with ease.

"Get those doors open!" she yelled, stabbing Soul Seeker forward and into the heart of another fiend. She felt strange as the creature's life force was sucked away and channeled into her veins. "The doors!" Ebonee yelled again, as Moss stared at the strange grin that was upon Ebonee's face as she hacked and stabbed at the fiends. He snapped free of his daze and ran toward the rear of the church and the mass of people gathered in front of the huge doors. Some of them screamed and banged and pounded on the doors begging for help. Others stared in amazement at the scene behind them. Moss pushed his way through the confusion and made it to the doors, only to be tackled to the ground by another fiend.

Moss felt the burning pain in his neck and chest as the creature clawed at him. He struggled to get his gun up, but the creature was incredibly strong. Panic filled Moss's racing heart as the creature's disgusting mouth opened, revealing rows of razor sharp teeth, descending for his neck. He screamed out, his hand forcing the creature's head back with a fear-inspired strength. He managed to get his arm up and put the muzzle of his gun to the creature's chest. The creature paused as the gun went off, taking a chunk of the fiend's chest with it, but missing its black heart. The creature howled angrily as it went for Moss's throat again.

"Fuck you!" Moss shouted, this time aiming the gun at the creature's head as he pulled the trigger. The fiend's head exploded as the hollow tip took half of its brain out of its skull.

Moss quickly struggled to his feet, his own blood covering the front of his suit as he inspected the huge doors. A thick chain secured the latch with a large padlock holding them secure. He fired a round at the lock, and then shoved the huge doors open as the people rushed out into the brisk night air.

Ebonee kicked the last fiend from her blade and stared upward. Her eyes fell upon Elijah. Blood and sweat glistened on his ebony skin as he hunched over, Enobe dragging on the floor at his side. He looked defeated.

She saw Dalfien stalking him, his spear raised high and a

triumphant grin on his ugly maw. Fear held her frozen. She couldn't scream, couldn't do anything.

The Protector waited calmly, swaying back and forth as the darkness fought to claim his consciousness. He was tired, so very tired. He staggered a bit as Dalfien approached.

"Ready to die, demon?" Elijah's voice was barely a whisper, but Dalfien heard him clearly.

Dalfien growled. Seeing the Protector with only one blade and barely able to stand, he stalked forward.

The Protector made no move—he couldn't.

Elijah watched through half-closed eyes as the glowing, red spear tip came forward. He didn't move—even as the tip of the spear pierced his side and continued through—even as the terror tore into his heart.

Elijah closed his eyes, concentrating on the smooth, subtle hum in his right hand, blocking out the terror, forgetting the pain that racked his beaten body.

Dalfien's smirk disappeared as his eyes went wide. He watched the Protector suddenly spring forward, the spear's shaft sliding through him as he closed the distance between them. With both hands the Protector plunged Enobe deep into Dalfien's chest, puncturing his heart as it passed through and exited the creature's broad back.

Dalfien gasped as he released his grip on the spear, and he felt his life being torn from him. His canine maw opened in a silent cry of protest as he fell to his knees, his eyes staring up at the roof of the church.

Ebonee felt the tears on her cheek as she watched the demon run through Elijah with the spear. Soul Seeker fell to the floor with a clang. Her shoulders slumped, and she felt her muscles constrict as she swallowed the huge lump in her throat. She watched as the demon fell and evaporated into nothingness. Then Elijah, too, fell to his knees, the Spear of

Suffering the only thing preventing him from falling out completely.

Elijah watched the demon fall and disappear, and then felt himself falling. He closed his eyes as he felt the pressure in his side as the spear held him up on his knees. The darkness grabbed at him, and he swayed. He could still feel the soothing vibrations of Enobe in his hand—so comforting. He then fell.

Ebonee snapped out of her daze and ran to his side, skipping over the splintered and broken pews. She dropped to her knees and gently lifted Elijah up as Moss stepped up to them.

"Ebonee . . ." Moss began sadly, as Ebonee rocked Elijah's still form in her arms back and forth. She glanced down through her tears at the spear; only a foot remained protruding from his wound.

She reached around and steadied herself, and then she quickly pulled it the rest of the way out. Her tears blurred her vision as she tried to speak.

"C-come on, Elijah," she whispered, as Moss stared down at them sadly. "Come on," she whispered again, unable to see through her tears as she clutched Elijah's head close to her bosom. She gently rocked back and forth, cradling his head in her arms as she wiped her tears in vain.

She stared down at the wound in his side, praying that it had begun to heal. A smile slowly worked its way onto Ebonee's tear-streaked face as she watched the wound slowly closing. Her tear-filled smile went up to Director Moss, who stared down at the wound in awe.

"See," Ebonee said softly. "He's going to be just fine."

Moss was at a loss; all he could do was stare and shake his head stupidly.

Ebonee sniffled and wiped her tears once more, gazing down into Elijah's light brown eyes, eyes that now stared back up at her. Her smile stretched across her face as he blinked and managed a weak grin.

Ebonee's beautiful face chased the pain away—chased the darkness away—as Elijah let his smile spread, feeling Ebonee's tears drip down onto his face.

"Cherry pie," he whispered weakly as Ebonee's tears began to flow unabated when she heard the words. She pulled Elijah close, squeezing him tightly in her warm embrace.

"Apple kisses," she whispered back through her tears, knowing that everything would be—cool.

Sneak Peek at

Sacrifice

Book Two in the
Demon Hunter Series
Coming Spring 2008

PROLOGUE

Elijah Garland staggered backward under the relentless assault, his twin blades, Enobe and Soul Seeker, blurring in their frantic attempts to keep the enemy weapons at bay. How many would come? How many had he already slaughtered this night?

His slender, black hands sent the twin blades into a spectacular dance, the ring of steel on steel echoing in his ears like thousands of tiny church bells being rung in his head. Rage spurred him on. A wickedly barbed spear tip came in from his left, too fast to be deflected by his preoccupied blades. Elijah spun as he felt the pressure in the left side of his abdomen. The tip of the spear drew blood, but continued on its forward plunge, its blade now past the swiftly moving Protector. Elijah brought Soul Seeker down hard with his right hand as he finished the spin, slicing through the heavy wooden pole, ignoring the pain from the new wound as Enobe followed in Soul Seeker's wake, her tip exploding into the foul demon's face and continuing through its black brain. The remnants of the spear clattered to the blood-soaked earth, the demon defeated, dead before it hit the ground.

It was replaced by three more.

Elijah's taut and chiseled muscles burned from fatigue. How long had he been here? How long had this battle raged? One demon howled madly, charging forward, seeking to bury the Protector under its weight. Elijah sneered, accepting a glancing blow to the back of his shoulder as he turned to face the advancing fool. He dropped to one knee, and Enobe sliced through the air in a wide arc. The demon's large, black eyes went wide as it fell forward, finding it suddenly had no leg below the kneecap to support its vicious charge. Elijah was up then, darting past the falling creature, Soul Seeker taking its head from its shoulders even as Enobe came up to block another attack.

The Protector's movements were a blur. He was rage incarnate. He was the hate amassed within his own heart. He was death.

His stark white hair, hanging below his shoulders in thick locks, was bathed red with blood, some his own, most not. *I am dreaming again.* It had to be a dream. The same dream. Sleeveless black leather armor fit snugly over a platinum chain shirt which hung down below his waist, split on both sides. Thick metal bracers, glinting red with blood, protected his bulging biceps, and armored leather gloves covered both hands up to his forearms. *Yes . . . a dream.* He was aware of the cavern then, dark and sinister, shadows seeming to cover every inch of the place.

With awareness came clarity. This place was his domain, created years ago as a sublet for his sorrow. He would come here often to give back the pain of heartbreak and loss, to repay the unseen demons within the material world into which he was born—a world he knew he did not belong to.

Enobe and Soul Seeker ceased their defensive dance,

their razor sharp edges dripping red with the blood of his attackers. Elijah's light brown eyes flared and now seemed to glow with a fire that burned within his soul. A single movement brought the twin blades to a reversed hold within his hands, extending along both arms up to the elbow.

The nearest demons, their elongated, sinewy arms carrying cudgels, swords, and spears, seemed to take note of the subtle change in the Protector's movements. Their disgusting faces, huge elongated maws filled with rows of razor sharp teeth, seemed doubtful, almost afraid . . . and justly so.

With a heart-wrenching, lustful cry, Elijah tore into the surrounding horde of demons. Soul Seeker and Enobe sliced through arms and pierced black hearts, decapitating and impaling demon after demon. *Yes . . . this is my place . . . this is my pain.*

Elijah felt a surge of pleasure wash through his body, like a never-ending orgasm. It saturated his being, caused his heart to flutter. Warm tears found his cheeks as the feeling continued to engulf him. His nostrils flared as he again reversed his grip on his blades, spinning in a breathless dance of death and destruction. *Take it back!* Elijah released the pain. He released the suffering.

The smell of sulfur suddenly became thick, and the air around him seemed to develop heaviness. His arms slowed in their dance. Demons scampered away from the Protector now, tripping and falling over the dead, which numbered in the hundreds. Elijah stood within the center of a circle now, his feet stumbling about the slippery ground, stepping on arms, legs, and torsos.

His heart was still pounding in his chest, and his knuckles ached from the death-like grip with which he held his twin swords.

Slowly he watched a narrow path open up as the minor demons tripped over each other to get out of the way. Their misshapen bodies cringed and hustled quickly away, their strange eyes searching in the direction the narrow forming path led to. Elijah could taste the silence; it was so complete. It laid upon the wide cavern like a thick wool blanket, suffocating all sound.

His eyes narrowed to thin slits, and his demeanor darkened further as he felt a powerful presence at the end of the path. Enobe and Soul Seeker at once began a vibrant hum, transmitting the truth of the unnatural evil through the hilt of the enchanted blades and into the palms of his hands.

Nothing changes here.

This battle had played out hundreds of times in his mind. Always it was the same, the weak demon fodder sent first to test him, to weaken him, perhaps. Elijah again reversed the grip of his blades and waited for the powerful demon he had named Reality to show himself and launch his attack.

His muscles tensed in anticipation. He longed to hack away at the powerful demon, to allow Enobe and Soul Seeker to feed off of its life force. The blades continued to hum, sensing the rage within their wielder. A grin found its way to Elijah's full lips, his thin white goatee framing it nicely. *Yes . . . come to me, Reality.* Confidence oozed from his aura, a confidence borne of repetition. He could never lose to this beast here, not in this place that he had created—not in his dreams.

He stood there for what seemed to be an eternity, waiting. He could sense the demon's presence, but it had yet to manifest itself. Elijah grew tired of waiting. His purposeful steps took him down the center of the sea of minor demons, along the narrow path. They stared at the Protector, fear in their eyes; some of them had tasted the bite of those terrible blades.

Elijah faltered halfway along the trail, his sure-footedness stolen away as a wave of unexpected dizziness washed through him. His eyes batted rapidly as he dropped to one knee, supporting his weight upon the tip of Soul Seeker. *What's this?* Confusion stole some of the bravado from his body. There was a weakness in his resolve, a weakness he knew well, but could not place. Elijah growled the dizziness away and resumed his march. He could show these beasts no fear.

The sea of deformed, grotesque demons closed the path behind him as he continued forward, their hissing snarls suddenly floating upon the thick, dank air as they momentarily sensed his trepidation. The path narrowed in on him, the closer creatures forced to come within range of Elijah's thirsty blades by their eager companions behind them who had not yet tasted their sting.

A flash of movement left three of them headless, and the path again widened. *Mindless fools.* Elijah frowned at the cowardly response of the beasts.

He was approaching the source. The path before him angled upward, a slightly steep slope within the cavern, leading up to a flat, rocky plateau. Around the flat elevated area, the sea of demons writhed, hundreds of them, thousands . . .

And there was Reality, a great and mighty beast of a demon, shoulders black as pitch and wide as a house. The demon stood nearly twice Elijah's six feet, four inches, and was almost just as wide. Its monstrous legs bulged with knotted muscles. A flaming sword, longer than Elijah was tall, lit up the area with bright orange flames. Ram-like horns sat upon the creature's grotesque canine head, and its teeth were like daggers.

Elijah ignored the inherent fear the creature's image triggered within his very soul, an image meant to stun its prey, to paralyze them. The terrible monstrosity's eyes burned blood red as it stared at this Protector who continued up the path, unfazed by the demon fear it projected.

Enobe and Soul Seeker led the way, their hunger for this demon's soul undeniable. Elijah gave in to their pull, forgetting the momentary lapse of resolve he had experienced a moment before. His heart pounded with the anticipation of battle as he closed the last few feet between himself and the creature. Only then did he notice the tiny form lying at the beast's hoofed feet.

Elijah's blood ran cold within his veins like ice water, his heart seized, and he was paralyzed. A low chuckle echoed throughout the cavern as Elijah fell to his knees, his eyes locked with those of the woman kneeling prostrate at the demon's feet.

Ebonee's tears glistened upon her cheek.

The rage flew from Elijah's being like thousands of animals fleeing a burning forest. *No!*

The fiery blade fell swiftly.

Stunned and motionless, Elijah watched Ebonee's head bounce along the rocky path toward him. It came to a stop before him, her lovely brown eyes wide, staring up at him. Her lips moved.

"I love you, Elijah."

Elijah screamed in denial, his hands releasing their grip on his only protection, his only comfort. Enobe and Soul Seeker clamored to the stone and were trampled by a thousand demon feet as they swarmed on the unarmed Protector, claws gouging, teeth biting.

Their snarls echoed all around him. He could hear their desire to take his life. He felt the pain, felt his skin being torn, felt their clawed hands upon his body, and he knew then, as darkness settled over his bloody corpse and the demons fed upon his remains, the weakness in his resolve. He knew the one chink in his armor. That weakness . . . was love.

About the Author

TL Gardner was born and raised in Philadelphia, Pennsylvania, where he lives and works today. His love for writing began after the passing of his grandmother when he was seventeen years old. Poetry was his first love and held his attention for many years. He spent several years in the military in the United States Army, traveling the world. Growing up in poverty, his young imagination became his only escape, and now he is putting that overactive imagination to use in his works of fiction.

LOOK FOR MORE HOT TITLES FROM

Q-BORO BOOKS

DARK KARMA - JUNE 2007
$14.95
ISBN 1-933967-12-9

What if the criminal was forced to live the horror that they caused? The drug dealer finds himself in the body of the drug addict and he suffers through the withdrawals, living on the street, the beatings, the rapes and the hunger. The thief steals the rent money and becomes the victim that finds herself living on the street and running for her life and the murderer becomes the victim's father and he deals with the death of a son and a grieving mother.

GET MONEY CHICKS - SEPTEMBER 2007
$14.95
ISBN 1-933967-17-X

For Mina, Shanna, and Karen, using what they had to get what they wanted was always an option. Best friends since day one, they always had a thing for the hottest gear, luxurious lifestyles, and the ballers who made it all possible. All of this changes for Mina when a tragedy makes her open her eyes to the way she's living. Peer pressure and loyalty to her girls collide with her own morality, sending Mina into a no-win situation.

AFTER-HOURS GIRLS - AUGUST 2007
$14.95
ISBN 1-933967-16-1

Take part in this tale of two best friends, Lisa and Tosha, as they stalk the nightclubs and after-hours joints of Detroit searching for excitement, money, and temporary companionship. These two divas stand tall until the unforgivable Motown streets catch up to them. One must fall. You, the reader, decide which.

THE LAST CHANCE - OCTOBER 2007
$14.95
ISBN 1-933967-22-6

Running their L.A. casino has been rewarding for Luke Chance and his three brothers. But recently it seems like everyone is trying to get a piece of the pie. An impending hostile takeover of their casino could leave them penniless and possibly dead. That is, until their sister Keilah Chance comes home for a short visit. Keilah is not only beautiful, but she also can be ruthless. Will the Chance family be able to protect their family dynasty?

Traci must find a way to complete her journey out of her first and only failed

LOOK FOR MORE HOT TITLES FROM

Q-BORO
B O O K S

NYMPHO - MAY 2007
$14.95
ISBN 1933967102

How will signing up to live a promiscuous double-life destroy everything that's at stake in the lives of two close couples? Take a journey into Leslie's secret world and prepare for a twisted, erotic experience.

FREAK IN THE SHEETS - SEPTEMBER 2007
$14.95
ISBN 1933967196

Librarian Raquelle decides to put her knowledge of sexuality to use and open up a "freak" school, teaching men and women how to please their lovers beyond belief while enjoying themselves in the process. But trouble brews when a surprise pupil shows up and everything Raquelle has worked for comes under fire.

LIAR, LIAR - JUNE 2007
$14.95
ISBN 1933967110

Stormy calls off her wedding to Camden when she learns he's cheating with a male church member. However, after being convinced that Camden has been delivered from his demons, she proceeds with the wedding.

Will Stormy and Camden survive scandal, lies and deceit?

HEAVEN SENT - AUGUST 2007
$14.95
ISBN 1933967188

Eve is a recovering drug addict who has no intentions of staying clean until she meets Reverend Washington, a newly widowed man with three children. Secrets are uncovered that threaten Eve's new life with her new family and has everyone asking if Eve was *Heaven Sent*.

LOOK FOR MORE HOT TITLES FROM
Q-BORO
BOOKS

OBSESSION 101
$6.99
ISBN 0977733548

After a horrendous trauma. Rashawn Ams is left pregnant and flees town to give birth to her son and repair her life after confiding in her psychiatrist. After her return to her life, her town, and her classroom, she finds herself the target of an intrusive secret admirer who has plans for her.

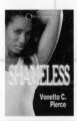

SHAMELESS- OCTOBER 2006
$6.99
ISBN 0977733513

Kyle is sexy, single, and smart; Jasmyn is a hot and sassy drama queen. These two complete opposites find love - or something real close to it - while away at college. Jasmyn is busy wreaking havoc on every man she meets. Kyle, on the other hand, is trying to walk the line between his faith and all the guilty pleasures being thrown his way. When the partying college days end and Jasmyn tests HIV positive, reality sets in.

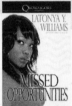

MISSED OPPORTUNITIES - MARCH 2007
$14.95
ISBN 1933967013

Missed Opportunities illustrates how true-to-life characters must face the consequences of their poor choices. Was each decision worth the opportune cost? LaTonya Y. Williams delivers yet another account of love, lies, and deceit all wrapped up into one powerful novel.

ONE DEAD PREACHER - MARCH 2007
$14.95
ISBN 1933967021

Smooth operator and security CEO David Price sets out to protect the sexy, smart, and saucy Sugar Owens from her husband, who happens to be a powerful religious leader. Sugar isn't as sweet as she appears, however, and in a twisted turn of events, the preacher man turns up dead and Price becomes the prime suspect.

LOOK FOR MORE HOT TITLES FROM

Q-BORO BOOKS

DOGISM
$6.99
ISBN 0977733505

Lance Thomas is a sexy, young black male who has it all: a high paying blue collar career, a home in Queens, New York, two cars, a son, and a beautiful wife. However, after getting married at a very young age he realizes that he is afflicted with DOGISM, a distorted sexuality that causes men to stray and be unfaithful in their relationships with women.

POISON IVY - NOVEMBER 2006
$14.95
ISBN 0977733521

Ivy Davidson's life has been filled with sorrow. Her father was brutally murdered and she was forced to watch, she faced years of abuse at the hands of those she trusted, and she was forced to live apart from the only source of love that she'd ever known. Now Ivy stands alone at the crossroads of life, staring into the eyes of the man who holds her final choice of life or death in his hands.

HOLY HUSTLER - FEBRUARY 2007
$14.95
ISBN 0977733556

Reverend Ethan Ezekiel Goodlove the Third and his three sons are known for spreading more than just the gospel. The sanctified drama of the Goodloves promises to make us all scream "Hallelujah!"

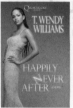

HAPPILY NEVER AFTER - JANUARY 2007
$14.95
ISBN 1933967005

To Family and friends, Dorothy and David Leonard's marriage appears to be one made in heaven. While David is one of Houston's most prominent physicians, Dorothy is a loving and carefree housewife. It seems as if life couldn't be more fabulous for this couple who appear to have it all: wealth, social status, and a loving union. However, looks can be deceiving. What really happens behind closed doors and when the flawless veneer begins to crack?

Attention Writers:

Writers looking to get their books published can view our submission guidelines by visiting our website at: *www.QBOROBOOKS.com*

What we're looking for: Contemporary fiction in the tradition of Darrien Lee, Carl Weber, Anna J., Zane, Mary B. Morrison, Noire, Lolita Files, etc; groundbreaking mainstream contemporary fiction.

We prefer email submissions to: candace@qborobooks.com in MS Word, PDF, or rtf format only. However, if you wish to send the submission via snail mail, you can send it to:

Q-BORO BOOKS Acquisitions Department
165-41A Baisley Blvd., Suite 4. Mall #1
Jamaica, New York 11434

*** By submitting your work to Q-Boro Books, you agree to hold Q-Boro books harmless and not liable for publishing similar works as yours that we may already be considering or may consider in the future. ***

1. Submissions will not be returned.
2. Do not contact us for status updates. If we are interested in receiving your full manuscript, we will contact you via email or telephone.
3. Do not submit if the entire manuscript is not complete.

Due to the heavy volume of submissions, if these requirements are not followed, we will not be able to process your submission.